Oklahoma Ghost Dance

Oklahoma Ghost Dance

Jeff Wilson

Copyright © Jeff Wilson 2015

All rights reserved. No part of this book may be reproduced or utilized in any form or by any means, electronic or mechanical, including photography, recording, or by any information storage or retrieval system, without permission in writing from the Author. Inquiries should be addressed to the Author. The characters and stories in this book are fictitious accounts of historic events. Any similarity to persons, living or dead is coincidental and not intended by the Author.

Book Editing by Becky Hawksley.
Formatting by Wendy Wilson Settle
Art work by Juan Padron, based on concepts
by Jeff Wilson.

Printed in the United States of America.
Library of Congress Cataloging-in-Publication
Wilson, Jeff D.

Paperback Second Edition
ISBN: ISBN-10 : 1500501913
ISBN-13 : 978-1500501914
Imprint: Independently published.

To Brett, Shane and Hannah.
I am so proud of you!
All my Love!

Jeff D. Wilson

Paperback Edition of 500

I would like to thank my wonderful family and friends. I really appreciate you always being there for me. A special thank you to my three children: Hannah, Shane and Brett, you are my heart and soul. Wherever you go in this world, please know I am proud of you and I am always here when you need me.

Thanks to Susie Sullivan for being so amazing and showing me what true love means. Without your love, this book would not have been possible. I am truly blessed.

I wish a very heartfelt thank you to the survivors and family of the Oklahoma City tragedy. Your determination to find the truth, was my inspiration when writing this book. Your courage against these acts of unspeakable terror gave everyone hope for a better future filled with peace. Thank you to all the firefighters, officers and emergency workers. Your dedication saved many lives. You are true heroes.

Merci beaucoup! To Mr. Peart, Mr. Lee and Mr. Lifeson for encouraging a thirteen-year-old "Rocker" to look up "Big" words in the dictionary and for providing the soundtrack to my life.

A big, Thanks to all my readers around the world. I really appreciate your continued support.

Inspired by true historic events, Oklahoma Ghost Dance is dedicated to the innocents that lost their lives on April 19, 1995.

Contents

1	Sheppard's Rod	11
2	City of God	26
3	Christian Identity	46
4	Dying of the Light	63
5	Millennial Rage	79
6	Fires of Insurrection	95
7	Geary Lake	108
8	Dreamland	139
9	Acoustic Shadows	166
10	Leaderless Resistance	180
11	Judas Redemption	195
12	Sand Creek	222
13	Perpetual Darkness	245
14	Trail of Tears	257
15	Jaci's Flowers	277
16	Snow Angels	296
17	Empty Chairs in a Field	312
18	Faith and Forgiveness	334
19	A Last Goodbye	339
	Bibliography and Historic Timeline	346
	Author Bio	375

Chapter 1

Shepherd's Rod

> "It matters not how strait the gate
> How charged with punishment the scroll
> I am the Captain of my fate
> I am the Captain of my soul."
>
> William Ernest Henry

April 19, 1993

Waco, Texas

Marissa

Originally designed by British Special Forces for the immediate disorientation of hostile combatants, the m84 stun grenades, also known as "flash bangs", unleashed instantaneous waves of deafening sound. Oxygen ignited the 4.5 grams of pyrotechnic aluminum powder mixed with magnesium and ammonium. It created a bursting flame the shape of a mushroom with a blinding light of one million candelas. The intense illumination in front of the Branch Davidian fighters, interrupted the signals from their optic nerves to their brains. It caused the last scene they viewed before the spark to loop repeatedly, as if time were stuck on rewind.

One hundred and eighty decibels of noise disturbed the three planes of motion in their inner ear canals, which helped keep balance on a constantly spinning earth. Severe sensations of the room moving beneath their feet, made it impossible to stand, while shooting back at the combined forces from the Bureau of Alcohol, Tobacco and Firearms (BATF) and the Federal Bureau of Investigation (FBI).

The exploding flash bang grenades ignited a stack of Coleman kerosene cans in the far corner of the partially destroyed gym, which were previously crushed beneath the tracks of an Abrams tank. The aluminum containers burst into walls of flames scorching everything within a twenty-foot circle. Ceiling tiles melted back into liquid form, as the fire raced through the Messiah's living quarters. Minutes later, a blaze flared up on the second floor when a tank fitted with a battering ram knocked over a lantern. The blaze continued to grow, while storming down to the gymnasium fire.

The sprawling U-shaped, Branch Davidian compound, situated itself cockeyed on seventy-seven acres and featured a series of square or rectangular buildings. It included a chapel, residence hall, a gymnasium, a four-story watch tower with a tornado shelter, a water tower, swimming pool and a large utility space, all hooked together with twisting corridors. An aerial view gave it the appearance similar to a gerbil habitat. The place sheltered upwards of one hundred at a time, with some families living here since the nineteen fifties.

It was always a peaceful existence, until sporadic violence erupted, as warring factions within, tried to wrestle control over this property named Mount Carmel. However, this was not the fertile, vineyard covered, coastal mountain range immortalized in the bible.

Blazes in multiple locations increased with each gust of twenty-mile an hour prairie wind. It howled through gaping holes punctured by the tanks during this morning's unsuccessful CS teargas campaign. Even though the FBI and the BATF used over four hundred cartridges, the desperate plan had failed miserably. Conditions inside the compound spiked to toxic levels, as thick, cyanide-laden smoke, released from the decomposing layers of powdered CS gas. Once the Branch Davidians kicked out windows attempting to escape, the flames drew in new air sources like bellows.

Marissa huddled in the center of the Chapel with a bedspread over herself and her three daughters. As memories flooded across her mind, it replayed the rare good times in a hard life. It seemed like a lifetime ago, when Marissa was a grade-schooler, walking home through the Iowa cornfields with her little brother. He would always wait until they were close to the house, before taking off and running the rest of the way. "Marissa, I beat you again!" Toby declared as if he had run the whole way.

That short span before her father died in a farming accident, was the best time she could ever recall. Months later, Marissa drifted down to Joplin, Missouri with her Mother and her new Stepfather, but that sturdy red farmhouse at the end of the dirt road, would always be home to her. *There are worse things than poverty*, Marissa would soon discover.

Thunderstorms still echoed in Marissa's mind, the night she climbed out a bedroom window and walked to the nearest truck stop. Although barely fifteen, *I will never look back*, was her resolution, to erase the pain associated with the inappropriate touches of her alcoholic stepfather. Running away would never placate feelings of betrayal, still left from her mother's accusations, that Marissa had enticed him.

Gregarious and clean-shaven, the young man seemed out of place with the older road dogs in the Truckers rest area. His casual smile offered Marissa a way out of this place, but his demeanor quickly changed at the next rest stop. He forced her into the sleeper cab and a blitzing rain provided ominous background music to a cowardice act. When Marissa realized that if she wanted him to quit hitting her, she would have to submit, she almost felt as much relief as shame. *At least it is not that drunken pervert back home doing this*, she kept reassuring herself. For a split second, the kid looked remorseful for his crime, but then grabbed a handful of Marissa's hair and flung her out of the truck.

"You only have yourself to blame," he declared, trying to justify his own reality, to the circumstances before driving off.

Lost and alone, from a concrete picnic table, Marissa watched the sunrise push the storm clouds west. Many strangers passed by without making eye contact with her, as morning turned to afternoon, before fading to night again. Her heart wanted to reach out for help, but pride roped her in. *If this is where my journey ends, then it is God's way. So be it,* Marissa thought, as her spirits waned.

That is when she met Tommy. Climbing out of a gas tanker with a broken odometer from too many miles to count, he walked by twice on the way to the restroom, before finally asking if she was okay. Marissa sported a swollen lip, black eye and scraped knees inflicted by the fall from the semi-truck to the parking lot. Although Marissa declared that she was fine, Tommy would not abandon her. *Maybe because I reminded Tommy of a daughter he once ran out on, whatever it was, made him decide not to leave again.*

Only the threat of having the police get involved as an alternative, finally got Marissa off the picnic table and into his tanker truck. The first hospital available was going to be the first stop, but it never turned out that way. Marissa would not go in. *They would only make me go home.*

They headed south to Texas after a quick run up to Coffeyville, Kansas. The first eight hours remained silent except the occasional squawk of a lonely trucker on the CB radio. Intermittently, Tommy played a few gospel cassettes to break the monotonous gallop of the rattling truck. Eventually, music from a Southern Baptist choir singing, *Amazing Grace*, opened the door to the secrets, Marissa was trying so hard to keep hidden.

She remained guarded, but in an inaudible hush, she began to tell her story. Thankful to have someone to talk to, Tommy listened patiently, without disclosing much of his own hard-living background, or his new life as a Seventh Day Adventist. With a deep caring voice, Tommy empathized with Marissa's situation, without sounding judgmental or preachy. Miles went by as comfortably as the conversation. When the trip was over and the next job started, Marissa stayed on with him. *Having no place to go and no way of getting there made the choice a bit easier.*

Tommy had a round face for a skinny man. Facial hair would only sprout up in certain splotches on his chin, so he settled for a goatee, when on the road. In his heart, the Lord Jesus was the answer; church was a nice sanctuary to escape from problems.

"Just give them over to someone else and move on," was his philosophy.

Moreover, Tommy lived life that way, constantly traveling, until stumbling upon the Branch

Davidian compound in a run through Waco, Texas. Besides, a little house in Monroe, Louisiana, recently inherited from his mother, after she passed away. If Tommy needed a rest, he always stayed at Mount Carmel. At first, Tommy thought Marissa was only gaining a few pounds from eating at all the greasy spoon dives along the way. Before long though, her stomach took on a plump egg look. She was pregnant.

Marissa denied she was going to be a mother, right up until her daughter, Serenity, was born in the passenger seat of the cab, just one hundred miles down the same highway conceived by rape.

Things really changed once Serenity arrived. *We became more of a family unit.* At least that is how they portrayed themselves at Mount Carmel. Nobody ever questioned it either. Even though Marissa's age barely increased, her maturity level rose tremendously with motherhood. She was beautiful. Tommy began to notice how her amber brown hair, curled down to highlight hazel, caring eyes, as her soft pink, pouting lips, counter-balanced a fair complexion.

It was not long before Tommy viewed Marissa in a different shade of light; less like a daughter and more like a young mistress. Effortlessly, boundaries fell on a lonely stretch of road through Texas, while hauling diesel down to Port Isabel. They stopped along the beaches of South Padre and pitched a blanket under the stars. *I loved Tommy, but I was not in love with him.* Not wanting to risk losing what they had together, she did whatever he wanted. *At least it did not hurt as much this time, was all I remembered of it.*

Tommy was on the road when his daughter, Chica, was born. He passed through less frequently until it was only one last Christmas. Then he never came back. Once again, Marissa felt betrayed. *At least I have my girls*, she resolved, while attempting to get over the loss.

Marissa had the church there to help. It finally felt as if she had a place to call home again. She could quit running away and settle down with her daughters among a brand new, loving and accepting family, which never asked about her past, but were always mindful of the future.

Based on a vision, the new Davidian leader, David Koresch, (formally known as Vernon Wayne Howell), sent for Marissa. Even though Koresch was married with children from several different women, Marissa was the next young girl blessed with his holy affections. Since Marissa was still two weeks shy of her seventeenth birthday, the unwanted sexual contact, amounted to child rape in the outside world. *The Lord must want me to have three children*, Marissa tried to convince herself, when realizing soon afterwar, that she was pregnant.

The pregnancy was taxing on Marissa's young body, but she still managed to achieve her High School GED. *Something I never thought possible.* Thankfully, it was an uneventful delivery after two hours of labor pains. Once the baby was born, Koresch rarely spoke to Marissa and never summoned for her again.

Marissa took to calling the baby "Little One" based on her premature delivery and Lilliputian size. As she grew stronger, Marissa considered other names, but her initial moniker stuck. Little One, had thin blonde hair similar to Chica, but with grayish green eyes, instead of brown. She rarely left Marissa's arms and would cry, if held by anyone else besides one of the girls. Every night, they all slept in a queen size bed together, with Little One on Marissa's chest and a girl at each side. Chica always slept next to the wall, because she moved around a lot and had fallen out of bed once. The closeness of having the girls in bed, was the best feeling, since her daddy tucked the covers tight before a bedtime story. He often fell asleep next to Marissa before finishing the book. *Until now, that was the last time I could remember being genuinely happy.*

Marissa tried to remain blissfully ignorant concerning the mounting troubles with the BATF, which recently rented a place up the road. They began infiltrating spies into Mount Carmel, to map the layout of the complex and to find information on where they kept their cache of weapons. Once word of a raid leaked from a reporter, to a mail carrier who happened to be Koresch's brother-in-law. The whole climate within the compound, began disintegrating into paranoia. To get outside and bask in fresh air, became a rare treat. *Nobody could leave without permission.*

Koresch's erratic behavior, grew borderline schizophrenic. His sermons changed from topics of love and the realms of heaven, to hate-filled rants of murder at hands of the government. It frightened Marissa so deeply; she decided to sneak out to a new life. Attempts to contact Tommy came to nothing. Several people thought he was in jail in Alabama on a parole violation. *At least he did not leave because of me*, she tried to assure herself. Up until that point, Marissa believed he might still come back and take them somewhere safe. It was a heavy blow, which took several days of tears to get over.

As rumors of an impending raid, coupled with frequent stories of Koresch molesting young girls, many began looking for an escape from the prison they once called home. Marissa was able to join some women going into town for supplies, but Koresch's inner circle of advisors made sure her children remained behind. While the rest shopped, she made one last ditch effort to leave the compound and called an aunt on her father's side. Shrill sounds of a wrong number tone, dashed her efforts. Marissa realized she was out of options. *I would rather die than call my Mom*, she thought, while hanging up the receiver and slinking back over to the group.

Within days, automatic gunfire rang throughout the compound, as the unconstitutional and poorly planned raid, slammed into heavy resistance from the Davidian's, protecting their rights. Marissa narrowly missed death from a stray bullet, while doing laundry. *Somehow, in my heart, I knew I would never leave this place.* Evenings became nightmares of strange lights and sounds, bombarding Mount Carmel. It took her hours to convince Serenity, that the disturbing squeals were not the result of bunny rabbits having their throats cut, as the gossip stated.

When things began to settle down, one of the Abram tanks, would pull forward in a threatening gesture, sending the whole compound into a constant drill for another assault. Sleep was unattainable except during the early evening, when a restless breeze crept in, through one of the few windows left unbarred. As darkness came, so did the sonic torture. Most pretended like it did not bother them, but others cracked under the pressure and were locked in the tornado shelter to keep control.

Day after day, Marissa's passionate requests to leave the compound came to nothing. When the latest blitzkrieg of CS teargas swept into the compound, Marissa figured this was the end. She and the girls used wet towels to block the nauseating effects. A momentary calm returned, until the tanks fitted with battering rams, slammed into the exterior walls, puncturing holes. Flash bang grenades, blasted into every opening, causing the merciless fires.

Koresch appeared from the fog like an angel wearing a sleeveless white undershirt. He had a blue and white plaid shirt hanging loose over his worn blue jeans. Marissa pulled out from beneath the bedspread, gave the frightened girls hand gestures to stay down. Serenity held the baby and Chica cried next to them. She covered them up while trying to block her mouth from the horrible tasting smoke hanging in the air. With so many different things burning at once combining with the CS gas, it created a suffocating death chamber, in several areas of the compound. The smoke was now spilling into the communication room.

"David! David, please help us!" Marissa screamed, into the tornado sounds of the inferno spiraling out of control.

Pieces of smoldering debris fluttered by like burning butterflies and left white smoke tails in the air. Marissa took a glimpse back to make sure the girls were okay, before forging ahead against the wind tunnel of heat. She caught up to Koresch along with Steve Schneider, his second in command. Desperately looking for a way to safety, a frightened group formed around them.

"Do not fear the flames, Marissa. They will cleanse you for the next life," Koresch replied in a dismissive tone, as he pushed away with Steve right behind him.

Completely grief stricken, most of his followers slumped into a fetal position, crying or praying aloud as their leader moved to the back of the room. He talked to Steve for a second before handing him an automatic weapon. With the AK47 to Koresch's forehead and an approving nod, Steve pulled the trigger. Koresch crumpled to the floor as Steve turned the gun on himself.

Loud explosions resonated throughout the compound from ammunition and other combustible items erupting in the flames. Marissa passed several people hurrying by in a bent-over fashion, attempting to stay as low as possible. Tears came to her eyes when she found the girls, who were barely conscious under the blanket. They perked up slightly having their mother back with them. Marissa looked around and found a thick cotton and polyester bedspread heaped in a pile of dirty clothes. She grabbed it and put an extra layer over the top of them. *I hope the fire department gets here? Please God, don't let my babies die*, she thought, as she huddled closer to shield them from the coming storm.

A thunderous crash of dust, expanded into the room, as large chunks of concrete floor in the chapel, buckled under the stress of a pounding tank. It crushed six women and three children beneath the layers. Nine Davidians crawled past the snipers and through the razor wire to safety, but the rest remained inside as fire spread to every building from all directions.

The blanket reached a critical mass temperature and burst into flames with the help of some floating embers. Marissa barely managed to remove it before it burned them. Her eyes stung and watered as she frantically looked for an exit. When realizing they were trapped in a swirling putrid oven, Marissa screamed out with such emotion it terrified the girls into a hysteric wailing.

"Please Jesus; don't let my babies' burn!" Her pleas spewed out with betrayal, before consumed into a dull roar of the abyss.

Growing woozy from the smoke inhalation and the extreme temperatures, Marissa began to slump backwards before her maternal instincts kicked in one last time. She huddled the girls closer and then lay over them to give them a few precious seconds of life. *In case, someone comes for us.* She reminisced about their last peaceful Sunday morning together before the siege. Under the covers, they were content on spending the morning snoozing and snuggling. As Marissa began to lose consciousness, a last wish came to mind. *I hope heaven will be like that morning together.*

Several tanks fitted with tractor blades, pushed the burning ruble back into the buildings, as a propane tank disintegrated with a deafening explosion causing a fireball to soar into the Texas sky. Finally, after a long delay, fire trucks started the process of extinguishing the smoldering ruins. Protesters cried out along barricades with anti-government chants, as the massacre of American citizens concluded.

The FBI agents at the scene decided it was a perfect opportunity to take surveillance photos of the crowd, to match against working cases. The lanky appearance of the young man with a military haircut made him seem taller than his 6'2 height. His erratic behavior made him stand out even more. He wore an orange hunting hat, along with a red and black checked shirt which clashed with his old camouflaged army shirt, with the name McVeigh stitched on the left breast. He was visibly outraged at the situation.

Repeatedly, he yelled profanities at passing BATF agents, when his attempts to shove past the spectator zone were thwarted. As if sensing someone was watching him, he turned and looked straight to the camera. Several frames clicked to capture his image. By placing the photos in succession, you could see him mouth the words. "Someone will pay for this!"

Chapter 2

City of God

"Every Government does as much harm as it can

And as much good as it must."

Nicholas Walter

December 10, 1994

Adair County, Oklahoma

Kara James

Traveling at over one thousand miles per hour, the asynchronous orbiting satellite, moved above its intended target. Using Keplerian mathematical data sent to an onboard processor, thrusters reacted to keep it hovering, high above the Ozark hills of Eastern Oklahoma. A series of rechargeable solar cells and batteries allowed it to run continuously. The Kh-12 satellite, equipped with a powerful lens that could pick up objects as little as six inches off the ground. It fulfilled its mission, by relaying raw information to the National Geospatial Intelligence Agency (NGIA) supercomputers. They combined the data to form three-dimensional photos of the Elohim

City Compound, before sending them on to the National Reconnaissance Office, headquartered in Chantilly, Virginia.

Elohim City came to the attention of the FBI, after they moved from Ellicott City, Maryland, to the four hundred secluded acres near Muldrow, Oklahoma, along the northern tip, just west of the Arkansas border. Founded in 1973 by Robert G. Millar, they practiced a new religion called the Christian Identity, based loosely on Carl Jung's racist theories of ancestral linage. They believe that Caucasians are descendants of the fabled, lost tribes from Israel, but Jewish people are half-devil creations, from the serpent seed of Eve and Satan.

After splitting from another group called the Covenant, the Sword, and Arm of the Lord (CSL), Elohim City was under constant investigation. They maintained close ties with The Order, also known as "Bruder Schweigen" or (Brothers remain Silent) a Neo-Nazi Organization active in the Pacific Northwest. The Order was responsible for a string of armored car and bank robberies from 1983 to 1984 until disbanding when their leader Robert Jay Mathews, died in a shootout with police.

Suspected of possession and sales of illegal automatic weapons, a major clash between the Bureau of Alcohol, Tobacco and Firearms (BATF) and CSL eventually came to a boiling point. After a short siege around their property in Elijah, Missouri, Millar negotiated a peaceful surrender for Jim Ellison and his followers on April 19, 1985. That date left behind unforgivable grudges with future Branch Davidian's living in Waco, Texas. The significance of that date was already important to right-winged patriots. It was the same day the German Nazi's burned down the Warsaw ghetto in Poland. It was also the day the "shot heard around the world" took place as American Colonies clashed with British soldiers in Lexington, the true spark of the Revolutionary War.

The disgraced leader of CSL and another former member Richard Snell, began plotting revenge for the perceived attack by the U.S. government. The plan included using a rocket launcher to destroy the Murrah Federal Building in Oklahoma City, but it misfired during testing and the misguided operation never came to fruition. Snell would later die of lethal injection on April 19, 1995 in Arkansas for murdering a State Trooper he mistakenly thought was Jewish.

After a relatively quiet end to the decade, a new investigation against Elohim City began when a series of brazen daylight bank robberies struck across the Midwest. Several agencies started files on "Reverend" Robert Millar, a charismatic, efficient leader that quickly built a large paramilitary cult. Millar walked a fine line between portraying Elohim City as a legitimate church, while also becoming a safe haven for others with anti-government sentiments. The FBI believed he was harboring these bank robbers.

The Kh12 rotated 90 degrees as the lens adjusted to get close up pictures of the license plates from the vehicles parked along the gravel drive behind the Elohim City meeting hall. The first plate was from Pennsylvania and belonged to Mark Thomas, the leader of the Aryan Republican Army (ARA). A former state chaplain of the Ku Klux Klan, Thomas modeled his secret military group after the small underground cells of the Irish Republican Army in the United Kingdom. With a goal of overthrowing the government and the extermination of the "American Jews", they would rob twenty-two banks and steal nearly $250,000 over the next few years attempting to complete their mission.

The next images were of a late 80's model; Ford pickup, belonging to Richard Guthrie Jr. a prominent member of the ARA and co leader of the Midwest Bank Robbers. Guthrie would eventually be the first suspect apprehended in Cincinnati, Ohio, and enter a plea agreement to testify against other members. After debriefing with the FBI and one week before his first court appearance, Guthrie was found hung in his jail cell in Covington, Kentucky. Despite evidence of foul play, his death was ruled a suicide. Guthrie would never get his book deal or have his day in court.

A slight adjustment of the satellite's lenses captured details of a black Chevrolet Tahoe with dark tinted windows registered to a high school dropout and leader of the Midwest gang, Peter Langan or "Commander Pedro" as he was known in the ARA. He would be arrested only three days after Guthrie was debriefed. Langan's violent shoot-out with police made national headlines. The authorities found Semtex explosives linked to the Oklahoma City bombing, pipe bombs, forged identification documents, a shoulder-fired rocket launcher, hand grenades, a cache of weapons and three prepaid calling cards from Fone America Inc. with the brand name "driveline" the ARA used to communicate with each other. A life sentence plus thirty-five years was waiting for Langan after a speedy trial and conviction for robbing nine banks in several states.

    As the satellite continued to photograph the compound, two men and a woman came out a side door of the chapel and a climbed into a dark blue pickup truck with dual wheels on the rear axle. It followed the vehicle as they drove past two white domed buildings resembling large igloos with aluminum sides and Confederate flags in the windows, before a slight turn south by a green van stalled out in front of a mobile home covered with wood siding. They paused for a few residents crossing the road after leaving a church, which featured an Israel flag as a floor mat and the "Iron Cross" band playing twisted versions of biblical hymns. Slowly the truck passed a field with rows of barbed wire and a lone fence post with a turkey-basting pan nailed to it for target practice during training for the coming apocalypse. They continued down the rocky, winding, gravel road to the entrance where camouflaged BATF agents staking out the compound snapped pictures for their reports. The satellite got a few more images as the truck paused on a covered yellow steel bridge leading out to the highway. Satisfied they were not being watched; they turned east and blended into the afternoon sun.

Kara James sat between Dennis Mahon, the leader of the White Aryan Resistance (WAR) and her current boyfriend, Andreas Carl Strassmeir, a German National in the United States illegally on an expired visa. Dennis, a stocky man with puffy flushed cheeks, drove under the speed limit, but also with purpose to reach the predetermined destinations. He wore a white cowboy hat over his thinning light-brown hair usually combed over to the right, a red satin jacket with a trucking company logo on the front left pocket that clashed with his camouflage hunter pants and brown leather boots. The conversation was limited to Dennis complaining the sun was in his eyes as they turned towards Tulsa. Neither man seemed anxious to say where they were going or to start any meaningful dialogue, so Kara sat there silently, holding Andreas's hand off and on. She tried to act as if she was unconcerned of their intentions, as if they were out for a quiet Sunday drive.

Thoughts of indecision and insecurity began to swirl in her head. *What if they found out who I really am? I am as good as dead. Do they know? Is that why they are so quiet? How am I going to escape from this?* Beads of sweat sprouted up on her forehead as her hands became clammy with the sudden wave of nervous tension.

"Are you hot or something, Love?" Andreas asked noticing the perspiration on her right hand.

"Well it is a bit stuffy; can we turn the heat down a bit?"

"Sure, no problem, honey," Dennis finally acknowledged turning some country music on in the same reach, before giving his full attention to driving.

Andreas patted her knee and gave her a little wink as he took a few swigs from a water bottle. He did not seem to have a care in the world.

Calm yourself down, they do not know. They cannot possibly know. We are probably just heading to Dennis's house in Tulsa, Kara thought to herself as she began to get her usual defiant nature back. Her mind drifted back to her "safe zone" as she liked to call the happy times in her life growing up an adopted, only child. Kara had a very close bond with her parents as they traveled during the summers of her school years. Her mother was a homemaker. She volunteered as a librarian at her school so she could have the same schedule as Kara. "My baby is not riding that bus with those other kids if I can help it" she was fond of saying.

Named Karina Michelle after her grandmother, it was abbreviated to Karen when she started school, but her father always called her Kara. *He loved that name for some reason.* She took on the last name James to pay respect to him when she joined the BATF and began going undercover. It was her way of trying to make things right for the years she spent spiraling out of control in her teen years. An abusive drug-dealing boyfriend was instrumental in Kara becoming addicted to cocaine and other assorted chemicals. However, the years of silence between the two would never be reconciled. Her father passed away in his sleep before she could complete her training and surprise him with her new career.

From the beginning, Kara stood out against the "beautiful people" as she referred to the perfect cookie-cutter specimens wanting to be the next generation of heroes. The instructors tried hard to make Kara quit, but after her father died, nothing in heaven and earth could have stopped her. Kara's past life in a counterculture drug world made her a unique candidate. It was easy for her to fall back into that lifestyle, except this time it was different. She was not dependent on anyone or anything. No matter how deep she got into "Kara James", Karen Howe was waiting for her on the other side. With a quick temper and tongue, she was a natural to infiltrate Elohim City and the Midwest Bank Robbers.

Kara began working on the turnpike tollbooth in the summer of 1993 to start her first undercover assignment. She made herself a regular at several of the bars Andreas was known to frequent and then waited patiently for her chance. The first two times he came in, he was preoccupied with others from his paramilitary group. As dumb luck would have it, the third time was the charm. Andreas came into Buzzards Gulch sports bar in Sallisaw and noticed her. Kara was in the middle of an altercation with a local she had beaten handily at pool. Not wanting to look foolish in front of his friends, the intoxicated man twice her size, decided to play the role of bully and grabbed her breast while backing her into the pool table as if he was going to mount her right there.

A cue ball delivered to his forehead ended the struggle as quickly as it began. Kara noticed that she had the audience she had wanted, so gave him an extra kick in the groin area to put an exclamation point to her statement. After years in an abusive relationship, she was not scared of any man. As a bouncer hauled the drunk out by his boot heels, Kara positioned herself at the bend of the bar and ordered a Seven and 7, drink for luck.

Michael Brescia, a handsome twenty four year old, part-time college student from LaSalle University, who once lived with Mark Thomas, was the first to approach. With a soft voice and slender build, he knew his advance was futile with Kara's first glance up at him. His claim for glory as a singer with an ultra-violent skinhead band could not help him this time around.

"Sweetie, I think it might be past your bedtime." Kara joked with Michael to let him down easy with the hope that Andreas would take a chance next.

"Hey, I was just going to buy you a drink. Don't kick my ass or nothing," Michael volleyed back.

"Don't worry Kid, I think I have reached my quota tonight. Besides, that guy was asking for it," she retorted, before being cut off by Andreas who stepped up between them and put an arm on each as if they were all old friends.

"Mikey Boy, who might your lovely companion be?" Andreas asked, relying on a cheesy smile on his tight gaunt face that sometimes worked on lesser women. He had neatly combed black hair that matched his sad, sullen looking eyes, which would perk up and get bigger when he had an idea. Dressed mostly in black, he raised one of his bushy eyebrows several times and then gave a little wink. "You are just striking..." he began to say, as he went into his usual routine that dripped with an international mystique he had developed over his travels.

"Excuse me, Pepe Le Pew, want to get your paws off me," Kara fired back, mocking his German accent as French. "Hey John, I will take a rain check on that drink. Be back in tomorrow when the clientele is a bit more upscale," she hollered to the bartender, while dropping a five-dollar bill on the bar and heading towards the exit.

"Hey, I didn't mean to offend you," Andreas tried to say, but received no reply. "Damn that bitch is cold," he confided to Michael, to try to save his ego.

Kara wanted to turn around and reel him in, but decided to keep walking to her car. *He has to come to me*, she thought, while trying to downplay the nervousness that she might have blown her only opportunity. Her worries were nearly confirmed, as two weeks went by without seeing the pair again. On a rainy night in July, they both pulled into the parking lot at the same time. Kara instantly recognized his maroon station wagon from the impound photos taken by the Oklahoma Highway Patrol, after Andreas was arrested by Trooper Vernon Phillips, for a traffic violation in February of 1992. She moved quickly into the bar and pretended not to see him. Once inside, Andreas wasted little time in shaking off the rain and sitting next to her at the bar. Before she could order, he did for both of them and flashed the money before she could turn him down.

"Don't I know you from somewhere, Love?" He asked in a hopeful tone, while playing down his earlier defeat to her sharp wit.

"Yes Pepe, I believe I told you to get your hands off me once before. Hey look, I am sure you are a nice guy and all, but I am not looking for a shadow at the moment."

"Slow down there, my little dove; just a drink and a spot of civil conversation are all I am asking for. Don't want to set you off on a bad trip or anything."

Kara could tell that Andreas was sincere so decided that if she rebuffed him again that he might stay away for good. She gradually let her walls down. *I am surprised at how fast the night passes and find myself liking him.* When closing time came, Andreas began to ask to extend the night before she abruptly cut him off.

"Wow, I can't believe I actually had fun with you tonight, but I have to work in the morning. So I guess I will see ya around," she said, while jumping up and immediately heading out leaving him stuck with the large bar tab. He tried to bring her back to no avail with a couple of old pickup lines, until she had the last word.

"Don't forget the tip," she said with a laugh, knowing he was hers now.

Kara avoided all of his known hangouts for a few weeks before seeing him back in the same bar where she had left him. Not knowing her name, he always asked the bartender where the "Cue ball chick" was. When Kara walked in wearing a light blue and white sundress instead of blue jeans, Andreas about fell off his stool turning his head to check her out. She passed right by him and talked with a group at the back of the establishment. After an hour of avoiding all eye contact with him, Andreas could not take it anymore.

"You owe me thirty six dollars for your share of the bill you hung on me, Love. I expect full restitution to this grievous indignation," Andreas explained in a business like tone, while maintaining a stone face.

"That is a big tab and a lot of big words, Mr. Le Pew. How long have you been practicing that speech?"

"Since you left me in a shambles last time," he finally admitted, showing a tender side that had not come out in a long time.

"Okay I will play ya for it," Kara decided, as she grabbed the rack and started putting a few stray pool balls into it. "Do you have fifty cents to get started?"

Andreas began laughing at her confident offer. He had never met a woman that seemed to walk the edge of life, but also was in perfect control of every situation she found herself tangled up in. "Okay, but if I win, I want the full tab paid, plus you have to come home with me."

"Not saying I will lose or anything, but that sounds a bit steep, considering if I win, it is only a few bucks that I already drank up anyway. Sorry, no deal."

"Okay, okay, how about you just tell me your name, if I win? Oh and you call me Andy instead of what you have been calling me, whatever that means."

"You know the cartoon of the skunk that thinks he is so suave and he chases around the cat," Kara tried to explain, but realized she was digging deeper the more she talked. "Never mind, it was silly anyway. All right Andy, you have a bet," she said, as she broke the balls up with a loud thud that sent three of the solid colored ones in the hole. "Looks like I am little ones. It is not looking good for you."

By the time Andreas got his turn, Kara only had one ball plus the eight ball to get in. Playing countless hours of pool on the base when he was an intelligence officer in the modern German Army called the *Bundeswehr*, served him well as he made up nearly all the lost ground. Kara made a lucky shot that was borderline "slop" if they were playing in a tournament, but against Andreas's protest, she took a shot for the win and slammed it into a side pocket.

"I guess that does it there Pep... I mean Andy. I hope there are no hard feelings. You did play a nice game though for second place," Kara quipped, with a laugh.

"You won fair and square, Love. At least tell me your name?"

"Nope sorry, a bet is a bet," Kara said, before nuzzling her face just under his left ear. "I might tell you in the morning over breakfast though," she said with a seductive twinkle in her eye. "I hope you are better at other things than you are at pool."

Andreas was stunned by the turn of events. He was a former Lieutenant in the Panzer Grenadiers and not used to being placed in a subordinate position in any form. *I have him wrapped around my pinky and he knows it.* Unable to muster any comeback, Andreas nodded his head with a grin plastered across his face.

They took Kara's Jeep and she picked the motel where she wanted to go. The next day, she dropped him back at his car and although promising to stay in touch, she never called. *After an incredible night together, I dropped Andreas cold.* With every day that passed, Andreas would become more hooked on her. He could never recall a time when he was treated as a one-night stand and then tossed away. Kara never did tell her name or anything about herself, but also did not seem interested in his past either. After a week of playing hide and seek with her, Andreas found Kara in the same bar they had left together. This time she was playing pool with another man. Andreas tried not to be jealous, but when the tall farmer in a cowboy hat went to the restroom, he made his move and slunk over to her.

"So how is it going, Love?" He asked, trying not to act too interested.

"Oh, hey there. You know, the same old thing. I have been meaning to call you back, but like I said, I ain't looking for nothing serious. Just having some fun for a change." Kara replied nonchalantly.

"Okay, well, let's go have some fun then," He fired back, while raising his eyebrows in a hopeful manner. "Last time was "fun" wasn't it?"

"Fair to moderate, I suppose," Kara, answered with a laugh, not giving him an inch to maneuver.

The farm hand came out of the restroom and was instantly annoyed by an interloper moving in on the girl he had invested twelve dollars in drinks and another three bucks in change for the pool table.

"Is this guy bugging you?" He asked, ready to toss Andreas out of the bar.

"Yes, he is. He is bothering me a lot," Kara replied, as she moved in and planted a big kiss on Andrea's lips to diffuse the whole situation. She kept kissing him until the other man got frustrated and left the bar in a huff of curse words.

"I just can't seem to work you out, Love. The pieces don't all fit. One minute you are humiliating me at pool, then the next, you are kissing me?"

"Let's go back to my place and see if we can make them fit. Shall we?"

"Whatever you say," Andreas complied, shrugging his shoulders, not knowing what else to say, but happy with the outcome.

Over the next few weeks, they spent a lot of time together, before he finally disclosed that he lived in Elohim City as their new security director. Kara remained guarded, until revealing her past in a night of drinks and lovemaking. *The more I gave of myself the more he trusted me.* Andreas found out they had a common interest in hating the government when she talked about being shuffled through countless shelters for battered women and other chemical dependency units.

Kara was the perfect yin to his yang and quickly rose up through the ranks after quitting her job and moving to the compound. No matter how hard she tried, Kara could not break into the inner circle and all the recent meetings behind closed doors. *Something big is going on, and everyone was keeping a tight seal on the plans.* On occasions of running errands off the property, Kara would check in with her senior advisors on the case and let them know all the players passing through. She would eventually make seventy reports, with thirty-eight audiotapes and two videotapes of illegal conduct at Elohim City.

Lately a young kid fresh from the army calling himself, Tim Tuttle, but with *McVeigh* stitched on his fatigues, began stopping in. Most trips he was with his much older, former army buddy, Terry Nichols, from Michigan. Rumors stated that Tim was there when Waco burned and was determined to exact revenge.

One weekend, Aryan resistance leader Pete Langan, brought in his entire crew including a rugged-looking guy from California that went by the name Vance Bradway. They trained secretly for weeks with Andreas. *Even though I am in the middle of it all, the closer I get, the farther I feel from knowing the truth.* Now it was just a waiting game as she compiled names and descriptions of their activities. *I was in complete control back then, now I don't even know what I am doing,* Kara thought, as doubts began to cloud her mind.

As they pulled into downtown Tulsa, Dennis made the first stop outside of the Internal Revenue Building. Dennis and Andreas got out without inviting her and stood outside talking for ten minutes or so. Dennis seemed disappointed for some reason and they jumped back in without disclosing their purpose of the stop. A few quick turns, had them in front of the Tulsa Federal Building, where once again they stepped out. This time, they took more time and walked to the front of the building. Andreas seemed more animated than the last stop, but Dennis did not like what he saw and shook his head. After a lengthy discussion, they both seemed impartial and got back into the truck in better spirits. They made small talk about a cold front passing through for Christmas just around the corner, as they left Tulsa and drove straight to Oklahoma City.

The traffic on the streets was minimal as they pulled in front of the Alfred P. Murrah Federal Building. Once again, the pair hopped out of the truck and spent twenty minutes walking around the building. Andreas kept pointing to the glass front of the building, while Dennis seemed more concerned with the side streets and parking garage. They both got back into the truck and stayed silent all the way back to Elohim City.

That evening Andreas was standoffish towards her. Kara tried to bring up the subject of their drive together, but he rolled over without answering. He seemed deep in thought, as if two separate forces were pulling from opposite sides. *I have never seen him so withdrawn.*

"I think I am going to visit my Mom for a couple of weeks over Christmas," she finally announced, to break the uncomfortable silence, as she paced the small room.

"What, oh okay, I had forgot all about it. I guess it is not as big of a deal as when I was younger," Andreas answered with a pessimistic tone, but seemed more willing to talk about this topic than anything else up to that point. "It is still a couple weeks out, what got you thinking about all that?" he asked, standing up and grabbing a soda out of a compact fridge in the corner.

"I saw Commander Pedro with that new guy Vance and he had a Santa suit for the kids. Funny, I never thought of him as the festive type. Reverend

Millar would be a better fit with that beard he has been growing.

"Sounds like it will be a lot fun around here, maybe you should stay close," Andreas responded with a comment, which sounded more like an order.

Kara instantly became defensive. The pressure of keeping a brave front, while missing all of her old friends and family had been tearing her apart. She could not hold it back any longer. *I just want to go home.*

"Andy, you can do whatever you want. I was hoping you would go with me, but I guess hate never takes a break."

"I am not like you, Kara. I cannot float in and out like the wind. I have major commitments that my life depends on, but you would never understand that. How about you just go have a drink and leave me alone."

"I understand things perfectly, Andy, except I can't turn my back on my family."

"I thought this was your family now, and that I...oh never mind. Once a barfly always-" he started to say before a slap across the face stopped him.

"Don't ever talk to me that way! I am not an alcoholic. I can control it."

Andy realized he touched on a bad memory for her and since the slap was more for effect than pain, he let it go. He had slapped her a lot harder before, when Kara was drunk and crossed the line into his business. Once Kara got into a fighting stance and prepared to take it as far as he wanted, Andy backed down and never touched her again.

"Hey look, I am sorry for that, but you don't understand what is going on. I cannot up and leave right now. You can go if you want though."

"Thanks for the permission," Kara answered sarcastically. "Sorry I slapped you. It is so frustrating that you will not talk to me. I mean…I have reveled stuff I never told anyone. I guess it is a one-way street with us. You can drag me all over Oklahoma and I am supposed to sit there like a Barbie doll and keep my mouth shut."

"Oh you know better than that, quit being so dramatic. Some things I cannot talk about. You know the score, Love."

"Fine, I will find a new place to stay tomorrow," Kara said with finality, to let him know she was serious.

Andreas paused to gather his thoughts, before answering carefully. "I will tell you everything soon enough, but right now all I can say is…" He stopped again to give her a serious stare with his brooding eyes, which caught her off guard. "The way I see it- life is blood for blood." Then he gave her a hug, as if it would somehow make all her questions go away.

Chapter 3

Christian Identity

> "A thief is more moral than a congressman
>
> When a thief steals your money,
>
> He doesn't demand you thank him."
>
> Walter Williams

December 14, 1994

Columbus, Ohio

Jericho Daniels

A Buick Regal stopped on the corner next to the First National Bank. Recently spray-painted forest green, several spots had already peeled with the morning rain to reveal the white beneath it. Pete Langan stepped out wearing a red Santa suit and carrying a red felt sack with white puffy fringe that matched his outfit. Dark sunglasses and a thick gray beard covered most of his face. Red batting gloves covered his hands. As he headed to the front door, a young mother with three kids came out. Practically programmed from birth to recognize jolly Saint Nick and associate him with receiving gifts, they immediately began hugging a disguised Langan. He tried to smile and push on by until the five-year old latched on to his leg, stopping his progress.

"I love you, Santa! Thanks for the doll last year, Miss Precious is my favorite."

He slid the sunglasses up and gave a little wink, as a broad smile opened up a hole in the tangled hair on his chin.

"No problem, you were a very good girl," he exclaimed diplomatically, while glancing over to the mother, who verified it with a nod, as she pulled the girl off his leg.

The other two were more concerned with getting their list into him while they had a chance. It included everything from new bikes, to the latest video game system. Children seemed to multiply as three turned into seven, with each wanting to get their wishes in. He turned towards "The Company" as he called his crew, and raised his hands in defeat. Giving every kid an equal chance to feel they made their best case to insure proper delivery on the special day, Langan let out a big "Ho, ho, ho," and tried to get away from the mob of toddlers. Just when he thought he had an opening, a pudgy little father of two, decided to save a long wait standing in the lines at the mall.

"What in the hell is Commander Pedro doing? We are already ten minutes behind schedule?" Richard Guthrie asked, from the backseat of the Regal. "I told him these outfits were an unnecessary risk to the job," he complained.

"Actually I kind of like them," Michael Brescia joked, referring to their green elf outfits. He was recently engaged to the granddaughter of Reverend Millar at Elohim City. "How about you Vance, do you like them?"

"They will make us popular in the federal penitentiary," Vance Bradway scowled back.

Bradway was a name that Jericho Daniels took as an alias when he went undercover for the B.A.T.F. He was a key informant in their investigation into the growing threat of militias. Jericho hoped to clean his past up so he could move on to a new life, but immediately regretted his decision when they put him into Elohim City. *Where are the cops? I gift wrapped this for the Feds and they don't even bother showing up?* Jericho wondered, getting more impatient by the minute.

The driver, Timothy McVeigh, who was using the alias of Tim Tuttle, let out a little laugh until he noticed Vance was not in a joking mood. Wearing the same camouflaged army fatigues he used in the Gulf War, was above average in height, in his mid-twenties, with a baby face and crew cut. Once a decorated veteran, McVeigh turned on the government after he watched the massacre in Waco, Texas. He decided to be quiet and not get in the middle of the debate. In the side mirror, he noticed the black Suburban carrying their associates, slide by and stop next to them.

In the Tahoe were two former band mates of Brescia. Scott Stedeford, eventually arrested in May of 1996 for the robbery of a Boatman's bank in Iowa, drove the Tahoe. Kevin McCarthy, who was also arrested for the same robbery, but received a lighter sentence of five years, before going into the witness protection agency, sat nervously in the passenger seat.

"What's with all the brats?" Stedeford asked, while glancing at his watch to note they were already behind schedule.

"It's that goofball Santa suit. I told that stupid bastard not to wear that dammed thing," Guthrie complained with frustration.

"I think we should scrap the whole mission." McCarthy stated, as he pointed to a patrol car that cruised past them only a few blocks down.

"You guys head on over to the dump off spot. We will handle this!" Guthrie barked orders. "Pop the trunk! Let's get this over with."

With that, Tim opened the glove compartment and pushed the trunk button. They all got out except Tim who left the car running. They each retrieved Christmas sacks the size of a golf club bag out of the trunk before approaching the small crowd gathered around Langan.

"Sorry kids, Santa has to go now," Guthrie interrupted, as he grabbed Langan's arm and shuffled him into the bank.

Immediately a guard came over to the group. "Sorry guys, you can't wear those-" he muttered, until Guthrie put a sawed-off shotgun with a black molded grip, under his chin. The elderly man dropped to his knees, while putting his hands in the air. "Please don't shoot!"

"Everybody, get down on the floor!" Langan commanded, as he jumped the protective glass above the counter and threw the employees on the floor, before they could activate an alarm.

"We will be done soon folks, just relax and nobody will get hurt!" Guthrie yelled out, as he removed an oven timer attached to three pipe bombs, out of his Christmas sack. He set the timer for five minutes, before placing it on a round counter with deposit slips. "You guys only have a few minutes until this whole place goes kablooey, so the longer you delay us, the less time you will have to get out to safety!"

Brescia and Jericho kicked several office doors open. They pulled out the branch manager and other financial officers, as Langan finished quickly before the tellers could attach any dye packets on the cash straps of various denominations.

"Okay folks; give us two minutes to leave. If anyone sticks his head out early, I will blow it off. Do we understand each other?" Langan hollered.

A few murmurs of yes came from the stunned group, as Guthrie pulled another pipe bomb wrapped in a Santa hat out of his bag. He used a compact blowtorch to ignite the heavy-duty detonation chord and rolled it back to the bank counter. "I changed my mind, you have ten seconds to say your prayers, Merry Christmas," he quipped with a laugh, as they filed out to the waiting Buick.

When they got into the Buick, Langan threw a small homemade device at the front of the bank. As they pulled out, it exploded into a burnt-crimson, mushroom of smoke. in front of the bank entrance. The shock wave mangled the bank doors and temporally stunted the electricity until the backup power surged to the alarms and automatic fire sprinklers. Only a few lights came on, leaving a majority of the bank dark as sprinkler water mixed with clouds of dust rolling in. The customers watched in terror, while the fuse burned down on the single pipe bomb. It fizzled and sparked, before letting out a stream of purple smoke.

The branch manager rushed over to the bigger bomb with only a minute left ticking away. His first instinct was to throw it out the front door, but there was not enough time left. Out of options, he tried pulling at several colored wires, attempting to defuse it.

"Don't touch it. It might be rigged!" The guard yelled out.

"What do we do?" The manager screamed back, as it dwindled down to seconds. "We have to at least put it in one of the offices..." he tried to say choking on the purple haze filling the lobby. He started to pick it up when the timer went off.

Shrapnel from another explosive device Langan tossed out, peppered the side of the Buick and shattered the front passenger window. The puzzle-pieced safety glass, left a few cuts on Jericho's face, before he could turn away from the blast.

"What a rush!" Langan called out, obviously pleased at the completion of another job. "Is everyone okay?" He finally asked realizing the fuse had been too short to leave enough distance for a safe escape from the blast.

"Are you trying to kill us?" Jericho asked angrily, while turning around in his seat and knocking Langan's Santa hat off. *I can't wait for you to get yours, Amigo,* Jericho thought to himself, as he used the reflection from a silver 9mm handgun to check the damage. "That shit practically blew up right in my face!"

"Oh quit your belly aching Vance, the job went perfect. It will make the evening news for sure. We are going to be more famous than the James Gang." Langan fired back unconcerned.

"Getting pinched by the Feds would make the news too." Guthrie retorted, backing up Jericho. "Seriously Pedro, I am dammed tired of all the circus antics. From now on, it is business only or I am out of the Company for good."

"At least we are getting some fresh air," Tim joked trying to lighten up the mood.

"Yep, that's right, always look on the bright side of things," Brescia agreed, while playing peacemaker, his usual role with the combustible personalities in the Company.

"What did you say? My ears are still ringing." Jericho chimed in.

A steady stream of water from the fire alarms drenched the customers huddled on the floor of the bank as they cowered in terror from the last pipe bomb.

"The bomb is not real. It is only a decoy…" the manager began to say as officers in full combat gear shoved through the shattered front doors of the bank.

"Okay, everybody freeze!" One of them yelled out, using his automatic weapon gun site, to scope out the layout of the bank.

"You guys are a day late and a dollar short," the old security guard informed them sarcastically, while climbing up off the floor. "How about you quit pointing those elephant guns at us and get these women and children out of this mess?"

After a short drive west, the Buick screeched in behind an abandoned warehouse next to Stedeford and McCarthy waiting in the black Tahoe.

"Here we are safe and sound," Tim chirped as they all jumped out.

"Nice job kid," Guthrie answered grudgingly. "But we aren't home free yet," he said referring to sirens screaming by on the highway a few blocks over.

"Make sure we have everything out of the car." Langan stated, as he pulled a can of green paint out of his bag leftover from painting the car. He stepped up on a few discarded milk crates next to a pile of trash and sprayed the letters F. B. I. on the brick wall.

"What in the hell are you doing?" Guthrie asked, stepping around to him. "I swear you have a death wish or something."

"No, my friend, I have a life wish," he answered with a laugh. "This should insure they have a happy holiday."

Guthrie shook his head in disgust. "Torch the car," he called out to Brescia, who quickly retrieved a gas can from the back of the Tahoe.

He drenched the Buick as Langan twisted the gas cap off and stuck a pipe bomb into the hole with the fuse hanging a foot out. He used his blowtorch to light it and dove into the passenger side of the Tahoe.

"Go, go, go!" Langan yelled out as Stedeford punched the gas, causing the tires to kick up clouds of gravel dust, before catching the pavement.

A glow of orange and red lit up in the shadowed alley behind them from the sparks igniting the fresh gasoline on the Buick. A few seconds later, a loud explosion rumbled out shaking the Tahoe. A smaller secondary blast followed right behind from the fuel left in the gas tank.

"You got the tags off didn't you, Mikey Boy?" Langan asked with a rare worried look, since the job had gone so smoothly.

"No. I didn't think we even cared about those bogus tags anyway." Brescia answered, in a concerned tone.

"Man, do I have to watch you every second?"

"No, you said that we-" he began to say, before Langan busted out laughing. "Oh shit. You had me going there for a second."

"I bet Bill Clinton from Arkansas, won't be too happy though, since the tags were in his name,"

Guthrie chimed in, revealing his distaste of the former Arkansas Governor.

The rest of the group got a good laugh, except Jericho of course. His thoughts were preoccupied, stolen by a sweet woman he recently married down in Mexico.

"Maybe they will throw that crooked son of a bitch in jail where he belongs," Guthrie added, showing how he felt about it all. Since receiving a court martial out of the Navy Seals for threatening George Bush Senior, he had a deep hatred for all Presidents of the United States.

Stedeford avoided the highway and took side roads to a shopping mall where four vehicles waited on the outskirts. They parked close enough to blend in with the other cars, but also far enough away from any security cameras that might be watching. Langan grabbed the Christmas sack, pulled out handfuls of cash and stacked it on the dashboard.

"Here is a little Christmas bonus for you guys before we go our own ways?" Langan chirped, separating piles of loose cash from the uncirculated bundles. "Here you go boys, an end to the means," he boasted while giving each of them, five new straps and a handful of loose cash. "Make sure you spread around the new crispies, they might try tracking those serial numbers. Stay out of bars and casinos with those. It is best to spend them in fast food joints that do not have any cameras."

"Yeah, yeah we know, this isn't our first rodeo," Jericho barked, interrupting the lecture. *After*

Langan's foolhardy displays of bravado in the bank, I am not in the mood for preaching. "I'm outta' here. You know my digits in Mexico. Catch ya later," Jericho scowled in a dismissive tone, directing it mostly to Brescia and Guthrie.

Langan started to say something before Jericho got out and shut the door on him mid-sentence. *Next time I hear from you Pedro, you will be behind bars,* Jericho thought, while jumping in a beat up 85' brown Chevy pickup truck he won in a poker game. *The drunken truck driver with the losing hand, tried to back out on signing over the title, until I persuaded him with a jab in the leg with my pocketknife.*

"Wow, that is one serious dude," Langan joked. "Okay here is your share for now. You know the deal. I will give the others their cut. The rest goes into the war chest for a rainy day. I will see you on the flipside. Don't be speeding or do anything stupid while you got this cash on you," he said giving one final order before sliding over to the driver's seat of the Tahoe.

They each got in one of the cars and went different directions. Jericho was already out on the highway heading west by the time the Company left the mall. The first stop was at a hole-in-the-wall liquor store. He made sure the only cameras in the place, pointed at the register. Before he went in, Jericho took two of the new twenties out of a band, crumpled them up several times and then stuck them down the back of his pants.

"That should take the new smell off them," Jericho laughed, as he went in and bought a few refreshments for the long road trip ahead.

A white Styrofoam cooler full of beer rode in the passenger seat for the next eight hours, as Jericho took sips from a pint of whiskey. Feeling a bit buzzed and tired, he decided to stop at a Company safe house in Herrington, Kansas. One night turned into two, as Jericho dipped into his newfound cash to buy several grams of low-grade cocaine at a biker bar. He decided it was time to move on when a discussion turned heated and guns came out. *Who needs those crazy speed freaks anyways?*

With the sun starting behind him, Jericho drove straight through to Kingman, Arizona, to the next safe house. Sleep eluded him as the place was overflowing with a group of Ku Klux Klan members, passing through to a rally in New Mexico. Growing up in an ethnically mixed neighborhood and marrying a Mexican wife, left him with no room to accept their racist views. *The same sentiments are prevalent in the circles I run in, but they do not run their mouth about it,* Jericho thought, as he pulled away from the neighborhood of mobile homes.

After driving for an hour looking at the same desert scenery, Jericho stopped to do a few lines off the dashboard for a pick me up. A pay phone caught his attention as he snorted the white powder. Several weeks had passed since talking to Maria, so he decided to call home. Realizing it took change, he fumbled under the seats of the truck on the floorboard until finding enough to make the call.

"Hey Maria, it's me. Thought I had better check in. I will be heading that way after I stop in Sacramento to visit my Sis and her kids." Jericho stated, in his sweetest voice possible. Several minutes passed before he could say another word.

"Maria, will you...but I told you I was going to be working...now come on don't be that way. Don't be saying a bunch of shit you cannot take back. You want a what? Whatever, you need to calm down. I will be down in a few days and we can straighten all this out. How am I supposed to stay down there and make a dammed living? If you want to be married to a ditch digger, I am not your man!"

As the voice on the other end got louder, Jericho began getting angry and stepped away from the phone for a second knowing he had heard it all before. When Maria did not take a break, he banged the receiver against the glass of the phone booth a few times to interrupt her.

"Can I just get one word in...can I...Maria, you know I love you. Now that is just a bunch of bullshit, I am not seeing anyone but you."

The anger built up in a familiar pattern. Jericho felt his face go flush while tension in his back and neck swelled up. *I tilted on the edge for a second, barely maintaining control; but since I was already irritated with the earlier altercations, I finally just lost it. Before I realized what I was saying, I threw away the most stable relationship I have ever had.* The phone booth received the brunt of the outburst as the receiver slammed down on the hook until it broke into pieces. Jericho's fist etched a large star-shaped formation into glass protecting the phone booth, before he got back into the truck and sped off. Not able to let it stand, he turned around, pulled the gun from the glove box and fired repeatedly into the payphone. *Nearly twenty minutes went by before I noticed my hand was bleeding from cuts on my knuckles.*

"Jack, it looks like it's only me and you from now on," Jericho confessed as he took another swig from a whiskey bottle.

The burning sensation raced down his throat and seemed to push the anger back where it came from. Jericho made a stop at a truck stop to clean his hand up and refill his cooler. Driving the rest of the night, he arrived in Sacramento four days before Christmas. *Instead of going straight to my sisters, I figure I had better cool down awhile to sort things out.* The first strip club he passed seemed like a good place to get some relaxation, so he pulled in. Sleep would not be on the top of the list as he drank and spent money recklessly with a bunch of eager new friends. Jericho stayed the night in a cheap motel while snorting through a new stockpile of drugs. *I tried to numb myself in an attempt to forget Maria, but I guess some things you cannot run from.*

When Jericho's latest playmate gathered her clothes to leave, he suddenly realized he had almost missed Christmas with his sister. They were going to celebrate early this year, before leaving for a trip.

Jericho finished off a bottle of rum, and then squirted a big glob of toothpaste in his mouth attempting to cover the smell, before stumbling out of the hotel room. Trying to sober up and balance himself from the sluggish effects of alcohol, he did a few more lines. More concerned with keeping the powder from falling back out of his nose instead of watching his driving, he backed into the side of a Cadillac, smashing the driver's door in. Surprised nobody heard the crashing sound of steel on steel, Jericho cruised out of the motel parking lot and never looked back.

"They are going to have a Merry Christmas when they see that little gift," he laughed, realizing he got away from the scene of the accident undetected.

The next hour blurred by as everything caught up to Jericho at once. The last thing he remembered was playing horsy with his nieces, before hearing crunching sounds of presents beneath his boots. Everything went in slow motion as he lost his balance and ended up falling into the Christmas tree. The room was spinning as he floundered about in a web of colored lights. A front door slamming in his face followed close behind. It took a while to figure out he had another blackout, until the memory of his nieces cowering away from him, scared and crying kept repeating.

Headlights of traffic passed in flashes as he rocketed up the highway, pushing the old truck to its limits. Soon Jericho was lost on the endless California roads. Suddenly on his left, another payphone caught his eye. A semi-trailer nearly jackknifed trying to miss him as his tired pickup tilted with the sharp turn into the deserted parking lot. Screeching to a stop in front of the phone, Jericho was oblivious to the screaming truck horn going on by. He stumbled out and tried to call his sister. Not remembering exactly what happened left him unable to have an excuse ready, so he hung up. *Then I dial the only other number I knew.* It rang repeatedly with no answer. He felt himself passing out for a second, before someone finally said hello. It took him a few more hellos before he could muster the courage to speak.

"Maria, it's me, please don't hang up. Please baby, I don't have anyone," he said, before a swell of shame overwhelmed him. "I am so sorry," he slurred out, between whimpers of pain. *The last time I cried was at my father's funeral. So I almost feel surprised when tears ran down my face.*

"What? I am somewhere in California, I think. Okay, I will not drive no more tonight, if you promise you will at least see me one last time. It cannot end like this. You are all I have in this shitty world. You are everything to me and I do not want to go on without you. I promise not to mess up anymore. Huh? No, I am not crying. Okay, I won't do anything stupid," Jericho answered, beginning to get control over his emotions. "Really, you mean it? All right, I will head that way in the morning. I love you, Maria. Bye."

This payphone got off a little easier than the last one did as Jericho hung the receiver gently on the hook. He pulled a bottle from the sun visor and took a few more drinks, before climbing into the back of the truck to lie down. An endless parade of stars marched counterclockwise until clouds fluttered in to fill the sky. A low-pressure front coming from the Sonora desert, mixed with the cool air descending east from the coast, to create a supercharged energy field, which ignited into an electrical storm. Sheets of rain doused Jericho, completely soaking him as he watched the show. Zigzags of splintered light, burst from every direction. Without warning, a bout of melancholy came over him like the thunderstorm sweeping over the rustic landscape. It was slow developing in its approach, but unforgiving and unbending in its designs. Jericho pulled out his gun tucked in the front of his jeans and put it to his temple. He clicked the safety off and pulled the trigger as a lightning bolt cut through the sky and struck a transformer on a light pole nearby. An eerie green light of fire from the charred wires illuminated the truck as he realized the chamber had been empty. *I was still alive.*

Chapter 4

Dying of the Light

"Do not go gentle into that good night

Old age should burn and rave at close of day

Rage, rage against the dying of the light."

Dylan Thomas

December 25, 1994

Nogales, Mexico

Jericho Daniels

Each young face beamed with an innocence unspoiled by time, regrets or failures. Minutes at this age seemed to last in dog years. All of the children sat on the floor Indian-style, listening to the daycare teacher read one of their favorite books, except for one girl with a soft white, chiffon dress on. She stood on the right side of the group clutching a plush bunny rabbit leftover from a recent Easter party. She was unconcerned with how Curious George was going to clean up all the suds flowing from an overloaded washing machine before the Man in the Yellow Hat returned home. Two long blonde curls hung down her round cherub face, parting enough so you could see her deep penetrating blue eyes, puffy and swollen from crying. The sweet girl kept looking toward the elevator, past the sign in desk, as if waiting for someone to return. As the pages turned, she became antsy and began pacing about. The teacher finally paused reading the story, to make her sit down with the rest of the group. Reluctantly, the girl obeyed the order after a couple of stern looks her way.

The rest of the children bounced and chirped out like little birds waiting for a worm, as they anticipated the ending of the story. As the page turned, a series of explosions crackled from above them rocking the entire building. The shockwave shook hand-drawn pictures off the wall, turned over desks and rattled the long white bulbs from the light fixtures. Another blast, exponentially larger than the previous, obliterated the east side of the daycare. A windstorm of shattered glass showered the group. The floor buckled upwards for a moment, then severed into three large slabs. The west chunk stayed in place, anchored firmly into the steel rebar of the building, as the other two heaved violently creating a jagged chasm between the circle of children, before they plunged downward and rested at ninety-degree angles. One by one, the terrified children slid into an angry abyss below. The girl in the white chiffon dress tried to hang on, as books and fallout tumbled past her. Slowly her grasp failed her and she followed her friends.

"Mommy!" She screamed out while sliding backwards, hoping this was all just a bad dream and her mother would be at her bedside to wake her up. Her beautiful face seemed frozen with dread as she looked into the blackness, but not surprised. It is as if she was expecting something bad to happen all along.

Jericho Daniels reached out within his dream, in a futile attempt to grab her. Shards of fire seemed to burst from all directions, swallowing him in a prison of ochre and crimson pain. Every nerve ending burned. *I welcome it as a payment for what I had done.*

Speckled in sweat, Jericho lurched up out of bed gasping for life and another chance to make things right. After several days detoxing from all the booze, drugs and painkillers, he could not tell if that was the reason for the constant shakes or the haunting dreams that seemed so real, he could almost smell the smoke. *I will never forget her face.* Whichever it was, Jericho knew he needed a drink. Anything would do, preferably something potent to dull the senses.

"Jericho, are you okay, Baby?" Maria called out, in a sleepy whisper, a vision of a resting angel, as the silk sheet clung to every curve of her body.

"It was only a bad dream. Go back to sleep sweetie, I am fine," He answered, while slipping out of bed and covering her back up in the same motion. Jericho fished around with his left foot, found his boxers under the bed and put them on as he left the room. He headed straight to the fridge where a bottle of vodka was waiting in the freezer. *I gulped it down like my morning coffee.* The clock on the new microwave he gave Maria for Christmas flashed that it was four fifteen a.m. *A bit earlier than I usually start drinking, but hopefully, it helps to get my mind off that nightmare.* Jericho stood there with the refrigerator door open until every drop from the clear pint bottle disappeared.

Their casa was compact with sparse retro furnishings from a long past decade. Two end tables on each side of a tan couch with broken middle springs, covered one wall in the living room, with a small imitation oak bookcase centered along the other wall next to the front door. A plump red-apple spiced candle burned on top of the bookcase slightly below an oil print of Jesus dying on the cross. Maria was Catholic and had only missed a handful of days at church since she was a kid. Jericho did not really believe, but went to church with her to avoid an argument. As Jericho stared at the flickering candle with the empty bottle in his hand, a strange comfort came over him. *I guess I am better off than him*, he thought, as he stared into the sad piercing eyes in the artwork.

The two-bedroom bungalow belonged to Carlos Espinoza, town mayor, police chief, developer and Jericho's new Father-In-Law. They hoped someday through perseverance, they could scratch enough money together to persuade him to sell it. *Maybe when he figures out I am not going to ditch Maria and actually be a good dad to her two young sons, he will not hate me with such venomous persistence.* Maria was devastated when Carlos did not attend their modest ceremony at the courthouse. *It is legal in this country now and there was not a damned thing he can do about it, except disown the both of us. He played that hand, so now he will have to live with all that hate to eat him alive from the inside out. I guess I should not expect him to believe I can change, when I am not sure I can myself. Drinking Christmas morning is not a very good indicator, that I am on the right track.* Jericho figured he had a few hours to relax and unwind before everyone else was up.

Briefly checking on his two boys, it seemed he could not take his eyes off them, as they lay entangled in each other and the covers. *What would I do if I lost them?* Jericho finally regained his focus enough to stumble out to his brown truck and retrieve the presents from the back, which amounted to a pair of almost new bikes for the boys and a vacuum cleaner to compliment the microwave for his new bride. *Rather boring gifts,* he thought, but that is what Maria wanted. *Maria was very practical that way.* She would rather have a few things to make it more of a home for all of them, than something extravagant for herself. *Just one more reason I love her so much.* Jericho placed the presents alongside the hunched over little tree, he had swiped by moonlight from a Boy Scout troop, selling them in a parking lot on the way down.

Once Jericho had everything staged in place, he stepped out and sat on the tailgate of his truck. *I need a smoke to get myself awake.* They had a big day of holiday festivities planned with Maria's family, minus her father of course, who conveniently scheduled a ski trip to Aspen, Colorado, as a present to himself. *I am happy as a clam in warm sand down here with my new wife and my boys, but I bet I could do some serious partying in that town,* Jericho thought, as his cigarette burned down to the filter within a few heavy puffs.

Jericho daydreamed in and out of reality while staring down the narrow, crooked street pock-holed with mini craters filled with rain, cluttered with old automobiles, homes of every size shape and color, overloaded trashcans, the occasional stray cat, but void of human life. It made him feel as if he were in a zombie movie where the government unleashes a plague that kills everyone on the planet. "I am the Omega man now, the last man on the earth," Jericho chuckled. *I do not think I have ever heard this town as quiet as it is right now.*

Besides a few random dog barks, the Ciudad was peaceful. No music, gun shots, or the dull buzz from the hustle and bustle of the poverty-stricken residents. Finally, the last smoke came out of the pack along with a half-burned joint partially sacrificed when celebrating getting across the border without a hassle from the Mexican Federals'. Jericho was more concerned with them finding the ten thousand in mixed bills stashed into the passenger seat covered with a suitcase and a weeks' worth of dirty laundry. *I would have more money without all my bad habits sucking the cash out faster than I can steal it, but it is still a lot of money in this shithole town.* Jericho hoped they could live almost nine months on it comfortably, while he picked up odd jobs so Maria would not get suspicious. *If she ever guessed, the money was from bank robberies, I would be out the door. She loves me, but I know I have used up all my chances.*

Jericho laid back and used a duffle bag to prop up his head. He couldn't remember when he felt so peaceful. The last time he looked at the stars was in the California desert when he tried to end it all. *Thank God, I failed...well if there is a God.* It is not that he did not want to believe in a higher power he surmised, but somehow could not believe without proof. Ever since he was a kid, one person or another tried to push him towards a religion or personal savior. Even the folks at the Elohim City compound did their best to convert him, to no avail. *How can they preach love while celebrating the Holocaust?* The more he thought about it, he realized Maria and maybe his sister Chloe were the only ones that ever accepted him for who he was and didn't try to change him. *They both lead by example and make me want to be a better man.*

"I am done with all of it!" Jericho said out loud to himself. *I am not going back up there again.* Something was telling him if he did leave, that he would never make it back alive. Another voice nagged him deep inside though. If he didn't head up to the States, he would be running forever from his past. *Maybe my horrible dreams are trying to make me realize that many lives are at stake?* Although completely disorganized, the Arizona Patriots were still dangerous. With the backing, training and lodging provided by Elohim City, mixed with the influx of cash from his Midwest Bank Robber gang, it would just be a matter of time before they got revenge for Ruby Ridge and the Waco massacre. Their hate only grew stronger with each government trespass on the Constitution. Immune from prosecution and media scrutiny, the government had unleashed deadly gas and tanks on its own citizens. Jericho knew a confrontation was brewing and every fringe element from skinheads to doomsday preachers were banding together for the coming apocalypse. *The President is as dirty as they come. A war is seething in the underbelly of the country.*

"Hell with it! It is not my fight anymore. I have everything I ever wanted right here. Let them burn the whole shit house to the ground for all I care." Jericho muttered to himself, as the effects of booze and drugs began to lull him back to sleep.

It started as a low clatter-trap rattle in the distance, slowly becoming more annoying as it grew closer. Every dog in the neighborhood took offense until the silence was irrevocably broken. Jericho tried to drum it out and stay within his own thoughts of a life with his new family, until the squeaky shocks and thumping rap music were upon him. He sat up as a four door rust bucket of a Lincoln Continental rolled up shining its only headlight practically in his face. The engine sputtered as the driver revved it one last time, before shutting the car off. As patchwork of Christmas lights from the neighbors illuminated the four passengers, they just sat and stared a moment.

Jericho felt a nervous tension slowly building, which always meant trouble. Jericho sold his gun so he would not have to explain the filed off serial number crossing the border. He still had a hunting knife in the truck under the driver's seat, but that seemed miles away. In unison, all four doors opened. His hopes that they were going across the street faded quickly as the shambled group stepped forward. Not knowing who they were or if they were armed, Jericho slowly pushed himself off the tailgate to his bare feet.

"Gringo, what you doing parked in my driveway?" A cigarette battered voice called out from a tall, slender, twenty-something punk pushing his way to the front. Colored tattoo ink covered every inch of his arms exposed from a white tank top.

Before Jericho could answer or even think of a response, an obese man on the left with a layer of gold chains matching his teeth, echoed the previous words. "Hey Chango, he is talking to you!"

In Jericho's mind it all played out. The two guys with red flannel shirts and baggy jeans on the ends had their right hands behind their backs, most likely ready to pull their guns at the slightest provocation. They were waiting for the cue from the leader, who wanted to make his point and gain rep with his homeboys. They wanted this to be personal by making him suffer, before the bullets finished the job. *In their arrogance, lay their ruin.*

"I live here with my wife and boys. So climb on back into that piece of shit and go back to whatever dirty Mamacita you crawled out of!" Jericho growled back, luring them closer.

"That is my Puta now, Holmes. She is my property! We are going to have a little party tonight with her after we cut your cojones off." The gang leader threatened, as he pulled a homemade shank from his back pocket. Consisting of a sharpened piece of sheet metal integrated into a wood handle and fastened with duct tape, it flashed ominously in the lone streetlight above them.

"I am not going to tell you Pendejos again. Go about your business before you piss me off!" Jericho volleyed back, cracking his knuckles while standing his ground.

They all laughed as their red bandanas fluttered from their belt loops. The gang spread out a bit as they approached. The two flannel clad thugs tried to flank him until Jericho took a step back. Their faces displayed a mix of excitement and anger, which soon changed to disbelief as Jericho got down on his knees in front of them. He looked a little less intimidating kneeling down in nothing, but his boxers as he looked to the ground. They were confused at first, almost sensing the trap until a drug-fueled hatred took over and they circled into a tight group.

Jericho put his arms in the air as if to surrender and closed his eyes. The neighborhood was quiet again and so were his aggressors, as they stopped the bravado and got in place to finish him quickly. *I hear them breathing. Every scuff of their worn cowboy boots on the dirt lawn seemed magnified. Closer...closer...until the group is right up on me.* The shank came up and rested between Jericho's eyes. The point indented enough into his skin to leave a mark, but not a cut.

"You're going to die tonight!" The gang leader laughed, obviously savoring his moment of power.

With his eyes closed, Jericho waited patiently. *I know the outcome already.* Between beats of his heart, the shank pulled from his forehead as the leader reared back to gain velocity for the deathblow. With a slight tilt of his shoulders, Jericho moved his head to the right as the shank whistled forward. *I felt the blade nick my left ear as it sped past.* As his eyes opened, Jericho's left arm came down and trapped the gang leader's arm. Using his own shoulder for leverage, Jericho pulled his right arm up and under, forming an arm bar above the man's elbow. *As I pulled down and flexed my bicep, I could hear the guy's tendons begin snapping from the pressure I was inflicting.*

Swiveling his hips, Jericho loosened the arm bar, before locking both hands onto the attacker's limp wrist. *I bent it backwards, shredding muscles, while ripping his shoulder out of its socket and forcing him to flop onto his back.* Jericho stripped the shank from the Leader's useless hand. With a deft move, he lunged towards the obese gangster and stabbed it twice into the potbellied thug's knee.

The flannelled gangster on right pulled his gun, but was too late. Jericho took the shank and jabbed it upwards between the kid's knuckles forcing him to drop the weapon, before slamming it down into his foot, pinning it to the ground. *With full force, I kicked my right leg straight back into the last dude's groin, before he could pull his gun. They are totally screwed now.*

The obese thug tried to regroup, while favoring his knee and threw a wild clumsy punch that connected solidly onto Jericho's cheekbone. *I did not even feel it, as the adrenaline surges through my veins. I jumped to my feet and delivered a crushing blow, that unhinged his jaw, knocking him out cold.* With the rage came the blackness. *It was like I was watching someone else use knees and elbows, to knock out teeth, break bones and smash faces.*

Red lights flashed as Jericho could hear Maria's voice screaming for him to come back to this world. When Jericho slowly slipped out of a trance, Maria's arms came up behind him to stop the fight. The fighting instinct was still in control while the Federals' guns pointed right towards his head, forcing Maria to step between them. *Then I was back.* Maria nudged him to go sit on the tailgate as she used her standing as the mayor's daughter to keep them from arresting Jericho. *Regaining my senses, I went around to the passenger seat and grabbed what I knew would seal the deal.* Jericho approached the closest Federal' and handed him ten new one hundred dollar bills, before he stepped past Maria and went into the casa. *American money is the only thing they understand down here.*

Jericho showered and lay on the bed until Maria came in and held him from behind. *I thought she would be mad instead of affectionate. I guess she knows I had no choice.* She was scared of the demon she witnessed fighting, but knew it was to protect her and the boys, so made peace with it. Maria kissed each one of his swollen knuckles on his left hand, until working her way to his midsection. She started to go lower until he pulled her up to him.

"Just hold me, okay?"

Maria smiled at his sudden tenderness. This was the part of him she loved the most. Somewhere buried inside, past the tough exterior, the anger, the pain, was a truly sweet and caring man. She felt safe for the first time in longer than she could remember. The moment flashed by like headlights on a deserted highway. Before they knew it the boys were snuggled in with them trying to get the day started. The presents under the tree were calling their name and they could hardly stand to wait any longer.

Jericho got up first and started some biscuits and iron skillet gravy for breakfast. *Just like my mom always made when I was a kid.* Maria was impressed. She could get used to the domestic side of Jericho. The boys tore through the wrapped presents and were outside on their new bikes before the bows hit the floor. Soon they had a ramp made from an old front door propped on top of a tire.

Maria was going to call the boys for breakfast, but decided to let them be daredevils a little longer. Jericho was unusually quiet, as if he was a million miles away. He never was much for chitchat or deep discussions; the words he did speak though carried a lot of weight.

"Breakfast is excellent, my love."

Jericho nodded in acknowledgement and kept eating his second helping. There seemed to be some distance between them and she did not like it. A few more bites in silence were all she could stand. Maria got up and pushed between him and the table. He resisted until she straddled him and began kissing his neck.

"So what is on your mind dear? I can tell you are thinking about something because your brow gets all serious and scrunches down," Maria asked, with a laugh.

"Oh, is that right?" Jericho volleyed back with a half-crooked smile.

"So, are you going to talk or will I have to get tough with you," She fired back, while reaching down between his legs and grabbing his crotch seductively.

Jericho squirmed at first trying to resist her, but knew that would never work. He stood up with Maria hooked to him and moved on over to the couch. He kissed her deeply a minute trying to find the words.

"So those guys out on the lawn...anyone you know? Because they said some shit they shouldn't have, as if they had intimate knowledge of you or something. Whatever it is, I know it's none of my business and it doesn't matter," he spoke softly, before she interrupted him.

"Hell no! Jericho, you are only the second man I have ever been with besides the boy's father. I was never with anyone else after his motorcycle accident. How could you even think I could be with that trash?" Maria fired back.

"No I didn't...that is not what I said. It is just-"

"Just what? They talked some crap and now you think I am a whore?"

Jericho could sense he was making it worse trying to explain. His words were failing him and didn't want to argue on Christmas morning, so he got up and went back in to finish his breakfast. *I want to leave, hide, anything but fight with her.* Maria was right; he felt jealous and had made a critical judgment of her character. While she tried to give him the benefit of the doubt over the altercation, he turned around and did the opposite. *I am such an idiot. I don't deserve her. Where am I going to go now?*

Maria could see all the worry and vexation creeping over his face. Jericho suddenly looked like a caged animal ready to run. After a couple of minutes, she began feeling guilty for raising her voice. She was still learning how sensitive Jericho was. In the time they were together, Maria always felt inferior due to her economic situation, but now it was Jericho who showed a jealous side. Maria casually walked over and put her arms around him. He resisted, trying to protect his space, until a kiss made Jericho relent his territory again.

"I am sorry I over-reacted. Yes, I do know who those guys are. They did not used to be that way when we were in school. For whatever reason, they took a bad path until my father finally put the hammer down on them. Maybe trying to ruin Christmas for me was a way to get revenge?"

"Not that he even cares about us." Jericho added.

"When the jobs dried up around here, all these gangs started forming. Nobody has anything worth stealing, so they just drive around, selling drugs and trying to recruit more kids into that life with them. That group has been the most violent."

"Well they won't be hurting anyone else."

"Thank you, baby. I feel so safe with you. I love you so much. Please don't ever leave us again. I know there is some work around here you can do. You can help my uncle at the restaurant, or construction with my cousins." Maria encouraged. "We can talk to them at the party today if you want? Everyone is looking forward to having you there." Maria gleamed with a proud smile.

For once in his life, Jericho felt like he had a home. *No sooner did I feel content in her arms, than that nagging voice started up again. I know I have to go back. If I don't stop The Company, who will?*

Chapter 5

Millennial Rage

"I was angry with my friend

I told my wrath, my wrath did end

I was angry with my foe

I told it not, my wrath did grow."

William Blake

January 1, 1995

Overland Park, Kansas

Pete Langan

Even with the recent decorative renovations, the overall ambiance of the hotel room still looked cheaply done. On the plus side, by utilizing all available floor space except for the plush green, carpeted aisles around the queen size bed, the room seemed larger than its modest square footage. Two days' worth of empty beer bottles gave the place the look of a hobo's shack. A stale, rotting barley smell indicated that room service had not cleaned all weekend.

Donna lay staring at the ceiling as a New Year's Eve companion snored with an irritatingly slow wheezing. Between that and the monotonous swishing sound of the ceiling fan, it created a hypnotizing effect, that brought on a deep sleep. Soon Donna's idle consciousness wandered back to restless days of youth. It was always the same.

In dreamtime, only a few seconds passed between Donna waking up in another world and springing out of bed as a young boy named Pete. An inner alarm clock told Pete it was long past breakfast and the punishment for not eating dinner the night before, was now over. He had been isolated in his room much too long for a five-year-old that was used to being the center of attention to a doting mother, four older siblings and a revolving staff of care-giving amah's that washed and dressed him in fine white linen outfits. The food, as he recalled, was not so bland that Pete would risk speaking back to his father, the absolute lord of the manner. *It was a way to get attention I suppose. A new yearning that I did not even know was there.*

Pete's parents had decided to go without their children to see *Lawrence of Arabia,* which was appearing in Saigon near the Royal Palace. It was a "must see" and all the rage back in the States. *I felt slighted for not being included in their plans.* Pete wanted to be with his family in the same ways other children interacted: normal everyday stuff such as hugging, laughing and wrestling about together. The only wrestling Pete received from his parents was an occasional pat on the head. Father gave all the kids an allotted amount of time on an individual, need to basis, almost as if it was on his things to do list. *Even though extremely limited, I always adored my time with him, brief as it is.*

As Pete rubbed the sleep from his eyes and headed downstairs to the kitchen, he noticed it was uncharacteristically quiet. *Where was everyone?*

"Mother, Father, I am up now. Can I come out? I will eat my dinner now," Pete called out, as he scampered up to the third level of the French colonial townhouse.

Pete could hear a dull uproar growing louder. He shuffled out onto the balcony which doubled as a playroom, a living area and bar for entertaining his father's important spy friends. The sun was bright and his eyes were slow to react, but Pete could make out the silhouettes of his family and several servants looking out over the wrought iron railing to the street below. They had a bird's eye view of downtown Saigon from this vantage point. Eventually, it was a front row seat to watch the city self-destruct into chaos and fire.

"What is everyone doing out here?" Pete asked quietly, but he received no reply.

Pete snuggled up to his Mother's leg to divert her attention from the circus of activity below. *Something big was going on today.*

"I was beginning to wonder if you were going to sleep all day." She inquired with a faint smile, while pulling him closer for a hug.

Pete was beginning to answer her when demonstrators grew in numbers from all corners of the city. He peeked up over the railing and was astonished to see a majority of the crowd dressed in orange flowing robes. Glistening, shaven heads irradiated a glare that seemed to make the whole scene sparkle. Although barely ready for kindergarten, Pete was well aware that Buddhist monks made up the bulk of the mob. The unfair treatment of the monks by the South Vietnamese government was the center of conversation recently at one of the many parties his parents hosted in their spacious dining room.

Looking up, Father seemed as tall as the blue sky above. He stood stiff as a statue with one leg slightly in front of the other, right elbow corkscrewed out, one eye squinting and the other peering into his camera, while it filmed the entire protest. His face stayed wallpapered with his "serious" look, but also seemed to have a bit of a nervous excitement at capturing history through the lens. The rest of the family did not seem as attracted to the increasing danger level.

A leader emerged from the crowd and sat down crossing his legs in a traditional style. Two followers approached from the rear carrying containers of fuel and doused the older monk as he prayed. With a choreographed kindness to it, he erupted in a rusted fireball that immediately filled the surrounding air with a putrescent odor and the taste of charred flesh. *I will never forget that burnt, salty coat that hung unto my tongue despite several drinks of tart lemonade from Mother's glass.*

The old monk closed his eyes, clapped his hands in front of him and sat unflinching as the merciless flames enveloped him in a cloak of death. Within minutes, he was an unrecognizable burning lump. Mother scooped Pete up and rushed to the illusion of safety within the house, as Father continued documenting the tragedy until running out of film. By the next morning, he had the negatives airlifted straight to President Kennedy, as a gruesome complement to his eggs Benedict.

Through the years, Pete would see himself as the old monk. Self-immolating, at the edge of sanity, but always going down fighting for something he believed in. It took him several stints in jail segregated from normal society, before Pete understood why the monk did it. The fiery death defined the religious leader and transcended his average life into one of a martyr. *In the end though, it changed nothing; he was just another useless death in that war.*

Back in the motel room, Donna felt a slight nudge from behind that woke her up. A hairy arm came over her left shoulder like a seat belt and lodged under her chin. *I was back to the real world again.* The man's face was rough with a five o'clock shadow going on ten. It sandpapered against Donnas' cheek as he began to grind with arousal. *I pulled away as far as his grasp allowed, trying to pretend I was still sleeping, but he shifted again while constricting his naked body next to mine. One hand went down my red lace bra while the other pawed at my black pantyhose with the back end ripped out of them from the night before.* Donna faced a pillow so not to breathe exhaled whiskey breath from this new friend. *My mind drifted past the faces of old lovers, weaving in and out of sordid sexual encounters, but always ending up trapped in a dimly lit prison cell. A strong black hand on the back of my head pinning me to the cold floor as it felt like my guts were torn out.* Without saying a word, Donnas' companion penetrated from behind, grinded and grunted for about five minutes, before releasing his last bit of pent up sexual energy.

While he rolled over on his back to savor the moment, Donna jumped up and duck-walked into the bathroom. *The reflection in the mirror was the other person inside me.* Donna's long brown hair was disheveled and flat on the right side, lipstick smeared, eyeliner bleeding down reminiscent of Alice Cooper, bra half off, rug burns on knees and elbows. *A wave of guilt and disgust from what I saw looking back at me, swelled up until it spontaneously combusted in a fit of rage. Before I even thought about it, I smash the mirror out with my forearm.* The crooked shards remaining in the frame, still gave off enough of an image that Donna could see a majority of the face looking back. It was Pete Langan. *Like the mirror, I felt broken and incomplete.*

"Maybe a shower will do me some good," *I mumble to myself as I got in without undressing.* A red line of blood ran with the water and circled the drain. *Two jagged slivers of mirror were lodged into my arm, but I felt nothing. Just like in life, I was consumed with a hollow nothingness. No room left for love, but plenty for hate.* Attempting to get one more spot of amber liquid out of the complimentary shampoo bottle, the glass drug across Langan's bare stomach, trenching out little cuts.

"Well hell, I guess I better get that out of there before I look like I was in a catfight." Langan talked to himself, while pulling the glass out and tossing it into the toilet. A shooting pain went up his arm that must have been saving up for the exit. *I welcomed it like a dear friend. At least I felt something. It meant that I was alive.*

Langan took off the bra and wrapped it around his bleeding arm, before removing the rest of his attire. *It felt good to clean up, sober up and snap out of the degrading whirlpool pulling me down.* A new year was ahead that offered different challenges and opportunities. *I am not going to blow it this time. Many people are counting on me to amount to something for once, including my family living back in Cincinnati, my adopted family in Elohim City, Oklahoma, and all of my brothers in the Aryan Republican Army.* The warm water had a rejuvenating effect, clearing a confused mind and allowing thoughts to focus on business. Langan sat down in the tub surround and tried his best to plan the next move, but the dreams from the night before kept coming back. *I had not thought about my father for a long time, but now could get him off my mind.*

It was difficult for Langan to rationalize an idolization of his father, to the man he really was. Many summer days passed as a kid running through the woods in Wheaton, Maryland, pretending to be CIA. Agent, Eugene Langan, shooting the enemy with a stick gun and single-handedly winning the war. Years later after his father's death, Langan and his sister found some of Eugene's old files. They had maps showing the secret tunnels from the Royal Palace. All of the documents were handwritten in his easily recognizable scribble, with the date of November 2, 1963. This pinned Eugene to the assassination of South Vietnamese President, Diem and his brother, Nhu, who was the Chief of the Vietnam military.

Seeing the photos of that day set off such a reaction. Langan could almost taste the teargas drifting in from the attacks on the palace, which crept into their townhouse in Vietnam. *I could never understand how my father, the most patriotic person I ever knew, could be involved in these murders?* It was the first assassination of many, Langan would soon find out. Other documents, trailed his father's politically motivated search-and-destroy missions from one village to another, leaving bodies and broken families. *Why did he not tell us that he was the lynch pin and the turning point in the war?* He shipped Mother and us kids off like useless luggage back to the United States soon after the revolt. Our family lived through hell once we came back "home". On the surface, we looked happy in our upper class home, but it was never like that. Things can be deceiving looking inward at other's lives. It is always what's beneath the surface that matters.* A knock on the bathroom door brought Langan back to reality.

"Donna, are you okay, baby?" A voice inquired, with urgency to use the toilet.

It took me a second to realize where I was, who I was and what I was doing in a shower with cold water spraying over me. It was not until Langan was dressed in a black Harley Davidson shirt along with army camouflage fatigues, with his hair pulled back in a ponytail away from his face, that he fully came out of the Donna character and the haze enveloping him like a drug. He pushed

Donna back into a dark closet of his inner thoughts. *She was always waiting for me.*

By the expression on the middle-aged man's face, Langan was not remotely the same person that went into the bathroom. As the hung-over companion clumsily sat up from the bed, Langan put one finger over his mouth, indicating that he did not want to be spoken to while gathering his gear. *I went over to the nightstand and grabbed his fat wallet. He started to protest until I give him "the look" which entailed a slight smile accompanied by a dead stare, meaning that I would sooner kill him than look at him.* The frightened man got the point and offered his watch along with all of his cash. Noticing it was just a cheap Timex with the incorrect time, Langan declined.

"Happy New Year, dumb ass," Langan exclaimed, as he walked calmly and deliberately out the door.

He could not get out of the hotel fast enough. Langan just wanted to hit the road and put last night, last week and his alter life behind him. *Where in the hell was I parked anyway?* Looking around the half-empty parking lot, which circled the hotel, Langan realized he had dumped his last car so it would not be traced back to him. *My mind chased itself around in circles, while I walked around the building.* Langan snapped out of it when he noticed Jericho Daniels waiting around back in his brown truck. *I took a second to reflect on the previous few nights. The guilt subsided and a new sense of, dare I say, "happiness and self-fulfillment" came over me.*

Langan still felt as if he was living a lie, but the opportunity to become someone else while attending the fetish ball party held by the K.C. Cross Dressers as his alter ego, Donna McClure, temporarily seemed to heal his soul. *It gave me a renewed energy to focus my nomadic life on one single goal. I knew I was going to make a difference in this world. The sacrifice of the innocent will be the catalyst for the American people to see the government for what it really is, a failed and corrupt system.*

"Hey Vance, how was your break?" Langan asked as he got in the truck.

Jericho Daniels sat there for a second as he adjusted to that fake name again. Finally, he shrugged his shoulders for an answer, started the truck and pulled out of the parking lot to begin the trip to the safe house in Kansas. Jericho made it obvious; he was not in a chatty mood. Jericho had a slight bruise under his right eye and his knuckles on both hands looked banged up.

"Did you run into some trouble, Vance?" Langan asked, trying to drum up some conversation to replace the clattering rhythm of the old truck.

"Nothing I couldn't handle. Did you?" Jericho fired back, referring to the small cuts on Langan's arm.

When Langan looked down, he noticed a slight tint of pink was still on the cuticles of his fingernails from the nail polish. *The way Vance stared at me when I got in the truck; it was as if he had figured it all out.*

"It was an accident, no big deal." Langan answered, trying to let the conversation tail off before the subject of his weekend came up. A hunger pang urged Langan to put some breakfast in his body to soak up some of the alcohol. "Hey, can you stop at the next place you see? I'm half starved."

The diner was a four-star, top-of-the-line restaurant when the Interstate first came through the area, but those days were long gone. Despite the uninviting appeal of the outside, Jericho pulled into the empty parking lot since it was the only place to eat for miles.

"I have to make a call…do what you need to do."

"Okay, Vance; it shouldn't take too long. This place is a ghost town."

As Langan ate the crisp bacon, runny eggs over-easy and cold toast, a flood of inspiration suddenly poured out through a pencil with no eraser, onto napkins from the fifties-style holder. *It is time to blow the doors off this revolution and bring in all the lost sheep to the cause.* His confidence as the future leader of these hordes of young white warriors building self-sufficient cells, grew when the words "armed, struggle, and underground" appeared on one of the waiting napkins. *With those three words, I have pretty much outlined our intent.* Langan hoped the "armed struggle" part would stir up a dormant sense of American pride in the audience, while the words "underground" gave the illusion of a wave of freedom fighters that would soon rise up and free this country. *We will pound out the messages of the Aryan Army and this historic cause.*

Standing there slack-jawed and chomping on a tiny nub of gum, the server slid the ticket under the corner of Langan's dirty plate stacked with crumpled unfinished ideas. He finally ran out of napkins and made his exit without tipping. Unfortunately, June Bug, as she called herself, was going to have to pay the piper for bringing an under-cooked breakfast. *Everything always evens out in life, even this.*

Langan went into the restroom and scrubbed at his fingertips to remove any evidence from his alter ego. Since the cloth towel holder only looped one dirty section after another, he left with his hands wet. Vowing silently to never return to this establishment, Langan walked to the truck where Jericho sat on the tailgate smoking a cigarette. A stiff cool breeze stirred up gravel dust in the parking lot and partially stuck onto Langan's wet hands before he could get them dried off on his jeans.

The air was a bit colder as a cloud front moved in and blocked the heat-giving sun. Almost in slow motion, Pete's master plan seemed to unfold in his mind as they cruised out of the parking lot. The pickup sputtered a puff of oily gray smoke when the engine moved up to higher gears to join the oncoming highway traffic. Before long, they were nearing Pittsburgh, Kansas.

Situated in Crawford County on the partially rolling prairie and forest of the Ozark Highlands, the peaceful coal town made a great central location to do their business, without interference from the neighbors, who kept to their own lives. They pulled down the badly rutted dirt road to the metal gate with a "No Trespassing" sign welcoming them to the property. Langan jumped out, put in the right combination on the lock holding a chain which secured the gate to a wood post and opened it up.

Once Jericho pulled in, Langan shut the gate behind them. A couple of twisting turns through a wooded area, led to an open pasture that was once home to a dozen or so dairy cows. The three-bedroom ranch style home was not in the best of shape. It looked lived in enough not to draw suspicion, but also run down to discourage anyone that happened past the gate. It sat facing east on a slight hill with a few dead scrub brushes decorating it. They drove around back to the walk-in basement and pulled alongside two SUV's with temporary tags, recently purchased in Arkansas.

Guthrie and the rest of the gang including Brescia, McCarthy and Stedeford arrived right after Christmas and celebrated New Year's Eve with a lot of booze, drugs and target practice using an assortment of new guns, courtesy of Andreas Strassmeir at Elohim city. They had more ammo, beer and confidence than ever before. *Everyone except Guthrie was in good spirits, which was typical.*

"Hey there, Commander Pedro! What's up, Vance?" Brescia bellowed out, as he stumbled towards them with a bottle of whiskey in one hand and a beer bottle in the other. The rest looked up from the college football game for a quick wave hello. Brescia gave Langan a one-handed hug before turning to Jericho, who quickly made it known he was not in a hugging mood.

"Did you guys get a phone hooked up yet?" Jericho asked, with a slightly hopeful tone.

The guys shrugged as if to say no before cheering for a big play on the television.

"Well shit, I would have stopped in town if I knew," Jericho replied, with an aggravated tone. "I guess I will go clean up," he mumbled to Langan, before making his way upstairs to the bathroom.

Langan could not wait to show his ideas to the Company, but wanted to put all his notes out on paper to make sure they would understand the significance of his thoughts. He dropped his bags to the side and ambled to the back room, which was already set up with a desk and war props in front of a stolen video camera. It looked like a military surplus store with boxes of ammo and a hodgepodge of old

World War 2 relics, including a swastika flag mounted on the wall behind the desk.

Langan worked on his notes through dinner, which consisted of macaroni and cheese with hotdogs cooked camp style over the open flames on the stove. By midafternoon the next day, Langan had his script ready that would change the world. He slammed several shots of liquor and chased them with beer until he had the right attitude. Langan put on a black ski mask and glared into the camera. Brescia pushed the record button.

"Our goal, is to overthrow the Government. To establish an Aryan Republic that will exterminate the Jews and deport all the blacks from this country. We will try to keep civilian casualties to a minimum, but in all wars…there is collateral damage."

This revolution will be bathed in the blood of the innocent, but that is the only way to cleanse the scourge that is controlling our country. My father was the spark of the Vietnam War and now it is my turn to start a revolution, Lagan thought to himself, as they finished filming.

Chapter 6

Fires of Insurrection

"Give me liberty

Or give me death."

Patrick Henry

January 18, 1995

Kingman, Arizona

Jericho Daniels

Living in the crevices of night, the Mohave rattlesnake leads a solitary existence. With a stare that is both mesmerizing and deadly, it strikes with blinding accuracy when provoked. As in life, the outline of a coiled rattlesnake on the yellow flag, warned outsiders to stay away. The Aryan Republic Army's banner seemed simplistic below the American flag, but the phrase of Liberty or Death on either side of the snake, brought to mind the revolution behind the stars and stripes ruffling in the scant breeze. Clumps of dead prairie grass surrounded the flagpole situated in front of a dusty beige mobile home perpendicular to the road. Several vehicles were parked in the gravel driveway close to the front door. The flags created shadows in a noon sun dominating the cloudless day.

Part of Jericho Daniels was glad to finally get to this place in the middle of nowhere for the big meeting, but mostly he wanted to get it over with and head back down to Mexico. *It felt like every time things started going well with Maria, some new bullshit came along and we are back to square one.* Curiosity got the better of him though, so now Jericho bounded past a threshold of this new twist in the road. He knew if he went on down the rest of the trail, he would find something evil. *It is not as if I am an angel or anything, Lord knows I have screwed up plenty, but these assholes want revenge in the worst possible way.* Maybe in the past, he was like them. Things were much different now. A happy new family gave him hope to live. *I tried to check out of this shitty life, but it wasn't in the cards. So there has to be some reason why I am still here?* That reason was at the end of the dusty street. No matter how much Jericho tried to turn the steering wheel and go home, something bad inside him took over. *Away I go.* As he pulled across the street from the Fortier's trailer home, an overwhelming urge for a drink boiled up. That rotten gut feeling that seemed to arise suddenly and take over all reason.

Jericho was reaching for a bottle in the glove box before he had really thought about it. Two gulps later, the sloe gin was gone and another flood of desire came over him. *It only made me thirst for more.* This time though, he thought it through and decided to keep his mind as clear as possible. *It is highly likely, that they will be tweaking out already. If I can stay somewhat lucid for the next few hours, maybe I can figure out a way to take these guys down and clear up my legal problems, all in one fell swoop.*

The arid climate felt like a gritty slap across his face, as Jericho got out of the truck and approached a small porch on the front of the modest domicile. Angry voices carried out to the yard, before Jericho made it to the front door. *Michael acts all tough with his women, but Laurie wears the pants in that relationship.* Laurie was usually the main breadwinner working in a beauty salon. She made up for a lack of a higher education, with above average looks. *I am not sure what Laurie saw in that lazy meth head, but she always stuck by him through one wrong choice after another.*

"God dammed, roaches! Laurie, I thought you were going to spray this dump?" Fortier asked, with a tone that put all blame on her. "I just found one of those suckers on the baby's head."

"I did spray. If you and Tim would clean up your beer bottles and empty pizza boxes, it might be easier to keep them from coming back." Laurie protested.

On cue, McVeigh stood up and headed for the exit. He could feel a major argument coming their way and was not in the mood to hear it. This visit was about business. As he came out the front door, McVeigh ran square into Jericho. Completely caught off guard, McVeigh jumped back into the doorway, while reaching towards a handgun in his shoulder holster. By his reaction, McVeigh had the distinct expression he believed it was Feds there to bust him.

"Holy shit, Vance; you scared the hell out of me!" McVeigh hollered out.

"I am here. Let's get this over with. I have other places to be."

"Hey, Mike, he is here. Let's go, dude," McVeigh ordered, as the air conditioning leaked out in moist cool waves from the open screen door. He skipped down the stairs and then slid behind the wheel of a rusted Impala on its last miles. "They should be there by now," he said, as Jericho got in the passenger side.

"So how do you know these tweakers?"

"Oh, no sweat Vance, they are a little weird, but they hate the cops as much as we do. The Patriots would never rat us out, or nothing like that…it's all cool. I need some help with the mix. If it is not right, this whole thing will be for nothing." McVeigh replied, as he scratched at the top at his buzz cut head, as if he was trying to think of something else to add to the uncomfortable conversation.

Where will it be?" Jericho asked, wanting to feel out how much he really knew about the outcome to these grand designs of terrorism.

McVeigh just shrugged, as if he did not know. It seemed like he could not keep still. First came the incessant sparking of his lighter, followed by a round of tapping on the steering wheel. Real life was in slow motion and every minute dragged on like days to him. He could not seem to live the moment fast enough. As he was about to honk, Fortier came out and slammed the door behind him. The wail of the baby and Laurie screaming something, were still clearly audible until McVeigh started the car and they speed off in a cloud of burning motor oil.

Fortier gave a sullen, hello nod from the backseat, before staring out the window into the desert and drifting off into whatever thoughts cluttered his mind. *He was pissed off and not in the talking mood. That suited me fine, but McVeigh stuttered and stammered on as we took one deserted highway after another. He never really answered any of my questions. They both carried themselves as a couple of martyrs to a new revolution, instead of a group of burnouts.* Similar to the Arizona Patriots, they lived a meager existence, on the far right fringes of normal society.

Driving as fast as the car could muster, McVeigh alternated his ramblings between a profanity-laced tirade of anti-government speeches and strange meanderings of science fiction paranoid delusions. He thought that he was an important lynchpin to changing the world and believed that the United States Army had inserted a computerized tracking chip in his left buttocks. *There was not a hint that McVeigh did not thoroughly believe every word he spouted.* By traveling constantly, McVeigh claimed to hide in dead zones of coverage from the Kh-12 satellites, which searched endlessly for him. *I did not really pay attention where we are going, but I notice the different directions the sun glared in at me, until it was finally behind us.*

A crooked gravel road led past miles of twenty-foot high chain link fence. It had barbwire curled along the top to protect an obsolete military base, left over from the Cold War. After a few quick turns and a long trail of gray dust, they pulled up behind a light green van. The added plastic top and bulky side doors hiding a folded ramp, indicated it was for someone with a handicap. The double doors opened in hurky-jerky movements and a silver ramp extended to ground.

Fortier and McVeigh climbed out and stood in the suffocating heat for several minutes until a little greasy man in a wheelchair rolled out. He took a hit from some sort of inhaler, as the harsh air induced a coughing fit. Although they had never met the forty-one year old paraplegic, Clark Vollmer's reputation preceded him. Besides the occasional loan sharking and meth dealing, Vollmer was very active with the Arizona Patriot militia. The Fortiers were regular loyal customers, as was Dennis Malzac, a local speed freak who assisted him out of the van. *It only takes me a few seconds to recognize the last person to join the party.*

Behind dark sunglasses and beneath a green John Deere hat, Steven Colbern tried not to draw any attention his way. *We had met Colbern once before through Karen Anderson, the girlfriend of an Arkansas gun dealer, Roger Moore. We stopped by Colbern's trailer in the deserted mining town of Oatman, twenty miles Southwest of Kingman, to pick up some cash he owed Roger. Whether Colbern has a chemistry degree from UCLA as he bragged about or was bullshitting us, he was unpredictable and I did not trust him.* Colbern's trailer was a cluttered collection of pornography, Nazi propaganda, stolen medical supplies, drug paraphernalia, beer cans and survivalist magazines.

Even though everyone knew his real name, he went by Bill Carson, a fake alias used after fleeing federal charges in California. *The four cops that finally subdued Colbern during the arrest would love to have their old friend back in custody. I hope I can make that happen very soon,* Jericho surmised, as he got out of the Impala and joined the rest.

McVeigh stepped up and shook Vollmer's hand, as a shaky Malzac, pushed him from behind. They all went down a rocky little trail until it was impossible for the wheelchair to go any further. On cue, Colbern presented a backpack stuffed with an assortment of bomb making materials, as McVeigh sat two milk jugs full of Nitro racing fuel mixed with ammonia fertilizer pellets, on a knee-high boulder.

Fortier seemed distant and paid little attention to Vollmer, as the little man instructed McVeigh to tape a small chunk of C4 borrowed from the Company, to the side of the bomb. McVeigh connected a round, homemade detonator and a string of Det-chord to it. Fortier slung the chord over his shoulder and doled it out as he walked the bomb out to the desert. He started to jog back, but slowed to a crawl due to the heat by the time he arrived. McVeigh had everything locked and loaded. He stopped for a moment, as if wanting to soak in the historic moment. *As if this is the spark to light the whole country on fire.*

"Are you guys ready to see this?" McVeigh asked while strutting around a bit, before finally settling close to the end of the fuse.

"Just light the damned thing!" Jericho ordered, growing tired of the theatrics.

With a broad smile, McVeigh cranked on a flame from an industrial sized fire starter, then touched it to the end of the fuse until it turned red hot and ignited. When it reached the bomb, nothing seemed to happen. As doubts that it was going to explode began to creep in, it went off. It is more bang than blast. Whether the mix was off, or the C4 failed to trigger a larger explosion, by all accounts, it is a dud. They walked out and inspected the damage, which turned out to be superficial. The smoke cleared enough to realize the boulder was charred and chipped, but suffered no major impact. Even if you factor in the exponential blast of increasing the bomb's mass, it was a failure. They wanted a "Big Bertha" of fertilizer bombs, not a market suicide popper. McVeigh seemed to take it the worst. He flew into a tantrum, which began by denouncing the government and ended up with the decision to terminate the entire mission.

"Hell with it! This soupy shit will not do anything, but make noise, maybe blow up a small car or something. It is over and I am out of here," McVeigh whined matter-of-factly, although ending with an up tone that left a little wiggle room for someone to talk him back into it. When nobody tried and it remained silent, he turned from a dissenter into a propaganda machine. "You know, I cannot do this whole thing by myself. We need more money, we need more soldiers for the cause and we need some more mix...a lot more!"

"Let's get out of here, in case somebody heard that." Jericho urged, unimpressed with McVeigh's pep talk and growing more uncomfortable by the second.

"Relax, Vance, It's all good. There is no one around here for a hundred miles," Fortier answered, before McVeigh could blurt out whatever was racing through his strung out mind.

"Don't tell me what is good. If you want to stand out here like a dumbass in this heat, go ahead. I am leaving right now. Give me the keys!" Jericho ordered, while turning and looking him right in the eyes. McVeigh started to protest that it was his car, but then relented as Jericho decided to make his point a bit more clear. "You want to cough them up or should I take them from you?"

"Okay, here. You can drive, but you are not leaving us here," McVeigh answered in a subservient tone, as he tossed over the keys."

"What is your problem, Vance?" Fortier asked, in his toughest voice before taking several steps back when Jericho turned towards him.

"You are my problem at the moment. This whole bullshit trip is my problem. I have places to be and yet I am here watching you idiots try to blow up a rock. You are taking too many chances doing this in broad daylight! You never know when some do-gooder might hear that explosion and phone the highway patrol."

Malzac and Vollmer had heard enough and headed towards the van.

"I will be in touch," Colbern added before they loaded up and slunk away in the opposite direction they came in.

McVeigh could keep arguing all day, but Jericho had reached his limit. *I was about to start swinging.* The stress was building up, slow and steady, until he could feel the muscles in his neck and back tighten up. That was always the first thing he did before a fight, crack his neck and back to limber up, then came his knuckles which popped as if he were shuffling cards. *Sudden violence was always my first choice for solving life's little problems.*

With a bad mood still lingering from his fight with Laurie, Fortier looked over at McVeigh to let him know he was going to stand up to Jericho. His bravery lasted only a second as Tim smiled to let him know he would have zero chance at any positive outcome. *Fortier has the heart of a coward and McVeigh knew it.*

"Calm down, Vance, everything is cool." Fortier relented and climbed into the backseat with McVeigh close behind.

Jericho paced back and forth, as he got control over the anger, which always lurked beneath the surface. *I had to relax and tune these meth heads out. The last thing I need on my resume is getting pinched with this bunch of anarchist and drug dealers.*

An optical illusion of swirling steam, produced by the heat on the road ahead, mesmerized Jericho. A disturbing movie kept playing and rewinding in his head as they drove down a desolate highway. *It was of a tan-faced rookie patrol officer standing next to the car, asking for my license and registration. A brief glimpse of shock in the young man's eyes as the .9mm shell ripped through his chest. That hollow feeling of shame as I drove off and let him bleed to death on the pavement. Was it real? Did it happen in one of my black outs? Sometimes, I cannot even believe my own thoughts. In a desert full of wannabe mass murderers, I was my own worst enemy.*

Jericho's thoughts drifted from happy times with Maria and the boys, to waking up in a cold California rain with his own gun to his head. Everything was a blur of regrets and bad choices that filtered in and out of focus, while McVeigh pointed the way to a dusty storage shed, on the outskirts of Kingman.

McVeigh hopped out first and urged Jericho to follow him to his unit. *Unless he had a cooler full of cold beer in there, I could give a shit less to what he was doing.*

"Vance, hey dude, you really need to see this!"

"He won't stop. Tim will stand out there all freaking day if he has too," Fortier warned, from the backseat. "He never stopped playing soldier after he got out. Seen too much and did too many foul deeds. The dude's soul is black."

"It better be worth it or I will leave him in that box," Jericho grunted, as he lumbered out into the humid oven. *My lips felt like they were cracking into pieces and my throat is parched to a point where I would settle for juice from a cactus, prickly thorns and all.*

"Okay McVeigh, what is this big secret, you had to drag me out to this dirt rag?"

For once, McVeigh was quiet while he keyed the lock, before opening the door. A loud creaking sound made it feel like a tomb of death, sealed a thousand years. As the light hit the contents, Jericho knew his initial feelings were right. It was filled with instruments of death. A large cache of dynamite, detonators and Primadet blasting caps stolen from the Marietta Quarry in Marion, Kansas, back in October. A couple of shotguns from a staged Roger Moore robbery in Arkansas, boxes of ammo along with several barrels of nitro methane racing fuel Terry Nichols bought under the fake name of Mike Havens, from a track in Dallas, Texas.

"This is just a start of what Nichols and I have collected. It will get a lot bigger than this. We just need Commander Pedro and those guys to get their shit together. I mean, Terry and I have been driving all over the place trying to piece this plan together and everyone else is coasting along or backing out. How will the BATF learn if we don't teach them?"

"Learn what? What the hell are you rambling on about, McVeigh?" *My patience was done, not that I was ever blessed with a passive disposition, but this was going beyond my personal record.*

"The American people will stop them from another Ruby Ridge and..."

"Is this stuff supposed to impress me? The Government has missiles, tanks and an army. And you are going to fight them with that? You better step down off your tripping' cloud Son, and come to terms with a little thing the rest of us call reality!"

"I make my own reality. They can track me with their satellites, but they will never catch me. Not out here in the desert. The entire planet will know my name soon enough. That is my reality, Vance!" McVeigh fired back in a condescending tone, that hit Jericho like finger nails over a blackboard. "Every revolution starts with a single shot and this will be the biggest blow to the country since John Wilkes Booth left Lincoln's brains all over that balcony at Ford's theater."

Jericho stared at McVeigh as he locked the storage locker to see if he really believed his own self-important hype. Without missing a beat, McVeigh launched into another long diatribe about the Waco massacre, as they headed to the car. This time, Jericho let him drive. McVeigh drove fast and erratically towards the next spot on the terrorist tour of the desert. Everyone was quiet except McVeigh, but Jericho was somewhere else. Mexico. *What was I doing with these losers, when the only thing I care about is down there?* All his instincts were telling Jericho this was a real dead end, maybe the last one ever. Jericho was thinking until McVeigh's crazy ramblings drifted into his consciousness and sort of took over. This time he was going on about a scheme by Richard Guthrie involving firing a missile at the Whitehouse to kill the president. *I think I wasted my time driving clear out to this desert. Their plans were dead.*

Chapter 7

Geary Lake

> "With an iron fist in a velvet glove
>
> We are sheltered under the gun
>
> In the glory game on the power train
>
> Thy kingdoms will be done
>
> And the things that we fear
>
> Are a weapon to be held against us."
>
> — Neil Peart

April 13, 1995

Junction City, Kansas

Pete Langan

Surrounded by native prairie grass and secluded public hunting grounds, the pristine lake was slowly refilled after a five-year drought, by the floodwaters of 1992. Being well stocked with bluegill, saugeye, bass and flathead catfish, made it a favorite spot for outdoorsman in the area. The rustic campsites and quiet secluded park grounds, made it a favorite hideout for the Mid-West Bank Robbers; a group recently named by the newspapers for their string of successes, which were only topped by the Jesse James Gang.

The "Company" as the main leader Pete Langan preferred to call his group of anarchist, thieves and antisocial racists, spent the last two days bunkered down on the east side of the state park. Morale and funds were at their lowest, after a failed armed car heist in the Phoenix area. *The more I tried to rally this group, the closer a split seemed eminent,* Langan contemplated, as he enjoyed the sounds of morning, sliding through a rolled down window in the Tahoe he was sleeping in.

Langan had several dust-ups with Richard Guthrie lately, who wanted to continue boozing and bank robbing, while Langan pushed an agenda for domestic terrorism. *I am going to be a key player in the coming revolution,* Lagan dreamed. Their visions for leadership could not be any farther apart. Guthrie lacked motivation to guide anyone, but objected to every plan, because he refused to take orders. His negativity and affection for alcohol led to several intense arguments within the group.

The date was set for their knockout blow to the BATF, who were located on the upper floor of the Alfred P. Murrah Federal Building in Oklahoma City. As the final days approached Elohim City's, April 19 deadline though, nothing seemed to be going according to plans. The Arizona Patriots failed to come up with a proper mix for even the most rudimentary explosive devices, leaving Langan to trust Tim McVeigh and Terry Nichols with the design. The pair forged a fragile alliance with a group of ex-Iraqi soldiers, who were planted in Oklahoma by the FBI, to infiltrate terrorist groups blossoming in the heartland. McVeigh met the Iraqis through his army friend, Jose Padilla, when Padilla worked at a Taco Bell in Florida. Padilla, had slowly worked his way into the inner circle of the Abu Sayyaf, a Philippine branch of Al-Qaeda. They also welcomed Terry Nichols to the group.

Terry Nichols used the guise of marrying Marife Torres to travel to Cebu City in the Philippines and set up several meetings with Edwin Angles, the Sayyaf commander. She was more than half his age and pregnant with another man's child.

Ramzi Yousef, the mastermind behind the future attacks on September 11, also attended the meetings. Yousef, whose real name was Abdul Basit, decided to contribute his expertise learned while building and detonating an ammonium nitrate fuel oil (ANFO) truck bomb, in the parking garage of the World Trade Center in New York, on February 26, 1993.

After several trips, Nichols volunteered to join a failed plan called the Bojinka Project, created by Mohammed Jamal Khalifa, the brother-in-law of international terrorist leader, Osama Bin Laden. Before Nichols had the opportunity to sacrifice himself in a hijacked commercial airliner, converted to a missile and aimed at key targets, the project fell apart. Ramzi Youself and bomb making expert Abdul Hakim Murad, caused a chemical fire, while mixing deadly components, which alerted the police to their Manila apartment. Nichols barely escaped back to the United States the same day the FBI arrived to question Murad, who was arrested at the scene of the fire.

Once back in the States, Nichols lingered around his brother's farm in Michigan between trips to Las Vegas to see his son and brief stays with his new wife. He eagerly immersed himself in the second part of the Bojinka Project. With his only friend McVeigh, acting as the puppet master, the pair crisscrossed the country to purchase, steal and acquire ingredients to build a massive ANFO bomb, much larger than the failed truck explosion in the parking garage of the World Trade Center.

Persistent rumors concerning double agents for the government, infiltrating Elohim City, worried Langan into many sleepless nights. The idle gossip left a general mistrust among the group camped out in the peaceful confines of Geary Lake.

Elohim City wanted to bomb the Oklahoma Federal Building since 1985, going so far as to acquire a hand-held rocket launcher to commit the destruction. Robert Millar's parish gave all the support they could; but with several agencies watching them closely, they were already making up alibis for the day of reckoning. Millar would bring the body of his Aryan brother, Richard Snell back to the compound for burial, after his execution for killing a pawnshop owner and an Arkansas State Trooper. Snell, a former resident of Elohim City, warned of pending doom, clear up to his last breath.

Andreas Strassmeir would be acting as a "Good Samaritan" by helping an elderly neighbor all day with yard work, giving him an ironclad alibi. The Company broke off all contact with Elohim City except McVeigh, who called them from Kingman, Arizona, on April 5th to set up a meeting with Strassmeir. Millar was already paranoid about the ongoing FBI and BATF investigations. McVeigh rambling on about spy satellites watching them on his last visit there, did not help matters much.

Langan felt his command challenged from all sides. He did not trust the Iraqis and the feeling was mutual. Their leader, Hussain Al-Hussaini mostly glared at him and refused to acknowledge any direction from "Commander Pedro" at all. Scott Stedeford along with Kevin McCarthy remained loyal soldiers, but the rest of the Company splintered into factions. Michael Brescia seemed unconcerned with his approaching wedding date with Ester Millar. He spent most of his time with Strassmeir and McVeigh partying and chasing women at the Lady Godiva strip club in Oklahoma,

Today is the day I take control of this operation, Langan decided, as the morning sun crawled across the lake, bringing color to everything it touched. He was quite comfortable sleeping in the back of the Tahoe, as he had on many occasions in the desert and woke up feeling refreshed. *I am determined to lead this mission and start this war.* He stepped over to the fire ring and tossed a few small pieces of kindling and some leaves to spark up the embers. He put a pot of coffee leftover from the night before on the grill to warm it up. Guthrie snored from the lawn chair he fell asleep in while still holding his beer. Langan gave him a nudge, but decided it was better to let him sleep. Guthrie made it clear he would not work with the Iraqis under any circumstances and planned to head back to the safe house in Pittsburgh, Kansas, as soon as he woke up. *Guthrie never could see the big picture,* Langan thought as he poured a cup of coffee to go along with his breakfast of two-day-old doughnuts purchased at a truck stop. *Everything will probably work out better without his constant dissidence.*

"Morning, Pedro," Jericho Daniels greeted from a picnic bench in the next site over, away from the group and did not participate in any of the partying.

"Oh...morning Vance, it is going to be a busy day." Langan acknowledged Jericho, by his only known alias. *I think Vance knows about my secret identity. If he tells the Company, they might leave me for dead here. I have to keep him close to me and away from the rest until Guthrie leaves.*

Jericho Daniels openly did not like, or trust Langan since their trip from Overland Park, Kansas, to the safe house on New Year's day, but he did not seem to like any of the Company lately. He especially loathed McVeigh after their few days in the desert together with the Arizona Patriots. Only the meek,

~ 113 ~

Terry Nichols, ever had much of a conversation with Jericho.

Terry Nichols was isolating himself lately, while attempting to back out of the plan along with Michael Fortier. Nichols had several arguments with McVeigh. He resented being relegated to a pack mule for hauling a majority of the fertilizer and racing fuel. Nichols also accused McVeigh of sleeping with his wife Marife, an allegation that Tim did not deny. Whatever the task, McVeigh would get his orders and pass them along to Nichols who reluctantly plodded ahead. Nichols was once more than willing to be a martyr in the Philippines; even getting caught boarding a plane with a stun gun and carpet knife on his last visit to Cebu City, but now reconsidered. He was content to move on and put his effort into his latest business selling used army surplus. As his son Josh grew older, their connection became stronger and Nichols never wanted him to find out about his dark side.

It was not long before Andreas Strassmeir showed up. He left from Elohim City that morning and arrived at the campsite before the rest of group.

"Hey Andy, it is a great day to start a revolution!" Langan greeted in his normal rhetoric, as Strassmeir stepped out of a borrowed charcoal-gray pickup.

"Yes indeed it is, Commander Pedro. I brought everything you asked for. Blueprints, code for the door leading from the parking garage. I could only get two "Guest" name badges though. So I guess you will have to figure it out if anyone starts asking questions."

Langan started to protest as an old mover truck clunked and coughed around the winding road to their campsite. Mohammed Chafti, a war-hardened soldier in the Iraqi Republican Guard, drove with Hussain Al-Hussaini sitting next to him in the passenger seat. A blue Chevy Cavalier followed close behind with Anas and Asad Siddiqy. The brothers had gone through the naturalization process with Al-Hussaini, via a Saudi Arabian refugee camp.

Strassmeir's whole demeanor changed once he realized it was Al-Hussaini. "I have had a nose full of that guy," he admitted, before walking over to the picnic table, where Jericho Daniels was working on a letter to his wife Maria in Mexico.

Langan liked Al-Hussaini even less and considered him a natural sworn enemy, but managed to find common ground in hating the United States government. *Once this mission is over, someone needs to make sure these guys take the fall for this*, Langan decided, as he greeted them with a friendly wave.

"Where is McVeigh?" Al-Hussaini asked, getting right to the point.

"Nichols, Brescia and McVeigh are clearing out the storage locker in Herrington, Kansas. They should be here soon. He got a late start after running down to Texas to get some pressure detonators and internal cutter charges for the job today." Langan replied briskly, trying to minimize the conversation.

"Did he get the new truck yet?"

"What new truck, Al?"

Al-Hussaini stepped back and talked with his companions, but never took his eyes off Langan. His indomitable stare exuded a combination of contempt and mistrust. It was obvious Langan was out of the loop of communication. "We will wait for McVeigh". Al-Hussaini snipped, before retreating to the Cavalier.

Langan stood there for a moment not sure what to do before Strassmeir stepped over and cleared things up.

"McVeigh reserved another truck. He called me from Arizona after he made the reservation on the fifth. That old mover is leaking transmission fluid. It barely holds the barrels the Iraqis mixed in their garage using auto paint respirators, so they would not breathe all the toxic fumes. There is definitely not enough cargo space for all the extra fertilizer Nichols and McVeigh bought. It can hardly take the weight now."

"Andy, so you think somebody should have told me this shit? Does McVeigh think he is running the show, along with his buddies over there?" Langan complained bitterly.

Moments later, Terry Nichol's truck with the camper shell removed, drove slowly around the bend. The rear end nearly touched the tires from the heavy load. Brescia sat in the middle with McVeigh sticking his head out the passenger window, while waving his long arms in the wind.

"Look at that idiot. Why doesn't he draw more attention to us?" Langan quipped sarcastically, as he pointed to several bass boats taking advantage of the morning fishing weather. "He is going to blow this whole thing!"

McVeigh barely waited for Nichols to stop the truck before he jumped out and greeted Al-Hussaini. They ignored Langan, as Brescia walked over to the tent to wake up Stedeford and McCarthy. Nichols slunk around a bit before moseying over to the picnic table where Jericho Daniels sat putting an address on the envelope for his letter and graced it with a stamp.

"Are we going to get this show on the road or what?" Langan called over to the Iraqis with a demanding question, that came out more like an order.

Finally, McVeigh and Al-Hussaini strolled over, purposely taking their time to show disdain for Langan. "Hey Andy, did you bring the stuff?" McVeigh asked, completely ignoring Langan.

"Yes, most everything I could. You will have to get some work suits or something for Al and his crew. I only have two guest badges and it might draw suspicion having you guys poking about in the ceiling and such."

"What about you, Tuttle? Did you make it down to Texas?" Langan asked, using McVeigh's alias name when he drove the getaway car on several robberies.

"Yeah, yeah; it's all good. I had to go to three different surplus dudes to get it all. Problem though, couldn't get enough of those cutter charges, so we will have to use some of the Tovex sausages, or C4 we scored from the Marietta quarry."

"I don't believe that will work at all..." Strassmeir tried to explain.

"Dammit, Tuttle! I knew you were going to screw this up!" Langan barked. "Andy gave you the exact list. If it is not right, it will not bring down the building. We cannot be leaving unexploded shit behind! We might as well leave our address."

"Hey Pedro, it is not my fault. As I said, I went to three different dudes. It is not like they have this stuff lying around in their showcases. I had to trade about a third of Roger Moore's guns to get it, plus all the cash we had from Terry selling his gold coins. If you don't like it "Commander", you can bail. We don't need your ass anyways." McVeigh chirped with confidence, like he was in charge now.

I have had enough of this punk! Who does he think he is? Langan decided, as he stepped toward McVeigh to give him an attitude adjustment.

"Bring it, Pedro!" McVeigh hollered, but took a step back behind Al-Hussaini, as the Iraqi crew immediately rushed over.

"What the hell is wrong with you, McVeigh?" Guthrie chimed in, after being awoke by the all the commotion. "You are nothing to this operation! We are in charge of this, always have been and always will be. You wouldn't have two dimes to your name if we hadn't been paying your crazy ass out of our war chest this whole time! If you have a problem with Pedro, then you have a problem with me. We will settle this bullshit right here and now!" Guthrie warned, as he slammed his warm beer to the ground causing a huge fountain of foam and stormed over.

Stedeford and McCarthy ran over to back up Langan as well. They were always ready for a throw down and saw the Iraqis as no better than foreigners polluting the country. Both groups circled each other spewing threats while daring the other side to cross an imaginary line in the dirt.

"You assholes want the whole lake to hear you? Maybe have some park ranger stopping by and noticing Nichol's pickup loaded down with fertilizer...get a big whiff of that mix dripping out of the mover truck. You can smell that shit a mile away. If you want to fight someone, then start with me!" Jericho Daniels demanded, as he clinched his fist and shoved in between the two groups. He took a step towards the Company to ward them off and then turned to the Iraqi crew. They still jawed towards the others with McVeigh heckling the most. Jericho pushed Al-Hussaini out of the way with a hard forearm to the chest causing him to lose his balance, before getting right in McVeigh's face. "I swear to God. I am going to beat your ass into the ground if you say one more word...just one dammed word!" Jericho threatened, as he grabbed McVeigh by the front of his shirt collar and reared back to strike.

"Everything is copasetic. No need for violence, fellows. We are all friends here. Isn't that right, Tim?" Strassmeir interjected, as he tried to worm his way in between McVeigh and Jericho. "Come now, Vance, let him go. It is just the stress of the job boys...stress of the job. Do not take it so personal and dance outside the lines."

Langan stepped over and gave Jericho a pat on the back to show appreciation for regaining order. Jericho finally let go of McVeigh's tee shirt at the same time he gave a little push. He stared at Al-Hussaini and his crew until they looked away from his angry eyes. Once he felt they had thoroughly backed them down, he sauntered over to the park bench where Nichols waited nervously.

"Okay now, that's more like it. We are all pals here. Everyone here can wear the fat pants today," Strassmeir regaled, with a crooked smile.

"You heard him, let's get moving on this thing. Al, you have your crew unload Nichol's truck. Give them a hand, will you?" Langan motioned towards McCarthy and Stedeford. "Andy, break out those blueprints so we can get this figured out. I do not want to be wandering around blind in there. Andy, you and I will head in first-"

"Oh no, I don't think so, Pedro. This is where the river forks for me. I cannot risk going in there. I am not even supposed to be in this country. I told McVeigh my legal situation."

"I am going in, Pedro; Al and I already scoped it out in March. We would have checked out the upper floors, but the lady in the daycare started getting suspicious so we booked ass out of there."

Langan thought about it for a second and realized he did not have any other options, so he relented. "Okay, you and I will take the badges. Al and his team will wear the jumpsuits. I am sure they can get some from the auto garage."

"Right oh, now that is all worked out, let's take a little gander at these prints." Strassmeir interjected, before another quarrel could ensue. He stretched out the original construction blueprints copied from City Hall. "The foundation is a slab, reinforced concrete, so there is no basement or anything like that. You will be completely exposed when you do the set up, but at least this floor here has a large vacant area to work in." Strassmeir flipped over to the sixth floor. "What we have here is three rows of columns, let's call them A, B, and C. The rows are thirty-five feet apart from each other, with eleven columns in each row. The columns are spaced at twenty-feet apart. The four corner columns are clam-shaped to accommodate the air duct system. They should be no trouble at all," Strassmeir explained, pointing to the plans.

"Okay, so how do we do this shit?" McVeigh interrupted.

"So what you want to do is put the high-velocity breaching charges at every odd column. Start with number 9 columns, because the blast from the parking garage should pretty much take out the first two columns in each row, the 10's and 11's, or at the very least weaken them." Strassmeir said. "There is a concrete slab-beam resting on the A columns, which supports the whole glass front of the building. The blast from the truck should buckle this upward. The shockwave, will push the air outward violently, to detonate those pressure devices attached on the explosives. Place them above the ceiling tiles on the bottom side of the seventh floor. Those charges will expand a blast with 8,000 meters per second impact, shearing through the tops of those concrete columns. At this point, the concrete slab beam will be too unstable to hold much weight. The entire front should collapse. That will sort of twist and pull on all the upper floors. With the parking garage blown away, all support on the north side will be gone as well and the weight of building will not be able to rest on the remaining columns of B and C. It will be like a house of cards my friends…a house of cards."

They all agreed it was a good plan until Al-Hussaini spoke up. "That is all good and fine Andy, but McVeigh already told you guys he couldn't get all the cutter charges."

Strassmeir relied on his demolition training with the German Army and came up with a solution. "Okay I see what you are saying Al, so…use the C4 gel packs from the quarry on the C columns. Detonate them with an onsite timer. That should be more than enough to weaken those columns. With the rest of the Murrah building rocked to the foundation, it should be like dominoes. C4, pressure detonators, truck bomb, boom, boom, and boom! Does anyone else have any questions?"

"I think we can handle it from here, Andy," Langan decided. "Let's get packed up and head out."

"So what are we going to do with this old piece of shit mover truck while we head into Oklahoma City?" Stedeford asked.

"We can't leave it here, it's too conspicuous. You, Vance and McCarthy follow someone from Al's crew in the mover truck back to the Dreamland. Park that stinking son-of-a-bitch as far from the rooms as you can. We will meet you there after we are done." Langan ordered with confidence that he was now in charge again.

Strassmeir and Brescia bid farewell to drive back to Elohim City to spend some time with their girlfriends and be as far away from Oklahoma City as possible during the set up. Terry Nichols pulled McVeigh to the side and the pair talked the whole time the rest of the Company finished unpacking his truck into the old mover. It irritated Langan that whenever there was work to do, McVeigh conveniently had a phone call or would find some other reason to avoid it. Nichols handed McVeigh a letter that he strung together with all the thoughts on their recent falling out. It explained clearly that McVeigh better not use Nichol's family as a bartering chip for control anymore. Nichols was formally out of the plan as far as he was concerned. McVeigh had other ideas and ways to pull him back in, but left it cordial and said his goodbyes as Nichols left for a military surplus auction in Fort Riley, Kansas.

Langan and McVeigh each changed their clothes before leaving the campsite. Langan put on some nice khaki slacks, tan shirt and a matching tie he pilfered from a lover on New Year's Day in Overland Park, Kansas. McVeigh put on his U.S. Army dress blues and his freshly spit-polished black combat boots. He figured he would blend in as he did before with a recruiting division in the building. The pair did not speak a word to each other all the way to Oklahoma City. *I think this is the only time I have ever heard McVeigh quiet,* Langan surmised.

They followed Al-Hussaini and the Siddiqy brothers to their auto garage. The minutes seemed to drag by as they waited for the Iraqi crew to come back out. When they appeared, the trio wore matching blue jumpsuits with the garage nametag removed from the left breast pocket. The brothers carried black backpacks filled with all the tools they thought they might need; a cordless drill, wire cutters, flashlights, a small ball-peen hammer, voltage regulator, assorted concrete anchor screws, extra detonation cord and homemade timers along with the pressure detonators. They loaded everything into the cab of a 1983 GMC High Sierra, stolen December 5, 1994, from Luke Conner. The Iraqis had stripped all GMC name decals from the brown truck and replaced them with Chevy insignia after painting it yellow. Al-Hussaini slid two aluminum stepladders into the back of the truck and gave a nod they were ready.

"What is the deal with that ugly yellow truck? Are they trying to look obvious?" Langan complained to McVeigh, who ignored him and looked out the window.

Once they reached the Alfred P. Murrah Federal Building, they cruised slowly down 5th Street and pulled into the parking garage. McVeigh jumped out with the plans before Langan could turn off the Tahoe. He stretched them out on the hood of the Iraqi's truck and took control of the operation. The group talked briefly before heading to the entry of the building. Langan caught them at the door and followed them up the stairs to the sixth floor. It was relatively quiet as they went about setting up the ladders and pushed the ceiling tiles out of the way to locate the columns they wanted. The Iraqis did most of the work, drilling small holes, installing anchor screws wound with support wire to hold the Royal Demolition Explosive (RDX) charges. The highly percussive sensitive, cyclonite explosives were delicate to work with; but after the first three were set, it moved along smoothly.

"Excuse me what are you men doing?" A woman named Darlene Watson asked, as she was coming back from lunch with her friend Jane Graham.

"They are working on some malfunctioning lines for the phone company. Do not worry, Miss. I am keeping a close eye on them." McVeigh answered, as he showed his guest badge. "You have a nice day," he politely dismissed the curious women with a wave of his army hat. "Keep moving guys, people are getting suspicious," he whispered up to Al-

Hussaini who placed the last pack on the columns of row B.

A majority of row C. columns were inaccessible due to the USMC recruiting office, so they rigged two C4 gel charges on the supporting columns in the vacant area of the floor. When Anas Siddiqy dropped one of the homemade timers in front of Army recruiters Arlene Blanchard and Marilyn Travis, as they walked down the hall, Langan decided it was time to go.

"That is going to have to be good enough. Let's head out." He ordered.

They quickly exited out into the parking garage, loaded up and headed north to Geary Lake, while Al-Hussaini and his crew drove to the Dreamland motel.

"You did a nice job in there Tuttle…I mean Tim. That was pretty fast thinking with that phone company bullshit." Langan praised.

It seemed to mend things a little between the two, so they made small talk in between McVeigh ramblings about wearing tin foil in his cap during the operation, so the satellites could not track him. It was dusk when the pair arrived at Geary Lake. Langan waited in the Tahoe as McVeigh tried several times to start his old Pontiac without success. After discussing their options, they decided to stay another night at the lake and get up early to buy a new battery. Langan drove McVeigh over to Wal-Mart first thing in the morning. With a fresh battery, the car finally started with a reluctant cough of oily black smoke, but ran rough all the way to Junction City, Kansas, as Langan followed close behind.

How in the hell is he going to use that old piece of shit as a getaway car, Langan thought to himself, as they pulled into the motel and the car died before McVeigh could get it parked. He coasted to an open spot and got out shaking his head.

"It was knocking so bad I couldn't hear the radio!" McVeigh hollered over, before popping into the office to rent a room.

McVeigh filled out one registration card with the name Bob Kling, but realized he left the fake driver's license Guthrie made him, in his army pack over at the Council Grove storage locker. It was also the name he used when inquiring about renting a new Ryder truck, so decided it would be best not to use the alias. The owner Lea McGown reflected a puzzled look when he asked for another registration card. McVeigh put the room in his own name using the Nichols family farm address of 3616 N. Van Dyke Rd. Decker, Michigan, along with the plate number from the Arizona tags. Lea McGown told him no several times as McVeigh dickered for a discount, but finally she relented and took eight dollars per night off for the four-night stay. McVeigh seemed happy with the deal and counted out eighty dollars in small bills to pay her.

McVeigh and Langan piled their stuff into Room 25 with Stedeford and McCarthy deciding they would be more comfortable staying put in their own room around the corner, than doubling up on the small uncomfortable twin size beds. McVeigh decided to work on his car instead of settling in. Al-Hussaini recognized the sound of the sputtering Pontiac and stepped out from Room 23 as McVeigh tried in vain to keep the car running. After they tinkered around on it a few minutes, they figured it was most likely the head gasket and the car would need major repairs. More than what it was worth.

"I'm going to trade this old piece of shit in. Be back later dude!" McVeigh called over to Langan, who was hanging outside the door to their room.

The Iraqi crew followed McVeigh in the stolen yellow pickup as he drove the Pontiac into Junction City to a Firestone owned by Tom Manning. The owner confirmed the head gasket was blown. Initially, Manning did not want to deal with a car he would have to tow away. McVeigh reminded him that he bought a car three years prior from the shop and eventually bargained for a faded yellow 1977 Mercury Marquise parked behind the business. After handing over the keys and an additional $250.00 to Manning, McVeigh changed out the license plates and cruised off the lot. He made a quick stop at Wal-Mart to return the unused battery for a refund before heading back to the Dreamland. They passed Jericho Daniels standing next to his brown pickup talking on a pay phone on the way back. McVeigh waved, but Daniels did not acknowledge him.

Langan was just dozing off when McVeigh burst into the room with enough energy for the both of them.

"We need to pick up that truck tomorrow so we can clear out the rest of the bags of fertilizer and gear out of the Council Grove storage locker." Langan said, half asleep.

McVeigh agreed and pulled the number out of his wallet to Elliott's Body shop in Junction City, Kansas, where he previously made a reservation. He was frowning when he got off the phone. "They won't have a truck with at least a 5000 pound payload capacity until Monday. They are closed on Sunday so I need to give them the cash tomorrow to make sure it will be ready for us."

"That is going to hold us to a pretty tight schedule. How in the hell are we going to get the load out of the storage shed now? It is too much for Al's truck and besides I do not want that canary yellow eyesore anywhere around there. I guess we can borrow Vance's truck since the Tahoe is full of gear. I don't know where the hell he is though?"

"I saw him in town on a payphone arguing with someone. He looked pissed off, as usual. I know he saw us, but didn't even give us a glance or nothing. The dude has a major attitude. I thought Fortier and me were going to have to kick his ass out in the desert. Luckily, he backed his ass right down when I got in his face."

Langan started to snicker at the thought of the two skinny beanpoles taking on Vance, until he realized McVeigh actually believed his own story. "Well, I will tell McCarthy and Stedeford to take that old mover truck and get a pull behind trailer to clear out Council Grove. Hope it doesn't break down."

McVeigh pulled out another number for his old roommate in the Army, John Kelso, who was living in Alliance, Nebraska. It rang several times until an answer machine picked up. "He's not home. He's at work." McVeigh explained while the machine recorded until he hung up. "I could call Andy; they have several trailers at Elohim City?"

"No bother, we will just rent a pull behind. They made it clear they are lying low this week. They have a lot of eyes on them right now according to Millar." Langan replied, as he got up and went down several rooms to tell Stedeford and McCarthy the new plan.

The former band mates did not seem too excited to load more fertilizer, but finally agreed. Loud screeching sounds echoed through the parking lot as McCarthy could not get the truck in gear due to the slipping transmission. Stedeford was also rusty on how to drive a manual transmission, so reluctantly Al-Hussaini volunteered to drive them. They stopped at a farm supply store outside of town and bought a used trailer for cash. Hussaini refused to fill out a bill of sale. They were back to the Dreamland in a few hours asking what to do with the square load wrapped in a dingy white tarp.

Lenard and Diane White, an older couple staying at the Dreamland while visiting their son at Fort Riley, walked by holding their noses. Al-Hussaini glared at them as he stepped out of the cab so they would not look too close at the contents on the trailer. The truck leaked transmission fluid all over the parking lot and the smell from the mixed fuel in the barrels wafted about in the breeze. It caught the attention of Eric McGown, the motel owner's son, who immediately instructed them to move the truck on the grass away from the motel.

"That old mover is drawing too much attention. You guys need to take that back to Geary Lake and set up camp. We will meet you there when we get the new Ryder on Monday." Langan decided, after smelling the strong diesel odor.

They all decided that Langan was right, so Al-Hussaini jumped back in the driver's seat with his crew. McCarthy and Stedeford followed behind them in the Tahoe. McVeigh ordered some pizza before leaving to run some errands, figuring he would time it out right for the delivery. Langan jumped in the shower to wash off a couple days' worth of camp dust. As he finished, the delivery person showed up.

"Got an order for, Bob Kling?" The delivery person asked, slightly surprised by Langan's long hair and clad only in a towel.

Langan noticed Jericho Daniel's truck out in the parking lot as he paid for the food. *It worries me that Vance seems preoccupied lately and does not put any input in this operation. I wonder if he has cut a deal with the Feds?* Langan wondered, as he closed the motel door. That night he had a hard time clearing his mind to go to sleep. Every detail kept revolving through his head, not letting him nod off. *It seems as soon as I fall asleep,* McVeigh was up fidgeting about, going in and out of the room to the pop machine next to the office, going to the bathroom and using the light to write out pages filled with dire warnings on the coming revolution against the U.S. government. McVeigh planned to leave his notes in a packet of doom in the getaway car once he dumped it. He figured the media would jump all over the juicy details and the exposure would help the cause. Langan, ever the showman, thought it was a good idea so he left McVeigh in charge of the war propaganda.

"I need some cash, Pedro," McVeigh asked, as he nudged Langan awake long before he was ready to get up. "Al is going to run me over to put that deposit down on the truck."

"Do you have the Bob Kling license?"

"Yep, got it out of storage, We are all set."

Langan lifted up his pillow and grabbed an ammo belt that held all the Company's money and counted out five hundred in twenties. "That should do it, bring back the change this time." Langan quipped, knowing McVeigh never would.

Al-Hussaini drove McVeigh over to Elliot's body shop and waited in the truck while he went in and paid the full rental amount of $280.32 to body shop owner Eldon Elliot, who gave McVeigh a military discount for two free days on the listed one-way trip to Omaha, Nebraska. McVeigh used the fake Bob Kling license with an issue date of April 19, 1993, which was the same day as the Branch Davidian massacre. It showed 428 Malt drive, Redfield, South

Dakota, as his address. McVeigh declined the insurance rider on the agreement, signed it and shuffled out of the office smiling.

The pair stayed gone the rest of the day bouncing around from club to club, until ending up back at the Dreamland, where they watched television on the loudest setting and drank beer until passing out. McVeigh was up and gone first thing in the morning, trying to find a place to get a haircut, to no avail. He called Nichols in the afternoon several times interrupting his Easter dinner with his family and talked him into helping drop off the getaway car in Oklahoma City.

Nichols was not in a very good mood and seemed distressed. He followed McVeigh south and they parked the Mercury around the corner from the Federal building. McVeigh put a little note on the dash to explain why the car was there, "**Do not tow, dead battery, will pick up on the 19th.**" He jumped into Nichols truck and they cruised slowly by the intended target. McVeigh attempted to strike up a conversation with Nichols, but he stayed quiet until they pulled into the Dreamland.

"Hey, Farmer," McVeigh quipped, calling Nichols by the nickname Al-Qaeda gave him. "We are getting the new Ryder truck Monday and transferring everything into it on Tuesday. I need you there to haul away any extra fertilizer we don't use."

"I told you in the letter, Tim… plain as day, I am out of this." Nichols replied, visibly upset. His neck would always turn a pinkish shade of red and veins would stick out on the left side of his forehead.

"You don't want the Iraqis thinking you're a quitter, do you? They might just have a talk with the boys in the Philippines. Marife still has family there by the lumber yard right?"

"Okay...I will be there, but this is it. In addition, you need to get the rest of the stuff out of my house once this is over. It is still in the crawl space and under the floor joist where we hid it. Come by when we are gone, so I don't have to explain anything to Marife, okay?"

McVeigh agreed to nothing and got out of the truck smiling smugly. He knew he had Nichols where he wanted and was not going to let him out so easily.

What is Tim up to now? Langan thought as McVeigh strolled into the motel room, grabbed his packet of newspaper clippings with his notepad, and went into the bathroom without saying a word. He heard a truck roll into the parking lot. Thinking it was Al-Hussaini; Langan got up and looked out the window. Jericho Daniels sat in his brown truck smoking a cigarette, staring at their motel room with a blank expression on his face. *Why is he watching us? I have to get control of this thing, or I will lose respect with the company and Elohim City*, Langan decided, as he went back to bed and attempted to get some needed sleep.

Langan woke up late afternoon and stepped out of the motel room to a slightly chilly and overcast day. He bought a couple of pops out of the machine and scanned the parking lot for any signs of McVeigh or the Company. As Langan turned back for the room, he noticed the outline of McVeigh walking in from the south entrance, since the main bridge into Junction City was under construction.

"Did Al make it back yet? I called the auto garage, but nobody answered. "McVeigh hollered, as he entered the parking lot.

"Nope...I have no idea what Al is up to. Must still be at Geary Lake?" Langan replied, shrugging his shoulders as he turned back to the room. *The sidewalk is cold on my bare feet and I do not want to be talking business out in the open.*

"We need to pick up the Ryder truck at four. Oh, the transmission was grinding in that piece of crap Mercury, before we parked it at the YMCA. I am so tired of these junkers. I have shitty luck when it comes to cars, Pedro." McVeigh chatted, as he entered the motel room.

McVeigh practically wore out the telephone calling anyone and everyone. He dialed 918-427-7739 to talk to Andreas at Elohim City in Muldrow, Oklahoma, but did not make a connection. Once again, McVeigh received an answer machine when he called 520-855-6491, a Ryder Truck rental in Lake Havasu, Arizona, to set up a truck to clear out the remaining storage lockers. With each busy signal or non-answer, he slammed the phone down and cussed. He checked the phone balance on the card by putting in the pin code of 118 then hung up again.

"Relax, order us some Chinese for lunch and find something on television to occupy the time. You're driving me nuts with that lighter flicking and that phone." Langan complained, as he went in the bathroom to clean up.

They ate some lunch without talking much and watched daytime soap operas. McVeigh stalked one end of the room to the other like a caged animal until it was after three p.m. "Screw it man, I am heading out."

"So you can handle it?" Langan asked skeptically.

"No problem, dude. It is all paid for. We just need to pick it up. I have the license number memorized on the Kling deal, so I don't need to risk showing it again." McVeigh fired back as he called the auto garage again. "I told Al I needed a ride today. It all comes down to me; it always does!"

"Okay, so call a cab. Make sure it drops you off…half way there. Do not link yourself to the body shop with that cab. Maybe, somewhere close so you can walk the rest of the way. Oh, and make sure there is a dolly in the truck. We need to move those barrels around and they weigh over four hundred pounds."

"How about that McDonald's where we had lunch the other day?" McVeigh asked, in a way that he had already made up his mind.

"That will work. If Vance or Al shows up, I will send them that way."

Cab driver, David Ferris, picked up McVeigh from a rainy Dreamland parking lot and shuttled him over to McDonalds. McVeigh paid the $3.65 cab fare with exact change and exited without leaving him a tip. McVeigh checked his watch, looked for any familiar vehicles then strolled in to buy a hot dessert pie and use the restroom. He lingered around until close to 4.00 p.m. before deciding to walk the rest of the way to Elliot's Body Shop. He made it about a hundred yards down the road when Al-Hussaini picked him up in the stolen yellow truck and took him the rest of the way. They entered to find a friendly smile waiting for them and the smell of fresh popcorn.

"I have been married longer than you have been alive," Vickie Beamer joked, making small talk with McVeigh, referring to the fake birth date of April 19, 1972, on his rental agreement. We have a 1993 Ford, twenty-foot cargo for you out of Miami. Vehicle I.D. number AVA26077. Tom is gassing it up and pulling it around now. Still a one way trip to Omaha?"

"Yes ma'am, it is." McVeigh answered politely.

"Just need to verify your license one more time...."

"It is out in the truck, but I have the number. YF942A6, Social is 962-42-9694."

She checked the numbers to the paperwork and they matched. Once again, McVeigh signed and checked off, **No,** for the insurance clause. "One problem though, we're out of dollys and I see that you requested one. Therefore, I reserved one at the Water's True Value hardware store around the corner. It is already paid for, but you will have to swing by and get it, if that is okay?" Vickie Beamer asked, assuming it was all right.

McVeigh turned to check with Al-Hussaini who nodded in agreement before answering, "Yes, I guess that will be fine."

Eldon Elliot and Tom Kessinger, a longtime employee, came in the side door after pulling the truck around. Whether it was Al-Hussaini's menacing stare, Atlanta Falcon hat sitting corkscrewed onto a pile of black curly hair, or the tattoo on his arm of a serpent wrapped around an anchor, he left a very negative impression on the group, as he left with McVeigh.

After a quick stop to pick up the moving dolly from the hardware store, they headed back to the Dreamland. When they pulled in, Jericho Daniels was sitting on the tailgate of his truck chatting with Langan about nothing in particular. When Al-Hussaini saw them, he quickly dropped off McVeigh to avoid them and parked at the far end of the lot.

"Let's go get some dinner and then turn in...going to be a big day tomorrow." Langan explained, with a cheerful tone as McVeigh moseyed over. *The revolution was coming.*

Chapter 8

Dreamland

"To kill the Americans and their allies

Is an individual duty for every Muslim

Who can do it in any county which

It is possible to do it."

Osama Bin Laden

April 18, 1995

Junction City, Kansas

Jericho Daniels

The colorful reminder to 1950's Americana sat perched atop a wall of stone. It displayed a large red star with **Dreamland** spelled out in white letters and silvery sparkling lights. Attached on a red pole rising skyward above the left corner on the red star, blinked the words **Motel** written in white scrabble-looking letters. A small white star accented the advertising sculpture. **Vacancy** and **Welcome** lit up at dusk to draw in tired travelers from the road.

Jericho Daniels woke up suddenly from a rare, deep, sleep when he heard a door shutting on the Ryder truck parked beneath the Dreamland sign. He peered out the window to see McVeigh fumbling about, adjusting the side mirrors and hanging his sunglasses off the sun visor. After a couple of times walking around the truck as if performing some kind of inspection, he went back into his room. Unsure what the day would bring, Jericho decided to make some over-due calls. He reached out to his sister in California first. It was two hours earlier there and he knew they would be asleep, but left a message anyway.

"Hey Sis, it was great talking to you on Easter. I hope everything turned out okay coloring those eggs. Make sure to tell the girls, Uncle J. said hi and I cannot wait to see them. No horsey rides this time though. It did not turn out so good last time. Sorry again about your Christmas tree." Jericho paused a second, not sure what else to say. "I want you to know that if anything bad happens to me, I tried to stop it. You know me and like you said, maybe there is a sliver of good in here somewhere," he explained with a laugh. "When I wrap this mess up, I am heading down to get Maria and the boys. We will head your way. Gotta' go..."Jericho paused again, before hanging up. *I wished I had told Chloe, I love her.* After thinking about it, he started to call back when the phone rang.

"Hey Vance, this is Pedro. We are going to get some breakfast in thirty minutes, before heading to the lake. Breakfast is on me."

Jericho did not reply and hung up the phone. He dug in his travel bag and found an old number he needed to call, but once again, he got an answer machine.

"Hey Dipshit, this is Jericho. My sister said you been calling her about my probation. I was under the impression the BATF cleared that up or did you not get the damned memo. So get on your little computer and get it done. If you got a problem call Agent McCauley. I have done everything they have asked, so take care of it! I don't think you want me to come visit you." Jericho warned, before slamming the phone down as his anger boiled up.

Jericho dialed the next number on the piece of paper and waited until the automatic answering system picked up. He pushed the numbers corresponding to the name he wanted. It rang to another answering system. Finally, he left the message.

"McCauley, not sure if you got my message from the pay phone the other day, but the shit is going down tomorrow. Have your team ready. McVeigh will be driving the truck right to the Federal building. I left a message for my probation officer as well. You need to clear my file as you promised. This is it, now we are square! I am handing you the Company gift wrapped with a bow. Do not screw it up!"

Jericho took a quick shower. The water pressure was low, but was hot enough to feel cleansed. *Maybe I should call Maria before I leave?* He thought, as he finished up and dressed in a hurry. He reached for the phone, but then stopped. *Nope, I better not. She will have me on the phone for an hour asking questions. Maria could always sense when I was tangled up in a bad way.*

When he walked out, Langan, Al-Hussaini and McVeigh were already in the Ryder truck waiting.

"Hey Vance, follow us, we are meeting up with Nichols." McVeigh hollered out in an upbeat tone as if he could not start the day fast enough.

Jericho agreed with a nod and followed them as McVeigh drove cautiously for a change. Nichols was waiting in his loaded-down blue pickup, when they arrived. Langan and Al-Hussaini decided use Nichol's truck and start out for Geary Lake, to make sure everyone was on the way. Nichols reluctantly jumped into the Ryder truck as Jericho followed along to the Santa Fe Trail Diner. It was a family owned restaurant known for "home cooking" and generous portions. The owner recognized Nichols and McVeigh from their many occasions eating together and came over to bring the check as they finished eating. When noticing the moving truck in the parking lot, she sparked up a friendly conversation.

"Where are y'all moving to, this fine day?"

"Oklahoma City." McVeigh blurted out without thinking.

"Oh really? M y daughter lives there. What part of the city?"

Jericho gave McVeigh a blank canvas stare meaning to shut up. At first, he did not get the message until Jericho dropped a fork down on his empty plate with an obnoxious clinkety-clank. The three of them sat in awkward silence until the curious owner decided to let the conversation drop.

"Sorry Vance, guess I wasn't thinking." McVeigh replied sheepishly.

I cannot wait to see these dudes locked up. Your time is coming, Jericho decided, as he got up and left McVeigh to pay the check.

When they got to Geary Lake, Al-Hussaini's crew waited impatiently with the old mover truck while Langan, Stedeford and McCarthy lingered by their campsite. *There does not seem to be any love lost between the two groups.* McVeigh parked the Ryder truck perpendicular to the old mover, leaving enough room between the two to slide down the loading ramp and transport the barrels over.

"Let's do this!" McVeigh exclaimed, obviously excited to build a massive weapon of destruction. He opened the back door, slid the ramp down and had the dolly out ready to go as the Siddiqy brothers put on their auto-painting mask and opened the back door on the old mover truck.

The smell was an overwhelming cross between rotten eggs and gasoline. A black barrel in the middle of the load, had a slight hairline crack that went unnoticed, until it leaked several gallons that soaked into the wood floorboards. The brothers struggled with the barrels until Al-Hussaini wrapped a t-shirt around his lower face and helped them get the first couple transferred over. Once they got to the leaking one, they left it out on the gravel driveway as they finished moving over the rest. McVeigh wanted to arrange the highly combustible barrels into a V. formation standing for "victory" as he had once shown the Fortier's using soup cans. When the first five barrels slid into place, they realized the width of the truck would not accommodate the design. After a quick discussion, they packed the front wall next to the cab with fifty-pound bags of ammonium nitrate fertilizer from Nichols truck and changed the pattern to a snake shape.

"Yeah, like a cobra that is coiled to strike!" McVeigh chirped, as he glanced down at the Iraqi's Republican Guard tattoos. They seemed to like the analogy and agreed it would work.

They left a two-foot section open at the bottom of the stacks of fertilizer bags packed against the front wall. Langan borrowed a cordless drill out of Nichol's truck and drilled the first hole from the cab into the storage area. After consulting with Al-Hussaini they decided to put a second, fail-safe fuse. It ran from the passenger side of the cab, along the outside and had it come into the detonators at the center from a side angle as well.

The Iraqis did not want a repeat of the World Trade Center failure and were being extra thorough this time around. They layered strips of demolition blasting caps and sticks of dynamite in between the fertilizer bags to ensure they would ignite, before packing four black barrels of mix tight against the wall of fertilizer. Once another black barrel and six white ones were puzzled-pieced into place, they focused on the leaking barrel waiting in the parking lot.

Nichols had brought along a couple of blue barrels with lids just in case. He was always worried about the "worst case scenario" and went to great pains always attempting to be prepared. Nichols put a small siphon pump down into the black barrel and when it drained close to the bottom, the Siddiqy brothers picked it up and poured in the rest.

"That one will be short now so let's put it in the middle and we will top it off when we fill up the truck for the drive to Oklahoma City." Langan decided. Al-Hussaini agreed and they placed it in the middle closest to the side door.

They formed a human chain and transferred thirty bags of fertilizer out of the old mover into the new rental. Jericho hung back on a picnic table and refused to help. Stedford started to say something, but Langan nodded it was okay.

Let those fools sweat it out because they are digging their own graves. I don't want any fingers pointing to me that I helped build that bomb.

Al-Hussaini used a moving strap to secure a welding bottle of liquid nitrogen, stolen from the quarry, to the middle barrel. They spaced sticks of dynamite within the bags, snugly conforming around

~ 145 ~

the barrels. With silver duct tape, he attached blasting caps around all the exposed barrel tops. McVeigh and Langan stretched out lines of sausage looking rolls of Tovex explosives along the front wall and then down the snake shape, before packing more bags on top to keep them in place. Al-Hussaini took ten sticks of dynamite, secured them together with tape and wrapped it with blasting caps.

"This should make a good detonator." Al-Hussaini quipped gleefully, as he taped it to the welding bottle.

McVeigh tucked C4 gel packs around the detonator as tight as he could, with one stick of dynamite beneath it. One fuse ran straight to the main explosive pack, with the side fail-safe, attached to the lone stick of dynamite. McVeigh moved the old mover up, so Nichols could park next to the Ryder truck. They unloaded the bags out of his truck purchased September 30, in McPherson, Kansas, using the alias of Mike Havens. The Company packed twenty more bags in every nook and cranny of the truck, leaving only enough standing room to top off the main blue barrel.

"So what am I supposed to do with the extra bags?" Nichols asked, with his typical worried look.

"Farmer, take them to your house with the other stuff for our next bomb. You will get your instructions very soon," Al-Hussaini ordered. "Your family...they won't be a problem, will they?"

Nichols knew it was a threat by the way Al-Hussaini said it. He looked over at McVeigh sporting that smug "I told you so look" and realized he was never getting out of this arrangement alive. "No they won't, Al." Nichols stammered out, while giving a meek goodbye nod and slunk over to his pickup. He pulled down the winding exit, never looking back.

"Let's load up and move out. Al, have your crew dump that old piece of shit mover truck. Burn it if you have to, but I never want to see it again. We will meet up with you tomorrow-" Langan started to say.

"No! I stay with truck." Al-Hussaini declared defiantly.

Langan stepped forward causing the Iraqi crew to go on alert and step behind Al-Hussaini. Stedeford and McCarthy hurried over behind their leader.

Not this shit again. Jericho thought to himself. *These idiots have a Ryder loaded with explosives and they want to have a pissing contest.* He stood up on the bench attached to the table and slammed his boot down with a forceful stomp to get their attention. "You assholes want to have a back yard wrestling match until the cops come, or do you want to get the hell out of here?"

"Vance is right, let's book." McVeigh agreed. "Hop in with me, Al. That's cool right, Pedro?"

"Okay whatever, but we will be right behind you." Langan agreed.

Stedeford drove the Tahoe and followed closely, as they headed back to the Dreamland in Junction City. McVeigh was hungry again, so he pulled into a Denny's on the way. Jericho kept going and went back to the motel to get some rest. *Tomorrow will be a long day.* He was nearly asleep when the familiar sound of the Ryder came roaring into the parking lot. Moments later, Langan's motel room door opened and closed. Five minutes later McVeigh left the motel room. *What in the hell are they up to now?* Jericho tried to roll over and get some sleep until the Ryder started up again.

Curiosity got to him and Jericho peeked out the window. Langan's Tahoe remained parked in front of his room, but the Ryder maneuvered out from below the Dreamland sign, down towards the south exit. With McVeigh driving and Al-Hussaini riding shotgun next him, they seemed to pause as if killing some time, before sliding out to the main road and out of sight. *If they are going now, I better follow them and stop it from happening or I am never going to be square with this shit.* Jericho got dressed in a hurry, jumped in his brown pickup and pushed toward town looking for any sight of them. He was almost to the Oklahoma City exit, when he noticed the back end of the Ryder, sticking out from behind the McDonalds.

Jericho passed on by, before doing a U-turn and doubling back. He parked in the shadows of a strip mall one business down. Jericho stepped out for a closer look. A charcoal-gray sedan with plain white plates featuring only five numbers, pulled next to the Ryder truck. *Definitely law enforcement or government,*

Jericho contemplated, while he moved without giving away his position.

Al-Hussaini stayed in the Ryder truck, while McVeigh talked to two men in matching suits. The shorter of the pair handed McVeigh a plain white envelop stuffed full. The agent looked visibly dismayed when McVeigh pulled the green contents and began counting out one hundred dollar bills, on the hood of their car. The taller man glanced around nervously to make sure no one was watching the transaction, before getting back into the driver's seat of the sedan. Jericho counted along silently until McVeigh reached twenty. *I will have to call McCauley and tell him there are other players in the game,"* Jericho thought, until he saw the face of a man he once trusted- Agent McCauley. *Why is that double-crossing bastard handing McVeigh two grand?* Jericho could feel the old familiar pressure behind his left temple, as the anger began to build up inside. He wanted to run over there and confront both of them, but decided to watch a bit longer.

McCauley stepped over to the Ryder and talked several minutes to coerce a reluctant McVeigh into opening the side door. He immediately stepped back in complete shock and shook his head, no. The massive size of the bomb apparently left McCauley confused, until McVeigh pulled at a long line of silver duct tape running along the bottom side of the Ryder truck. He showed McCauley a loose unattached Det. Chord, before covering it back up and shutting the side door closed. McVeigh smiled confidently and talked fast using many hand gestures. He finally made whatever point he was trying to make. McCauley checked his watch and shook his head in agreement as McVeigh held up four fingers. The pair walked to the front of the Ryder, where McCauley handed him a small, location transmitter. McVeigh quickly attached it behind the front bumper.

Jericho thought about what to do next all the way back to the Dreamland. He never came up with a solution, before dozing off into a restless sleep. When McVeigh and Al-Hussaini arrived back to the Dreamland, they noticed that Jericho's brown pickup was in a different spot. Al-Hussaini felt the hood and realized it was still warm. The pair talked a few minutes, before slinking back into their rooms.

For a brief moment, Jericho was back in Mexico holding Maria, as the sun came up. Every kiss left him longing for another, but with a loud knock at the motel door, she faded away. *I woke with a rotten feeling in the pit of my stomach...like I am never going to see her again. I have to figure a way out of this or the BATF is going to bust my ass along with the Company*, Jericho resolved, as he jumped up and got ready. He thought about heading south, slipping across the border to his family and never looking back, but changed his mind. *I have to see this through to the end...no matter what.*

Langan and McVeigh hovered above a map while Al-Hussaini did final preparations on the truck. Stedeford and McCarthy both looked hung over as they poured themselves from their room and crawled into the Tahoe.

"Are you riding with us, Vance?" Langan asked, as McVeigh finished mapping the route to Oklahoma City.

"Nope, be best if I follow along." Jericho answered in a dismissive tone, leaving no room for a rebuttal. *I need to keep my options open.*

"Let's roll!" McVeigh hollered with excitement, as he eagerly got in the Ryder. He was only in the truck less than a minute before jumping out and dashing over to drop the motel keys off in the night deposit box. He gave the thumbs up when he returned.

The caravan moved out with Langan driving the Tahoe to lead the way. McVeigh cruised cautiously in the middle, with Jericho bringing up the rear. They traveled south down Interstate 77, crossed into Oklahoma and stopped at Newkirk to meet up with the Iraqi crew. Mohammed Chafti drove the blue Cavalier and waited along with the Siddiqy brothers who wore matching workout suits. Anis Siddiqy spent part of the morning doing timed practice runs in front of the Murrah Federal Building. After several tries, he had the distance from the parking garage to the south corner where they would pick up Al-Hussaini, down to the precious seconds needed for their getaway.

As Siddiqy finished his test runs, a bomb disposal truck pulled to the front of the building to check the first floor before letting workers enter. The

Siddiqys waited around the corner as the BATF called off their stakeout and declared the Murrah building safe before taking the rest of the day off. Langan parked the Tahoe in a far unused corner of the lot. They loaded their gear into a white four-door sedan that McCarthy and Brescia recently purchased in Arkansas from monies gained out of the staged Roger Moore robbery. Once everyone was ready, the caravan headed south.

Langan decided to stop for breakfast at the Loves truck stop in Ponca City. Al-Hussaini filled the Ryder with fuel one last time before opening up the side door to top off the middle barrel and reconnect the fail-safe fuse. McVeigh purchased a couple breakfast burritos as Langan bought doughnuts for the Company. Jericho was not hungry, but decided to have a cherry pastry with some black coffee to settle his upset stomach. He lit a cigarette and watched as Al-Hussaini fiddled about beneath the front of the Ryder truck until finding the location tracker.

"You want a doughnut, Vance?" Langan offered, to no reply. He handed Jericho a walkie-talkie preset on the same channel the rest used. "Check, check, can you all hear me?" Langan's voice squawked. When the crew nodded in agreement, he motioned to move out.

Being careful not to speed, they turned west on interstate 44. As they slowed on the exit ramp, Al-Hussaini rolled his window down. Jericho could see a brief glimpse of the location transmitter in his hand, until he tossed it into a clump of sagebrush. They passed the State fairgrounds and continued at a leisurely pace towards Oklahoma City. *I knew I should turn off on an exit, lose them in traffic, anything except keep following. Maybe it was that haunting dream I had of the little blond-haired girl in the building. Staring at me with those blue eyes that dared me to look away, but I couldn't. Just like I could not stop driving. I tricked myself that I could stop it at the last minute as we rolled past the city limit sign. Somehow, it was going to be okay. Then I could go home.*

Langan checked his watch and realized they were ahead of schedule, so he turned down towards Brick Town to get ready for the final run. They were only parked a few minutes when a warehouse supervisor, David Snider noticed the Ryder truck. Believing it was for an overdue delivery, he waved at McVeigh to back into the dock.

"Hey Pedro, are you seeing this guy waving at us?" McVeigh called into his walkie-talkie. "I don't think he wants us to deliver what we have in this truck."

"Copy that. Move out." Langan ordered, as he instructed McCarthy to drive north several blocks until they saw an old gas station converted to Johnny's Tires. McCarthy yielded to the side of the road to let the Ryder take a large section of the limited parking available in the square corner lot.

Mike Moroz was working on an alignment for a new set of tires, when he noticed the Ryder truck pull in. It almost caught on a line of colored flags stretching from the business, to a tall post with

Uniroyal and Johnny's Tires signs. When the two occupants did not get out, he decided to see if they needed some help.

"McVeigh, here comes a man. Better get rid of him." Al-Hussaini stated in a cold tone, as he glanced down at McVeigh's Glock 45mm handgun loaded with special Black Talon rounds, hanging from his shoulder holster.

"Al, I will talk to him first, before I shoot him down," McVeigh joked, as he stepped out to head off the curious worker, before he got too close to the truck.

"You guys need some tires?" Mike asked in a friendly tone, even though Al-Hussaini was glaring at him from the passenger seat.

"No, just got a bit turned around a little and needed some directions.

"Sure, where are you guys headed to?"

"5th and Harvey," McVeigh blurted out streets he could remember.

Jericho slowly backed out while the rest of the group was preoccupied watching McVeigh. He turned down an alley to a pay phone and quickly dialed the only other number he thought might be of some help. The Department of Justice's phone rang several times, until Executive Secretariat; James Miller finished typing the last lines of a report and answered the phone.

"Department of Justice, this is Miller."

"The Federal building is going to blow up in twenty minutes."

"Who is this?"

"Get those people out now!"

"And how do you know this?"

"I am standing across the street." Jericho answered with conviction. He wanted to say more, but McVeigh pulled from the tire lot, so he left the phone hanging off the hook and hurried to catch up.

The Iraqis broke from the caravan and sped off to the auto garage where Mohammed Chafti got in the stolen yellow pickup. He drove through light traffic left over from the Mayors' annual breakfast at the Myriad Convention Center and waited with the engine running on the corner of 5th and Robinson for Al-Hussaini.

McVeigh cruised slowly street by street beneath colored banners highlighting the upcoming Festival of the Arts, before stationing the Ryder in front of the Regency Towers, building just up from the target. Realizing they were still early, he decided to go into the convenience store on the first floor to quench a morning long thirst.

"You need anything, Al?"

"Smokes."

Langan was immediately annoyed that McVeigh was shopping instead of following the script. He was about to call the Ryder on a walkie-talkie when a relaxed McVeigh strolled out with a couple of Cokes and packs of cigarettes. Let's move!" he ordered, while motioning to drive ahead of the truck. McCarthy pulled the white sedan into the Federal building garage and paused, sideways across a couple of parking spots. They quickly realized the Ryder was too tall to enter.

McVeigh parked cockeyed hanging out into the street until Al-Hussaini pointed to an alley between the Federal building and the courthouse. McVeigh started forward again, but realized he was blocked by a Highway Patrol van driven by Tom Hunt, the head of protective services, who was delivering an inmate to a trial. Langan decided they were running out of precious time and called for McCarthy to pull out and save some spots in front of the building. Langan jumped out to guide McVeigh into place as if he was landing a plane, before practically diving headfirst back into the sedan.

"I can't believe they are going to do it? Where is the BATF?" Jericho called to himself, while stomping on the gas pedal to coax his old pickup into a U-turn, before pushing north to the rendezvous spot.

McVeigh waited until Al-Hussaini was ready, but accidently dropped the ignition key on the side step of the truck as he got out.

"Should I leave the key?" McVeigh asked.

Al-Hussaini shrugged that he did not really care, so McVeigh locked the driver's door and ambled across the street to the Mercury that Nichols helped him stash behind the YMCA building on Easter. He was relieved that it started on the first try.

Glen Grossman, an employee of the Oklahoma Department of Securities, noticed two men park a Ryder truck in front of the Murrah Federal Building.

He had a perfect view from his office on the fourth floor of the Journal of Records building. It caught his attention when the driver got out, left the truck behind, seemed to wipe the truck key with his shirt, before tossing it into the alley next to the YMCA. The driver hastily got into an old yellow Mercury, with a big primer spot on the driver's side and cut northeast across the parking lot. He gave the passenger sitting in the truck, a thumbs up and when he turned his attention back to driving, the Mercury was heading straight for a dumpster.

McVeigh yanked the steering wheel to the left to avoid a collision and jumped over the cement medium leaving a trail of sparks from his muffler hitting the street. The car sputtered a few times as it picked up speed east down an alley, then cut hard to the left heading north on 6th street. He put a set of earplugs in as he ran a stop light. Al-Hussaini paused another thirty seconds, that seemed like ten minutes, as he waited for McVeigh to leave the scene. He mumbled a quick prayer to Allah, thankful for the opportunities before him. Without remorse or hesitation, he lit the fuse.

Daina Bradley waited by the front glass windows of the Social Security office on the first floor of the Murrah building. She had a busy day planned and changing her son's S.S. card was the first thing on her list. It was a curious sight to see a Ryder truck pull up directly across from her. She was momentarily distracted, as her sister asked her a few questions, before getting back in line. When she turned, the passenger stepped out and looked her way. His eyes seemed to stare right at her with such hatred. The olive-complexion man with short curly hair, clean-cut, wearing a blue Starter jacket, blue jeans, tennis shoes and a white hat with purple flames, captivated her attention with his nervous, mysterious movements. First stepping to the back of the truck…looking around, then to the front, before walking briskly down the sidewalk out of view.

Al-Hussaini gazed Daina Bradley in the eyes for a brief moment, already knowing what her future would bring. Once he was to the stolen pickup, he felt relieved it was done. The farther away they drove, the distance made it seem like a dream. He started to doubt that everything was working out as they planned when he heard the first series of blasts that changed the world forever. Twenty miles from the Murrah building, the Oklahoma Geological Survey in Norman, Oklahoma, registered several cataclysmic events at 9:02 a.m. for roughly ten seconds followed by a major event that spiked nearly off the charts.

Jericho pulled on a service road from Interstate 235. He heard a loud rumble to the south as he drove down to the meeting area off NW 23rd in an industrial park. Langan's crew was waiting as he slid down next to them behind a loading dock. Nobody said a word. They stood and watched a mushroom cloud of black, snarling smoke, rolling up over Oklahoma City and begin to drift southeast in a slight breeze.

McVeigh screeched around the corner in the Mercury. He seemed giddy and nervous at the same time.

"I have to lose this tag. Too many people saw me pulling away." McVeigh said, with a screwdriver already in hand. The front plate was left in a storage locker with a set of Arizona plates from the Pontiac he traded in. The lone back plate with number PTA-811 belonged to Phillip Douglas. Terry Nichols stole it after a gun show from a car driven by Douglas's daughter in Fort Smith, Arkansas. McVeigh took the plate and tucked it up under the front tire of a Semi-truck next to them.

"So what are you going to do?" Langan asked, staring down at the spot where the plate used to be.

"It should be fine until we get back to Geary Lake to dump this piece of shit," McVeigh answered.

"Okay, follow us. Vance will bring up the rear. Let's move out," Langan decided.

Jericho watched McVeigh and felt anger coming over him. *Look at him strutting around, but he does not have the guts to look back at what he did. Coward!* Jericho thought as the smoke above the city grew, with forty car fires adding to the devastation.

The caravan moved north on Interstate 35 through light traffic. After twenty miles, the Company turned off to go pick up the black Tahoe in Newkirk, Oklahoma. McVeigh gave them a wave and sped north to the Kansas state line. *That idiot better slow down,* Jericho thought as they passed a State Trooper pulled over to help two women with car trouble. Jericho followed behind, but slowly lost sight of the Mercury as McVeigh drove faster, cruising in front of a white Winnebago doing the speed limit.

A few miles past Perry, Oklahoma, Jericho noticed the same trooper creeping up in the passing lane behind him. *I did not even look over as he went by.* Trooper Charlie Hanger weaved in and out of a few cars until catching up to McVeigh. On a long straightaway, Jericho could see the Trooper pace along next to the Mercury for a mile, before sliding behind and hitting his lights. Once McVeigh pulled over, the Trooper Hanger stayed behind the protection of his car door and ordered him out of the Mercury.

There was a seemingly long pause, before McVeigh complied. He opened his door and put both feet out to the ground, but sat sideways a few more seconds, before finally stepping to the back of the car. The Trooper asked for registration, proof of insurance, and his driver's license. When McVeigh reached for his license, the Trooper Hanger noticed the bulge of a weapon. As Jericho drove closer, he could see the Trooper immediately draw his service revolver and place McVeigh under arrest. He quickly had McVeigh in cuffs as Jericho passed on by the scene.

Al-Hussaini directed Chafti to an apartment complex they previously staked out to dump the truck. Virginia King watched from her apartment as they backed up to the fence surrounding the property, seemed to wipe down the inside and door handles, before locking the truck. They hopped in a Blue Cavalier with the Siddiqy brothers. The Iraqi crew stopped by the auto garage and dropped off Al-Hussaini, while picking up their duffle bags to leave the country. An All-Points Bulletin was out on the Cavalier, by the time they were on their way to the airport. Although the trio were all quickly arrested before they made it on their flight, Chafti and the Siddiqy brothers were never questioned about the bombing, before a direct FBI order, allowed them to fly out of the United States.

Jericho met the Company at the safe house in Pittsburgh, Kansas. When he pulled in alone, Langan expected bad news.

"Where is Tuttle?" Langan asked, already knowing the answer.

"State Trooper got him... dumb shit was hauling ass with no plates on his car."

A quiet cloud of panic lingered over the Company. They had three radios and a television on waiting for any information concerning the bombing. *I could feel my anger boil up when I saw the first images of the Murrah building and watched as rescue workers pulled dead babies out of the rubble.* Langan was visibly perplexed as the FBI made a beeline to Elliot's body shop in Junction City the next morning.

"They seem to already know who they are looking for." Langan declared, realizing the entire operation was compromised from the beginning.

Once Terry Nichols turned himself in to police, Langan knew it was time to run. As the Company packed up everything that looked important or incriminating, the FBI launched the largest manhunt in history by offering a two million dollar bounty for the arrest of John Doe #2. Jericho left in the middle of the night without saying a word. He crossed into Colorado by dawn. The days all blended as he tried to stay oblivious to the media that began putting out false information fed to them by the BATF. He thought about sneaking across the border in Texas until hearing on the radio they were looking for an old brown pickup, so he headed west to California. *Many times, I thought about calling my sister and explaining it all, but I am not sure she would believe me.*

When money started running low, Jericho decided to drive south down Highway 5 through San Diego. He camped a final day on June 10 at Chula Vista. *I tried to enjoy the friendly town square and abundant sunshine, but something is telling me not to cross over the border. I missed Maria more than I have ever missed anything in my life, so I ignore all the bad feelings.* Jericho almost made it through the checkpoint until a message to detain him printed out in the supervisor's office. Eight hours later, he was staring at the white cinder block walls of jail cell 709A at the Oklahoma City Federal Transfer Center.

Bland meals came through the slot of the pink prison door as Jericho lost track of time in between brief naps. *I wish I could dream of Maria and be home again, but I never do.* Keys rattled at the door, a lock turned and three large guards intruded into the cell.

"Get up Bradway, someone wants to talk to you!" The haggard looking vet of the group barked, as he grabbed Jericho up and pushed him out the door in one motion.

They did not wait for Jericho to put on his issued slippers and quickly herded him down several halls of the pod into the shift office. Jericho was escorted inside and shoved into a chair with his left hand zip-tied to it. Two men in suits hovered about the office as a Shift Lieutenant with the prison scanned over a manila folder with the name Vance Bradway written on the tab with black marker.

"So...the FBI has a few questions for you-" The Lieutenant began to say.

"I am not saying shit. I want my phone call."

Jericho did not see who was behind him, but felt a nightstick bludgeon him between the shoulder blades. *It felt like both my arms went limp for a minute.*

"Who else was with you the day of the bombing?" One of the agents demanded as he puffed on a cigarette that was half-smoked.

When Jericho refused to answer, the next blow was harder. It struck Jericho in the back of the head and caused him to black out, until smelling burning flesh. He was still groggy as an intense pain from burns surged from his left shoulder. Jericho realized two of the guards were leaning him forward in the chair and holding him face down over the desk, while the lead agent touched a lit cigarette to his bare skin.

"I suggest you tell us everything!"

Jericho screamed in pain as he sprang up from the chair. It caught the group of guards by surprise and Jericho was to his feet swinging wildly with his free arm, before they could react. Jericho grabbed the agent burning him and judo flipped him onto the desk. Jericho punched him in the face several times until the veteran guard jumped on his back. A nightstick forced against Jericho's throat, as they pulled him off the agent. With a surge of adrenaline, Jericho broke free again while using his left hand to swing the chair as a weapon. He knocked one of the guards down, as he kicked the desk so hard, it toppled over onto the Lieutenant.

Jericho ran out of the office with most of the broken chair hanging from his left arm. There was nowhere to run in the segregated pod, so he ducked back into his cell and slammed the door shut. The guards were there in seconds. Jericho used a piece of the chair to brace the door and keep them from coming in.

"You guys need to find Agent McCauley. He is your man." Jericho yelled, through the thick rectangle window of double safety glass.

They looked confused for a moment, but eventually left. *Pain was coming from every part of my body all at once.* Jericho barely made it to the bed before collapsing as bruises began forming all over his arms and legs. *Even the soles of my feet were starting to swell.* The memory of the beating during the interrogation slowly came back to him. *While it was happening, I had somehow put my mind somewhere else.*

Vision from his left eye became clouded as blood from a large gash along his brow streamed down into sanguine puddles onto the bed and floor.

Maria and the boys will think I had a part in that bombing. They are all going to think it was me, Jericho contemplated, as a wave of shame came over him for being in this situation. *I have to tell them the truth.* Jericho looked in the empty cell for something to write on and found nothing. He stared at the wall a moment before deciding to use the only thing available. Jericho touched his index finger to the gash in his eye and used blood to start his message. He wrote "My Famlia" as the lock clicked and the cell door burst open, before he could get back over to brace it closed.

It was in slow motion. Every bone in his hands, were shattering as he swung. Jericho nearly had them out of the cell, when his foot slipped. It was the only break the guards needed. The haggard vet put a line of zip-ties around Jericho's throat, which suffocated him with every movement. From his knees, he could see the guard pull a jagged-edged knife from a sheath on his right shin. Jericho did not feel anything. He was with Maria and the boys opening presents Christmas morning. *I was finally home.*

Chapter 9

Acoustic Shadows

> "The keenest sorrow
>
> Is to recognize ourselves
>
> As the sole cause of
>
> All our adversities."
>
> Sophocles

Mustang, Oklahoma

April 19, 1995

Anthony Motavato

Built with sturdy logs of Loblolly pine, with an interior trimmed out with Saw Tooth oak, the cabin was of modest size. The original dirt floors were replaced with a concrete slab in the 1940's, Polished, Eastern Red cedar floors were installed a few years back, along with new energy saving doors and windows to give the place a modern feel to it while still honoring its history.

Lonely Bear was born in the southwest corner bedroom of the cabin and raised by relatives. He could afford to move to a much larger place, but decided to stay in the place created by the hands of his great grandfather instead. Everything in the cabin was passed down, accumulated over time or seemed to have always hung on the wall. Even the most modern conveniences, a gas stove, microwave oven and a hi-fi stereo system were still functioning although nearly obsolete. Along with the peaceful acres and a fishing pond, the cabin was a part of him now. The garden where his grandmother Rain Cloud grew their food over the years was still in the same place it always was. Lonely Bear grew special herbs and spices along with special plants he used at his healing center in a small part of the original plot.

This place was home and the only one Lonely Bear ever knew. Now his grandson Little Hawk Soaring, who went by Anthony Motavato, lived here as well. His Americanized name of Motavato paid homage to their distant ancestor Chief Black Kettle. Anthony was trying his best to settle in for the night, but sleep came stubbornly to the boy on his first night here in the cabin. Losing both parents in the previous week left him melancholy, lonely and a bit confused at how he ended up here. *I always loved going to the Smoke Shop and visiting Lonely Bear's cabin. I especially enjoy all the treats I got to eat,* Anthony remembered, as he lay on the couch tucked in blankets. Those happy visits were rare due to Lonely Bear not approving of the lifestyle of Anthony's father. Lonely Bear was a mythical figure to Anthony. He was tall, proud, and always carried himself with more dignity than anyone he ever knew.

Flames from behind the cabin danced through a windowpane leaving wild shadows on the cabin walls, while illuminating the heads of stuffed deer gazing ominously down at Anthony. When the rhythmic chants from Lonely Bear seeped into the cabin, not even pulling the covers over his head could keep the unbridled fear of Anthony's darkest imagination at bay. Curiosity won over self-preservation and Anthony got up and made his way to the rear of the comfortable home. *I have to see if Lonely Bear is okay*, Anthony thought to himself, as he carefully opened the back door to sneak out into the waiting darkness.

A chest-high bonfire pushed the limits of the stone fire pit surrounding it as Lonely Bear faced the raging flames. He meditated a couple of minutes until singing to begin the next interval of the sacred Ghost Dance. Created by the prophet Wovoka and passed down through Lonely Bear's grandmother, the dance helped him connect to his family in the spirit world. "Only through peace and love can the threads of the past bind us to the present." Rain Cloud always taught.

Lonely Bear bent over slightly, arched his back with his arms to his sides as he began. "Love is coming, love is coming....the eagle brings this message to us." Lonely Bear sang with a soft voice that drifted for a brief moment before being enveloped by the crackling sounds of the burning logs.

Lonely Bear stutter-stepped twice with his right foot while extending his long arms into a breeze that stoked the fire into churning blues and oranges. A single eagle feather in each hand created the sacred symbols for faith and forgiveness into the ghoulish gray smoke. He repeated the pattern with his left foot. Stutter-step, tap, tap, before gently planting his bare foot to the ground. On the turn, Anthony noticed that Lonely Bear's face glowed with color. White pigment streamed down in three lines on the left side of his face representing light, purity and peace. Two green lines running sideway across his right cheek represented healing and harmony. He danced methodically and purposefully around the fire as it grew with an influx of cool air.

Lonely Bear was on the thin side, but well-toned and exuded strength of character in everything he did. He wore only hand-sewn pants with different colored beads and eagle feathers hanging from leather strings around his waist. They fluttered a near perfect circle when he spun counter-clockwise as he began the next verse.

"The crow is coming, the crow is coming…sad are his black wings."

As Lonely Bear finished the song verse, he pulled the hat from his head once belonging to his son Black Hawk Soaring and paused in the Ghost Dance. He bowed slightly and recited an old prayer so softly only the fire and angels above could hear it, before casting the hat into the flames. The cowboy hat landed on a half-burned log and smoldered a bit before catching fire. A single hawk feather blew in the breeze as the hat burned until the leather strip tethering it to the hat turned to ash and it released into a vortex of heat.

Anthony watched the feather surrounded in flames before emerging above the fire unharmed, then continued upwards with an upstream of wind into the night. At that moment, Anthony realized he would never see his father again, at least not in the living world.

"Rest in peace my, Son. I hope you find the love and happiness that eluded you in this lifetime. Be brave and know I will always be here for you." Lonely Bear prayed as his voice nearly gave out with emotion.

A few tears escaped and ran down Lonely Bear's face creating green and white droplets on his chest. He finished his prayers and turned to Anthony gazing at him with sadness mixed with tenderness. With slow, deliberate movements, Lonely Bear closed his eyes, threw his head back and extended his arms out forming a cross in front of the bonfire. It frightened Anthony. *I have never seen Lonely Bear in a trance before.* The fire spread until it trapped Lonely Bear within a circle of flames as it had with the hawk feather. It was so bright Anthony had to shade his eyes for a moment and when he looked over again, a young girl in a white chiffon dress was holding Lonely Bear's hand. Only five years old, the same age as Anthony at the time, she seemed brave and without fear of the fire snarling around her. She stood there peacefully as Lonely Bear stepped from the circle towards Anthony before the flames burst skyward in a churning, burning sphere.

Anthony tried to run to the sweet girl with the haunting blue eyes nearly hidden beneath blonde curls. *I wanted to save her until Lonely Bear stopped me.* Anthony struggled against the firm embrace even when he realized it was futile. *She was gone.*

"Little Hawk, I would change places with her if I could," Lonely Bear lamented. "It is...how it is supposed to be. She is safe with our loved ones now."

The flames grew so bright Anthony had to close his eyes. Even in blackness, he could feel the heat from the fire and the images forever trapped into his memory. Suddenly someone was tugging him from sleep.

"Please save her from the fire!" Anthony cried.

"Save who, Daddy?" A sweet voice answered.

Anthony opened his eyes to see the beautiful face of his dreams. His daughter Jaci Rae sat on the edge of the bed pulling at him to wake up. His mind was confused and stuck between two worlds. It took him a few awkward seconds to respond to her.

"Nobody baby. Daddy was just having a bad dream. It is okay, everything is okay. There is no fire." Anthony reassured her.

"What fire?" Sonja asked as she came around the corner and stepped into the bedroom to finish getting ready for work. *Sonja always looks like a statue of perfection.*

"Daddy was having a bad dream. It's okay Mommy, I woke him up just in time." Jaci Rae explained with a proud smile, as she gave Anthony another hug for good measure. "I think he is going to be okay." She reassured, while feeling his forehead for a fever in the same manner Sonja always did when Jaci Rae was not feeling well.

"That is a great job sweetie," Sonja praised. "Now that you saved Daddy, you better go eat your breakfast. I already poured the milk on your cereal."

"Okay mommy, I don't want it soggy," Jaci Rae answered as she pushed her bouncing curls away from her ocean blue eyes. She hopped off the bed and headed into the kitchen with a slight swagger from feeling happy she had helped her father. *Jaci always loves to feel needed.*

Sonja lay down next to Anthony and snuggled against him. Sonja's inner clock was ticking away, telling her to get ready for work, but she wanted to make sure he was okay. "You look like you saw a ghost, my dear. That must have been some dream huh?" She inquired while nuzzling under his chin.

Anthony started to say something before getting lost into his own thoughts. *What did my dream mean? Lonely Bear predicted at the Smoke Shop that Jaci Rae was in danger, but I ignored him. Maybe I should have listened instead of storming out as I did?*

When Sonja did not receive a reply, she sat up and looked at him. She knew Anthony better than anyone and could tell he was very worried about something. "You are starting to scare me, Anthony?

Is it the same dream you had the night before...with the fire and stuff from when you were a kid?"

"Well kind of, but I am sure it is nothing to worry about-"

"Was Jaci Rae in it again?" Sonja asked getting right to the point.

Anthony wanted to tell Sonja everything and almost did before pausing. *I had better not tell her everything right now, Sonja is already worried about me recording my first album and going on the road with the band. The distance between us lately seems to be growing by the day with all the new changes with my career.* "Everything is fine, Sonja. I think I just have cold feet after signing that big contract. It is everything I always wanted for us."

"To be honest, I have been worried too. I don't want you to find some dream girl to take my place when you're a big star."

"Sonja, you are my dream girl....you really are," Anthony declared as he rolled over on top of her. "You are my best friend, my best everything. Half my songs for the album are about you and how much I adore the life we are building together. It is the best stuff I have ever written. Without you and Jaci Rae, I am nothing. I never would have pushed ahead after having the door slammed in my face so many times with so many bands."

"You did that all on your own. You and that old guitar of yours make a magic people can relate to. You really have a special gift, my love. I know I should have said this more, but...I really am proud of you. Jaci Rae is proud of you as well. You are her hero. I even caught her singing in the mirror the other day."

"She was?" Anthony asked with pride.

"Yes, and she was very good. Jaci Rae must get her sweet voice from you, because I can't hold a tune for nothing," Sonja admitted with a laugh. "Just promise me you won't stay gone too long. We need you around here."

I won't, babe. Uncle Bijou booked the tour in short sections with a three-week break in between. I will have almost a month after we cut the album to hang around and bug you. Bijou knows how tough it is to live on the road from his blues days." Anthony promised, as he gave a soft kiss to seal the deal.

"I know it was really hard on your Aunt Jo with Bijou gone so much. That is why I don't want us to be like that."

"We won't be. Aunt Jo made sure he put lots of down time in there for the band. Dominique wanted more gigs, needless to say, he lost that argument."

"I know he is your brother and all, but he doesn't have a young daughter. One that needs her daddy around for things like taking her to day care today…as he said he would."

Anthony drew a blank for a moment until remembering their last conversation, which entailed more responsibility on his part to take some of the load off Sonja. "Yes, that is all true, and I will be more available, starting tomorrow. Dominique is coming over to practice and finalize the song order and stuff and-"

"Okay, dear!" Sonja interrupted, with a slightly irritated tone that quickly melded into acceptance. "Well, I better get a move on then. I cannot be late again this week. I am already on thin ice and we need my job right now."

"You are the best! I will take Jaci Rae every day until we go into the studio. Does that sound fair enough?"

"That's fine, just don't be making any promises your body can't keep." Sonja fired back seductively, while kissing Anthony's neck.

She always knows the exact place to get to me. "Okay, you started something now! Looks like you will be late after all." Anthony joked, as he pounced on Sonja while tickling her midsection.

Jaci Rae heard the laughter and came running in to join the fray. She had changed out of her nightgown and now wore a white cotton dress with chiffon lace highlights. It was meant for Easter Sunday, but she decided today was a good day to wear it. She climbed up on the bed and pushed between the pair while giggling along with the fun.

Anthony had his eyes closed as he laughed and teased Sonja. He grabbed Jaci Rae and started wrestling her until he opened his eyes and saw the dress. Anthony stood up and was barely able to speak.

"Jaci Rae, where did you get that dress?" He asked trying not to worry them.

"Auntie Jo bought it for me for Easter Egg day."

"What is wrong, Anthony?" Sonja asked, immediately noticing his dramatic mood change. "I said she could go ahead and wear it to get some use out of it as long as she didn't rough house or get it dirty."

Anthony wanted to explain that the dress was identical to the one in his dream. Words escaped him though as he relented with an approving nod.

"Are you sure everything is all right with you? You look spooked or something?" Sonja inquired again, as she felt his clammy, trembling hand.

"It is probably because I am still half asleep."

"Okay, if you say so." Sonja finally decided and refocused on not being late for work. "We have to go, baby." She stated while scooping Jaci Rae up off the bed.

"Why can't I stay with Daddy?"

"Because Daddy has to work today and he won't get anything done with you underfoot." Sonja replied as she scooted them closer to the front door.

Anthony walked the pair to the car and helped Jaci Rae get buckled in tight. He gave her a loving kiss on the forehead and then an extra one on the cheek. "Daddy sure loves you, baby. I am so proud of how pretty and smart you are. I hope you know you are my whole world, my sweet angel."

Sonja overheard Anthony's sentimental goodbye to Jaci Rae as she was getting her morning coffee, work binder and purse all situated in their places. It seemed as if they were leaving for good, by the way he was fawning over her. After waiting for her turn for affection, she hugged him and gave him a tender kiss.

"Sonja, drive safe today...don't be speeding or anything to get to work. I love you guys so much-" Anthony tried to say, before choking up with emotion.

"Hey, what in the heck is wrong with you this morning?" Sonja asked with concern. "We will be fine and I will follow all the traffic laws." She joked trying to lighten the mood.

Anthony pulled his long black hair away from his eyes and quickly wiped away a tear at the same time. "I just want you guys to know how much you mean to me. Be careful okay, something does not feel right. Maybe I am jumpy because of all these dreams?"

"We are fine and we both love you too, my darling!" Sonja replied, as she gave him another hug and got into the car.

Anthony waved as they pulled out of the driveway before heading back into the house. He paused on the first step and tried to hurry back out to stop Sonja, but it was too late. They turned the corner off Juniper Drive onto S. Mustang Road on their way to Oklahoma City. *I feel like someone punched me in the stomach.*

"What is wrong with me today? I need to get it together." Anthony murmured to himself as he went inside.

Anthony felt a little better after a quick shower, a bowl of cereal and a cup of coffee for breakfast. He tried to refocus on his music and all the new possibilities that were fast approaching. Anthony picked up his old guitar and strummed a few familiar chords to settle his nerves. It was a hollow-bodied acoustic with a few hawk feathers and a dream catcher hanging from the tuning gears. The feathers used to belong to his father, Black Hawk Soaring. They hung down the back of the black cowboy hat that he always wore. The dream catcher once hung above his mother's bed for the many years she battled various illnesses. She believed that sleep was filled with dreams both bad and good. By hanging a dream catcher nearby, all the pleasant ones would pass through to your consciousness. The scary ones would entangle within the strings and be vanquished into dawn's morning light. *Unfortunately, none of her good dreams ever came true during her lifetime. They were always with me now, just like this old guitar that never left my side.* Anthony strummed a few chords as he thought about the song Lonely Bear would sing during the ghost dance so many years ago.

"The crow is coming, the crow is coming..." Anthony paused a second trying to remember the rest of the verse from his dream. "Sad are his black wings..." he stumbled out as a loud repetitive knock on the front door startled him from his music.

It stopped for a moment before starting up a little bit louder with a sense of urgency to the knocks. *Who in the world can that be? Probably Dominique wanting to jam before we head into the studio next week,* Anthony surmised, as he set his guitar down and ambled to the door. When he opened the front door, the sun's glare temporarily blinded him until a familiar face came into view.

Aunt Jo stood on the porch wearing a nightgown with her car parked sideways in the yard. Her long red hair barely moved in the breeze. She had tears welled up under her sad eyes. Aunt Jo looked as if her whole world had ended and could not muster enough courage to say what she came over for, so she just stood there glaring at Anthony with such melancholy it made him weak in the knees. *She did not say a word but her eyes told me that nothing would ever be the same.*

Chapter 10

The Judas Redemption

> "I shall not see the shadows
>
> I shall not feel the rain
>
> I shall not hear the nightingale
>
> Sing on, as if in pain
>
> And dreaming through the twilight
>
> That doth not rise nor set
>
> Haply I may remember
>
> And haply may forget."
>
> Christina Georgina Rossetti

May 5, 1995

Sacramento, California

Chloe Daniels

An infrared beam hit its target before returning the raw data to a processor, which quickly calculated the distance traveled, multiplied by the speed of light. The coordinates determined the magnification of a zoom lens. It adjusted a focusing mechanism that allowed light onto a semiconductor sensor. Nearly four hundred thousand, light-sensitive photosites, evaluated the illumination. Hue levels measured out in red, blue and green before mixing into the full color spectrum to give an accurate portrayal of the gruesome image photographed. Recording many frames per second gave the illusion of movement on a three dimensional plane.

The first few seconds were blurry until the "dressing room" as the director of the funeral parlor liked to call it, came into clear focus. It was a cramped, sterile room with sections of stainless steel covering the bottom half of sad, drab olive, walls. A faint whiff of assorted chemicals overpowered the bleach smell lingering from a freshly mopped white and black checkered linoleum floor. A round white speaker in the ceiling played an endless supply of depressing organ music with very little singing. It was loud enough to bore into a person's subconscious and give the whole place a morbid feel to it, although not audible enough to cover the drone of florescent lights across the ceiling.

Jericho Daniels lay dead on a stainless steel table at the center of the room. It commanded such a position, that you could not help but glance down at his rubber-looking, gray skin and the horrible expression coerced onto his face. He looked anything, but peaceful. The first images recorded showed an overview of the room, before panning to a steady shot of the body, mostly covered with a cheap, standard white sheet. Purple discoloration of rigor mortis splashed over a majority of Jericho's high cheekbones not covered by slanted trimmed sideburns. His brown hair, peppered with a touch of gray, combed over to the left instead of straight back in his usual custom, making it evident, someone not familiar with Jericho was the last to brush it. The sheet flowed nearly flat as his barreled chest elevated evenly with his muscled abdominal section. At just under six foot, Jericho stretched across the whole table with clumps of hair hanging off one end and his feet with only a half an inch to spare on the other side.

A zipper-looking pattern ingrained deeply into the skin, ran the full length around his neck. Two inches below, was a gaping wound from ear to ear, separating his Adams apple into two sections. The chasm hung open enough to see clearly into his throat and was speckled with a red stain left behind from a quick cleansing. Jericho's eyes seemed slammed shut, with the left one puffy and severely bruised around a gash across his eyebrow.

Although his sister Chloe saw the condition Jericho was in the day before, she still gasped and covered her mouth attempting not to cry before turning her eyes away.

"Chloe, are you okay," Jason, her coworker asked, while he hit pause on the camcorder.

"No, not really, but give me a second. I nursed Jericho several times after fights in bars, but usually it was only a scrape or two. Nobody ever got the best of him that I ever saw. Okay, I am going to be fine,"

Chloe, stated firmly, trying to convince herself as much as the other two.

"I see why you called me; this is not like any suicide I have ever worked assisting the coroner. Even though we are only getting started, the official story is not adding up. Let's just slide this sheet down a bit and I will give Jericho a complete once over," Chloe's friend and confidant, Rod, blurted out with an enthusiastic tone, which sounded eager to uncover all the secrets the body held. After realizing that his upbeat tempo came off as unsympathetic, he slowed to a more professional pace. Rod worked on many cases Chloe handled as a prosecutor with the Sacramento County Superior Court. He respected her immensely and did not want to hurt her feelings. "This examination might get a bit graphic…I already see the tell-tale signs of torture," Rod explained.

"Are you sure?" Jason asked, realizing the implications of the statement.

"Yes, unless Jericho was in the habit of putting out cigarettes on his own shoulder. In addition, these elongated bruises look similar to a police nightstick or maybe a broom handle. It would be nearly impossible for him to put these marks on his own back like that. This might take a while. I hope you have plenty of film."

"It has about forty-six minutes left on the tape." Jason replied.

"I suppose we should start at the top and work down. Here, get a close up of his face to show the injuries while I go over them."

Jason stepped around to film a close-up shot. As he pushed the zoom button, Jericho's battered face came into focus. He pushed the record button as Rod began.

"Hello, this is Rod Thompson, Assistant Coroner in Sacramento County. I will be performing the autopsy of Jericho Daniels. Suicide by hanging is the official cause of death, but as of this date, that remains unconfirmed by the Oklahoma City Medical Examiner. My initial findings as to the cause of death though, indicate a severe blunt trauma to the head and a massive throat wound, which led to a fatal loss of blood. I am very confident this recorded tape and my report will verify these findings and this death will be reclassified as a homicide." Rod stated with a certain, calm delivery before motioning to stop the camera. He wanted to give Chloe a last chance to leave the room. "Are you sure you want to stay for this, Chloe? There is no way to sugarcoat this. Considering the circumstances, I don't think you want me to."

"I have seen worse," Chloe replied, with a tinge of irritation at the kid gloves treatment she was receiving. "Let's get it over with please."

"As you wish," Rod answered while giving a nod for the recording to proceed. "Beginning at the head of the victim. We find three separate deep lacerations, accompanied by slight fractures to the back of the skull. The left orbicularis oculi muscle, has a two-inch gash along the eyebrow. The zygomaticus major muscle, has severe bruising on the right cheek. There is visible blunt- force-trauma, to the nasalis muscle in the nose, along with several hairline fractures. A small square indention, possibly from a ring, is present on the frontal epicranius muscle on the forehead."

Jason moved around to get different views as Rod paused.

"You can plainly see extreme damage on both ears and the right eardrum, ruptured beyond normal functionality. Moving down to the neck...there are three separate injuries. The first is a diagonal bruising that would be consistent with a nightstick leveraged against the windpipe. Within that generally area, there is a tie-strap, zippered mark that wraps around most of the neck, which also matches perfectly to the marking on the left wrist." Rod stated, as he lifted and displayed Jericho's wrist for the camera. "A deep laceration of the jugular trunk measuring twenty-four centimeters long by six centimeters wide, slants across the neck in one fluid motion. The physical evidence completely disputes the account of Jericho, using a toothpaste tube in an unsuccessful attempt to cut his own throat, before hanging himself in the suicide proof cell. The wound is eight centimeters deep and would cause immediate death."

As Rod continued his work, Chloe felt a dizzy spell coming on, so decided to sit on a chair in the corner until they finished. *Who could have done this to him?* The remorse she felt for the way their relationship deteriorated the last few years, overshadowed the pain of losing her brother. Chloe did not want to admit the truth, but she was a little ashamed of Jericho and wanted to limit his exposure to her children. For years, she stood by him, until the final visit on Christmas, when Jericho stormed in unexpectedly. Coming down from a weeklong drug binge, he was so intoxicated, that he collapsed into the tree after trampling the girl's presents with muddy army boots. Never a happy-go-lucky drunk, Jericho only left the house when Chloe threatened to call the police. He knew he would go to jail for violating parole. *Jericho could not afford to call my bluff.*

The girls loved their Uncle J. and took it the hardest. They did not understand why he was so angry. The mean snarl that usually greeted the rest of the world, melted into a loving smile when the girls were around. They would ride him around the house like a horse or force him to participate in tea parties and board games until it was bedtime. *There seemed no limit to his patience with them.* To Jericho, he was able to relive the childhood experiences that always eluded him. With all the good Jericho was capable of, always came the bad. *Something was just missing with him.* Although possessing great compassion and love, he was always unable to see the negative consequences his actions brought onto others.

It started in fourth grade. Jericho's teacher disciplined him for flirting innocently with a little hazel-eyed girl he liked. Feeling unjustly singled out when the rest of the kids were also talking; Jericho took a defiant stance that turned nasty. The principal and gym teacher forcibly removed him from class. Blessed with a natural strength that would have transferred well into athletics, it was all they could do to restrain him until his father showed up.

Jericho never cried when getting a whipping with the belt and afterwards, declared he would not be going back to "that bullshit place". *It would be the first incident in a string of violent outbursts. There was no end to his anger when provoked.* When Jericho made up his mind, nothing could change it. It was a bad turn of events that led to truancy, running away and eventually joining a local gang. This was a disheartening blow to Jericho's father, who traded being a second generation coal miner in a rural Pennsylvanian town, to a white collar life in the California suburbs, only to have his son fall into all the traps of city living. *Jericho was always out of control with no direction at all.*

Running around with a gang resulted in a juvenile arrest sheet several pages long, ranging from assault and petty thefts to possession of a controlled substance. *It was too much for our father to bear and he died from complications associated with a heart attack.* Jericho took it the worst; he knew that he was directly responsible. Jericho never forgave himself for the way he treated the only man he ever respected. After the funeral, Jericho disappeared into the wind, until news arrived that he was in a Federal Prison for bank robbery.

Losing all freedom went against Jericho's wild, restless soul and it took several years to adjust to conditioning by the prison system. *Then one day, Jericho just showed up.* He would not elaborate on details of his release, but when pressed admitted; "I made a deal with those bastards, I am one of the good guys now," Jericho stated, with a begrudgingly prideful smile. Almost immediately though, Jericho was at odds with his probation officer, who was not aware of any prior arrangements and would not let it slide when he showed up for an interview with beer on his breath. Jericho's stance was that he served his time and if he wanted a drink, undercover status should allow a bending of the rules.

Frustrated that they still treated him as a criminal after he helped break up several minor drug rings, Jericho left for Mexico. Maria Emelda Sanchez, a young woman with two sons from a previous relationship, gave Jericho the stability and love he always yearned for. They married in a small ceremony with only her disapproving family members present. The lethargic Mexicali tempo combined with low paying jobs soon chased Jericho back across the border into familiar patterns. When Jericho did happen to pass through for a visit, he always possessed more money than his pockets could hold, but never a legitimate origination to the windfall. Sometimes it came from the sale of a couple of junk cars for the scrap heap, or sometimes he had recently wrapped up a construction job. *Jericho always changed the subject in a terse way, that meant the conversation was over and do not bring it up again.*

The stressful situation and the sterile smell of the room began to take its toll on Chloe. A steady rumble snarled deep within her stomach. Her face felt a quick hot flash as she leaned her head back against the wall and closed her eyes to focus on better times. Her daughter's heroics of a last second goal during a soccer game, became something better to think about until her mind drifted back to Jericho. *I have to remember a happy time with him to help balance out the bad*, but nothing came to mind. Instead, Easter Sunday dwelled on her thought process.

Eight coffee cups were lined up in no particular order of the colored vinegar inside, although the red and blue had the most eggs dropped into them. The solution instantly shaded the egg to that color, but if you wanted it to be permanent, the egg had to "marmalade" in there according to Sarah Jean, Chloe's six-year-old trying to explain the process.

"The word is "marinate", stupid," Casey, four years her senior, pounced, quickly capitalizing on the mistake. *There was no way she was going to miss an opportunity to make fun of her sister.*

"Hey now, let's not be that way," Chloe responded, coming to Sarah Jean's defense. *Although I wanted to laugh at the cute mistake, I knew I had better portray a strong front or the entire egg-coloring project would descend into a chaotic, bickering mess.* "Sweetie, I am impressed that you remembered that big word. You were so close."

The praise seemed to work and the assembly line continued. A clear crayon spread snippets of good holiday cheer, before the eggs are dipped and dunked in the liquid. Once dried, the girls decorated the eggs with stickers.

"Nice job girls, keep on-" Chloe began to say, before the phone interrupted her. "I bet that's your dad telling me he is going to be late. He should have been home an hour ago," She quipped with a sarcastic tone, while pulling the phone from the charging cradle on the built-in desk. "Hey sweetie, don't tell me you are running late again, I guess we will go out for dinner," Chloe answered both curtly and sweetly at the same time. *I wanted Richard to know they we are waiting for him, but also not add extra pressure during a large project for his architecture firm.*

"Yeah, I am going to be real late. Better late than never," a familiar voice laughed, at the obvious mistake in identity.

"Jericho, is that you?" Chloe asked, recognizing her brother's deep raspy voice from years of smoking. "Where are you at? Are you in town?"

"No, not exactly, but I will be passing through that way soon. I need to wrap up a few things...then I am heading west. Or maybe south."

"Your probation officer made his annual call looking for you. Must have been in February I think? With work and all the girl's activities, it seems like the days have been blending into one another lately."

"Oh don't worry about that clown. I am clearing that up once and for all this week.

Hopefully, this will settle the score with those bastards and they will leave me alone in peace." Jericho stated emphatically.

"Should I even ask what you are involved with now?" Chloe said, with such a starchy concern it went through the phone like a slap across the face.

"Sis, I can't get into all of that right now. I will just say...I am going to take down some hard-core dudes. It is a bad situation."

"Jericho, I don't like the sound of that. Why don't you let me help you? You know I can make some calls. If you turn yourself in, that would go a long way towards getting you back out sooner."

"Please...I am not going back to prison. Like I said, this should square things up for good." Jericho started to say something else, before being interrupted by a car horn in the distance and the sound of a moving truck starting. "Listen, I need to go, but tell the girls that Uncle J. said hi and that I love them."

"You have to go already? We just got on the phone. So when will you be here? Everyone will be glad to see you."

"Well, not everyone," Jericho laughed referring to his feud with Richard.

"Oh, that has blown over. No grudges or vendettas are against you. You know we love you right? All of us!" Chloe said with conviction to let Jericho know she forgave him once again. *It also helped to alleviate lingering guilt from throwing Jericho out on Christmas.* "I mean it okay, and let me know about making some calls for you also."

"Sis, I am the one that is sorry. Sometimes, it is as if I am standing back and watching some other person living my life and totally wreaking havoc on everyone that I ever loved. I am in a good place right now with Maria. I almost made the biggest mistake of my life, but I guess there must be some good in there somewhere, because I could not walk away and let innocent people get hurt again. Some things are just… I don't know…too evil," Jericho muttered, before the weight of his decision choked words back and left his thoughts incomplete.

"There is a lot of good in you, Jericho, please don't ever think there is not. Things will work out for you. Whoops, hang on a second. Casey don't let your sister drink that stuff," Chloe tried to say to no avail as Sarah Jean took a big drink of purple from a coffee cup. The instant pucker and frown made it clear that it did not taste like the Kool Aid Casey convinced her it was. "Oh, honey, go wash your mouth out in the sink," Chloe encouraged as the concoction trickled down Sarah Jean's chin, onto her shirt and she began to cry. "Sorry about that, even Easter is a challenge around here," Chloe admitted into the phone to get back into her conversation. However, the line was dead. "Jericho, are you there?" she asked again. Chloe waited a few seconds without hearing a response before hanging up. *I was very disappointed that I did not get to say goodbye. It would have hurt even more, if I knew that it would be the last time we would ever talk.*

"Chloe, we are all finished over here," Rod informed her. Noticing she was in a bit of a daze, he snapped his fingers and repeated his sentence.

"Oh, okay, thanks a lot for coming down. I really do appreciate it." Chloe finally answered, still half caught up in a daydream.

"I have all of my notes. I will get an official report typed up for you. Hopefully this will help you resolve this and they can find the ones responsible," Rod stated, as they both came forward and gave Chloe a reassuring hug before leaving.

"I am really sorry about your loss," Jason declared on the way out.

Chloe was glad this part was over. *Little did I know that it was just the beginning of my fight for justice.* She always thought of herself as helping the good side, place the final stamp on their war against crime. It was hard for Chloe to reconcile all the outstanding officers that put their lives in danger every day to ones that would do this. *It does not make any sense.* Right from the first call from the Acting Warden of the Federal Transfer Center, the official story was confusing. He kept referring to a Vance Bradway, an alias Jericho used during his bank robbing days. *It was as if he was talking about a completely different person.* Only when he mentioned the name Maria Sanchez as next of kin, did Chloe realize the Warden was actually talking about Jericho. *When I questioned him as to whom exactly Vance Bradway was, the conversation stalled to an uncomfortable silence.* As Chloe convinced herself this was some strange mistake, she heard papers shuffle and the Warden asked if she was related to a, "Jericho Daniels".

Immediately, Chloe knew something was afoul when they listed the cause of death as suicide. He also seemed overly eager for permission to cremate the body. Supposedly, it was a precaution to keep blood-borne pathogens from infecting his officers. *Only when I mentioned my current position and dropped a few names of judges did the Warden back off from this idea and agree to ship Jericho's body at my expense.*

Months would turn into years as Chloe's case pushed through the court system. An initial feeling of vindication over winning a million dollar judgment in a wrongful death suit against the United States Department of Justice, Bureau of Prisons, dissipated to frustration, as the government spent eleven million dollars overturning the decision in the 10th circuit Court of Appeals.

Nearly three years after they laid Jericho to rest by their father's burial plot, Chloe walked out of the gothic, marble covered Judicial building, disillusioned with the legal system and overcome with guilt at not finding Jericho's killers. *Even in death, I am sweeping up the pieces from his mess*, Chloe grieved inwardly to herself. She could not help but glance back at the team of highly paid attorneys responsible for squelching her case, filing out with smiles and cheerful moods. A sick feeling came over her. *Does the truth even matter anymore?*

Chapter 11

Leaderless Resistance

> "We pledge to do all we can
>
> To help you heal the injured, to rebuild this city,
>
> And to bring to justice those who did this evil."
>
> Bill Clinton

Muir Beach, California

August 26, 1998

Kara James

Like puppets on invisible strings, steady rolling Pacific waves pulled by magnetic gravity fields between the earth and moon, flatten and swell before cresting in frothy white caps onto the sandy beaches accented with granite boulders. A mother Gray whale and her calf came up between waves and called out a song of love, as they continued their journey north to Puget Sound. Not to be outdone, a rag-tag group of seagulls provided a chorus, as they squabbled over the last few scraps left on a dead fish washed ashore. Monarch butterflies fluttered to the edge of the rocky cliffs. They pushed to their limits against a summer breeze, before settling back in the quiet pine trees along Red Wood Creek winding through John Muir National Forest, nestled around the edges of pristine beaches.

Sydney watched a few boogie boarders working against the tireless surf until she shifted her gaze to a bank of silvery clouds passing by. The puffy cotton balls floating past looked angry and brought the smell of rain along with a salty taste almost bitter to the tongue. A Monarch butterfly came down and landed on her bare knee. It tickled a little, but she did not want to move in order to prolong the grace of its swirling colors of beauty. One quick flicker from ambitious wings carried it off to another resting spot. This was Sydney's most favorite place she could ever remember. *It seemed like it was always calling me to be here even when I did not know where "here" was.*

On her way to a safe place in Oregon, Sydney's car broke down along the coastline. Without phone service and nobody to call that cared, she decided this was home. A setting sunset melting down into the ocean water captivated her until the darkness kept her from venturing any further up California Highway One. When the morning's light painted the natural scenery, she could not bring herself to leave. *No place could be better than this,* Sydney decided.

It turned out to be a perfect spot to forget the life of mistakes she left behind and start a new journey to find out who she really was. Sydney figured that if the people still looking were going to track her down, this was a good spot to end the chase. *I am tired of running away and blaming myself for what happened in Oklahoma City. I know there was nothing I could do.* Sydney made peace with her new life as a bartender at a local tavern, which kept her from digging too much into her rainy day fund. Then a phone call shook her back to reality. *I never should have stopped running. Was it that easy to find me? Do I even care anymore?*

A combination of fear and self-preservation came over her. *Why did I agree to meet like this? I have no protection, so vulnerable to whatever is going to happen.* As Sydney decided to make a break for it, a black compact car with rental tags looped through the parking lot. It cruised slowly by the weathered walking bridge that separated her from the unknown. *I am tired of this. I have to face it. Whatever happens, I guess this is how it is supposed to be.* Sydney felt like that butterfly. Able to fly, but caught in the endless winds of resistance, with no control of where she would land.

The car parked in one of the many open spots. After a few seconds, a trim and confident woman a few years past middle aged, stepped out. She went into the backseat before emerging with a handful of folders stuffed with papers. Her long red hair blew in every direction for a brief moment, until she put it into a ponytail. She surveyed the area before spotting Sydney sitting alone at a picnic table and started in that direction. Dressed in casual brown dress pants, a tan cotton blouse with a matching sweater around her waist, she seemed caught between a business meeting and a weekend of relaxation. Even though Sydney did not look her way once, the woman came right to her and sat down across the table.

"Kara James?" She asked, getting right to the point as she put her hand out for a friendly shake to start things off on a good note.

Sydney sat there, unable to answer or to pull her eyes from the mesmerizing waves, which had grown considerably in size since she arrived.

Suddenly feeling unsure that she had the right person, the woman repeated her question as she pulled up her sunglasses to scrutinize the situation a little more closely. When no reply was forthcoming, she grabbed her stack of papers and stood up to leave.

"Okay then, I suppose…I have come all this way for nothing." The woman announced with an air of defeat that did not hide her frustration at feeling ignored.

"I do not go by that name anymore," Sydney finally answered, so softly the wind and crash of the surf almost muffled her words.

"So, I do have the right person then? I am Jo. We spoke on the phone-"

"Look, I am sorry for your loss and all, but like I told you, I have nothing to say. It is nothing I want to relive or be a part of anymore."

"I understand how you feel. I don't like reliving the sorrow every single day either." Jo fired back, letting her feelings show even more. "I don't want to be here either, but I want answers!"

"I don't have any answers for you. I thought I was clear about wanting to be left alone. Then you call me from the San Francisco airport and tell me you are here? How did you even find me?"

"Oh I see. You want me to respond to your questions, but-"

"Very bad people are still looking for me. I am risking everything I have built here, to sit on this bench and acknowledge who I used to be." Sydney admitted, with more stress in her voice. She looked as if she could bolt from the table at any second. Her eyes shifted and moved looking for any signs that someone followed Jo.

"I found your name in some BATF reports you filed that had not been redacted…well, your alias name, after you changed it from Karen Howe. An ally in the CIA led me to you. It was not very hard, to tell you the truth. If I can find you-"

"I know they want to kill me, okay!" Sydney stated, while pushing the blonde hair from her face. I could have gone into witness protection, but I figured what was the point. Why trust the very people that betrayed me and were responsible for the events I ran from?" Sydney declared with an air of defiance.

"Kara…I mean Sydney. I understand what it is like to feel vulnerable, exposed, not knowing who the enemy is; because I have been stalked by both the Iraqis and rogue factions within the FBI. Each had its own way to intimidate me, whether it was calls in the middle of the night, to finding my front door wide open, when I came home from the grocery store.

They do not want me to find the truth. Nobody does."

"They did that to you?" Sydney asked.

"Yes, I have never been more frightened. I am all alone in this, and have nobody I can trust or turn to. Every dead end trail is paved with lies." Jo admitted.

Sydney looked eye to eye for the first time and in a way saw herself. She knew exactly what Jo meant. "So why do you keep going? Why come all this way from Oklahoma City?"

"They took everything that I held dear," Jo replied, as she pulled a photo from the pile of paperwork. "This was my niece, Jaci Rae."

Sydney looked down at the photo of the sweet, smiling young girl, opening up a bright package, on the last Christmas she ever had. She remembered seeing her name on the list of victims. *Putting a face to it changed everything.* Guilt swept over her like one of the sudden rainstorms swelling up from the ocean. "That is a beautiful name for such a pretty girl."

"Thank you, she was my beautiful baby. Her name means "Moon" in the Tupi Indian language, spoken along the Brazilian coast, before conquered by the Spanish. She was my moon, stars and universe." Jo confessed with pride.

For once in a long time, Sydney was not afraid. Seeing the resolve that Jo used to push ahead from the tragedy, gave her a bit of confidence. "So what exactly do you want from me? I mean…how can I help you, Jo?" She replied, with genuine warmth.

Jo perked up realizing this was her chance to get past the walls Sydney had around her and wasted no time digging into folder after folder, to pull her long list of questions from her research. "Let me see now," Jo began, as she fired an endless barrage, that immediately overwhelmed Sydney.

"I don't know that. I mean maybe I do, but I am not sure. I am still confused about everything that happened. It is all so blurred as to who did what, or who knew what before and after the bombing."

Jo could tell Sydney was feeling stressed and did not want to lose her cooperation, so she changed tactics. "Sydney, how about we narrow the focus down a little. I have read most of your reports from Elohim City, including the ones afterwards when you had your troubles. I need to know how the Iraqis, specifically Hussain Al-Hussaini, fit into everything.

Sydney felt a cold chill come over her when she heard that name. "I am not sure exactly, but I do know the Iraqis designed the main bomb. It was almost a blueprint copy from the one used in the World Trade Center bombing in 1993, according to my former BATF sources familiar with both terrorist attacks.

Jo sat stunned by the new information. "I don't understand? Nichols and McVeigh did not build it alone? Why has the government spent so much time and effort trying to prove it?" Jo asked, while barely looking up from her notebook as she scribbled into it.

"Honestly, I don't think those two were capable of building anything at all. I mean, I only met the odd pair a few times at Elohim City and then at the Iraqi's service garage in Oklahoma City. Nichols failed at everything he touched and McVeigh, well, I do not think he could focus past a few minutes at a time. There was something seriously off about him. His boyish looks sure did not match his real personality, I guess you could say."

Jo rustled through a few more folders and found the one titled **Iraqi Connection**. "This is a lot to take in. Would you mind if I tape the rest of our talk?" She asked, while pulling out an older model cassette tape recorder.

Sydney hesitated at first, but decided what more could it hurt. *I am hiding in plain sight and wanted to get this over as quickly as possible.* "That is fine I suppose."

"And what about Al-Hussaini, did he help build the bomb as well? I figured he was involved. That man really scared me, but I never backed down."

"Not exactly, he was mostly a facilitator, a sort of go between with the other ones that knew how to mix all the components. He met Nichols through his connections in the Philippines and monitored him. Al-Hussaini seemed to grow close with McVeigh. He was with him a lot towards the end when they decided McVeigh was the glue between all the groups with the same goal. You met him, face to face?" Sydney asked.

"Yes I did. It was soon after they broke into my home. I was able to track Al-Hussaini down through a television report by Jayne Davis on the Iraqi group before pressure from the FBI forced her off the air. From that, I found them at a seedy strip joint and walked into the place with a picture of Jaci Rae. I sat down right at Al-Hussaini's table and looked him face to face. I didn't say a word though, just held the same photo that I showed you and stared at him."

"My goodness Jo, you are so brave. These men are trained killers. They are about as cold and heartless as they come. What did he do?"

"Al-Hussaini glanced down at the photo and tried to dismiss me. He waved to a couple of his friends to throw me out, but I would not budge. Finally, he told them it was okay. When they walked away he looked at the picture again and it almost seemed like he was sad, or maybe it was guilt eating him up inside. He got a tear in one eye before turning away from me. I did not understand his reaction at all. It ranged from intimidation, all the way to the point, where I felt like I was the one badgering him."

"Al-Hussaini was a paid informant for the FBI. He was supposed to make sure the bomb did not go off. Actually, McVeigh and Al-Hussaini were both supposed to, but apparently McVeigh must have had a second fail-safe fuse."

"What? They were informants, all this time? No wonder the government has tried so hard to bury what happened." Jo exclaimed with a mix of outrage, but also relief at putting a few more pieces together. "Here, let me grab my notes," she responded mostly talking to herself as she fumbled through pages of notes and newspaper clippings. "Let's see here. Al-Hussaini was part of Saddam Hussein's Royal Guard, the equivalent of a Navy Seal, until captured during the final push of the Gulf War when Saddam left them to die. Al-Hussaini and others in that group quickly made deals to switch sides. He helped find sleeper cells in Bagdad and provided info for a few low-level missile strikes against Al-Qaeda. The United States put him through more training and brought him over here after the first New York towers bombing in '93, to root out the terror cells forming in the heartland." Jo said.

"I suppose that explains why the whole bunch of them were allowed to waltz right out of the country, despite the fact, their so-called work visas were long expired. They were never even questioned, even when their faces were posted all over the evening news." Sydney replied with disgust, as the motives for the cover up sank in. "I reported him along with the whole group working out of the phony auto garage in Oklahoma City to my handler, but soon as I mentioned that name, the whole conversation turned combative. I was reassigned to a biker gang passing meth-amphetamine around town. It made no sense at all."

The sun emerged from the clouds like a welcome friend before ducking behind a rolling mass of gray. Sydney began to talk more until a few sprinkles blotted the papers in front of them and a gust of ocean wind nearly swept the table clean. The clouds turned darker. A few streaks of lightning illuminated the area as a loud boom of thunder sounded deep into the forest and then echoed back.

"Oh my, just my luck!" Jo called out in despair. "It is all starting to come together for me, but there are still so many loose ends," She stated while gathering up her notes and putting them into a plastic grocery bag.

Sydney thought about the situation for a minute. *It feels good to let out some of my secrets.* "I tried in vain, so many times, to tell the truth to my supervisors, but those reports were quickly discredited. It was all for nothing I am afraid."

"Oh, I wouldn't say that. Those reports helped me find you," Jo reassured.

"Jo, where are you staying while you are here?"

"I do not have a place. I did not plan that far ahead. I was kind of surprised you showed up."

"I was surprised I was here too" Sydney quipped with a rare smile. "I'll tell you what. I only work about three hours tonight to fill in for my friend. How about you meet me around dinner time and we will talk some more?"

"That would be great. Thank you so much!" Jo replied, as she put out her hand again for a friendly handshake. This time she received it.

"Try the Pelican Inn. It was the first place I stayed when I hit town. I will meet you in the pub around eight." Sydney called out, as she stepped away.

Sydney walked over the wooden bridge and went down a side trail leading to an open area next to an isolated park road. When she looked back, Jo was still sitting at the bench looking towards the beach. Jo had a few tears she brushed away. She held Jaci's picture and looked both sad and relived she had made the trip here. *It feels nice to help Jo. I wish I was that strong,"* Sydney contemplated, as she reached her car and went back to her new life.

A hanging wood sign with a pelican painted over a blue background, welcomed Jo as she pulled up to the quaint English cottage. It sparkled with a new coat of white paint with green trim to start the tourist season. Neatly manicured hedgerows across the front, made perfect right angles to the stone chimneys at each end. Jo quickly checked in with the friendly girl at the desk, before ambling around to the back patio. A misty, salty breeze wafted through hanging plants to greet her. An outdoor fireplace and sandalwood scented candles, illuminated tables filled with lovers on a holiday from their normal reality.

Jo made her way inside to the pub. It was intimate and cheerful. The place felt authentic to a far off Scottish tavern of dreams, with its wood-paneled bar, black and white framed pictures capturing moments in history from the area, along with various old plaques. Jo sat at a small round table with a half pint of lager sweating down onto a bar napkin. She waited nearly an hour watching the sun struggle through the clouds, before smoldering into the waiting ocean. Time seemed to get away from her and Jo did not notice Sydney was running late, until she fluttered in the side door. She was dressed casually and gave Jo a smile, as she weaved through the tables of patrons, before sitting down across from her.

"Sorry I am late, Jo. It was supposed to be a short shift, but of course, two people called in. It finally slowed down enough, so my manager let me get out of there." Sydney explained, still wearing her work outfit consisting of a red t-shirt and jeans. "I did not get a chance to change."

"No bother. I have enjoyed the scenery here. It is so beautiful. I can see why you love it so."

"I thought you might like this place. They really make you feel like family. I spent about three weeks here. I even helped a bit, to pay off some of my bills, until I found another job, which hired me without asking too many questions."

"I have not checked out my room yet, but I bet it is lovely."

"Oh it is. I am sure you will be comfortable. I notice your drink is about gone. Can I get you another one? I think I will have one as well. It's been one of those days."

"Well, okay then. Yes, it has been one of those days," Jo agreed with a smile.

They made small talk for a bit as if they were old friends reacquainted after some lost years. Both talked a little about their past without revealing much and wandering into any topics too hurtful. Each avoided the event that brought them together, until Sydney noticed Jo did not bring her notes or recorder to the meeting. It made her feel at ease to open up a little more into past lives that seemed so far away. *It almost feels like someone else lived them.*

"Jo, I have not had a drink...in at least a few weeks," Sydney admitted with a sly smile. She wanted to say a longer timeframe, but changed it to the truth at the last moment, before the words left her lips. "I guess I had to prove to myself that I didn't "need" to drink or anything else anymore. You would think working in a bar would be the last place I should be, but actually, it has helped, because my customers have been supportive. I do not want to be lost to the bottle. It was too much of a crutch in my life. Moreover, I do not want to be that person anymore. I am not that person anymore." *I hope I am not that person anymore.*

"Yes I completely understand, dear. I lost my nephew Anthony to alcoholism. When Jaci Rae was stolen from us, it destroyed him. Finally, he took off without a word to anyone that loved him. Anthony did not say goodbye to his wife Sonja, who was recuperating from the bombing, or his Uncle Bijou who raised him. Not even his grandfather, Lonely Bear, whom he idolized, knows what happened to him. It was as if we lost two people that day." Jo explained, as her voice cracked with emotion on the last sentence.

"I am so sorry, Jo. It sounds like your family was hit really hard?"

"Yes we were. After the funeral, we each fell into our own private hell to mourn. Anthony drank; Sonja went numb and hardly spoke; even Lonely Bear, stopped seeing his patients at his healing clinic for a while. As for myself, I got angry. I have always been a "short-fused firecracker" as my momma always liked to say, but this was much different. It is hard to describe. I vowed to Jaci Rae as she lay in that little coffin with that beautiful white dress on, I would find these people and do whatever I had to. I want to make them suffer as much as I am." Jo declared, with a defiant smile that was mostly in her green eyes.

Sydney was caught off guard by Jo's candid admission. *I know those types of feelings all too well and how dangerous they are.* When she could not come up with a response, Jo finally spoke up to break the uncomfortable silence.

"Excuse me, that came out wrong."

"No need to apologize, Jo. I know what you meant. The people you are dealing with, those responsible and the ones that covered it up for political gain, they deserve everything they have coming to them. Honestly though and please do not take this wrong, I do not think they will get justice in this world. I know that is not exactly what you want to hear."

Jo turned away for a moment and looked to the ocean highlighted by a few beach torches and an endless shining blanket of stars. She knew Sydney was right. This quest was a way to deal with the pain. To fight back, so it did not consume her like it did the others. Nothing would bring Jaci Rae back. She was gone to a better place. At least that is what everyone tells you to make it seem like a peaceful transition to the next life. It still hurt though and it always would. After Jo reflected a moment she seemed to regroup herself and find that fire that continued to burn for justice. She closed her eyes, took a deep breath before turning back toward Sydney.

Sydney could see all the hurt in Jo's eyes, she knew it was fresh and would likely never go away. *I have to help her in any way I can*, she thought. *Jo deserves that.*

"Not to bring up a subject that will ruin our nice time, because I really am enjoying visiting with you. I have to keep pushing forward. I have to see this through to the end. I have a promise to keep, no matter the cost."

"I understand, Jo. Please ask me anything. It seems you have researched this thing and know more about it than me, but maybe something I say will lead to something else, that might open more doors."

Jo perked up to the direction the conversation had turned. She realized all her notes were in the car and pondered what to do for a second, before deciding to try a new way instead of the interview tactics she used before. "Sydney, you mentioned that McVeigh and Al-Hussaini were informants. How did you know this?"

The question caught her off guard. Sydney hoped she did not have to talk about Al-Hussaini again. *When I think about someone coming to find me, it was always his haunting face and those hollow, hate-filled eyes that came to mind.* It took her a second to gather her thoughts before blurting out, "Andy told me they were informants for the CIA."

"Andy? Do you mean Andreas Strassmeir, the one you were…investigating?"

Sydney could tell by the way Jo paused, that she was aware of the personal relationship they had before the bombing. *I got too close to him.* Feeling of embarrassment and betrayal washed over her, before Sydney could muster an answer.

"Yes, that is who I was talking about."

"And when did he tell you this?"

Sydney realized this was going to go into a past she wanted to keep buried. This time, she turned to the ocean for solace to soothe a tired soul. After a couple of minutes of contemplation, she went back to a dark place.

Andreas woke her up with a nice kiss on the cheek as he whispered into her ear. "Morning Love, it is time to get going. I need you with me today."

Kara James stretched a second, trying to go back to sleep. They had drinks late into the night at a local bar and she wanted to sleep it off a while longer. After he shook her a few times, she finally opened her blurry eyes and rolled over to where he lay inches from her face. He always talked too close and this was no exception, only now he seemed to have a purpose. Andreas fidgeted at the covers and looked around as if being watched.

"We have to go before it is light out. Pressing matters, Love, pressing matters."

"Honey, what are you talking about?" Kara asked, with an irritated tone."

Andreas did not say another word as he began tugging her into an upright position. She barely had time to brush her teeth, get dressed and fix her hair, before they were creeping slowly down the rutted gravel driveway leading out of Elohim City. He stopped the black Tahoe and looked both ways several times to see if anyone was waiting outside the gate to follow them. When satisfied they had a clear road ahead, he pressed the gas and turned towards Oklahoma City.

"Andy, where are we going so early? I thought you were helping Dennis with the new recruit training today?"

"We have to meet some people in the city. I do not want Dennis to see us leave. I don't trust him," Andreas responded in a dismissive tone, that meant the conversation was over for the moment.

Kara had a slight headache and nursed a bottle of water she managed to grab, before they left in a hurry. Her eyes felt too heavy to keep open and after a few miles down the road, she fell back asleep. Her rest was deep and dreamless until the car door on the driver's side shut and woke her up. Kara cracked some of the stiffness out of her neck, as she sat up and tried to get her bearings. Nothing looked familiar and it took a few seconds to realize they were sitting in some sort of car lot.

Andreas knocked on the glass front door featuring a closed sign, which looked like it had always been there. For a business, there was nothing inviting about the place, it almost seemed to say, "Keep out". From the thin layer of dust on the cars for sale, to the weeds cropping up in every crack in the parking lot, it was obvious car sales were of little concern to them. Without looking back, Andreas entered the business and closed the door behind him.

When five minutes turned to twenty, curiosity and impatience got the better of Kara and she decided to go into the business. She refrained from knocking on the door, partly so Andreas would not tell her to wait in the Tahoe, but mostly in hopes to slipping in undetected and eavesdropping on whatever was going on. Her eyes had trouble adjusting as she entered into the first office. A pair of crusty desks sat across from each other with yellowed papers and car parts stacked on them. The girly calendar on the wall had been there at least since the seventies, according to the date above the model holding a can of motor oil while she relaxed on a beach in a pink bikini. An elbow turn lit with a single hanging bulb, led to a larger garage with three car hoist lifts. It was empty of vehicles and people. Belts, tailpipes and assorted mufflers hung from the rafters that were once in demand, but never used. Kara could hear a few voices coming from an open side door leading to the back of the auto garage. As she made her way to the doorway, she noticed stacks of ammonium nitrate farm fertilizer, next to some brand new fifty-gallon plastic barrels. They looked completely out of place when compared to the used tires piled close by. She peeked out the back, but could not see anyone.

"Dr. Khalil, when will the truck be here?" Andreas asked.

"Al-Hussaini confirmed they would be here this morning. He did not answer the phone in his room at the Dreamland, so I don't know where they are." The much older man answered with a thick Israeli accent. The slow deliberate way he spoke made it more like a direction instead of an answer. "I also spoke with Commander Pedro. Seems the Arkansas robbery went off as planned. The money from those guns should be enough to cover any of the "Farmers" extra expenses for the high octane racing fuel. If not, I will make a call to Mohammed or Ramzi. They have pledged their full support."

"So the place and date are set?"

"Yes, Wednesday, April 19$^{th.}$ The Murrah building here in town will be the first target. The long paper trails from the Mena drug smuggling and Iran Contra debacles will be shipped over from the courthouse in Little Rock by then. Key evidence from the Whitewater land trial and Hillary Clinton's Federal indictment papers, along with the all the BATF's evidence concerning the new Waco indictments They will be swept away in the wind. It is important these fragile alliances remain intact until the rest of the operation comes to fruition."

"The rest?"

"Not of your concern, Andy. You and the Reverend will be justly rewarded for you cooperation in these matters."

"Not a problem at all. We all want the same thing, or so it seems."

Kara strained to lean out the door and get a look at Andreas's companion. Her heart beat so fast it seemed to echo out into the empty garage. She instantly recognized Dr. Khalil as the keynote speaker from a Muslim jihadist event at the Oklahoma Convention Center six months prior. She thought it was strange at the time that Andreas wanted to go there. Now she understood the connection.

"What are you doing, woman?" An angry voice demanded, as a firm grip clamped onto Kara's left arm. "Who sent you? Answer me now!" The man ordered with intensity, as he yanked her straight out the back door and flung her violently onto the ground.

The mid-day sun was bright in the cloudless sky and made it difficult for her eyes to adjust, even when trying to shade them with her empty hand. Kara could hear the familiar sound of a bullet cocked into the chamber of a handgun. Probably a 9 mm she figured, by the smooth graceful loading she remembered during her training. She felt a hard kick in the side that mostly got her stomach as a barrage of foreign language mixed with cuss words berated her.

"Hey now, you need to back the hell up and I mean now! She is with me!" Andreas hollered, as he stepped between the aggressor and Kara. Although Andreas was much taller than the stocky Al-Hussaini, he seemed a little unsure of himself, but bluffed anyways. "Don't touch her again, Al, or you will deal with me!"

"She was spying! I seen her with mine own eyes. What group you with, you traitor bitch?" Al-Hussaini demanded again, while pointing the gun down towards Kara's head.

"Put the gun away!" Dr Khalil, the obvious leader, ordered. "You are embarrassing yourself in front of our new friends. Why are you late?"

All the faces came into focus as Andreas helped Kara up. He used his right hand, while keeping his left on the gun tucked in his waistband. After a few tense seconds, Al-Hussaini lowered his gun down and put it back into his holster strapped to his right ankle. His eyes burned a hole right through Kara, as he answered the previous question.

"That piece of shit mover truck broke down twice on the way here. It is leaking antifreeze and coolant among other things."

"The last two hours on the road we didn't have any air conditioning and the heat off the motor about fried our asses!" A voice chimed in behind the group, as the lean young former Gulf War soldier walked up.

Kara recognized him from frequent visits to Elohim City. She knew him by the alias of Tim Tuttle, which contradicted the McVeigh name patch on his green camouflaged army shirt with the sleeves ripped off.

"Very soon, the air conditioning will be of no consequence." Dr. Khalil answered, as he gave a welcome nod towards McVeigh.

"Okay, if there is nothing else, we are heading out." Andreas interrupted, while ushering Kara away from the meeting.

"That is fine, my friend; seems all is in good hands. Until next time…" Dr. Khalil's voice called out from behind them, as Andreas and Kara quickly stepped through the garage and made their way to the Tahoe.

Kara was still half-winded and her side was hurting from the vicious kick. Nothing was making much sense to her until she noticed an older model mover truck parked on the side street next to the auto garage.

"What are you guys blowing up?"

"Just get in the car, Love. Now please," Andreas asked in a firm voice.

Kara started to protest before another car pulled up with four dark-skinned occupants. Al-Hussaini appeared at the front door to greet the new crew. He never took his eyes off Kara and continued to stare until they turned the corner a few streets away. Kara tried to act as if she did not notice that deadly gaze, but she did. *It frightened me a lot more than I let on.*

"Are you okay, Love?"

"I will be when you tell me what is going on? Who are those people?"

"Let it lay."

"Andy, I want some answers now! I mean it. You said there would be no secrets between us. Or was that more of your sweet, double talk."

"You and I are on the same team. This is not something you can be involved in, Love. When we get back I want you to pack up your stuff-"

"I am not going anywhere!"

"Your people should pull you now, it is too dangerous. I don't think I can protect you anymore. I do not even know if I can protect myself, too many wild cards. Who is who, has become too blurred."

Kara paused for a second. She was confused and was not sure what to say. "What "people" are they, Andy? You know my family does not care-"

"Oh, stop it! You know exactly what I mean. Now Al-Hussaini knows it as well. This is bad, Love, this is really bad." Andreas explained, as he nervously looked at the rearview mirror. "Why didn't you stay in the car? I thought you trusted me?"

"You are worrying me Andy. What are you talking about?"

Andreas snapped into one of his fits. He slammed the brakes on as he steered the Tahoe half off onto the shoulder. "I know who you are, Karen

Howe! I have always known who and what you are. I was instructed to come back to the bar and bring you in. A sort of truce between the people I am with and the BATF."

Kara wanted to lie, to deny or start to cry, anything, but admit her cover was exposed. *I am the one that was played?* Finally, it all came out. The mix of personal feelings that felt like love. The betrayal she felt from her supervisors, all of it. "So you have known this whole time?"

"Yes, of course. Now they all know." Andreas admitted.

Andreas resumed driving back towards Elohim City without saying another word while Kara looked out the window trying to piece all the events together. *What hurt the most is that he never loved me. I want to break down and weep, but held it in. Just as I always did, except this betrayal was harder than all the rest.*

Tears welled up in her eyes as Sydney finished telling her story to Jo. A salty evening breeze cooled her flush checks as she wiped them into a napkin. Jo put a comforting hand on hers to show appreciation for revealing such a personal defeat. They moved down to the beach as the lights on the deck dimmed to let the patrons know it was closing time. Jo was the first one to kick off her sandals and step into the chilly Pacific surf.

"I was always suspicious of Andy, but I let my personal feelings cloud my judgment. Things confused me about him. For instance, how he entered the United States on a six-month visa with no known address and why the BATF and FBI stopped investigating him after his work visa expired. Andy paid for everything on some credit card with no name on it, that he never made payment on. He confided to me that he trained with the Israeli intelligence agency, Mossad. Andy also said he worked with the GS9 antiterrorism unit in Germany as well. I did not understand how Andy managed to infiltrate Dennis Mahon's W.A.R. and other factions of the K.K.K. so easily. I guess now I know the truth."

"So have you heard from Andreas since the bombing?" Jo asked quietly.

"I only received one phone call from him. It was right before his friends smuggled him across the border into Mexico and onto a plane back to Germany."

"Why did he do all that if he was working for the government as a provocateur?"

"My guess is that it was not supposed to happen like that. The bombs were supposed to take the building down the night before and the BATF would be on site to catch them…except."

"Except McVeigh and the rest, double-crossed the BATF and set the charges off in the morning with all of those innocent people in the Murrah building." Jo surmised, as she stepped from the water and sat down in the wet sand, not worrying about her clothes. The truth hit her much harder than what she could have imagined. "It is such a horrible tragedy.

How could they do it knowing my Jaci Rae was in the daycare?"

Sydney sat down next to her. The pair exchanged glances and realized there was nothing more to say. They watched a few clouds roll in past a waning moon and disappeared into their own thoughts of grief. Together, they quietly mourned the lives they were trying to leave behind.

Chapter 12

Sand Creek

"Although wrongs have been done me I live in hope."

Chief Black Kettle

December 20, 2001

Mustang, Oklahoma

Anthony Motavato

A droopy orange sun, skittered behind the pine trees of the Wild Horse park, leaving shadows of darkness over the rectangular cinderblock building across the street. A light sensor within a timer triggered a surge of electricity to the circular sign on the front of the business. Steady currents flowed into a socket, before transferring on through a pair of contact pins located on the ends of three long cylindrical tubes. Voltage sprinted to a coiled electrode that heated up from the energy. Instant warmth changed a small dot of mercury from liquid form into a vapor, which collided with inert gas within the bulbs. It produced a white light visible to the human eye, that bounced off a metallic silver surface on the backside of the sign, pushing radiant luminescence through a sheet of hard plastic. With a couple of spastic flickers, the words **Indian Smoke Shop,** finally stayed illuminated. The sign gave off a continuous buzzing sound of a hundred lightning bugs captured in an old pop bottle.

Anthony Motavato had leaned against the wall for hours not sure what his next move would be. *Although I was born and raised in this town, I feel like a stranger here.* A sudden burst of a yellowish, red light from the sign above seemed to break him from distant places. Over the last two weeks, a draining ride aboard a cargo vessel shipping out from Bristol, England, carried him to an overcast and gloomy New York port. From there, Anthony had spent eight hours in the economy section of a Greyhound bus, before hitching rides with truck drivers that wanted a little conversation to help break the monotonous grind of eighteen wheels over asphalt.

Soon after, Anthony witnessed a pair of jet liners crash into the World Trade Center. An urgency to come home, replaced a vow of never returning to Mustang. The weeks since watching the shocking images on a small television in the tavern Anthony worked at while living in its crowded stock room, seemed to pass with a blink of his bloodshot eyes. *I know how the families of the victims feel due to my own anger left over from tragedy and broken dreams. It is something that never leaves you. A permanent melancholy,* Anthony thought to himself, while finishing his last cigarette.

After mustering the remnants of courage in his worn out heart, Anthony decided to enter the building he practically grew up in. A few new cigar stickers graced the door over the old ones, but nothing else had changed.

Jesse Spotted Owl pushed the dark hair from her face, as she looked up from behind the counter. Now in her mid-twenties, she could not hide her worried glance when noticing Anthony's frazzled appearance. Her fawn brown eyes warmed up a little when she recognized the ghost from her past. Still unsure if her instincts were trustworthy, she withheld a greeting and pretended to fill empty slots on the cigarette dispenser above.

Anthony hesitated a second before moving any further, as if an invisible force field of guilt prevented him from the task. Taking a mental inventory of what was the same from his youth, to the things that did not reconcile to memories gradually moved him into motion. His rattlesnake skin cowboy boots came unglued from the floor and slid in a slow deliberate shuffle allowing him to explore.

For the modest size of the seven hundred fifty square foot establishment, the Smoke Shop seemed bigger by using every available inch of floor space. Lacking modern updates, it was nearly the same as Anthony left it. To his right were three coolers, two of which were crammed full of soda, milk, eggs, lunchmeat, juices and various brands of beer. *The third cooler never worked for as long as I could remember.* The doors were removed and stuffed full of dry goods, firewood, fuel cans with heating oil, lawn mower parts and auto accessories.

Above every isle, were multi-colored Indian blankets mixed with hand-made dream catchers, like the one hanging from Anthony's acoustic guitar strapped across his back. *It always swayed in perfect rhythm when I played.* On the end caps, t-shirts and camouflaged hunting jackets in plastic bags, hung alongside each other. Kiln-fired sculptures made from red clay prevalent in the area, lined the tops of the shelves full of cans of food and about anything else, someone passing through might want or need.

A slight hunger pang forced Anthony to grab a stick of buffalo jerky made from the beef of a local butcher. It was all dressed up with spices and then dehydrated with a special machine that owner John Spotted Owl bought from a late night infomercial. After lackluster initial sales, he added the name "Buffalo" to the title helping it blend in with the mystique of the Smoke Shop. Anthony took a large bite from the jerky, but instantly grimaced in pain with the first chew. A molar on his top right side had been tender for quite a while. *I guess it has been too long since visiting a dentist.* Chewing gingerly on the opposite side, he finally made it to the back of the store.

Anthony took a long pause outside a door leading to an attached building addition. This was where his Grandfather Lonely Bear operated his lifelong holistic healing business. Roughly the same size as the original building, it was constructed in the mid-sixties after Lonely Bear won a dispute with a County Prosecutor, who was out to see his name up for Governor in the next election.

While racial clashes between African Americans protesting against an unjust system and white police raged on, Native American rights were being systematically diminished. In the prosecutor's opinion, Lonely Bear was a fraud operating a den of sin. His charges included; illegal heath care (holistic healing), tobacco and alcohol sales, ammunition (shotgun shells for hunters) and gambling, which consisted of an old Poker slot machine in the corner, that nobody ever played. The ones that did would be disappointed if they did not read a tattered sign on the front declaring maximum payout in the event the (1 in 675,000) odds of a Royal Flush hitting, was fifty dollars in store vouchers. As the prosecutor's bad luck would have it, the Circuit Judge in which he pled the case, happened to be a close friend of Lonely Bear. The prosecutor's case was abruptly thrown out of court. Judge Dean had finally repaid the special care his granddaughter received for her asthma attacks.

After the dismissal of the frivolous lawsuit, Lonely Bear followed the path his vision quest revealed to him at the age of ten. When Lonely Bear turned sixty, his career was further legitimized in a series of essays in a Boston Medical Journal, on native herbs and remedies. The essays highlighted his biannual, sabbaticals to the four deserts of the

Southwest to replenish dwindling supplies and reconnect with the Mother Spirit.

Anthony sauntered down the narrow hall and passed by an elderly woman who suffered more from loneliness than medically. He smiled to acknowledge the tight fit as she pushed by, but did not even receive eye contact as a reply. Anthony reached for the doorknob. He froze up as guilt came along with the memories of last time walking through this door on a nice spring morning, when Anthony brought his daughter Jaci Rae here for treatment. Usually she was such an active, happy five year old, except on this day, she woke up with a scratchy throat and a whooping type cough. Lonely Bear was able to cure the symptoms with two baby aspirin and a few cherry flavored cough drops. Something else troubled him.

"Jacie Rae has a shadow over her life force," is how Lonely Bear tried to explain it. Disregarding these predictions of harm coming to his daughter, Anthony stormed out without facing the truth about her future. *When I left here, I could never have imagined how much our lives would change and that I would be gone for so long.* It turned out to be a crucial mistake. *I will never forgive myself.* In the aftermath of the Oklahoma City bombing, it hit the entire family hard, even Lonely Bear cursed his natural gifts. For the first time in his life, he temporarily lost all faith in his abilities and even in the Mother God as well. Lonely Bear felt he should have saved Jaci Rae somehow.

"Come in, my Son!" Lonely Bear called out, acknowledging the familiar presence waiting outside.

Tears of disappointment and separation changed to happy tears, as Anthony slunk into the office and saw Lonely Bear, who wore a generous smile across his gaunt face. The smile was crooked to the left, while subtly cascading down to a stubbly, prominent, dimpled chin. Lonely Bear was a bit thinner and his gray braid noticeably longer, but he still stood tall despite the passing years and a haunch from a strained disc in his back. He took a few steps toward Anthony, while unfolding long frail arms to beckon a hug.

"This is the first step in making the bad years go away, my boy."

"I am so sorry-" Anthony stammered out, as he hugged Lonely Bear.

"Oh, nonsense," Lonely Bear interrupted. "The past can't touch us anymore. Welcome home my son. Long has your journey been," he declared with an air of optimism, that life was on the upswing to better days.

"Yep, some tough times are behind me now. Glad I can't remember them," Anthony smirked, to acknowledge the mirthful moment. *It feels good to have a flame of hope, even if it is fleeting,* he thought to himself as the embrace ended.

"Anthony, I dreamed of this recently. I was lost in the sands of the Mojave and a cold desert wind was picking up while the sun went the opposite direction. My hope was waning. Suddenly, you rode up from around a dune on a brown and white painted pony. I knew it was a sign as soon as I awakened."

"I had to practically beg, borrow and sing my way here," Anthony admitted.

"Like my Grandmother Rain Cloud always said, the difficulty of the travel will soon be forgotten, when the destination is reached," Lonely Bear replied, with a proud tone for the woman whom raised him after his parents died of small pox.

"She sounds like a very wise woman," Anthony volleyed back, to acknowledge respect for his own heritage.

Anthony always loved hearing about the family he never knew. It brought back all the summer nights spent around a campfire behind Lonely Bear's cabin as he retold tales from Rain Cloud, who had passed the stories down from her own Grandmother. When Lonely Bear told about the massacre of Rain Cloud's family along the Washita River, Anthony would always get chills as if he were standing in the bloody snow next to her. *The images will never leave me.*

"So I reckon you haven't talked to your Aunt Jo or Uncle Bijou yet?"

Anthony's black straggly hair bounced down in his face as he shook his head no in a casual manner, obviously not wanting to make an issue of it.

"After you get cleaned up a bit, I will run you over there. You know where the shower is, plus your stuff is still in that south closet."

"Oh okay, yep I could use a hot shower," Anthony agreed since his last bath was out of a sink at a truck stop in Hazard, Kentucky.

"Anthony, wait a second. Let me get a look at you while I have you in my crosshairs," Lonely Bear requested, as he tapped the leather examination table between them. "You look a bit worse for wear, I hate to say."

"I'm fine really, just tired and a tad hungry..." Anthony started in protest until a stern look made him sit his duffle bag down, prop his guitar next to it, before hopping up on the table.

Lonely Bear grabbed a small examination light on the counter behind him to check Anthony's eyes first. They were a deep defiant brown, but also slightly jaundiced, which was an early sign of kidney failure. Anthony was pale with poor muscle tone, from the combination of malnourishment and alcoholism. Lonely Bear lifted up Anthony's shirt, which had the smell of beer and a hamper full of dirty clothes. A heavy, negative energy made Lonely Bear's hands tingle, as he ran them across Anthony's side.

"How long have you been in pain Son?" he asked, but received only a slight grimace as a reply. "No wonder you have not been eating right," he deduced while finding himself in a quandary to keep silent or risk another fallout by disclosing Anthony was terribly ill. After a quick pause to ponder the dilemma, Lonely Bear decided to keep the peace, well that is, unless asked directly.

Anthony turned away, unable to look Lonely Bear in the eyes. Without realizing it, Anthony had divulged that he already knew his dire situation. Lonely Bear continued his duties by moving his nimble fingers across Anthony's face to locate unhealthy energy coming from there.

"So how long have you had a toothache?"

Anthony flinched, which confirmed Lonely Bear's initial diagnosis. "I don't rightly know. The days have kind of run together. It has been tender a week or so, maybe longer if I had to guess."

"Open your mouth and let me see."

"Ahh..." Anthony croaked, while titling his head and opening his mouth.

"I am looking at your teeth, not your tonsils."

"Oh, sorry," Anthony replied sheepishly.

Lonely Bear examined the decayed tooth using a small magnifying glass on the end of a stainless steel handle.

"Yes Sir, plumb rotted to the core. It is going to have to come out," Lonely Bear surmised, as he turned to a cabinet behind him. "The rest would look okay if you brushed and flossed occasionally. I would give you something to numb the pain, but it looks like you have already taken care of that," he said in a disappointed tone in reference to Anthony's breath, still pungent from a half-pint of Southern Comfort consumed in the parking lot. Lonely Bear fumbled in the drawer a moment before shutting it and moving down one. "My good friend William gave me all of his tools of the trade when he retired. Poor fellow passed away right after that and never enjoyed his golden years. Reminiscent of your father, Black Hawk Soaring, who drank his life away," Lonely Bear stated in a glib tone at losing his only son to his demons, but also in a patriarchal cadence to make sure Anthony was following his opinion on the subject.

Lonely Bear slipped a curved needle nosed instrument into Anthony's mouth and clamped onto the tooth. With an even pressure leading to a quick snap of his wrist, he extracted the offender.

"Did you get it out," Anthony began to ask, before a sharp pain and a slight taste of blood answered his own question.

"What was left of it," Lonely Bear replied, as he held it out for inspection.

"Okay, you're all done. Why don't you get ready and we will have some supper over at the diner. They still have the same old stuff."

"All right," Anthony agreed, as he remembered some of the best chocolate cream pies in the area. In an instant, he was in a mini daydream as he watched a big wedge of fluffy heaven come from beneath a glass cover and float over to their table. How his mouth watered as each step the server took seemed to take forever. The first bite was always the biggest and squished between his cheeks a few times before swallowing. The bites would grow progressively smaller, savoring the taste, while rationing his milk to the end. "They still got that pie?"

"Yes they do, even though I try not to notice it on a regular basis. Been watching my sweets intake lately," Lonely Bear answered with a slight smile, as he began to recall the many meals shared together, having hamburgers and pie. "Well, you know where the shower is. I will go get you some shampoo and other necessities."

Anthony gave him an appreciative nod for the care received, before grabbing his gear and stepping out the door. He turned left two steps to a small room used as a kitchen, bedroom, laundry and stockroom. The door was always a little off-centered, so Anthony gave it a nudge with his shoulder. It let out a shrill creaking sound as it stubbornly opened up.

On his left was a closet with white maple-finished sliding doors. The backroom featured a white enameled kitchen sink built into a pine cabinet painted black. Metal shelves stacked full of various items including a shoe box full of bank receipts, cleaning supplies, can goods with an inch of dust on them and paper goods, stood on both sides of the sink. Anthony stepped over to the shower base and pulled the white nylon curtain, which gave the illusion of privacy, while barely keeping the water from splashing out onto the floor. A rattling series of thumps knocked against the wall when he started the water. The first few sprays were rust colored as the iron pipes cleared out the old water. While the water warmed up, Anthony decided to find a new set of clothes from the closet, since he had worn everything in his pack several times on the trip here. Lonely Bear stepped in and handed Anthony a bag full of stuff.

"Let's not get too dressed up, it is just Sandy's Diner." Lonely Bear joked, in reference to the outfits in the closet. "Holler if you need something else."

Anthony turned and relented to a spontaneous outburst himself as he saw the pair of zebra-striped pants, left over from his heavy metal days of the eighties. He began looking through the clothes, most of which had not fit him since high school. A brief pause was made at his old stage jacket. It was blue denim, smattered with patches from groups of the day, Iron Maiden, Rush, Van Halen and several from his own garage bands.

"Did a lot good shows in you, old buddy," he said proudly, while tucking it back into the past. Satisfied nothing in the closet was going to do the trick, Anthony slid the doors shut and moved over to a three-drawer dresser situated between an old army cot and a set of shelves. It served as a barrier between the kitchen and bedroom. He removed a clean pair of socks and underwear from the top drawer, and then skipped down to the last one to retrieve a pair of blue jeans, a long sleeved black t-shirt and a towel. A *shower sounds good. It is going to be nice to wash the road grunge off, maybe try to sober up a bit for Lonely Bear's sake. Well, as sober as possible,* Anthony resolved, by adjusting his expectations to his will power.

Anthony dumped the sack of personal items onto the cot. He picked out a bar of Irish Spring soap, shampoo, conditioner, toothbrush and toothpaste. After staging everything in place, Anthony peeled his clothes off and made use of the toilet to relieve a day's worth of drinking. It had become progressively more difficult to urinate lately, but this time went smoothly and pain free.

Stepping into the shower seemed like stepping back into another life, as Anthony immediately drifted away in dreams, not thought of since leaving the States. It was the night he met Jaci Rae's mother, Sonja Christie. *The night I fell in love with the woman of my dreams. We made love for the first time in this cramped, dated shower.* Meeting after one of Anthony's shows, there seemed to be an instant chemistry. She had a wild side, tempered by a very loving personality. Sonja's shoulder-length blonde hair lifted and bounced every time she laughed with a deep laugh all her own. Sonja's crystal blue eyes, so full of charm and grace, could never tell a lie. Moreover, she never did. *Not that I ever knew at least.* She was "tall legged" as his Uncle Bijou, was fond of saying about the natural born beauty, with a body that was a perfect combination of voluptuousness in build and also athletic.

Anthony reached his right hand through the water. In his mind though, he was touching her cheek, getting ready to kiss Sonja for the first time. It felt like the second their lips touched, there was an unbreakable bond between the two of them. *Nevertheless, it did break,* Anthony's subconscious interrupted, to snap him forward to the last time showering here. *The day I walked out on Sonja.* The day Anthony gave up and succumbed to the overwhelming guilt he felt for losing Jaci Rae, the light of both their hearts. Anthony could not face those blue eyes looking at him, while attempting to hold back the hurt. Sonja still loved him, but they had only so much room for anguish in their hearts. *There was nothing left to give to the other to ease the pain.*

Anthony's knees became shaky when a wave of sorrow washed over him as if he were lying on a beach of broken glass. *It hit me hard.* He wept on one knee until the shower turned chilly. Not a day went by he did not miss them, but before it had just felt like a dead past life belonging to someone else.

Now Anthony began to realize that it was in real time, not rewind. The water turned frigid by the time he finished scrubbing up and washing his hair twice to get it back to long and straggly. As Anthony stepped from the shower basin, he felt like a new man. It had been cleansing to his appearance and his soul. Even if only temporarily. Anthony shivered as he dressed in a hurry. He sat down on the end of the cot to put on his socks. After getting the left on, he lost his balance on the right one. He tumbled over. He started to sit back up before his body pulsed gratifying messages to his brain. With a slight stretch, his shoulders neck and back all crackled in unison. It had been days since laying out flat on a bed. The only sleep came with his head against a window on the bus, or huddled in the cab of a truck.

The discolored ceiling panels above kept his eyes attention, while his mind wandered. *Where am I going to go when I leave again?* Although Anthony had just arrived, something in his restless soul was pushing him to go. *Am I just nervous about everyone seeing me in this condition, or is it something deeper?* In his heart, he knew it was more than the fear of another failure. If he stayed, he would have to face all the mistakes he ran from. Anthony blinked once, and then a second time a bit longer in duration. The third time was too much for his tired blackened eyelids to open up again. His thoughts began tricking him, "*just relax for ten minutes then you will feel refreshed*". Ten minutes would eventually turn into fourteen hours.

Lonely Bear kept busy locking up the Smoke Shop as Jessie Spotted Owl counted the meager cash receipts behind the counter. She switched the breaker on the panel to turn off the outside sign before moseying on home. A few hunger pangs reminded him the restaurant would be closing soon. The opportunity for pie was disappearing fast. The absence of a running shower gave Lonely Bear the inclination that Anthony must be close to ready. He gave a knock on the door as he entered the room. A deep, nasally snore resonated throughout the room that immediately let Lonely Bear know it would be supper for one tonight, as usual.

"A long rest will do you a world of good Little Hawk," he said quietly, while turning out the lights and leaving Anthony to the fate of the dream he in.

Even though the television screen jumped occasionally while the black and white picture was a little fuzzy, the program achieved the desired reaction from its audience. Anthony laughed out as Yogi made a futile attempt to swing down on a rope, right under the Ranger's nose and take a picnic basket.

"Boo Boo tried to warn you, silly bear," Anthony called out, as if talking to actual friends. "See, now you're in trouble again," he squealed, jumping off the apple-green velvet couch.

The plastic footings in his pajamas stirred up sparks in the lavender shag carpet of their residence. Technically, it was a mobile home, but it had never gone anywhere for the six years since Anthony was brought here from the hospital. He was a happy baby, or so it seemed in the only surviving photo of Anthony's childhood. All bundled up in a red blanket featuring a panoramic scene of wild mustangs running through a mountain valley, all stitched out with colorful threads. Most days, these cartoons were his only friends since Anthony's parents failed to register him for kindergarten. When his mom called him from the back bedroom, he figured it must be about dinner since his stomach was growling. The bowl of dry cereal he had for lunch had worn off.

"Anthony?" Her despondent voice laced with an urgent tone, called out to him again. "Honey, please come in here."

"Okay, just a second," he replied, trying to stall until the cartoon ended. A commercial for the latest toy he could only wish for came on next. *Maybe if Santa does not get lost this year, he will bring me one of those*; he schemed quietly to himself, swishing down the hall and into his parent's small bedroom.

The king-size mattress and box springs lying directly on the floor, took up most of the room. A nightstand at the head of the bed, blocked an overfilled closet behind it. Boxes of belongings that remained unpacked from one of the many moves out of her parent's basement, still resided at the foot of the bed, piled along with bags of clothes that always seemed too good to throw out. His mom lay in the middle of the bed wearing a plush cotton nightgown that she alternated with her other two since falling ill.

"Yes Mama. Do you need a drink of water, or for me to turn on the fan again?"

"No, but listen this is important. Honey, go down the street and tell your Daddy to come here right now, okay? Can you do that for me sweetie?" she asked, with a deep raspy cough that interrupted whatever else she needed to say. Unable to catch her breath she just motioned Anthony to leave.

Anthony left the room, skipped his way out of the trailer and onto a bare, dirt patch of front yard that also functioned as a place to stack old car parts, before shuffling on down to the Lucky Nines bar. Nobody ever really knew why they called it by that name, especially considering no other reference to the number or luck appeared anywhere on the building. A major ice storm had weighed down the old sign causing it to crash to the ground. The saying went that if you knew where the Lucky Nines bar was located, you had probably been there. The surrounding urban area did not invite many strangers to want to investigate what was in the sheet metal clad building.

As Anthony passed another mobile home on the way, two young girls came from around the side and hung out on the front steps. Although they did not say anything, the sisters laughed and stared at Anthony as he passed their yard. One made a swishing sound by puckering her cheeks in, while blowing out air in short intervals. Immediately, Anthony realized they were mocking his blue Cookie Monster pajamas. It was definitely too early in the evening to be wearing them, especially in public. Not only did it embarrass him, but also it made him feel different. *Like somehow I was not as good as those girls with a nicer home and actual grass in the front.* He heard a few laughs call out until he reached the door to the bar and the music from inside overwhelmed all other sounds. A slice of stale, burnt smelling air rolled out as he opened the flimsy wood door. *It took a second for my eyes to adjust to low wattage bar signs lighting the place.*

Every face in there appeared hollow, as if they had always been there and always would. At the bend in the bar, he recognized the laugh and the long braids that danced beneath a black cowboy hat with a feather of a hawk tacked onto the left side of it. Anthony scotched over to him and tugged on his brown flannel shirttail that hung out over faded blue jeans.

"Daddy...Momma said she needs you," Anthony chirped, still tugging to get his attention while his father finished his story.

Black Hawk Soaring gave a drunken laugh at his own joke, before turning his attention to his son. "Run along home, boy, tell her I will be there shortly," he replied in a demeanor that started with a nice welcoming tone, then ended with a dismissive order.

"Okay," Anthony answered, unable to muster enough courage to convey the urgency of his mother's request.

Anthony turned around and left not wanting to make eye contact with anybody else in there. The only thing he worried about now was how he was going to tell his mother her request was denied. "shortly" to his father, could mean in an hour or in a day or two. He floated in barely enough to be able to call this place his residence and never made a difference in their lives.

Anthony was glad to see the front porch was now empty of the tormenters when he passed the double wide. As he stepped into the living room of his own home, Anthony could hear the whimpered cries coming from the bedroom. He zipped around the corner and down the hall. As he came into the room, his mother's desperate eyes caught him by surprise. *She looked so sad.*

"Where is your father, Anthony? Is he coming? Does he know that I need him right now? Does he know baby?" She asked, directing the question to the ceiling due to her head titling backwards as if the very task drained off most of her energy.

"He told me to go home, but to tell you he will be here in a little bit," Anthony recounted, trying to sugarcoat it to cheer her up.

"He's not coming?" She responded, in a voice filled with so much anguish at the realization of the answer, that it seemed more like a final personal disappointment to her empty life.

Anthony's mother gave out a short cough, gasped for air for a second and exhaled one last time. Having never been explained the meaning of death; Anthony assumed she was only sleeping. All examples came from cartoon figures hit by an anvil, then sprouting wings. They always sang and played the harp as they floated skyward to a happy place in the clouds. The message played out with a simplistic approach. The good character went to heaven, while the bad ones went to a place of fire.

Two hours passed as Anthony's mind drifted along with the dream worlds of television shows. His father came in and immediately went to look in the fridge for a beer that he knew was not there, but the temptation was so great, it made him hope for a chance at finding one. Neither one spoke as they went about their own business. Eventually, the big man stumbled back to change his clothes, from the same ones he had been wearing since yesterday.

"Anthony!" he called out with such a demanding bark, which meant, if he hurried, there might be a chance he would not be in trouble.

"Yes Daddy," Anthony replied as he skidded into the room, feeling he had hustled the best he could.

"Why didn't you tell me she was dead? You said to come home. Not that your Momma was dead. What the hell is wrong with you boy?" He growled, letting Anthony know he better stay back from arm's length of he might catch a smack upside the head.

With one short question, Black Hawk Soaring transferred all the guilt he should have felt for treatment his wife while she was alive, onto his son for not comprehending the gravity of the situation. Although Anthony understood he was not directly responsible for her death, he still felt ashamed. Over the years, it would slowly consume him. Anthony went into his room to stay out of sight until hearing the sound of the front door slamming from his father's departure. Laying on his back staring at the bare walls, tears welled up in his eyes at a profound realization. He was never going to see his mother again, until joining her in heaven. Two days later, years of alcoholism finally caught up to his father, when he passed out and drowned face down in a mud puddle outside the Lucky Nines bar. Anthony closed his eyes and hoped to dream of better days.

Lonely Bear shook Anthony lying on the cot in the storeroom, until he finally sat up and opened his puffy eyes. He was back to the real world.

"Come on wake up. Get yourself cleaned up and we will get some lunch at Sandy's diner. I will be in my office."

What did he mean by cleaned up, Anthony started to wonder, before the clammy sensation in his groin area, alerted him to a large urine stain on the front of his jeans. Anthony was increasingly worried about his health problems and now, he felt completely humiliated that Lonely Bear saw him in such a pitiful condition. *Once again, I felt like that little boy in pajamas, laughed at by two mean girls on a porch.*

Chapter 13

Perpetual Darkness

"Men fear death as children fear to go in the dark

And as that natural fear in children

Is increased with tales, so is the other."

Francis Bacon

December 21, 2001

Mustang, Oklahoma

Uncle Bijou

Skilled nimble fingers, danced over the black and white keys of an upright piano, in perfect timing to a steady rhythm from the drums. The sweet notes mixed beautifully with a standup bass and a slide guitar. The music swirled around the crowded little Kansas City jazz bar, before drifting up through the wood planks in the ceiling, into the upstairs hotel room. It was reserved for traveling musicians to catch some rest between sets. It was a sparsely furnished room, but colorfully decorated with hundreds of advertising handbills from singers and players through the years. A neon sign outside the club blinked the words "Kitty Cat Club" in bright blue. It illuminated the room intermittently through a shade-less window.

The boy lay asleep on his left side facing the wall, until hearing a key jiggle in the lock. A few seconds later, the door opened and a table lamp came on.

"Pops, is that you?" He asked in a sleepy tone with only one eye open.

"Yep, Bijou, sure-nuff is me. I need to get some medicine, for my lady friend and me. Then we be on our way. Go back to sleep now, ya hear?"

Bijou managed to get his other eye unstuck from the "sleep crunchies", as Pops called them. He gazed over at Pops with love and pride. Pops was of medium build, never too fat or too thin, average height and bald-headed from shaving it with a straight razor. "If the good Lord is going to take most of my hair, I might as well give it all to him," Pops reflected nearly every time he shaved. His smile was his trademark and was a stark contrast from his dark coffee colored skin. It was always there. Pop's smile was so toothy it made strangers feel like friends. Ladies in particular seemed drawn to that "magic" smile. Pops played the saxophone because he figured, "if I have to have such a big mouth, I might as well use it for something besides eating" he always joked, with a loud chicken-cackle of a laugh.

Pop's female companion stumbled about, until he sat her down, in one of two chairs in the room. *I still remember her stained barmaid smock and how her blonde hair kept creeping down over her pale face, making it hard for me to get a good look at her. I ended up getting more view than I wanted, as her short skirt hung open with her uncrossed legs. She did not seem to care that her pink panties were showing to Pops and I.* After a minute or so, she started to light a cigarette before Pops took it from her.

"Not if front of the boy. He is a bit light-winded in his lungs," Pops explained, with a slow Georgia crawl of an accent.

Growing up a sharecropper's son for the first ten years of his life, Pops caught an empty boxcar and never looked back. Although he missed his five brothers and his Momma, he would not miss the steady stream of drunks she bedded down with regularly after his father took the same rails out of town. Unable to support himself, he took to playing a harmonica lifted off a sleeping hobo to make a living. Self-taught, Pops played the notes out of that thing, before saving enough money to purchase a saxophone from a Louisiana pawnshop. If the song called for it, he would pull that harmonica out of retirement and let wail those blues he always carried in his heart.

Bijou fell in and out of sleep until the familiar smell of a candle, along with Pops special medicine, filled the room. Bijou made a few shadow animals off the wall, as the flickering candle provided enough light to make a dog, duck, and a very rough outline of a pig. *I started to succumb to the will of tired eyes until I heard the clumsy crashing sound of the barmaid falling off her chair. Turning over, I could see her slumping in Pops arms as he tried to pick her up.* With all the help Pops could give her, the delirious woman came out of her trance long enough to shuffle over to the door.

"Come on now, Hunnie, don't ya be fading out on me now. Bijou, I am going to go tuck my lady friend in and I will be back in a bit," Pops stated in a calm voice, before lugging her down the hallway.

Between random flashes of blue from the sign, Bijou could see that Pops left his medicine kit open. Curiosity got the better of him and in a hop and skip; Bijou was fumbling through Pop's stuff. Inside the cigar box waited a syringe, matches, extra candles, a blackened spoon and a red bandanna rolled up into a thin rope. *I should have left it alone, but then I noticed a piece of foil tucked inside an envelope. It had unraveled enough to see the contents.*

"Pops has some chocolate," Bijou whispered quietly to himself.

Bijou opened the crumpled foil to reveal a silver dollar size hunk of black substance, sticky to the touch. He sniffed at it a few times, before giving it a little nibble. *At first I decided to put it back before remembering Pops saying,*

"What's mine is yours."

The first few chews were definitely not, what Bijou was expecting. *It tasted worse than the cough elixir I drank to sleep at night.* Instantly, it latched onto his teeth like ivy onto an old brick wall. It began to taste bitter, so he quickly swallowed the entire batch. *My stomach rippled with nausea for a minute or so before a euphoric calm came over me. All of my fingers and toes tingled something funny. Then I felt light as cotton*

Neon blue from the sign outside, streamed into the room in the shapes of flowing water. *It seemed to splash over me.* It reminded Bijou of seeing the ocean for the first time, on a recent trip down to Florida with Pop's blues band. *Except this water is a shining, glistening blue.* A calm happiness filled his heart, which continued to beat faster as if it could not keep up with itself. Bijou opened the window to swim into the light. *I seemed to bounce right up into the open window with the easiest of effort. I wanted to take off and swim away.*

As Bijou started to release his grip to venture on into the night, a cold stiff wind pushed in, causing him to lose balance. The room was spinning as he fell backwards. The left side of Bijou's head, slammed hard against a chair, as he collapsed to the floor. Everything turned fuzzy for a few minutes. *My consciousness was drifting about the blue room, but my body was lying on the floor. I look down and can see myself.*

All of the colored posters seemed to bleed right down the walls into liquid puddles of paint. *I have never seen colors so vivid.* The hues kept glowing brighter until they were so overbearing it was like staring into the sun. *Light was all around me.* Bijou felt like a force was gently reaching down and picking him up. As he rose to the ceiling toward an intense light, an awful dread of missing Pops came over him. *I could not leave him behind.* In an instant, Bijou was back to the floor as everything went black. Drifting through dreams and reality, he slept on the floor until Pops came back around dawn.

"Bijou, wake up partner," Pops called out in a worried tone as he simultaneously tried to shut the window. "Oh come on boy, don't you go leaving me now. You have too much in front of you, son."

After several attempts to revive him, Bijou finally woke up. *My head hurt and my whole body was stiff. I shivered so hard during the frigid night, my muscles felt plum worn out, except for an occasional spasm.*

Everything remained dark when Bijou drifted out of the haze. *I rubbed frantically at my eyes trying to clear the sleep crunchies away, that are caused by my allergies, but nothing held my eyelids shut this time.* Even though Bijou could feel the warmth of the morning sun as it snuck into the room, nothing was in front of him except an empty blackness. *I rub through tears of panic, but still cannot see anything.*

"Oh stop foolin' Son, there is plenty of light to get your wits about ya."

"Pops, I can't see! It is so dark in here."

Nevertheless, Bijou did have his wits enough to come to an understanding right then. *The blindness was my sacrifice for coming back for Pops. I reckon the colors of light were too holy to see. No person witnesses them without giving something back in return.* Bijou stopped crying. *I was at peace with it. I have only cried twice in my life since then; the first time happened when I finally had to let Pops go. He passed over because of his infliction, fueled by the guilt of my blindness. Years later, it would be after losing my beautiful niece, Jaci Rae, during the senseless bombing of the Murrah building in downtown Oklahoma.*

It struck Bijou as strange, that he thought about Jaci Rae, as he gracefully awoke from an afternoon nap on the sofa. *I snapped back to the "regular world" as I call it. I thought I had buried all that pain long ago.* Bijou's mind began to trick him into thinking it was Jaci Rae's sweet voice. She was calling from a better place to wake him up, until the doorbell rang again. A loose wire gave it a wounded ring, which quickly became annoying if left unanswered.

"Okay, hold on! I hear ya out there," Bijou called out, to buy some time to get to the door.

The layout of the house remained permanently etched into his subconscious. Bijou stepped right through the living room and opened the front door.

"Hello out there. What's your business?" Bijou inquired in a no-nonsense voice, to let the visitor know that he was sightless, but far from helpless. "I said, state your business!" Bijou repeated, as he reached to shut the door and go back to his nap.

"Uncle Bijou, it's me, Anthony," a timid voice crept in to his ears.

A long pause of uncomfortable silence prevailed until Anthony spoke up again.

"I was passing through and wanted to say hi. I will leave you be."

"Anthony Motavato? Is that you, my boy?" Bijou asked softly, nearly too stunned to speak the words. Memories of Anthony as a boy intertwined into other thoughts of Jaci Rae. He remembered the last time he spoke to Anthony. *It is funny how some things will leave your memory, but you can always remember the last time you were with someone, before they are torn from your life.*

"Yes, Uncle Biscuit...I am here," Anthony answered with an upbeat tone, trying to reconnect after all of the lost years.

Anthony could never quite say Bijou when he was a kid, so it always came out sounding like biscuit. *Eventually, I got used to being called Uncle Biscuit. It has been a lifetime since I heard that name.*

Part of Bijou was still upset that Anthony left without saying a peep to him, or his Aunt Jo. *We nearly fretted ourselves to death.* Jaci Rae was the glue that held their whole family together. *We all lost our special light that day. Her death left us with nothing inside but sorrow.* Anthony was hurt the worst of all. It killed him slowly. There comes a point when things are not going to get better, only worse every day. The losses kept mounting for Anthony, as he drank away a lucrative record deal, while blowing the signing bonus. Then he lost his true love, Sonja Christie. *He was in some sorry shape back then. I think that is why he finally took off. I hope he is better now.*

""Well, come on in, Son. No use standing out of doors. How long have you been in town?"

"Oh, not too long. I blew in yesterday from overseas. It was a very tiring trip to say the least. I don't think I have adjusted to the time change yet."

"Where abouts are you coming from? If you don't mind me asking?"

"I took a ship over from London. I had a steady gig over there with lots of cash rolling in. I saw those planes crash into the towers and it made me want to come home. I thought maybe I could try and make things right for once."

"Things is right between us, son. Please, don't give it another worry."

"And what about Aunt Jo and Dominique? How are they doing?"

"Oh fine, I suppose. Jo busies herself over one thing or another. Dominique works at the car dealers installing stereo equipment. He seems to like it okay."

"Do you guys still play?"

"What? Oh no, not much at all since..." Bijou paused, wishing he had not gone down that path of conversation. "Well, I did get my Pop's harmonica out the other day. It still had the same ol' tricky notes in it. However, as far as getting together and playing formal like, nothing of that sort. How about you? Still got that old guitar of yours?"

"Actually, yes I do. I have it with me right now. I always have it with me."

"Okay, you get warmed up, while I fetch Pop's harmonica," Bijou decided, with a spark of hope and inspiration in his voice. *I always hoped I would get to play music with Anthony again and now that day has arrived.* It almost seemed like a dream as Bijou walked into the bedroom and got the harmonica off the nightstand. *I always keep it right where Pops did when he was not playing on a stage. I do not recall how many nights he sent me off to sleep with a slow cry of the blues.* A few chords from worn guitar strings twanged up the hallway.

"Here we go!" Bijou called out, as he gave the harmonica a burst of air. The polished silver instrument responded with a familiar perfect pitched "hello" to kick things off.

Bijou stepped over to his favorite high-backed chair with a pillow to sit on.

"What do you want to play? I will try my best to keep up with you," Anthony interjected, as he stretched his fingers with a series of scales. He threw in a few marvelously blended notes, before hammering out a few random chords to end the warm up session. "Here, how about you see if you like this new one that was bouncing around in my head on my way home."

It drew silent, before he started with a raking of the strings with a steel slide. It caught Bijou off guard, because they had never practiced it together before. The music was bold, but not loud, raw and yet cleverly composed, bluesy and still full of hope. Anthony seemed to be melding a wide-open Spanish flamenco strumming style with a gritty-edge blues, coming from deep within him.

"That sounds great, Son! Let me see if I can mess it all up," Bijou joked, before joining during the second chorus. *I felt clumsy and out of place at first, until the right notes seemed to come out at will. It was as if we have never been apart.* Anthony played several standards from their club days. For a second it almost felt like they time-warped back to happier times. There was something missing though Bijou started to wonder, until he heard the screen door open and the heavy-footed shuffle of Dominique. *At first, I could hear Dominique just tap his foot to the 4/4 beat. Then the riffling hits of drumsticks onto the sofa cushion. A bass and snare drum it was not, but it did fill a void, while keeping Anthony and I on the same rhythm count.*

Anthony began to play stronger and with more zest after Dominique joined in. He saved the best for last as he ripped into a powerful version of *Kansas City*. Bijou could not recall ever playing that one together, but the old harmonica remembered it though. The song had fond memories associated with it due to Pops playing it every time they toured there. *That is where I died and was given another chance at this concert called life.* This time around, the song had a healing power, which united the trio. The nearly perfect beat that Dominique tapped on the glass tabletop merged with every note Anthony struck. *The music seemed to help erase a bad time in our lives.* Bijou's notes began lost and weak sounding, but ended bold and meaningful. He felt alive again. *I know every song must have an ending though, and then comes the darkness.*

Chapter 14

A Trail of Tears

"In my beginning is my end."

T.S. Eliot

December 22, 2001

Mustang, Oklahoma

Sonja Christie

Nearly full term, the baby, soon to be named Julia Beth, squirmed and kicked until finally resting in an awkward position that put pressure on a full bladder. Although mentally and physically exhausted, Sonja was soon clomping into the bathroom, one eye closed and the other barely half open. Her aching back cracked a bit as she sat down on a clammy toilet seat. *It felt like a bag of popcorn kernels were bursting within my stomach,* Sonja decided.

"Sonja, is everything okay?" Her husband Blake called, from the warm bed she reluctantly vacated.

"Yes dear, just have to pee, yet again."

"Third time is a charm I suppose," he responded with an agreeing tone, laced with a tinge of irritation for being kept awake all night.

"Well, I can't help it! Do you think I like hauling this wiggling watermelon around? Why don't you try sleeping when your kidneys are getting kicked around like soccer balls?" Sonja complained.

Sensing another no win situation, one of many during this trying pregnancy, Blake remained quiet as if he had fallen back to sleep. Sonja started to give him a second barrel full, when her mood suddenly changed to guilt for the way she had snapped at him.

"Sorry Blake, hormones and all. I think since I am up, I will go ahead and get my bath. My feet are swollen up so bad. Maybe a nice warm bubble bath will help them come back to normal size."

"That sounds good honey; I will go ahead and get some breakfasts going for you. I love you…!" He swooned, drawing it out to a full breath.

"Darn, I knew he was faking sleep to avoid my wrath," Sonja chuckled to herself. *I did feel remorseful for the way I had treated him lately. Blake has been so sweet and patient with me. I know this is hard on him as well.* As she removed her fuzzy yellow bathrobe, which gave her a slight resemblance to Big Bird, Sonja's thoughts quickly focused on another new stretch mark across her battered stomach. *That stupid lotion the doctor gave me has not done a bit of good. I look like I am being pulled apart at the seams.* "You better be worth it, sweetie," Sonja confided softly while rubbing her bloated belly. Julia Beth must have liked the combination of warm, soothing, water and the caressing, because she stopped squirming and settled in for a nap. *She always liked it when I talked to her, letting her know, she was not alone in her journey to this world. I knew she can hear me in there.*

As Sonja swooshed around trying to wet her upper half, she was glad Blake had won the argument in the home improvement store to purchase the over-sized tub, instead of the cheaper, standard-sized one. He was so practical in that sense, as if somehow he envisioned they would need it someday. Sonja knew he was probably buying it more for the romance than for her comfort during these uncomfortable times, but she was still glad he had won. *This is the only place I do not feel clumsy and off balance.* Using her trusty bath cup, Sonja wet her shoulder-length hair down and began to suds it up with some special aloe shampoo she had treated herself to. *Blake would kill me if he knew I spent forty-five dollars on this stuff. As tight as money was, I would not blame him, but I felt like I deserved something nice for going through all of this. Well, besides a beautiful baby girl.* As she began to massage the suds on the back of her scalp, a prickly sensation shot up her pinky finger on her left hand.

"Honey, can you bring the tweezers in here. They are in the medicine box in the tall cabinet in the kitchen," Sonja hollered out the bathroom door.

"Yes dear, I know where they are at. I put them back the last time," he volleyed back, with a nice tone."

As Sonja waited, she gently poked around with her right hand to locate the offender, while rinsing the small blot of blood off her pinky. "There you are," she said keeping a finger on it until Blake came in.

"Okay, where?" He asked unenthusiastically, while rubbing at his bloodshot eyes with deep dark bags under them.

"Right here sweetie, I have my finger on it. You got it?"

"Well not yet, hang on a second. Now tilt your head back and rinse some of these bubbles out of your hair. Umm… is that the expensive shampoo again? It sure smells like it?" He inquired, already knowing the answer.

"Did you get it, don't lose it. It already got my finger once," Sonja replied, ignoring his question about the shampoo.

"Yep, got it. It is just a little piece this time. I cannot believe you still have remnants of glass in the back of your head from the accident. Hopefully this will be the last of it." Blake consoled sympathetically, as he kissed her cheek.

"I hope so too. I dread having to worry every time I wash my hair."

"You have plenty of time. Here is your bath pillow. Why don't you try to lay back and relax. I will bring breakfast right to you."

"Oh, you are so sweet. I feel like such a burden lately," Sonja blurted out, as she felt unbridled emotions going crazy again.

"Nonsense. I have the easy part of this deal," he whispered, kissing her rotund stomach protruding out of the water like a barren island. "I will be right back with some breakfast for you two."

I feel like the luckiest women in the world when he turns on the charm with me. Until Sonja met Blake in a chance encounter outside a local bookstore, she never thought it possible to ever love another man after Anthony left. She had resigned herself to being alone in this cruel world, but the wicked hands of fate dealt her a queen of hearts this time instead of the Old Maid card. Sonja turned on the hot water to warm her toes for a minute. *My circulation was working overtime and had not felt like getting around to my feet. It seemed I was either hot or cold, nothing in between. Now I was cold. Funny how good warm water feels on your frosty toes. Oh, the simple things in life,* she thought, finally feeling acclimated to her surroundings. Methodically, Sonja rinsed off before easing back and resting her head on the waiting bath pillow. Two deep inhales followed by relaxing exhales made her eyes too heavy to hold back from closing. Her consciousness drifted to dark dreams.

"Can I push the button, Mommy?"

"Well, okay Jaci Rae, just this once and just because I love you so. Leaning down Sonja nuzzled to her sweet face. Heart to heart and soul to soul. *She was the best thing that ever happened in my life.* Pressing her lips against Jaci's soft cheek, the after smack sounded as the bell dinged for the floor.

Stepping out of the elevator, Sonja picked her up while kicking the bottom of her heels as if she was booting her out of the elevator. Jaci Rae's contagious laughter echoed out into the lobby.

"You have the cutest laugh I ever heard, you know that, sweetheart," Sonja praised, as her arm slipped around Jaci Rae and escorted her along.

The first thing Sonja noticed was walking on marble looking tile instead of the plush carpet of the America's Kids daycare on the second floor. "Whoops, honey we are on the wrong floor," She exclaimed looking at the words Bureau of Alcohol, Tobacco and Firearms. We better jump back in," Sonja declared, as the elevator doors shut behind them. "I guess we will catch the next one." Her words seemed more pronounced and carried through an unusual silence not expected for a busy, governmental entity on a weekday. "Wow, where is everybody? I don't think it's a holiday."

"What's a holly day, Mommy?"

The doors opened and Sonja waited until they got on before answering, "That means days like Christmas or Halloween. People don't work on those days, sweetie."

Jaci Rae's face lit up by mentioning Christmas. It was her favorite.

"Do you think I have been good this year?"

"I don't know babe, you are quite the troublemaker. I think I am going to have to send Santa a bad report for next Christmas," She dictated in a stern voice, that quickly melted into a chuckle.

"Huh uh, I have too been good," Jaci Rae proclaimed, knowing she was being teased, but still wanting to insure presents were on the way just in case.

"I am only getting your goat; you have been very good in fact. Okay here we are. Let's get you signed in quick or I am going to be late for work again."

Jaci Rae suddenly seemed to linger instead of moving forward. Her mood changed from jovial to reluctant and sullen. "Mommy, I don't want to go today. Can I go home with Daddy?"

"What? Are you feeling sick? You don't feel warm," Sonja, answered in a quizzical tone. She could tell Jaci Rae was not ill, but something was definitely on her mind. "Tell Mommy what is wrong? I really have to get going, Honey."

"I don't want to go today. I don't know why, but please Mommy, I don't want to," she called out, beginning to get more upset and desperate.

Sonja nudged her forward and signed Jaci Rae's name next to her printed name on the clipboard. "Okay Baby, head on in. I will see you real soon; maybe I can get off a little early or I will have Daddy pick you up after lunch."

"No Mommy! Don't make me, please, don't make me!" Jaci Rae cried out, as tears began to stream down her face leaving little wet stains on the collar of her white chiffon dress. Her hands clamped onto Sonja's shirt and soon Jaci Rae was down holding onto her leg so she could not walk away.

"My Lord, what has gotten into you?" Sonja asked, with a bit of frustration at the drama unfolding in front of several of the children and daycare staff. "Please tell Mommy what is wrong?" She inquired again with slightly softer decibel level.

"I don't know, but I am just scared."

"Scared of what, Jaci? You have been coming here for a while now and have lots of friends waiting for you."

"I don't know why," Jaci Rae, answered sobbing and wheezing harder.

Glancing down at her watch, Sonja quickly did the math in her head and realized that at best, she was already ten minutes late. "I will call and check up on you after lunch okay? Bye Sweetie, love you," Sonja announced with an air of finality to it, letting Jaci Rae know she was really going to leave. She pried Jaci Rae off her leg and shuffled her off to the beloved and always smiling Brenda, the team leader, before quickly stepping to the elevator.

"No Mommy, don't leave me!" Jaci Rae's cries called out from behind, as the doors opened and Sonja stepped in.

I pushed the button, but then held my hand out for a second to stop the doors from closing. Tears streamed down Jaci Rae's face as she tried her best to pull away and run. Sonja blew Jaci Rae a kiss and waved until only her own face gleamed in a silver reflection off the doors. *I had not seen her carry on like that since the very first day. What a tearjerker that was. This incident was so unexpected and intense.*

As Sonja excited the Murrah Building, she could not shake the feeling that something was wrong with Jaci Rae, either real or imagined. *I paused, turned and began to head back in, until the voice of my boss telling me that I needed to be more punctual sprang from my memory.* With that extra motivation, Sonja hustled to her car. *My little voice was telling me I should go back and get her, but my mind seemed to be made up, because I started the car, checked for traffic in the mirror and then pulled out.* Everything was clear except for an approaching white sedan with a Ryder truck close behind. They passed with a rapid speed and whipped into the parking garage. The Ryder followed, but was too tall so parked awkwardly in the street. *They must be running later than me,* Sonja thought to herself as she moved a block ahead to a red light. Sonja did a quick check of her hair and makeup in the rearview mirror. As she finished primping, the Ryder caught her attention again. *Its two occupants talked for a moment, before a lanky young man with a military haircut leapt from the driver's seat and made a beeline across the street to the YMCA building. A stocky, Middle Eastern man with a blue jacket on stayed in the cab for a minute or so longer. He exited the passenger side, stepped to the back of the truck before walking briskly to the end of the block where he jumped into a yellow pickup, before speeding away.*

"What in the world was that all about-" Sonja began to say, when a series of loud cracking noises blasted out from the Murrah building with such power it toppled the Ryder truck. On the turn, the Ryder disappeared into a massive ball of fire, pushing the rear axle over five hundred feet in the air causing it to land on top of maintenance man, Richard Nichol's red car, a couple of blocks down the street. The entire glass front of the building disintegrated into nothing.

It almost seemed like I was watching a slow-motion movie in the mirror as an all-consuming shockwave sprinted towards me. The whole rear of the car lifted up simultaneously as the back window obliterated into a tornado of glass. Orange flames, flashed from every direction and enveloped the airborne vehicle for a moment until it came crashing to the pavement with such a force, it slammed Sonja forward and backwards several times, bouncing her head off the steering wheel until she blacked out. Sonja became conscious enough to realize someone was pulling her out of the smoldering wreck, before gently placing her on the sidewalk next to the street. Her eyes creaked open, but then closed several times. With each attempt, they managed to stay open a little longer until finally her eyes were able to send disjointed images to her confused brain.

An older man in a business suit covered in ash, hovered over Sonja like a pale and bewildered angel. His kind face had round circles of clean skin where his glasses must have protected an area surrounding his tearful eyes. The man talked to Sonja, but she could not hear anything at all. It was complete silence. She pulled at her ears and even fiddled her index fingers into them to clean out any obstruction. Sonja sat up and tilted her head to one side as if trying to drain water out, but remained in a deathly soundless limbo. *Nothing worked.* After coughing on the thick dust in the air, she could taste her own blood. *Touching my face, I could feel a gash, along the hairline of my forehead.* Sonja removed a tattered shirtsleeve and wiped her face off, while trying in vain to stand up. *My equilibrium was off, as if the ground is still rumbling beneath me.* After several attempts, Sonja made it to her feet and focused on the surrounding chaos. The man that helped her was gone.

Sonja could not believe what she was seeing. *It was as if I had fallen into a war zone of a third world country.* Every car around her was on fire and blanketed with debris. There was so much fallout swirling around in the wind, it gave the illusion of a ticker-tape parade. Every building on the street had their windows blasted out and were peppered from collateral damage. As she turned around, the sight of the Murrah building was so grotesque it overloaded her facilities to comprehend. Sonja could feel her body drain of energy as if she was going to black out again. *At that moment, I knew I had lost my baby. Maybe I still had some scrap of hope, fueled by love and maternal instinct, but in my heart, I knew. Jaci Rae was gone forever.* The whole front of the building was missing. A gaping sinkhole collapsed in the center where the top of the pillars were severed from cutter charges. Layer after layer caved in on top of itself creating bloody people sandwiches.

A massive crater dominated the street where the Ryder truck was and slowly began to pool up with red water, as broken pipes spewed out into trickling little streams of coppery crimson. Giant widow maker, concrete slabs, hung precariously by threads of steel rebar, while stunned and battered victims tried to climb down from the upper floors. *People were running in every direction and not seeming to get anywhere.* There was nowhere safe to go. *It was surreal.* Several dusty ghosts lumbered by. Some motioned for Sonja to turn around instead of moving forward. *I had to find my baby.* Something sharp poked up into her right heel, which made Sonja realize she had lost her shoes. She was walking barefoot on glass and mangled shrapnel. Sonja left blobs of sanguine tracks in the dust, while stumbling forward, to where the front doors used to be. *I screamed Jaci Rae's name repeatedly until my throat became dry and ached. It was like shouting into a hurricane, nobody could hear me, including myself.*

Then I saw my precious baby. Limp as a rag doll in the arms of an Oklahoma police officer. *Jaci's hair blew about covering her face, but I recognized the white chiffon dress.* Sonja struggled toward them screaming her name. *When I got closer, I noticed the back of Jaci Rae's head was stained red and had splattered on Officer Yeakey's uniform. I could tell by his demeanor that she was gone.* Officer Yeakey was trying to put on his bravest face, but he had two daughters about the same age. Nothing in his years of training and experience could keep the emotions back. This one was personal. Tears darted down his rugged face as Sonja grabbed onto one of his arms. He escorted them along to a semi-clear patch of grass and placed Jaci Rae down. *I collapsed next to my baby hugging her, kissing her and pleading with God to put the spark back into her.*

"Please take me instead," Sonja sobbed, in an uncontrollable whimpering.

A rescue worker tried to pry Sonja up and head for safety, as a second bomb report came in due to unexploded charges inside the building, but she clung tight, never wanting to let go. Sonja felt her body release all its energy as everything turned a cold black. *I hoped in my heart that I was leaving for heaven with Jaci Rae. I did not want her to go alone. We would make the journey together. It was my fault; I should have taken her out of that daycare. Jaci Rae always had a sixth sense about things and if I had trusted that, she would be alive right now.* Something pulled Sonja back to this world and blocked her from leaving. As a rescue worker administered CPR, she felt her soul crashing back down into her body. *I will never forgive myself.*

"Honey wake up, you are dreaming," Blake pleaded as he nudged Sonja's shoulder. He repeated it again until she awakened.

"My baby-" was all she got out before falling to pieces.

"I know sweetie, I know. Let it out. I am here for you," Blake consoled, as he helped her out of the lukewarm bath and into the yellow robe.

"It was my fault!" Sonja blurted out as she began to regain her composure.

"Honey, we have gone over this a million times. It was not your fault. There was no way for you to know. Besides, like the doctor said-" Blake began to explain, before Sonja lit into him with a furry.

"I am so tired of you throwing what the doctor says in my face all the time! She does not understand what I carry in my heart. Worst of all you will never understand how I feel inside either. Just lost and empty. How can she fix that with a few sessions?"

"I understand more than you think." Blake answered solemnly.

"Oh and how is that? Did you lose your baby?!"

"No thank goodness. You know that I did not lose anyone. Although, I have to watch the women I love, live with pain and guilt every day of my life. So yes, I am a lot closer to this than you give me credit. We have a precious daughter on the way. Do you really want all this to hurt her like it does us?" Blake asked, as tears began to trickle down his face.

Sonja had never seen Blake cry before, not even at his own mother's funeral last fall after she lost her fight with colon cancer. He got drunk that night and was melancholy for several weeks, but she never saw him shed a tear. He was taught that real men do not show weakness. Crying was something he never did, until now. At that moment, Sonja realized how strong their love was. *My pain had spread like a disease. My loss was truly his loss as well.* Sonja knew she had to break this cycle somehow. They could never have a fresh start with all this hurt binding them down. *I am not sure how I am going to get through it, but I have to try.*

"You are right, Babe, I have to let it go. I just don't know if I will ever be able to though. Jaci Rae was my world. I miss her so much," Sonja, sobbed onto his chest.

"I never said to just get over it. What I am saying...is that you need to forgive yourself. Please, I love you. It was not your fault. Okay?" Blake pleaded as he cried a little more. "Please say you will forgive yourself. Please, for us."

I knew he was right, but I could not push the words through my lips. "Give me some time. I honestly cannot say that right now. I want to, but in my heart that would be a lie and I never want any lies between us. Does that make sense?" Sonja asked in a way that was more like a confession than a question.

"Okay you have ten minutes," Blake joked softly, as he kissed her forehead. He flashed a cute smile, while squinting out a half wink. "I love you this much-" He started to say, before letting his stretched out arms finish his sentence for him. "We will get through this together, okay, Sonja?"

"I love you too. I am sorry I brought this on us. I promise, I will deal with it and put it behind me. I am ready to move on with our new life together," Sonja declared, as she pulled away and rubbed at her stomach. Julia Beth responded with a nice kick to her bladder. *Not terribly hard, but with enough zest to make it clear she was getting bored being in there by herself.* "Whoa, let's settle down Sweetie. I think she is a bit anxious something big is about to happen."

"Yep, it won't be long now. She is strong-willed...like her mother," Blake responded, while giving Sonja another warm embrace. *When he hugs me like this, I feel safe from the past.*

The next hour seemed to skip by almost without Sonja having to tune into it. A quick breakfast started the day and they did not talk much after that. There was nothing much left to say, so even when Blake dropped her off at work, they only hugged and gave each other that certain look, which meant they were both on the same wavelength. She blew a kiss goodbye as she waddled into the front entryway. *I was at my desk in my own little cubicle for nearly thirty minutes, before my thoughts caught up to my body in real time.* Sonja really did not have a lot left to do, because management was already thinning out the workload to her lucky coworkers. Sonja had at least been trying to look busy, as if she was giving it her all, right up to the due date. She ruffled a few papers around pretending to be searching for a number on a sales contract before dialing Blake's work number. *I want to tell him thanks for being so understanding.*

"Excuse me miss. You have a…well… a visitor who is asking for you up front," a young security guard stated, as he touched her shoulder from behind.

"Oh jeez, you almost scared this baby right out of me!" Sonja burst out indignantly, nearly jumping from her double-padded office chair. Even though he did not know she was making a personal call on company time, it still felt like being caught in the middle of something dishonest.

"Oh I am sorry. I did not mean to...umm... to startle you," he stammered out as his face turned a light red with embarrassment.

"So is this your first day on the job?" Sonja asked, already knowing the answer. His baggy uniform gave him away. The new guys were always stuck with hand-me-down uniforms that usually never fit until their own came in.

"No it's my second," he replied sheepishly. "My supervisor would have called, but we only had a first name to go by and there are three Sonja's in the building. You are the only one with blonde hair, well mostly blonde, so I thought that it might be you."

"Oh, thanks for noticing my dark roots," Sonja replied with a chuckle. She could tell the teenager was getting more uncomfortable by the second, so decided to let him off the hook and finish his mission. "Where is this visitor?"

"The man is right in front of the building. He would not leave his guitar, so he decided to wait outside with it."

"He had what with him? Did you say he had a guitar? What kind was it?"

"Oh, I don't know what brand. It just looked like an old wooden acoustic, with a dream catcher and brown hawk feathers hanging off it."

"Did he say his name was Anthony?"

"Don't know for sure. I do not think he ever really said that. He kept repeating your name. He kind of had an attitude and would not take no for an answer. He looks like your run of the mill street person I suppose."

"Please take me to him. Hurry, before he leaves," Sonja demanded, as she bounced up and pushed by the guard leading the way. She was already in the elevator and pushing the ground floor, before he caught up. *Could it really be Anthony after all of these years*, Sonja pondered quietly for a few seconds, until the doors opened. She left the guard behind.

"Miss, do you need me to look after you-" A voice called from behind, as she maneuvered through the revolving glass door.

Sonja did not see Anthony at first. *My heart sank with disappointment momentarily, until I saw a cloud of smoke puff up from behind one of the concrete pillars. I was not sure if it was nerves, adrenaline, or only fatigue from sprinting down here, but I felt light-winded and a bit discombobulated.*

"Anthony?" Sonja called out quietly. *My lungs felt empty and my mouth was so dry it took me a few seconds to muster enough energy to call out again.* As Sonja started to speak out again, he stepped around towards her. His eyes immediately went from her face to her pregnant stomach and when they returned, a hint of disappointment filled them. *He always did wear his emotions on his sleeve.*

"Sonja is that really you?" Anthony inquired meekly while composing himself from the initial letdown.

"Yep in the flesh," Sonja quipped back, as she stepped closer. She was trying hard to conceal her own feelings as well. When Anthony left, he was young, healthy and had a rock star aura about him. Now he looked as if he was at death's door. His hair was stringy; skin was a pale yellow, eyes sunken back with dark rings above and below his pupils. *I almost did not recognize him, except that he was wearing the same jacket as when he left to "sort things out" away from her.* The next minute was silent and awkward, with neither of them really knowing what to say. *Something took over inside me and I found myself slowly drifting towards him, until I had my arms around him. I could feel all the anger, frustrations, hurt, love, hate and bitterness boil up inside until they melted into one ball of tears.*

"I have missed you so much, why did you leave like that? We thought you died because you have been away so long." Sonja wailed onto his shoulder. *The next thing I knew my fist were clinched and I was hammering at his chest.* "Why did you do that? I thought you were dead!"

"I did die. The same day we lost Jaci Rae. Since then I have been wafting about like a ghost, with no direction at all. But not a day has gone by that I did not think about you." Anthony volleyed back, as he grabbed her hands to keep from being hit again. "I am so sorry! It was my fault. If I would have watched her that day…she would still be here with us. We lost it all because of me," he moaned out, trying to fight back his own tears. "You two were my world and without you, I have been…well I am…nothing."

Sonja was speechless. *I had always thought Anthony blamed me for what happened.* Anthony completely shut down after the accident. He stopped playing music and disappeared into a bottle. Sonja was barely out of the hospital, when he began staying drunk. It got so bad between, them she left to spend a few days with her mother. She hoped it would give Anthony a chance to figure out what he really wanted in the future. *Then he was gone from my life.* Anthony left without an explanation, apology or phone call. *Just like my Jaci Rae did. It was more than I could bear.* Sonja pulled her hands free and hugged him again. Anthony stepped a little to the side, so the baby was not between them. *I have waited a lifetime to hold him again and I am never letting go this time.*

Chapter 15

Jaci's Flower Garden

> "Now I lay me down to sleep
>
> I pray the Lord
>
> My soul to keep."
>
> Children's Prayer

Mustang, Oklahoma

December 23, 2001

Aunt Jo

Measuring only four foot square, it was a small piece of heaven next to the tool shed in the back yard. Currently it was only a soggy dirt pile, but it represented far more than the sum of its parts, which included weeds surrounded by round fence post lying on their side, outlining the patch of ground. In spring, new life would come with the cool rain to give a genesis to the seeds that lay dormant beneath the earth's surface. One row of azaleas, a row of blue bonnet, one with marigolds, two rows of roses, both white and red, with the back row reserved for sunflowers, which were Jaci Rae's favorite. The wooden sign in the front was becoming weathered and tilted to the left after a run in with the lawn mower.

Aunt Jo stared out the sliding glass door at the little flower garden, as she did most mornings. The lack of color out there and the crisp misty weather seemed to personify the depression Jo felt. She knew it was probably unhealthy to relive a brief moment of her life every day, but she did anyway. *It makes me sad and happy at the same time,* Aunt Jo contemplated. She was glad to have that special day nearly as much as she wished she could go back to it. *You only recognize defining moments of your life when they are gone forever. When I closed my eyes, I am there.*

"What's wrong Baby, why did you stop digging?"

"I dun' kno," Jaci Rae answered.

"Well you best keep at it my hard little worker, or we will never get these seeds planted before it is time for bible study tonight." Aunt Jo encouraged, to no avail. She waited for Jaci Rae to turn a few more scoopfuls of rich black potting soil into the red Oklahoma clay, but she was getting more on her sandals and pink work overalls with white flowers, then on the shovel. She knew something was on her bright, active mind and until it was discussed, there would be no work from her little helper. Aunt Jo stepped down on her shovel so it stayed in the ground and feigned going into the house before cutting back around behind Jaci Rae. She picked her up and kissed her face and neck before spinning a few circles.

"That's it, you are fired! You will never work in this garden again," Aunt Jo laughed, as she spun until they were both a bit dizzy. She loved Jaci Rae's laughs of excitement and wished she could have kept going, before crashing back down to the soft grass, which made a perfect landing spot.

"You're funny, Aunt Jo, cuz' I didn't want to work no more anyways," Jaci Rae fired back, as she took the offensive and started tickling Aunt Jo's sides.

Jaci Rae's hands did not do much damage at first, until finding the right tickle spots. Aunt Jo tried to push her off, to no avail. She began laughing so hard, she almost went into a coughing spell.

"Okay sweetie, you win! I give up. You can have your job back with double the chocolate chip cookies as payment."

Jaci Rae stopped the tickle war, but still sat there with a slightly quizzical look. Something big was on her mind. *Once she got an idea in her head that was how it was going to be.* Finally, Jaci Rae was able to put her thoughts into words and disclosed what she was thinking.

"Aunt Jo, I don't wanna hurt your feelings, but....you is making this garden all wrong. You won't get nothin' for your canning day in the fall."

"Oh is that so?" Aunt Jo laughed. "Okay, so what exactly am I doing wrong?" She asked humoring Jaci Rae, since she was trying her best to fix an imagined problem. Aunt Jo tried to keep a serious business look, but she had to turn away a few times not to laugh when Jaci Rae scrunched her brow in deep thought. *She is so darn cute!*

"Well, you have the corn first instead of the beans," she explained while picking up the little wooden signs. "And you have the water melon thingy's before tomatoes." Jaci Rae declared, showing the pictures of the seed packets stapled to the signs.

"So what is wrong with that?" Aunt Jo inquired with a skeptical glance.

"Cuz' B. comes before C. does and T. comes before the W. silly, everyone knows that." Jaci Rae declared, as she stuck the signs in the alphabetically correct order. "And you don't even have a place for flowers. I want to plant the balls I got."

Aunt Jo was dumbstruck, she could not decide if she should laugh at her own naiveté or feel embarrassed for being out-witted by a preschooler. She stood up on her knees and motioned for Jaci Rae to come to her. "You are right my dear, I am so glad you caught that. We would have had a lot of empty jars without your quick thinking." Aunt Jo praised as she hugged her tight to show appreciation. *I never want to let go of her.* "I am sorry dear; we don't have enough room between the fence rails to plant anything extra I'm afraid."

"What about over there?" Jaci Rae asked, while pointing to the trash can spot next to the tool shed. "Flowers are prettier than trash cans aren't they?"

Aunt Jo could feel the pride welling up inside. "You are smart as can be! That is another fine idea.

We do have all the flower bulbs...I mean balls you picked out. It would be a shame not to get them in the ground." Aunt Jo got up and headed to the bright red tool shed, painted up like a small country barn, complete with a fake window on the side. "Please give me hand with this stuff she asked, while dragging out a leftover post, a small hand saw and a tape measure.

Jaci Rae jumped up with a squeal; she loved diving into a new project. She was more than happy to hold the tape measure, put a pencil mark on the post at four feet, more or less and then, she held the end of the rail while Aunt Jo sawed them to size. They moved the trashcans and laid out the post in a square before using some extra bags of soil to fill in the space. Using the soon-to-be patented "Jaci's Alphabetical Planting System" they put the bulbs into the waiting top soil.

"Here, I have one more idea," Aunt Jo declared, stepping into the house for a moment and coming back out with a bottle of red nail polish. She grabbed the last wood sign and wrote "**Jaci's Flower Garden**" on it. They both took turns blowing on it to dry the paint and Jaci Rae stuck it in the perfect spot.

"Well sweetie, I think that is about as good a flower garden as I have ever seen." Aunt Jo beamed with pride. She was impressed how it came together from leftover scraps and even more impressed with Jaci Rae for thinking of it in the first place. "You amaze me, my sweet little darling!"

"Aunt Jo...will you miss me when I am with Jesus?" Jaci Rae asked out of nowhere, with a sudden worried look revealed from her blonde curls by a splash of fresh April wind.

"Oh my! Why would you ask me that? I mean, of course baby, you are the best flower planter ever, but I think I want to keep you around a little longer." Aunt Jo replied, trying to gloss over a serious subject. "What made you think of something like that?"

Jaci Rae shrugged her shoulders. "Will you water my flowers too?"

Aunt Jo could feel a sick sense of panic come over her at the mere mention of that dark topic. She was not sure why Jaci Rae was asking such morbid questions and did not like it. "Oh, don't be silly. How about we water them together?" She asked grabbing Jaci Rae's hand and scooping her up in one move.

As Aunt Jo contemplated the past, she could feel a single tear make its way down her left cheek before she wiped it away. She had set up her Christmas tree for the first time since the tragedy and promised herself she would not cry today. Aunt Jo tried to change her mindset to a happier time, but it was too late. Her thoughts shifted back into familiar guilt and self-pity. *It was my fault. If I let her stay one extra day and finish the vegetable garden, she would still be here. They could have found someone else to help with the church rummage sale or Jaci Rae could have gone with me. Why?* Aunt Jo started to question the past for the countless time, when the doorbell rang to interrupt her thoughts. She started to ignore it until the familiar "shave and a haircut" cadence rang out. *There is only one person that did that. I do not know why he bothers to ring the bell, this is his home too. I guess it still is?*

"You could have used your key," Aunt Jo started to say as she opened the door.

Bijou came on in, "I would have Sugar, but I went off and left my keys on the nightstand before we walked on over here," he answered, in the nicest tone he could muster. Although Bijou could not see the look on Jo's her face when she saw Anthony, he knew it was not hospitable. He could feel Anthony's pulse race as he held his arm. "Well, look who I found!" Bijou declared with a big smile, trying to try and change the current mood. He could hear the door creak slightly as Aunt Jo was leaning to close it on them, before deciding to let them in.

"Come on in, but be careful, I moved the furniture around when I decorated for Christmas." *How could he show up with Anthony?*

Bijou felt at home. The temperature was set at seventy-four degrees, as she always had it; one degree either way made her uncomfortable. A sensation of peach tea lingered in the air from a coffee cup sitting in her favorite spot at the kitchen table. Jo had sprayed some air freshener a few hours ago to cover up burnt toast with her eggs this morning. Jo always managed to burn the toast somehow. Bijou offered to buy her a new toaster many times, but it once belonged to her Mother so Jo would not part with it. *It was worth a bit of "scraping off the burn" to keep a little part of my childhood. Mom always did the same ritual for Dad.*

Anthony led him around the brown plush loveseat that now sat diagonal to accent the room and make a space for the Christmas tree next to the fireplace. Bijou stepped to the tree and gently ran his fingers down the shining silver garland, before fluffing up some of the branches slightly mashed down from being packed in the box for years. He felt along the lights and found one that was not working. He could tell it had a short since it was not warm.

"Anthony, grab me one of the…" Bijou paused to feel the light in his hands. "Give me one of the green bulbs so I can fix this string of lights."

The bulb was actually red, but Anthony decided not to say anything. He handed Bijou a red bulb to match the rest. Bijou started to plug it in and paused feeling the bulb. "This smells like a red one. Are you trying to trick me son?"

Anthony's eyes got big as he stared at Aunt Jo with a "how does he do that look". He grabbed a green one and stepped over to Bijou. "How did you-"

"Oh stop teasing him Bijou; you already knew darn well they were all red. You were with me at the department store when we bought the tree." Aunt Jo quipped with a laugh. *Bijou always knows how to make me laugh.*

"Okay you got me on that one Uncle Biscuit."

The mirthful moment did not last, as Aunt Jo realized she was still mad at Anthony. *He was not going to get off as easy as he did running away.*

"Bijou, can I talk to you outside for a minute."

"But Honey Pie, I am just starting to warm up from the walk," He began to answer, but figured it would get a lot colder in here if he did not capitulate.

Anthony moved forward to help him, but Bijou put his hand up to signal he did not need assistance. Bijou memorized the entire floor and with a few brisk steps, he was outside with Aunt Jo.

A yellow sunflower stuck onto one of the bedroom doors caught Anthony's eye. He knew even without a closer look whom the artist was. He was present when Jaci Rae stuck it on the door of her "room away from home" that Aunt Jo set up for her. Jaci Rae could put all the dresses, dolls and toys Aunt Jo spoiled her with in there so it would be their secret. Anthony looked at it closer. Bold colors swirled in a circle highlighted with a happy-faced sun looking down. Jaci Rae was going to be an artist when she was not busy saving sick ponies as a veterinarian.

Curious how Jaci Rae's room looked now, he went on in. One corner still displayed her toys and favorite baby dolls, but the rest became an office with a large map of the United States on the wall. Stacks of handwritten notes on white typing paper covered piles of books in every corner. Anthony started to leave the room until noticing the handwriting on the map. Oklahoma City was circled with the date April 19, 1995, in red. As he looked closer, there were initials and dates all over the map. Aunt Jo had the entire bombing plot mapped out and the terrorist's movements nearly down to the day.

Turning back to the desk, countless papers and photocopies of witness statements formed a bed for a stack of bound notebooks. He thumbed through them trying not to be too nosey, but was unable to resist. Within the pages, the entire cover up was written out in detail. Beneath the binders lay a personal journal. He tried his best not to violate her privacy as he did so anyway. There were pages of notes on the Timothy McVeigh trial she attended daily, all the way to his execution by lethal injection in Indiana. *"He was cold, heartless, and remorseless to the bitter end."* It stated with what looked like teardrop stains on the paper. She had her personal thoughts on the Terry Nichol's "monkey trial" as she called it. In the back was a Christmas card from Nichols and a little note. Aunt Jo dismissed his apology and finding Jesus in a final entry in the journal. *"Why did God wait until now to guide his life? How can someone like this live when my baby is gone?"*

"What are you doing in here?" Aunt Jo asked in a quiet tone, which seemed more like screaming when he looked up and saw her face as he held her private journal. "Did you get a good laugh at my expense?"

Anthony tried to talk, to deny, to say something, anything to change what it looked like, but his words failed him. He stood there looking right into her piercing eyes. He was too ashamed of himself for the past and the present, for leaving as his own father did to him. Anthony knew he should have been here with her while Aunt Jo fought for the truth as a corrupt judge, federal agents and especially the Clintons, buried the truth under mountains of bureaucracy and misdirection. Aunt Jo had never stopped fighting for justice for Jaci Rae and the rest of the victims. It was her passion and obsession. She had followed every lead no matter how small. She traveled to Elohim City in Oklahoma where the plot originated. Even when faced with automatic weapons pointing at her, Aunt Jo pushed ahead down the gravel road of Elohim City. She went to church service with their grizzled old leader, but refused to step on the Israeli flag lying in the entrance as a floor mat.

Aunt Jo drove to Herrington, Kansas, to Nichol's home along the way to Patriot camps in Arizona, to find the truth. She had looked McVeigh square in the eye at his trial with such a fiery stare, the killer felt it to his bones and turned away, which was no doubt a slight moral victory for her. *I wanted McVeigh to see what I had lost. Everything!*

She had sat across the table from Commander Pedro Langan as he tried to look tough, while handcuffed to the table and sporting an orange jumpsuit. Obviously scared he would end up hanging in a cell like his buddy Guthrie, he talked in riddles. In between the bravado though, Langan told her all she needed to know in able to piece the plan together.

Aunt Jo had confronted Al-Hussaini in a strip club in Oklahoma City. Even when he brandished a gun, she was relentless for the truth. She hammered away at him by remaining silent and showing a picture of Jaci Rae until he drank himself into a stupor and she could not understand his babble anymore. Police would find him passed out behind the wheel of his car later that night.

Aunt Jo flew out to California to talk with Kara James, a former BATF agent turned informant, who had warned of the bombing nearly a year before it happened. On the three-year anniversary of the bombing, Aunt Jo visited Terry Nichols in prison. She glared a hole through him until he cried for forgiveness. The last trip was out of the country and down to Nogales, Mexico, where Aunt Jo traced a dead-end lead on a Jericho Daniels, who was using the name of Vance Bradway, a known Elohim City regular and one of the Midwest Bank Robbers. She took comfort in being around his family and the two young boys he left behind. *They were about the same age as Jaci Rae would have been....if only.*

Anthony gazed into her deep jade-colored eyes until everything became blurry. He had not eaten much today and had not had a drink out of respect for Lonely Bear, since he arrived. He could see the room move for a second, before it all seemed to buzz like a light when the filament burns out. In a desperate attempt for stability, he clawed at the air to find something to hold on to as he tumbled forward onto the desk, slid off the side and crashed to the floor bringing a pile of papers on top of him. When he woke up, Aunt Jo's eyes were still fixed on him. This time they held concern and love, as he looked up from the loveseat in the living room.

"Aunt Jo, I could say that I am sorry for leaving and how I hurt you when you needed me the most...but...I guess that is who I am. Daddy was right. I let my Momma die. I let Jaci Rae die, it was my fault. I should have let her stay with me that day. I have hurt everyone that ever cared for me. I lost Sonja and I lost myself. I am completely ashamed and hopefully won't have to deal with it much longer."

Aunt Jo was speechless, so she hugged him. She kept hugging him even after it became awkward and only let go when he started smiling.

"All this time I thought it was my fault. Jaci Rae wanted to stay and finish helping me in the garden. I was so wrapped up in trying to help others and do the Lord's work, that I missed a chance to save her. So now, I have done everything I can so she did not leave us in vain. It has been this trap of sorts. Well, I do not know how to say it...the more I tried to find the truth, the more I lost myself in the lies. I guess we both ran away from ourselves."

"Aunt Jo, I saw your notebooks and maps," Anthony admitted. "You did not run at all. I am so proud of you. I think you are the bravest person I know. You have always been my hero and you were Jaci Rae's as well. She loved you so much."

Aunt Jo could feel some tears building before pushing them away. "I am not a hero. I turned my back on the church. I have been consumed by hate and wanted revenge, exactly like the people who did this. I turned my back on the man I love. Bijou supported me all along until I wanted to go to Germany and track down a saboteur named Strassmeir. He was working for the Government all the while he helped to plan the bombing. *I completely lost myself and Bijou knew it.* He could not take that road with me anymore and I was starting to hate him for it. The way he is always happy. I resented his faith in the God that betrayed me. How could Bijou just move on with his life? That is why he left me."

"Uncle Biscuit left you? I wondered why he was staying at Dominique's."

"Actually, Bijou helped Dominique get that house. Bijou wanted to find the closest place he could, that is why he is only one block over," she explained with a laugh. "He told me he would be waiting for me on the other side of the hell I was going through, but he couldn't walk with me anymore."

"Where is Uncle Biscuit anyways?"

"He left with Dominique after they put you on the couch. Bijou said he had an appointment with a man about a thing, whatever that means?" Aunt Jo smiled for a moment, before starting in on Anthony again. *I am not finished speaking my mind.* "Next week Lonely Bear has an appointment set up for you with a specialist he knows. The initial blood work came back and was very encouraging, good enough to move to the next step in the donor process."

"What doctor appointment, donor and blood work are you talking about?"

"For the kidney transplant that you need. You have nearly drowned the ones you have in booze. Anthony you look yellow and brown as a week old banana. Lonely Bear told me on the phone the other day when I called about you, if you don't stop with the drinking and get a transplant, we will be burying you before Jaci Rae's flowers come up."

"How did he get my blood?"

"Off your tooth he pulled out. Lonely Bear saved the tooth and a swab for a test. He is a match, but they are very concerned about his age. I think if he passes the physical test, he might be able to push it on through. He has a lot of pull at that hospital from donating a small fortune over the years, helping terminal kids."

"I am not going."

"Oh you most certainly are! You are not going to run away and die in some ditch. Or a mud puddle, like that no good for nothing father of yours." Aunt Jo stated, as she could feel her temper flare up. "Do you want to hurt me again?"

Anthony knew he was not going to win this argument and felt grateful that she still cared enough to want to help. He was not sure if he meant it, but finally stammered out, "Okay, Aunt Jo. I will check it out. Whatever you think is best. I love you and I don't want to ever cause you a bit of pain ever again."

Aunt Jo did not fall for it so easy and looked him straight in the eyes. *I could sniff a lie from a mile away, especially from Anthony.* The one and only time he tried to lie was when he was nine and was riding his Big Wheel in the garage after being told not to several times. Unable to stop in time, he crashed into Aunt Jo's pop bottles she always saved up for the ten-cent return money. They tumbled down the stairs to the basement, causing her to have to wait another two months, before getting a fancy new hair dryer with three settings. Anthony ran out of the garage just as Boots the cat walked in for a perfect patsy. Aunt Jo did not say a word. All through dinner, she stared right at him with that look. It slowly pulled the guilt out of him until he exploded with a tearful confession. *He never fibbed to me again.*

Before Aunt Jo could be sure, a familiar car pulled into the driveway. She could hear Bijou whistling, as he walked up the sidewalk to the front door. Once again, he rang the doorbell and waited until she answered. Anthony and she shared one last hug, before she got up and opened the front door. "I wonder who this could be?" Aunt Jo teased.

Bijou stood there with a big toothy smile, a red Santa hat on, along with an armful of packages. Dominique waited two steps down with a green elf hat on that was at least a size too small. He carried the bulk of the presents and gave Bijou a little nudge to move on, so he could set everything under the tree.

"Ho, ho, ho and a Merry Christmas to all!" Bijou called out with a chuckle, obviously proud of himself for the big surprise. "Everything is for someone and I have something for everyone!" He laughed in such a contagious way the rest could not help but get excited. *It has been too many years since we felt the Christmas spirit around this house.* Before they could start unwrapping the gifts, Bijou huddled them into a circle. He knew exactly where they were standing by their breathing and pulled them in close.

"Our father, we give you a most gracious thanks for bringing us together to honor your son, who died for our sins. In your name, with peace, love and forgiveness, amen."

The rest did not say amen, but gave a clap to show support and not ruin the happy moment. Aunt Jo could feel a sliver of guilt leave her with the prayer. *It has been a long time since I have heard the good word.*

"Okay, Dominique my jolly good elf, if you will do the honors and pass out the gifts, including the ones I bought for myself," Bijou laughed.

Aunt Jo began unwrapping and opened up a new combo DVD and VCR player to replace the one Bijou tried to fix. He took it completely apart, but when she accidently moved the pieces around, the schematic in his mind was not the same as the one lying on his kitchen table. Anthony found himself the owner of a new jacket and a couple of pairs of jeans. Dominique got some new drumsticks of course and a new car stereo that he had his eye on at work.

"I have two more left," Bijou stated triumphantly as he pulled the first from behind his back. It was a fraction of the size of the others with a white bow. He handed it to Aunt Jo as he got down on one knee in front of her.

"What are you doing you crazy ol' coot," she said defensively, while blushing like a girl being picked to dance for the first time. It sparkled in the Christmas lights when she opened it. "Oh my goodness, Bijou, what is this? I thought we had our understanding and what not?"

"Jo baby, you is the apple of my eye. My good one that is not as blind as the other...." He paused with a smile. "I love you more today, than the first time you threw me out of your bar at closing time for pestering you. We is a true match if God ever did create one. I do not want you to walk one more step in this world without me by your side. So, will you be my girl...forever?"

Aunt Jo paused, nearly so stunned that she did not know what to say, until his sweet words wiggled their way past the wall she had built around her heart. *It had blocked all the hurt, but also all the love and now outlived its usefulness.* She sprang up off the couch with Anthony and hugged Bijou so hard they almost fell back into the Christmas tree. Luckily, Dominique's bear hug was waiting instead and he joined in. Anthony sat there reluctantly a minute until Bijou seemed to look right at him and gave him a wink to pile on.

"Okay, I guess that was a yes, my dear." Bijou spoke up tired of being smothered in love. "I just have one more gift to one of the best darn bluesman I have ever heard in all my days of honky-tonkin' and caterwauling. Here you go, my boy," Bijou praised as he tossed the last gift to Anthony.

"Uncle Biscuit, I can't take this. I mean, thank you and all, but this was your Daddy's harmonica."

"Yes, it was. He passed it down to his boy and I am passing it down to mine. I would give it to Dominique, but he would just beat the thing with his drumsticks." Bijou explained, with a proud pat on Dominique's back to show he was equally proud of him. "Well, don't stand there holding it like a puppy; slobber on that darn thing!"

Anthony was overcome in the moment. He could not think of a song until one he learned to play in the fourth grade on a school-issued recorder, came to mind. It had been a lifetime since he blew those notes. He sucked in a breath of air and tried his best. After he played the first chorus, he started it again and the others joined the sing along.

"Silent night.....Holy night...All is calm...All is bright....Round yon Virgin Mother and child....Holy infant so tender and mild....Sleep in heavenly peace."

This is the best Christmas ever, at least since the last one with Jaci Rae, Aunt Jo thought while singing and admiring her new ring. *Sleep in heavenly peace, my sweet baby.*

Chapter 16

Snow Angels

"Nobody can bring you peace

But yourself."

Ralph Waldo Emerson

December 25, 2001

Mustang, Oklahoma

Anthony Motavato

With a turbulent bounce, the warm extratropical cyclone air, climbed above a massive cold front, barreling down from the Rockies. The vapor trapped within the churning gray clouds formed ice crystals, which expanded until they were too heavy. They fell to earth in white cottony blankets. By morning's light, the world was a frozen paradise, with glistening icicles bending the sun into beautiful colors and surf like snowdrifts, burying everything shorter than the mailbox.

Jaci Rae watched through the living room window as she balanced on the arm of the couch. Three days of being inside due to inclement weather, had her stir crazy. She daydreamed of bobbing through the snow like all of the squirrels that had passed by as they went about their day. Her dolls were bored and did not feel much like playing today. Most of her other toys seemed uninterested in doing much either. Her favorite movie, in which she sang along to every song, was finishing up on its' second showing of the morning. It had failed to keep her interested like the winter scene playing outside.

Anthony sat in the recliner trying to work on a new piece of music, but the guitar seemed out of tune enough to make him adjust back and forth between scribbling musical notations in his writing pad and tuning it. The chord progressions fit the lyrics he wrote down although they were as lackluster as his motivation from being housebound. He stopped several times to warm up his coffee in the microwave and help Sonja clean up the breakfast dishes. The sweet scent of blueberry syrup and cinnamon banana pancakes, still wafted about the kitchen. Sonja reorganized her recipe book for the third time this week. She tried to keep busy on housework and getting a big jump on the spring-cleaning chores, which dried up when she finished the exciting job of relining the kitchen cabinets with shelf paper.

"Honey, I think I will go shovel the walkway and the drive, before it melts down and refreezes," Anthony stated randomly to break the boredom.

"Do we even have a snow shovel? You borrowed Aunt Jo's the last time it snowed?" Sonja asked in an upbeat tone, which hinted she wanted to help.

"Yep, I think it is still in the garage next to her lawn mower," he answered sheepishly, as he came up behind her and kissed her neck. "Well, unless you can think of something more fun to do to break up the grind today?"

"I think you have "broke up the grind" enough lately," Sonja laughed, pushing him away. "Besides it is too early for her nap, we would not have a minute to ourselves."

Suddenly, shoveling snow did not sound all that fun to Anthony compared to what else was on his mind. "Well, with that snow drift against the front door, I doubt I could even get outside anyway." He wavered, trying to change the subject.

"Oh, no you don't, Mister! I think you had a fine idea. I will need to get out tomorrow for work. I doubt they will close the office again. So you better get to it." Sonja snipped with a smile, realizing it was a big job and Anthony had already changed his mind.

"It does sound fun and all, but I am right in the middle of a song...so I best get to it." He volleyed back, as he quickly stepped into the living room. He made it as far as the couch when Sonja jumped on his back. The unexpected sneak attack sent him tumbling gently to the floor. Jaci Rae quickly picked a side and dove on him too.

"You have been playing the same sad notes, in the same sad tune, for days now. I think some hard labor will do you some good." Sonja teased, as she pounced and wrestled around with him trying to hold his arms down so Jaci Rae could get in the middle of the scrum.

"Okay, okay, you two win again. No fair ganging up on me!" Anthony laughed as he admitted defeat. "It will be nice to get some fresh air anyway."

"How about we give you a hand....well that is if Jaci Rae wants to go out in the snow?" Sonja asked with a big smile.

"I do Mommy, I do!" She replied with a squeal, as she bounced on Anthony a little more to make sure he was really giving up. *Jaci Rae was always determined in everything she did. An attribute she inherited from her mother, no doubt.*

In a flash, Sonja had her bundled up in a pink snowsuit with matching mittens and they were pushing out the back door. The wind came from the northeast with the storm, so most of the backyard received the fallout as it missed the brunt of the ice. The temperature warmed up nearly twenty degrees, making the snow perfect for packing snowballs. Anthony found this out when the girls tagged him several times before he could dodge the onslaught.

"Jaci Rae, why don't you help me build a snowman?" Anthony asked, as he dropped down on his knees and started rolling one of his snowballs into a bigger ball. *It was the first snowman I ever built,* Anthony reckoned.

Sonja could not help but admire the pair as they squished and slid around trying to build the perfect base. It was more egg-shaped than round, from pushing too much at one angle, but they did not care. When it got too big to roll, they stopped and left it there in the shade of the biggest walnut tree in the backyard. They started with a fresh patch and made the middle. It soon was the right size and Sonja helped with the lifting as they packed some fresh snow between the base to help hold it in place. Jaci Rae rolled most of the head section herself and did not want any help. Sonja went into the kitchen and found a carrot that was destined for stew, an old scarf that was heading to Good Will, two Maraschino cherries for the eyes and a box of raisins that stretched out into a big smile. Anthony and Jaci Rae found a few small limbs down from the storm, which made wonderful arms, even though the left was much shorter.

Mr. Frosty, (an obvious name) was lumpy, disproportionate, a bit lopsided with a few skid marks of brown grass and dirt mixed in his white body. He looked happy to be here though and seemed to say, "Welcome to winter".

"Hang on, let me get the camera so I can take a picture of my two expert snowman builders," Sonja called out as she zipped into the house.

The pair kept shaping, patting and cleaning off blemishes, until Sonja came back to line them up for a snapshot with their chilly creation. Sonja could never have imagined, it would become her most cherished picture.

"Come here, Baby. I want to get one more of you," Sonja asked, as she grabbed Jaci Rae's little hand and led her over to a pristine bed of white snow. "Okay, now go straight back with your arms to your side," she explained while lowering Jaci Rae down to the snow. "Now spread your arms and legs at the same time...just like a bird flapping."

"Mommy, I can't fly, silly," Jaci Rae teased.

"Here Baby, like this," Anthony explained, as he lay next to her and started forming a pattern in the snow just like he remembered from a cartoon he watched as a kid. He had never actually done the process before, but tried his best.

"Like this, daddy?" Jaci Rae asked as she started in motion with all her limbs.

"That is perfect my little angel!" Sonja praised, as the shutter snapped and caught the defining moment in time.

Then Anthony was back to the real world, so far from that special moment.

"I miss you, baby," Anthony slurred out, as the snow sprinkled down and melted on his face. He stuck his tongue out in an attempt to catch a few flakes, before giving up and gulping a drink out of a vodka bottle. It was cold and dark in the parking lot of the Smoke Shop. Anthony lay on his back moving his arms and legs as if he was making snow angels in the backyard all those years ago. *Part of my mind knew I was a lifetime away from that day, but I hoped that if I kept drinking, I could go there forever.* Headlights flashed on him as his legs kicked two empty pints onto a dry spot and broke them. "I love you Sonja-" he tried to say before losing his train of thought and went back to making angels on the wet snowy black top.

Jessie Spotted Owl was on her way home, until she noticed someone in the parking lot of the Smoke Shop. When the lights hit the shadowy figure, she realized it was Anthony lying on the pavement wiggling around. Although Jessie's family did not celebrate Christmas, they still used the occasion to have a family dinner, while they retold joyful stories of the past. Her father, Chief John Spotted Owl, was in poor health as of late. His words held extra meaning this year when telling the story of how he met Jessie's mother, Lana. It always made Jessie happy to hear about the woman who brought her into this world and left her too soon. Three summers after Anthony's mother passed away, Lana lost her long fight against cancer. Jessie was too young to understand the transition to another life her mother experienced, but she did understand that her she was gone. She also knew why Anthony always seemed to have part of his happiness missing, a melancholy that only others with the same circumstances understood.

Jessie loved Anthony before she even knew what love was. Anthony loved her as well, but like a younger sister. She was always Anthony's biggest fan during his band days. Jessie started singing and writing music in some part, to get his attention. At first, Jessie was extremely jealous when Anthony met Sonja, until she saw them together. Watching how happy Anthony was, slowly helped Jessie move on and wait for the person the Mother God wanted her to be with. So far, no great candidates had proven themselves to her or her father. The one she always loved, crumbled beneath tragedy, before disappearing for what felt like, eternity. Now Anthony was lying in the middle of his own private hell, as if he remained caught between worlds. This hard reality and the one he wanted to go back to so desperately.

Jessie shut the car off, but left the lights on. She stepped around some broken glass and knelt down close to Anthony, making sure to stay away from his moving wingspan.

"Anthony, can you hear me? Please come back to this world?" Jessie pleaded softly.

Anthony stopped making angels and looked up with red blurry eyes. "I love you Sonja," he said as he reached up to hug his imagined ghost from the past.

Normally it would have wounded Jessie to hear those words from Anthony except the only thing that mattered was to save him from himself. Jessie came around and tried to lift his shoulders from the back. With little help from Anthony, she managed to get him to sit up. He immediately tried to take a drink out of the bottle before she grabbed it out of his hand. Anthony still went through the motions as if he was quenching his relentless thirst. Jessie shook, pulled, pushed and cajoled him until somehow he was on his feet. She practically carried him as far as the car before Anthony lost his equilibrium and pulled them onto the hood. Jesse finally got control and steered him back towards the Smoke Shop.

Jessie opened the front door as Anthony slumped to the ground, halfway inside with his legs hanging out. She turned the alarm off and came back to navigate Anthony far enough into the Smoke Shop to get the door closed. When he did not answer after she shook him, she went out and shut the lights off in the car. Jessie sat in the driver's seat a moment trying to figure out her next move. A misty haze of accumulation glazed over the window before she gathered her thoughts. The first call went out to Lonely Bear, who did not answer. She called Bijou and Dominique and left a quiet, but frightened message when they did not answer. Jessie picked up the receiver to call for an ambulance when Anthony began mumbling. She hung up and rushed to his side as Anthony laughed while grabbing his stomach as if someone was tickling him.

Jaci Rae grew tired of snow angels and decided to take up the battle royale that was taking place in the living room before they came out. The anticipation of the pounce had her giggling before she reached Anthony as she slugged through the snow seemingly in slow motion. "I'm gonna' get you, Daddy!" Jaci Rae warned, only seconds before tumbling safely in his waiting arms.

"I love you, my snow angel," Anthony fumbled out, as he opened his eyes enough to see Jessie talking to him. Her lips moved side to side, up and down, without a sound piercing though to the place he was.

"Anthony, can you hear me? Are you okay? How much have you had to drink, I really need to know?" Jessie called out as she gave him a kiss for comfort on his forehead that somehow seemed to snap him out of the foggy lucidity.

"Jessie...what 'cha you doing in my backyard?"

She laughed slightly at his sudden sweet charm and decided to go along with it. "I came to see you and make sure you are okay?"

"Fine, fine...fine," he slurred badly, as he drifted back in to a semi-conscious state. *I miss you my angel, I miss you my sweet angel,* Anthony repeated in his mind, which echoed into a vast blackness of nothing.

At a complete loss at what to do, Jessie sat down and let Anthony lean against her. It had been a long emotional night realizing this was probably the last Christmas she would have with her father. This business with Anthony was too much for her. It was like an overwhelming static that her brain could not process. For a second, Jessie's eyes were growing tired and she was slipping into her own dreamland, until the headlights flashed of a car pulling up in front of the Smoke Shop. She looked back as a big shadow came over them.

"Hey Jessie, we got your message," Dominique stated for a hello, in his usual low deep voice. "How is he doing?" He asked, kneeling down on one knee to check on Anthony.

"I am not sure what to say besides, that I know he is drunk. Whatever else is going on with him, I will leave it to Lonely Bear or a hospital. I called him, but got no answer.

"Don't worry; Uncle Bijou was going to keep trying him. Let's get Anthony to the cot in back, so we can make him comfortable until Lonely Bear gets here," Dominique decided, as he tossed Anthony over his shoulder and stood up in the same move. He could not believe how light Anthony was. He was probably the same weight or less, that he was in high school, when they wrestled around together. It was never really a fair match, as Dominique had always been twice his size growing up. Many coaches over the years tried in vain to recruit him for various sports., but the drums were the only thing Dominique had a passion to pursue.

Drumming was a part of Dominique, from the first night when he hid in the closet from his mother and tapped a shoebox to the rhythmic sounds of the rain against the windowpanes. Music was his sanctuary. The only place he felt safe growing up with an addict, who alternated between tears for her poor parenting skills and anger at how useless her life was. By third grade, Dominique was big enough to fight back, but he refused, she was still his mother. It was hard for him to remember any sober times with his mother, before Bijou adopted him permanently. Bijou never approved of his neighbors lifestyle, or the way she raised Dominique. He tried all the legal channels to save him. *His desperate requests went unanswered since Uncle Bijou is not directly related to Dominique.*

Finally, Bijou rescued Dominique despite the court's opinion. A goodbye hug after dropping off some food ended up being the last straw. Bijou could feel that the back of Dominique's shirt was wet. When the horrific gasp from Jo alerted him it was not water, Bijou carefully ran his gentle hands up the back of Dominique's shirt. A few open wounds, mixed into scars, all from a heated wire hanger. Uncle Bijou cried as he held on. Dominique never really knew what happened to his mother after that last night in the squalid apartment with more drugs, drunks and drifters than there ever was food. Dominique took out his anger on the drums, until he practically beat them into the floor and never thought of her again.

"I got here as quickly as I could." Lonely Bear announced, as he came into the room still clothed in his flannel pajamas, house shoes and a winter overcoat. He was shocked when he saw Anthony's dire condition. "Oh my, he is plumb full of poison." He declared sadly, with a tone of defeat in his voice.

Jessie noticed Lonely Bear's despondent demeanor and knelt down to Anthony's side. She grabbed his hand and whispered in his ear. "You hold on. Keep fighting, Anthony, we will get you some help." She stood back up and collapsed into Lonely Bear's chest crying. "You have to save him!

We just got him back. Please, there must be something we can do for him?"

Lonely Bear paused to think about the situation. He stepped into his office and came back with a handful of baby jars with various herbs along with a bucket. "This won't be pretty, but we need to evacuate his stomach and get as much of the alcohol out as we can." He explained as he popped open a can of ginger ale and filled a glass half full. Lonely Bear mixed in some black goop that smelled like spoiled milk and a few pinches out of each jar. "Dominique and I will work on things from this end while you call in some back up. Anthony's kidneys have all but shut down and are not cleaning the waste from his blood. Boy, he has really done it this time," Lonely Bear lamented while shaking his head with disappointment.

Jessie gave Anthony a final hug. She left the room to use the phone as Dominique propped Anthony upright. Lonely Bear used a wooden tongue depressor to open Anthony's mouth and poured most of the liquid down his throat. The concoction immediately expanded in Anthony's stomach until it pushed so hard there was only one direction for it to travel. Dominique held the bucket.

"All we can do now is hope for the best," Lonely Bear stated glumly, as he wiped Anthony's face with a cool wet cloth, while Dominique laid him back down.

Anthony was oblivious to his situation. He drifted back to a winter memory. Jaci Rae would have played in the snow the rest of the day except for the arrival of the next wave of ice. What started as a light sprinkle quickly turned into sleet, which put a slick glaze over everything including Mr. Frosty. When Mr. Frosty's scarf began to freeze to his midsection, Sonja decided it was time to warm up with some hot chocolate. A great way to end a day of snowman building, Anthony and Jaci Rae reluctantly admitted, as they headed inside.

"You have enough marshmallows," Sonja teased, as Jaci Rae piled them two inches high.

"Umm...maybe a few more." Jaci Rae decided, as she went for another handful of the little round confections, made from gelatin and sugar.

Sonja began to stop her from over-doing it, but changed her mind and figured there was no point in saving a quarter of a bag anyways. It was past Jaci Rae's normal naptime and Sonja began thinking about Anthony's previous offer.

"Hey Honey, you better get on that driveway like you said you wanted to." Sonja chirped in a serious tone. She could tell by Anthony's frazzled look that he was worn out.

"Okay, go ahead and put the rest of my hot chocolate in my coffee mug and I will warm it back up when I get done...if I get done," Anthony replied unenthusiastically, as the sleet turned to marble-sized hail and pinged against the roof. He got up slowly dragging it out as much as possible, even giving a slight groan while reaching for his wet snow boots. Anthony hoped she would let him off the hook, but

Sonja did not say a word. *Darn me and my big snow shoveling mouth,* Anthony thought as he slipped into the first boot and bent over to tie it.

"Would you rather put Jaci Rae down for a nap instead of shoveling?" Sonja whispered in his ear seductively, as she came over and hunched down close to him.

"Nope. When I say I will do something...no matter how dangerous, I will stick to it for you, Baby." Anthony whined in a melodramatic whimper, that soon faded when she kissed the nape of his neck. "On second thought," he smiled, as he kicked the boot right off. "Nap time Jaci Rae," is all he got out before the fight was on.

Jaci Rae was wide-awake and was having no part of the N. word. Her sugary marshmallow buzz was kicking in and the only way she would agree to even head into her room was if Daddy lay down too.

"I will be waiting for you when she nods off." Sonja promised with a wink.

With new motivation, Anthony scooped Jaci Rae up and had her tucked in her bed in record time. He tried to sneak out early but, her left eye popped open and caught him.

"Daddy, you said you would take a nap?"

"Okay, Sweetie," Anthony answered, trying not to sound too disappointed she was not out like a light yet. He lay back down and snuggled while trying a different approach. Anthony began combing his fingers through Jaci Rae's apple blossom-smelling hair. He softly sang one of her favorite songs from the video that had been playing for days on end.

Dominique and Lonely Bear watched as Anthony patted at the air, while he slurred out a kids song they had not heard in years.

Anthony's voice cracked a little and grew softer as if the energy was draining out of him with each verse. "I love you....You love me....We're a happy family. I love you so much, my sweet Snow Angel," he sputtered out, before it all went dark.

Chapter 17

Empty Chairs in a Field

"The weak can never forgive,

Forgiveness is the attribute of the strong."

Mahatma Gandhi

Oklahoma City, Oklahoma

April 19, 2002

Uncle Bijou

Selected from over six hundred entries, the design was simple and breathtakingly beautiful. With the memorial museum on the north side of the property, where the Edward P. Murrah building once stood, a peaceful orchard with Chinese pistachios, Bosque elms and Amur maples, mirrored the spring colors off the reflecting pool that was once N.W. 5th street. Two bronze covered gates with interval units of time marked the borders on the east and west sides of the Outdoor Symbolic Memorial. The time 9:01 was etched on the east side, symbolizing the last minute of peace for the victims and 9:03 on the west end, which stood for the first moments of recovery for the families.

One hundred and sixty eight chairs

represented the innocent souls taken, with nineteen smaller replicas for the babies. An American elm, which survived the blast, nicknamed the "Survivor Tree", offered a shady peaceful place to take in the magnificence of the surrounding park. *I think this is Jo's favorite place in the memorial,* Bijou decided, as he led her and Anthony over to the landmark tree.

They skipped the National Park dedication on the five-year anniversary. Aunt Jo did not want to be a part of a ceremony with some of the same shameful officials that participated in a cover up, which included a demolition of the building, before all the bomb evidence could be collected and analyzed. It was another knife in the heart for the families of the lost, when the Red Cross volunteers opened letters to steal donations, while the FBI and BATF shook down witnesses, confiscated video footage, destroyed evidence and created a false narrative to hide the truth, concerning the worst domestic act of terrorism in the country's history. Jo would finally stop fighting against their big lie, because it was destroying her. Nevertheless, she would never forget what they did. Jo felt they were just as guilty covering it up as the ones prosecuted.

Uncle Bijou spread out a blanket as best he could, in a nice spot and made sure Aunt Jo was comfortable, before he offered to show Anthony around. Bijou knew pretty much every inch of the memorial from dozens of visits over the last two years. On many occasions, he visited with Aunt Jo or Dominique and other times on his own. For a three-acre site that had unspeakable terror and suffering within its grounds, it was cleansed with love and tears. *I feel close to Jaci here. It is a sort of connection to her wonderful new world in heaven.*

"Jo, baby, you be okay if I show Anthony around a bit?"

"Yes I would actually appreciate that. I do not think I am up to seeing her chair today. Tell Jaci Rae I am missing her though."

"Will do, Darling." He replied, as he bent down and gave her a tender kiss on the forehead, before he grabbed a hold of Anthony's arm. "Just follow me Son; I will take you right there."

They took a few steps down the hill to the granite slabs outlining the reflecting pool. Anthony paused to breathe it all in a moment. The clouds mixed and melted over the fixed image of the west gate they came in from. Between the two gates it would forever be 9:02, the exact time the world changed.

"Uncle Biscuit, how do you know the way?"

"Oh don't worry, Anthony; I have this place blueprinted out in my mind." Bijou answered confidently, as they made their way to the first rows of golden bronze and etched glass empty chairs. "There are nine rows, which show which floor your loved one was on. They are also gathered in the blast radius of the main bomb, which did most of the damage. At first, it messed me up because there are five extra chairs for the folks that perished outside of the building. Here it is, Anthony," Bijou explained, as he arrived to Jaci Rae's little chair and ran his hand across her name on the glass to make sure. He knelt on one knee and said a quick prayer, before ushering Anthony around to the front. Bijou could tell by Anthony's pulse, that his heart was beating hard with anxiety. He could hear a slight change in his breathing and could tell Anthony was most likely crying, so Bijou stepped back to let him have a moment.

Anthony took the dream catcher with a silver cross in the center of it off his guitar and hung it on the monument. It was always Jaci Rae's favorite and she marveled at it every time he played for her. "I hope all your dreams are coming true, my Sweet Angel." Anthony whispered softly, as he strummed her favorite song for her.

They were the only ones in the area today. It was peaceful. A slight wind from the east carried the scent of a fresh bouquet, placed in honor of a loved one. Bijou turned his head so his left ear was facing toward Anthony. His right ear was always next to the drummer all those years in a band and could not pinpoint voices very well, unless they were up close. He listened for only a few words and instantly felt guilty for eavesdropping on Anthony's conversation. He walked to the reflecting pool and sat down on the ledge. *I enjoy running my fingers in the cool water while I think about things. Jaci Rae would love this tribute. It is so peaceful.*

It was a little easier every time Bijou came here. He knew Jaci Rae was happy and that it would be only a flash before his own journey to join her. Bijou could not contact her directly, as if to have a conversation, it was more of a warm feeling that came over him. *I feel so close to her here.* He closed his eyes behind his dark sunglasses and let the cool breeze surround him while momentarily losing his thoughts in a meditative state of tranquility. His mind drifted to a familiar place.

"Uncle Bijou, will you read me a story?" Jaci Rae asked, in order to stretch out bedtime and stay up a little longer. The books were not in brail, but she would climb up on his lap and he would "read" her a story anyway. Jaci Rae loved the tales of velveteen rabbits, lost puppies that found their way, princesses and unicorns.

"Sure, I will read you a story, baby girl." Bijou answered, enjoying the moment as much as Jaci Rae did. From the day she was born, they were best friends. *And always will be.* They both had the same kind of positive and loving energy about them, which meshed perfectly from the first time he held her in the delivery room. Jaci Rae stopped crying right after birth and gave Bijou a little smile, permanently sealing their bond. *She was my special girl, oh how I miss her so.*

Bijou could hear Anthony walk up to him after finishing his visit. A slight swish of his jeans alternated with an ever-so-slight scuffing, as he dragged his left foot a bit every step. "So, did you have a nice talk?" Bijou asked, to start up a conversation.

"Well, I talked and I hoped she could hear me."

"Oh I am sure she can, son," Bijou assured him. "Jaci Rae is always with you in your heart and only a thought away. She is also with you here today in spirit. I can feel her sweet soul, just as I did when you were in the hospital. It was soon after your transplant when you were losing ground from that post-op infection. You and Lonely Bear were both doing great, until the fever came over you. I could sense you leaving us, Son, until...I felt this calm. This might sound funny, but I could feel Jaci Rae there with us." Bijou confided, to only silence at first.

"How did you know she was there with me that morning, Uncle Biscuit?"

"Same as I know she is here. I can feel it in my bones." Bijou reassured him.

"I still don't understand it, because I was out cold with a fever, but I could see everything in the room, including myself lying in the bed. I turned and looked back as I was walking to a doorway where Jaci Rae waited. She was surrounded by an overwhelming light that seemed so bright, I should have to shade my eyes away from it. I slept with tubes in my arms, blankets tucked tight under my chin. I looked sad, but I did not feel that way. I was at peace with it and ready to go with her. As I turned back around, the light was waning and Jaci Rae just smiled and shook her head no. It was not time for me, I guess. In the next instant, I was swept back into my body and waking up to a long painful recovery."

"I was in the light once and like you, it was not my time. I could almost see to the other side. It was a moving, swirling, kaleidoscope of color, so intense it took my sight. That was the tradeoff to be able to come back to this world and be with Pops. *Best trade I ever made.* Anthony, your deal is to live your second chance without regrets from the past. You need to make the most of your talent and help others that are in a bad way."

"I will, Uncle Biscuit. Thank you for believing in me enough to set up all the places for us to play. I doubt that I will ever have a six figure record contract like before, but I am thankful to be able to do what I love again."

"That's the right attitude, my boy! Oh and Aunt Jo did most of the work on the phone. I only passed along a few numbers for my friends that are still around."

"I promise I will do my best. I have not had a drink since before the operation, when it almost killed me at Christmas. Lonely Bear said his kidney had been fine all those years without alcohol and that he would take it back if I polluted it." Anthony explained, with a smile.

Bijou felt a familiar presence and stood up as she arrived. "Sonja, how are you my dear?" Bijou asked, towards Anthony's direction.

Anthony turned around as Sonja was walking right to him. Sonja carried a precious bundle held papoose style against her chest. She looked radiantly happy. Motherhood seemed to be a blessing. She was in a good place for the first time since her accident, so close to this very spot.

"Hey there, Sonja, it looks like you brought some company with you?" Anthony asked, as he gave her a warm hug and a congratulatory pat on the back,

"Yes I did. This is Julia Beth. She is doing great. It is hard to believe she celebrated her three month birthday already last week."

"Sonja, you better watch out or she will want to run off with a musician like you did," Bijou joked, as he gave Sonja a kiss on the cheek, because he had missed her all the years she was not around.

"I am going to let you two get caught up while I check on Jo." Bijou decided, sensing the sudden awkward pause in the conversation. He turned and started counting steps in his head to find his way back to the Survivor Tree. *I bet they have a lot to talk about.*

"That is fine, Uncle Biscuit; we will be over in a bit." Anthony called out, before they slowly made their way up to Jaci Rae's memorial.

This time Anthony felt more comfortable with Sonja by his side. She tried to be brave until Jaci Rae's name came into focus. Sonja paused a second getting her courage up. Coming here was never easy for her. Anthony put an arm around her in a show of support as they made the final few steps together. They stood in silence as several other visitors walked about leaving mementos and flowers.

"Uncle Biscuit says he can feel Jaci Rae's

presence here…and that she is happy." Anthony stated quietly, trying to comfort Sonja as she did her best to hold back any tears still left from her cry this morning, knowing it was the anniversary date.

"I know she is, but I sure do miss her. Jaci Rae always wanted a baby sister-" Sonja started to say, until catching herself, as she realized Anthony pulled his arm off her. Anthony always wanted another baby, but Sonja worried she would be alone with two babies, while he was on the road supporting his first album, so she never wanted to try. She figured they had plenty of time. "I'm sorry, I would have left Julia Beth with Blake, but he was called into work. I am sure all of this is uncomfortable for you since we never tried."

"Oh no dear, I am fine really. It is good you brought her along. Julia is beautiful like her mom," Anthony admitted with a wink, to show he was okay with everything. "I really am happy for you, Sonja. That is all I ever wanted. Maybe in another life we could have…well, I think you know what I am having so much trouble saying. You always could finish my sentences for me," he teased.

"I know how you feel. To be honest, I never wanted to let you go again when you came up to work that first time. If things were different."

"Sonja, it is okay. I messed things up and I have kind of made peace with it. We can only go forward from here. There is nothing in the past for us anymore."

"Just so you know. I love you, Anthony…and

I always will. You and Jaci Rae are in my heart no matter where I am. You will always be part of me."

Anthony felt a cleansing feeling come over him. It swept away the last remnants of guilt, he still carried for his mistakes. He stepped over and gave her another hug. Like the last time they hugged, he had to step a little to the left because the baby was between them, and as before, Sonja did not want to let go. It made him feel good that they would always have a bond of love and friendship between them. *Not even all the tragedy they went through could break it.*

"Sonja, you will always be my best friend and I promise to stay in touch when we get out on the road."

"Oh yes, that is right. Aunt Jo said you are playing again. I am so proud of you. And you had better keep in touch! I thought I lost you in the hospital there for a while. You gave me such a scare."

"Well, let's just say, I had a little angel that showed me the way. I hope to make the most of this chance. I have wasted so much of my life in self-pity and blaming myself for what happened. Finally, I decided the only ones to blame were the terrorist that did it and that it will never make sense. Those pieces will never fit. That kind of evil is on such a different level, it is probably good we don't understand it."

"I suppose you are right. I am sure they will pay somehow. I am impressed that you seem to be doing so good now." Sonja praised.

"I tried to run from it; drown my sorrows; even gave up on myself and everything else, but it did nothing to take away the pain. Lonely Bear explained that the only way to beat it was to learn to live with it. Turn it into motivation for something good. So that is what I have been doing, taking it day by day and turning all the hurt into new lyrics and music."

"I wish I could be strong like that." Sonja confided. "Some days I still fall apart at the seams over the littlest things. I feel like I am never going to be whole again."

"You will dear. Julia Beth will remind you along the way, that love always wins over hate," Anthony declared, with a new resolve.

"I am glad you came back and faced everything. It does make it better for all of us. Hope you know that."

"I never meant to hurt you. I was lost and I never wanted to be found again. But yet, here I am," Anthony replied with a smile.

"Yes, here you are and I am so thankful. You promise to call me?"

"For sure, I will call you three times a day." He joked, as he gave her another quick hug and made funny faces to coax a smile out of Julia Beth.

It worked for a little, but she woke up hungry and soon let them know with a pitiful whimper, as if she had not been fed in days. Her lip crinkled under the top one and her brown eyes teared up enough to make Sonja feel sorry for her.

"Don't you ever feed this sweet baby?" Anthony teased.

"Nope, poor little thing only gets to eat whenever she wants and I guess she is ready. Oh baby, that is the saddest cry I ever heard," Sonja comforted her in a baby talk voice, to let Julia Beth know she was going to be okay.

"We can head back over to the shade tree and meet up with them," Anthony suggested, taking one last look at Jaci Rae's chair before turning that direction.

"That sounds good. I want to say goodbye to Aunt Jo before you guys leave."

They took the long way around and admired the reflecting pool again, which mirrored a different scene from before, with the shifting light of the sun. Julia Beth was not amused and reminded them it was past lunchtime, so they continued over to the blanket where Aunt Jo immediately stood up and hugged Sonja.

"Oh my, I have to hold Julia Beth," She exclaimed, as Sonja pulled her out of the fleece carrier and handed her over. "What is the matter Sweetie? You look so sad."

"She woke up hungry and has been letting us know about it," Sonja explained, as she found a comfortable spot to breastfeed her.

Aunt Jo gave a few more kisses on the top of her head before passing her down to Sonja who sat on a bench waiting. Julia Beth latched on with such enthusiasm, that it made Sonja grimace for a second.

"Ouch, please slow down a little. Gosh, she has me so sore lately. I guess she is worth it though,"

Sonja praised, as she swaddled Julie Beth in a baby blanket.

"So how have you been?" Aunt Jo asked as she came and sat next to Sonja.

"I have my good days and then, well…the rest, if you know what I mean?" Aunt Jo said.

"I do honey, for sure I do," Aunt Jo sympathized. "I can't believe it has been seven years. Where does the time go to?"

"I am kind of glad some of it is behind me. I still get headaches occasionally. Blake is so sweet and patient with me. I am lucky to have had two wonderful men in my life," Sonja confessed, as she buttoned up and gave Julia Beth several soft pats on the back until she let out a big burp. "That's a good job, baby. Oh you are so cute, yes you are!' Sonja gleamed with pride.

"Speaking of wonderful men," Aunt Jo hinted, as she held up her left hand featuring a new ring on prominent display. "Look what I got for Christmas from Bijou."

"Congratulations you two, it is beautiful! When is the big day?"

"It's already on paper. We went to the courthouse and afterwards our church had a wonderful reception for the wedding and also to welcome me back."

Sonja understood completely, the bombing and aftermath had pushed her faith to the limits, but she did not break. Although Sonja did not attend as much as she wished she could, the church was always there for her. "I will get you an invitation for Julia Beth's baptism, now that I am thinking of it. Probably be towards the end of June, when she has grown a little more."

"We would love that. Do not forget you are still kin to us and more than welcome anytime for supper or even just to talk. I will have some fresh veggies this year and fresh flowers from Jaci Rae's garden. I will get some over to you guys."

"Thanks, Aunt Jo." Sonja replied with a smile.

"Okay, Jo baby, we best get a move on. Anthony needs to get on the road. Don't want him missing his first gig, now do we?" Bijou asked, as he reached out for Aunt Jo's hand to help her up.

"Do you need a ride somewhere, Sonja?" Anthony offered, as he stepped around to the group.

"Thanks, but actually we are good. I think we will hang out here a little longer. Blake can swing by when he gets off work."

They all made small talk for a few more minutes, not wanting to say goodbye until Bijou started wrapping it up. *If I do not get things moving we are going to be late*, he thought as he bid his farewells and best wishes.

"Don't forget your promise to keep in touch," Sonja reminded him, as she gave him one last hug and kiss on the cheek for good luck.

"I will call you for sure. It has been great to see you two." He answered with a glint of love in his eyes for her that would never fade.

Three more rounds of goodbyes went on until

Bijou started pulling Aunt Jo in the right direction. They were mostly quiet as Jo drove them to the Smoke Shop where Lonely Bear was out on a ladder fixing a loose wire in the big red sign on the front.

"You be careful on that thing before you break your neck." Aunt Jo teased out the car window as they pulled up. "I don't think you are supposed to balance on top of the ladder like that."

"Either me or this ladder, has shrunk and inch, since the last time I fiddled with this old sign," Lonely Bear volleyed back, as he finished up and the sign flickered on, buzzing with a continued hum.

"You better get out there and help him before he has a fall." Aunt Jo decided.

"Okay, which direction do I go?" Bijou asked.

"Oh not you silly." She laughed.

"I got it covered," Anthony replied, as he jumped out and helped Lonely Bear back down to solid ground, after which, he received a hearty pat on the back as thanks.

"Thank you, Anthony; things were a bit shaky for a moment." Lonely Bear admitted, as a shining new van rolled up with a couple of quick honks to accentuate the surprise arrival.

It was a touring edition painted bright metallic silver with extra headroom and all the extras. Dominique sat behind the wheel with Jessie Spotted Owl hanging out of the passenger window.

"Hey handsome, do you need a ride?" Jessie hollered out, while pointing right at Anthony. Her hair was down from her braids and blowing in every direction. Jessie looked amazing.

Anthony was not sure if he was more stunned by Jessie's beauty, or the implication they would be traveling in style. He stood there slack-jawed unable to come up with any kind of response, so finally Bijou came over.

"So what do you think, Anthony? She's really something, don't cha think?" Bijou asked, as he could smell the new car scent from the leather seats and the tire sheen. He ran his hands across the hood, feeling the perfect smoothness of the high-gloss lacquer finish. In his mind it looked much different, more like the souped-up Model T's he used to watch from the hotel windows, in whatever town his Pops played. *If only I could have driven one of those babies*, he lamented a moment, until two car doors opened. The one on his right shut right as Dominique's big paw of a hand grabbed him and pulled him in for a rare hug.

"Thanks for everything, Uncle Bijou. I wish you were going with us to round out the horn section." Dominique gushed with praise.

"I am too long in the tooth for the road anymore. Besides, I have a pretty girl that waited a lot of years for me and if I keep her pining away any longer, she might up and find herself a new dance partner." Bijou declared with enough volume, so Aunt Jo could hear he was talking about her.

"I don't understand, Dominique, where did you borrow this from?" Anthony asked, as he stepped closer for a look.

"Oh, it is not borrowed," Lonely Bear

interrupted, as he handed Anthony an envelope with the title and insurance cards for all of them to split the driving. They were a band now and the paperwork was in all their names. "The entire tribe, Jessie's father, along with Jo and Bijou all chipped in. We are proud of you guys and know you will be a big success. Please don't stay gone too long this time, okay?"

"Hey now, Bear did his part, don't let his modesty fool you. It was all his idea and he put the whole deal together with an old patient. Well that is if you guys really want to take this instead of my 75' baby-blue Caddie."

"Oh Bijou, leave those kids alone. They do not want that worn out old boat. That clunker has more miles than you do, my love." Aunt Jo teased.

"Maybe so, but she still purrs like a kitten and can get up and go…just like me!" He fired back, with a big whoop of a laugh that cheered everyone up even more.

As Aunt Jo went another round with Bijou, Anthony walked over to Jessie, as she stepped out of the van. When Jessie smiled, something happened to him. Anthony finally saw her as a beautiful young woman for the first time. *It was confusing and amazing at the same time.*

"It looks like you got your braces off?" Anthony fumbled out, before he knew what he was actually saying.

"Yes I did, almost sixteen years ago, but thanks for noticing," Jessie joked, as she sensed something different was happening between them. It was as if Anthony was seeing her for the first time. The real Jessie, the part she always tried so hard to make Anthony notice.

Anthony's faced turned red from embarrassment, at his clumsy attempt to flirt and make small talk. "Umm...well, they did a good job."

Jessie looked right into his eyes, so full of hope and at that moment knew she had him. Anthony was tongue-tied as he pulled at a loose string from a belt loop of his jeans. It was awkward between them, as neither really knew how to take the turn of events, so they stood and gawked at each other with goofy smiles.

Aunt Jo was the first to notice and alerted the group. She squeezed Bijou's hand and whispered, "Jessie and Anthony sitting in a tree....k.i.s.s.i.n.g." in his ear to let him know why it suddenly went silent.

"Say what, Jo baby? Jessie and Anthony are kissing each other?" He blurted out, which embarrassed them even more.

Dominique jumped in to save the day. "Not yet Uncle Bijou, but they might as well get it over with. Jeez, all this mushy stuff is going to get old fast," he teased, but was happy for the pair of old friends.

"Well, I'll be. I sure didn't see that coming." Bijou interjected as he started laughing at his own good humor. His happiness was infectious and his clucky laugh irresistible, especially to Aunt Jo who came around for a hug.

Jessie leaned over and gave Anthony a peck on the cheek, to let him know this was the start of something good.

"Little Hawk, you better not stand there too much longer with your tongue hanging to the pavement." Lonely Bear called out, joining in on the teasing. "Did you get all packed up like I told you? That is right; you have been packed up since you got here. You might want to take your stuff with you though."

"Huh? Oh yes, I am ready. I will go in and grab my duffle bag."

Lonely Bear followed him into the Smoke Shop to have a last talk. He waited by the poker machine, while Anthony retrieved his stuff. He reached in his pocket, found some change, and decided to play it once since he never had. With a click of the "Deal" button, five cards came up. An ace of hearts was the only thing worth keeping, so he saved it and had four new cards dealt to him. Two more aces came up for three of a kind. "That is what I call a winning hand!" He murmured to himself, recognizing the strange coincidence with his loved ones starting a new life together.

Anthony came out with his bag, an extra jacket and the new cowboy boots he received for Christmas.

"So are you sure you are up for this? Doctor gave the okay, but said no alcohol, no smoking, watch your soda intake and sweets. Also, drink plenty of water every day. Oh and don't be eating the normal junk you usually do."

"I will be careful, so don't worry. I might even have a salad once in a while," Anthony countered with a respectful smile.

"I gave Jessie Spotted Owl a copy of your dietary needs and also a list of specialists and hospitals along your tour route, in case any more infections sprout up. I have you added on my health insurance as well. Your new card is in there along with a credit card for any "in betweens" you guys might need."

"In betweens?"

"That is what Bijou calls it anyway. Stuff like food and gas that you might need "in between" being paid. I think they have it all worked out. Now all you have to do is the hard part and sing. You have all new gear and a couple of new guitars you were eyeballing at the music shop last week, already packed in the van with your old one.

"Thank you so much, and I mean for everything. I don't know how I can repay you?" Anthony inquired, in a worried tone.

"You are my family. The last one of us left. So, it is all on you how we are remembered. That is how you pay me back."

"That sounds like a lot of responsibility," Anthony quipped. "Can't I just pay with a few songs?"

"I am proud of you, Little Hawk, and all that you have overcome. Somehow, you dragged yourself up from a very dark place. In doing so, you also pulled all of us up with you." Lonely Bear praised, as he gave a stern proud hug. Not being to resist, Lonely Bear ran his hands around to check Anthony's aura. He could feel a strong core this time. Anthony was still weak physically, but stronger in spirit than ever before.

"I will do my best." Anthony promised, as the horn on the van honked a few times to let him know it was time to leave.

"Well, go on now before they leave you stuck here with me."

Anthony reached out and shook Lonely Bear's hand with a firm handshake, to show respect to his hero, before heading on out. Lonely Bear watched until Anthony's silhouette disappeared in the abundant sunshine coming through the front door.

Dominique and Jessie already said their goodbyes and were waiting in the van. Although there was plenty of room in the back, Jessie picked the front middle so she could be next to Anthony.

"Goodbye honey, and don't forget my address this time around." Aunt Jo declared, while trying to hold back all her happy tears. "You drive safe and have some fun. I am sure you will be terrific as always."

"Thanks Aunt Jo. I will call you when we get to Kansas City. I love you!"

"Love you too, Baby!"

Uncle Bijou did not say a word as he walked Anthony over to the van and gave him a pat on the back. His smile said everything he wanted to say. *I sure am proud of you, Anthony.*

Anthony watched in the side mirror until the Smoke Shop went out of focus. He could not believe he tried so hard to leave that place and now was already homesick. He started to have doubts crop up for a moment until he turned and saw Jessie's comforting smile.

"Everything is going to be okay," Jessie assured as she reached her hand over and placed into his.

It was a perfect fit.

Chapter 18

Faith and Forgiveness

"Only love, can help the blind to see

Only hope, will heal a broken heart

Only forgiveness, can light a path

Away from dark places

And only faith, will guide you to

A peaceful spot in heaven

That you can always

Call home...."

Lonely Bear

Mustang, Oklahoma

July 27, 2005

If you are reading my poem, know that I have passed from this middle world to the next one. Please do not weep for me, because my struggle was long and I lived more lifetimes than most people do. I am at peace with my decisions. Many days, I wanted to give up when things became impossibly difficult. Sometimes it hurt so bad I was unable to write the words onto these pages. I guess, in some roundabout way, those days of tragedy made me stronger and prepared me for my journey to the Mother Spirit. With a stubborn perseverance, I overcame my demons. Escaped a dark time in my life. That is just part of life and everyone goes to the dark place sometime. A place where all hope starves, while your dreams rot away to nothing.

Some never find the light to better days and the blackness pecks at their soul like a ravenous murder of crows. They become so disoriented, that the path to happiness sinks into a quagmire of lies that once resembled a normal life. Lifelines from people that love you dangle out of reach in the opaque gloom, while fear preys on self-esteem until it owns you. Numb to the pain, they welcome anything that will make them feel something close to real. Or…they choose to never feel anything again.

My key to freedom, came from two words: Faith and Forgiveness. Simple words that are used, abused, forgotten and sworn against. I had faith, that my loved ones were waiting for me in the next life. That part was easy when compared to the challenges of learning to forgive. How do I forgive those who trespassed on my happiness, by taking what I loved most, without a shred of remorse? Even more so, I had to learn to forgive myself. Let go of the hate and guilt that was drowning me in the shallow waters of loneliness.

Words are the only thing eternal in the infinite fabric of time. They will exist forever once they are spoken or written. All of us have a unique story to tell with the words we choose, but we only get so many chapters in our life's book. We spend the brief time we have adding pages of memories. With each day being a new blank paper to write our life as we wish. Some pages are filled with laughter and defining moments that we hope to never forget. Other times are so sad, we want to close that chapter and never look back. Some get such a short book, their families are left behind wondering how a different ending might have been. If only...they could have more time.

  With the relatively long story called my life, I always tried to give more love than I took. A lesson passed down from the unknown generations before me, through my sweet and loving grandmother. When I was a child, my fondest memories centered on dinner and the evenings listening to my Grandmother Rain Cloud tell stories from her life's book. She had a way of making the lowest points of her journey have meaning. That somehow, the terrible pain she lived through was....as it should have been....to someday teach me the lessons she paid for in tears. Generations of my family passed into my heart though her kind and meaningful stories. They lived within me, always there to guide the way through the hardest of times when I felt I could push no further. As my grandmother often explained, some things in life do not only hurt you, they take a piece of your spirit that you can never get back. Maybe it makes you stronger that you found your way through the darkness, or it makes you numb to it, until the pain goes away. I hope my words, as hers did, might help someone down the road that feels he cannot go on. The lessons that I paid for with my own tears, will be a lighthouse in the storm, raging within their hearts.

They say that truth is only a perception of the person hearing it. Lies become truth if you believe them and truth become lies if you turn your back to it. Somewhere between the fictions spun from others with an agenda to hide the truth and true reality, is my story. The years since the tragedy have accentuated special times and became the distance needed to forget some of the painful memories, to keep them buried where they belong, but this is what I believe. It is my truth so therefore my reality and I will own it. It is my life book…and I humbly pass it onto you.

I will start somewhere at the beginning with a day mostly forgotten except from those that escaped the horror. It is only a blurb in the history books now. The real story is condensed down to a politically correct, whitewashed footnote, written by the victors, as is most history. For the innocent lost that day, there are no words to help them now. They will never again add pages to their life book. I take comfort knowing this story holds truth, faith, love, forgiveness and is dedicated to their memory.

When you escape the dark corners of your mind as I have, you are always different when you reach the other side. You leave something behind.

The more you go there, the more it steals your essence, your innocence, your hope and beckons you to stay. If you choose to take this journey of truth with me, there is a price to pay. Some scars never heal...and some fires will burn forever.

Chapter 19

A Last Goodbye

"You laughed quietly at

My innocence and naiveté

But you knew I had to take the journey

And when I returned you would guide the way

Some of the storms were heavy

Through it all, I could see your light

I always stayed on course

By knowing wrong from right

No matter if, the distance is far or short

Your love is my compass

To navigate me back to port."

Lonely Bear

Little Hawk Soaring

Sand Creek Massacre National Historic Site, Colorado

August 1, 2005

It was an unusually chilly July day, when I lost Lonely Bear. Although there were clear skies leaving fresh sunshine unabated to brighten the morning, a cold front blanketed the area pushing out the hot humid weather from the weeks before. Lonely Bear never told anyone the day that he would pass to the next life. *I am sure he knew.*

Their last conversations happened at the Smoke Shop, when the band returned from tour. They could not wait to tell Lonely Bear the secret news, that Jessie and Anthony were expecting a baby. Anthony would not be the last man in their family tree after all. *We had sonogram pictures to prove our first son was on his way.*

Lonely Bear knew the second Jessie and Anthony walked into his office. He sensed it and his wonderful, caring, gifted hands gave him pictures of our baby. Lonely Bear also knew he would never see the birth. In that few minutes he ran his hands over Jessie's stomach, he closed his eyes and he connected with his future legacy on a different plain, that we could never understand. Lonely Bear opened his eyes and smiled at us as if he knew we had many happy times ahead, better than we could have dreamed.

"Your son is strong and is as rare, as a cool breeze on a summer day." Lonely Bear exclaimed with a big smile, before they could tell him the big news.

It was such a special day, even though for the first time Anthony could ever remember, Lonely Bear looked tired. Of course, he aged as all people do, but his spirit was so young that most never noticed that he changed over time. He knew his time was brief by the way he said goodbye. He hinted that all his important papers were in his top examining desk drawer. Jessie and Anthony felt this was a last goodbye. I wanted to ask more questions, anything but leave. The last hug he gave me, would have to do until I saw him in our next lives.

"I know you are with me today, giving me the strength for what I have to do." Anthony whispered to the wind, trying to gain the courage to respect his last wishes.

Anthony's hand was shaking so bad, he could not seem to use my lighter. The slight smell of gasoline wafted up with little dirt devils, which suddenly burst through with the cool breeze. It was a perfect day, just as Lonely Bear predicted it would be. Although never sure what day would be his last in this middle world, he knew how it would be. He once had a vision of joining with the spirits of his ancestors on a peaceful summer day. Lonely Bear wanted it to be the same place they left this world. It was also the resting place of his Grandmother Rain Cloud. She chose to pass to the Mother Spirit here.

Dedicated as a National Historic Site many years ago, the tranquil spot along the Washita River remained nearly unchanged since the massacre. I knew that I was committing a crime on federal property by respecting Lonely Bear's wishes, but it was a promise that I would not break. It took a couple of days to find the right trees to build the scaffold for his body. Normally he would pass to the Mother Spirit in a state of open burial. Lonely Bear knew the park rangers or a Good Samaritan would stumble onto his memorial and take it down. Therefore, he chose to have Anthony burn it on the second day, after a proper pass-over period.

Anthony was finding it impossible to let go. *How could I say goodbye to someone that gave me so much, including a second chance to right all the mistakes of my past.* Lonely Bear gave him a way to reconnect with my roots and family. When Anthony found his journals, I saw he had never given up on me. Even when Anthony was halfway across the world, lost in my own private hell. Every day he said a little prayer for me.

Anthony found one of Lonely Bear's last poems tucked away in an envelope with his name on it, along with his will and testament. Hand written and well creased, Lonely Bear wrote it for Anthony, so he could always find his way home. Now I hoped the same words help him on his journey. Along with his medical books and notes, Anthony found the manuscript for their story. Lonely Bear used Aunt Jo's meticulous research to complete most of it, so there would be a record of truth, that he could leave behind. Anthony knew it must have been difficult to write, since he missed Jaci Rae so very much. *I am sure he knew I would finish it for him.*

As Anthony gathered his courage to ignite the funeral pyre, a park ranger truck pulled up. A young man no older than nineteen, was the first to jump out of the passenger side. He dressed similar to the older dark complexioned man, but did not have a full uniform with all the patches.

"What is going on here?" The kid asked, with a tone of authority, as he picked up the small red gas can and realized it was now empty. "You can't burn that thing in here-" the young ranger blurted out before his supervisor interrupted.

"How old was our brother when he was called to the other side?" He asked with a sympathetic voice, which surprised me.

"I am not sure exactly how old Lonely Bear was? He said in his journal that he would never be a hundred, but he had no regrets. His life was as long as it was supposed to be."

"Did he have a healing shop in...Mustang, I think it was?"

"Yes, my Grandfather practiced his life's purpose for over sixty years. Did you know him?" I asked, wanting to know the connection.

"When I was just a boy, I was very sick. My grandmother took me there to heal me. I will never forget his kind eyes and how he helped our family."

"He saved a lot of kids, including myself many times over the years." Anthony answered, with a proud smile. "Even when I was older. I lost my way and he gave me everything he could to get me on the right path again. I don't know how I am going to go on without him." Anthony admitted, doing my best to hold the emotions back.

"You do know, it is not our custom to burn the burial platform?"

"I wasn't sure. I am just going along with his final letter. Lonely Bear was worried someone would find it and drag him into a morgue. Or even worse, desecrate it and create a bad karma over his journey."

The Ranger thought about the dilemma of losing his job to break the rules or repay a debt from his childhood. It was obvious his younger apprentice did not think it was a good idea at all. After a moment, he reached his hand out for the lighter. *I was reluctant, until he smiled to let me know it was okay.*

With a couple of quick flicks, the spark lit the tender pile of brush and the wood soaked in gasoline, flamed up with a giant "whoosh" as it bellowed a black cloud nearly straight up in the air until drifting north in the breeze.

As they stood and watched the pyre burn, Anthony thought of a letter Lonely Bear placed with this manuscript. *I read it often, especially when I start missing him.*

Little Hawk, sometimes stories don't have happy endings, they only have endings that are better than what you hoped for. If you find your way through the darkness on those troubled roads and make it to the other side knowing you did not give up, sometimes that is all the comfort you will get. Nothing will ever make up for the losses of those special people that shaped our lives;

the only thing that makes it better is knowing you will see them soon enough. They will thank you for keeping them alive in your heart and say that you were the one that had the hard part, because you had to keep that spark of love alive, even during your saddest days..... your loneliest days. Always let love be the spark, to light a fire, which will burn against the cold winds of heartbreak. I am proud of you my son. I will be waiting with Jaci Rae, until we see you again.

L. B.

    The three of us watched the fire smolder into a beautiful sunset, with colors so vivid, it seemed the Mother Spirit created them just for today. The Rangers bid farewell and final condolences to leave me to my thoughts. *I could feel a gentle calm come over me.* A slight gust of summer wind felt like Lonely Bear's strong hand on Anthony's shoulder, telling him it will all be okay. The hurt will pass. You will always have the scars from your past and some will never heal. Love is the fire that burns so bright, it helps you through the darkness and some fires will burn forever....

Bibliography

Books:
- Bell, Randall with Phillips, Donald T. *Disasters, Wasted Lives, valuable Lessons.* D & F Scott Publishing. ISBN 193081943-0 (2005)
- City of Oklahoma City Document Management. *Final Report: Alfred P. Murrah Federal Building Bombing April 19, 1995.* .Stillwater, OK: Department of Central Services Central Printing Division. ISBN 0-87939-130-8.(1996)
- Brownell, Richard. *The Oklahoma City Bombing: Crime Scene Investigations.* Lucent Books. Farmington Hills, MI. ISBN 976-1-59018-843-9 (2007)
- Crothers, Lane. *Rage on the Right: The American Militia Movement from Ruby Ridge to Homeland Security.* Lanham, MD: Rowman & Littlefield. ISBN 0-7425-2546-5.(2003).
- Figley, Charles R. *Treating Compassion Fatigue.* ISBN 1-58391-053.
- Giordano, Geraldine. *The Oklahoma City Bombing.* New York: The Rosen Publishing Group, Inc. ISBN 0-8239-3655-4. (2003)
- Gumbel, Andrew and Charles, Roger G. Oklahoma City-*What Investigators Missed and Why it still Matters.* William Morrow. New York, NY. ISBN 978-0-06-198644-4
- Hamm, Mark S. *Apocalypse in Oklahoma: Waco and Ruby Ridge Revenged.* Boston: Northeastern University Press. ISBN 1-55553-300-0. (1997)
- Hamm, Mark S. *In Bad Company: America's Terrorist Underground.* Boston: Northeastern University Press. ISBN 1-55553-492-9. (2002)

- Hamm, Mark S. *American Skinheads: the Criminology and Control of Hate Crimes.* Westport, Connecticut. Prager Publishers (1993)
- Hinman, Eve E. and Hammond, David J. *Lessons from the Oklahoma City Bombing: Defensive Design Techniques.* ASCE Press. New York. ISBN 0-7844-0217-5. (1997).
- Hewitt, Christopher. *Understanding Terrorism in America: from the Klan to Al Qaeda.* Rutledge Publishers. ISBN 978-0-415-27765-5 (2003)
- Hoffman, David. *The Oklahoma City Bombing and the Politics of Terror.* Feral House. ISBN 0-922915-49-0. (1998)
- Irving, Clive. *In Their Name.* Random House ISBN 679-44825. (1995)
- Jones, Francis. *A Circle of Love.* IPD Printing. ISBN 9653320 (1997)
- Jones, Stephen and Israel, Peter. *Others Unknown: The Oklahoma City Bombing Conspiracy.* New York: Public Affairs. ISBN 978-1-58648-098-1.(2001)
- Keith, Jim. *OK Bomb.* Illuminet Press. Lilburn, Georgia ISBN 1-881532-08-9.(1996)
- Kellner, Douglas. *Guys and Guns Amok: Domestic Terrorism and School Shootings from the Oklahoma City Bombing to the Virginia Tech Massacre.* Boulder, CO: Paradigm Publishers. ISBN 1-59451-492-5.(2007)
- Kight, Marsha *Forever Changed.* Prometheus Books, Amhurst, New York ISBN 1-573922382 (1998)
- Knight, Peter. *Conspiracy Theories in American History: An Encyclopedia.* Santa Barbara, CA: ABC-CLIO. ISBN 1-57607-812-4. (2003)

- Linenthal, Edward. *The Unfinished Bombing: Oklahoma City in American Memory.* New York: Oxford University Press. ISBN 0-19-513672-1. (2001)
- Marcovitz, Hal *The Oklahoma City Bombing.* Chelsea House Publishing ISBN 0-7910-6738-6 (2002)
- Meyers, Paul and Jim Ross. *Dear Oklahoma City, Get Well Soon.* Walker and Company, NY New York (1996)
- Michel, Lou; Dan Herbeck. *American Terrorist: Timothy McVeigh & The Oklahoma City Bombing.* New York: Regan Books. ISBN 0-06-039407-2. (2001)
- Miller, Richard Earl. *Writing at the End of the World.* New York: University of Pittsburgh Press. ISBN 0-8229-5886-4. (2005)
- Mustaine, Dave. *Mustaine.* Harper Collins Books. New York, NY. (2010)
- Oklahoma Today. *9:02 am, April 19, 1995: The Official Record of the Oklahoma City Bombing.* Oklahoma City: Oklahoma Today. ISBN 0-8061-9957-1 (2005)
- Oklahoma Bombing Investigation Committee. *Final Report.* ISBN 0-9710513-0-5
- Paul, Michael *Oklahoma City and Anti-Terrorism in Today's World.* World Almanac Library. Milwaukee, WI. ISBN 0-8368-6558-6 (2001)
- Prichard, Evans Ambrose *The Secret Life of Bill Clinton.* Regnery Publishing Inc. Washington D.C. ISBN 0-89526-408-0 (1997)
- Sanders, Kathy *After Oklahoma.* Master Stategies Publishing. ISBN 0-9766485-0-4 (2005)
- Serano, Richard A. *One of Ours: Timothy*

McVeigh and the Oklahoma City Bombing. New York: W. W. Norton & Company. ISBN 0-393-02743-0. (1998)
- Sherrow, Victoria *The Oklahoma City Bombing, Terror in the Heartland.* Enslow Publishing Inc. ISBN 0-7660-1061-0 (1998)
- Spignesi, Stephen *Catastrophe.* Kensington Publishing Group New York N.Y. ISBN 0-5065-2558-4 (2002)
- Stein, R. Conrad *The Oklahoma City National Memorial.* Scholastic Inc. ISBN 0-516-24205-9 (2003)
- Stickney, Brandon M. *All-American Monster: The Unauthorized Biography of Timothy McVeigh.* Amherst, NY: Prometheus Books. ISBN 1-57392-088-6. (1996)
- Sturken, Marita. *Tourists of History: Memory, Kitsch, and Consumerism from Oklahoma City to Ground Zero.* Durham, NC: Duke University Press. ISBN 0-8223-4103-4. (2007)
- Time Magazine *80 Days that Changed the World.* Time Publishing NY, New York ISBN 93227302 (2003)
- Treanor, Kathleen and Candy Chand,. *Ashley's Garden.* Andrews McMeel Publishing Kansas City Mo. ISBN 0-7407-2223-9 (2002)
- Wright, Jon D. *Hate Crimes.* Mason Crest Publishers. Broomall, PA. ISBN 1-590843797 (2003)
- Wright, Stuart A. *Patriots, Politics, and the Oklahoma City Bombing.* Cambridge; New York: Cambridge University Press. ISBN 978-0-521-87264-5. (2007)

Internet Resources:

- Baker, Al. Dave Eisenstadt. Paul Schwartzman and Karen Ball. *Revenge for Waco Strike Former Soldier is Charged in Okla. Bombing.* New York Daily News. (April, 1995)
- BBC News. *Call to reopen Oklahoma bomb case.* (March 2, 2007)
- Bennett, Brian. *Where Moussaoui is likely to spend life in prison.* Time magazine. (May, 2006)
- Berger, J.M. *Did Nichols and Yousef meet?* Intelwire.com.
- Bierbauer, Charles; Susan Candiotti, Gina London, and Terry Frieden. *McVeigh execution rescheduled for June 11.* CNN. (May 11, 2001)
- Blejwas, Andrew; Anthony Griggs and Mark Potok. *Almost 60 Terrorist Plots Uncovered in the U.S.: Terror From the Right.* Southern Poverty Law Center. (July, 2005)
- Caesar, Ed. *The British Waco Survivors.* The Sunday Times (London). (December, 2008)
- Candiotti, Susan. *Federal Building Demolition.* CNN Interactive. (May 23, 1995)
- Church, George J.; Patrick E. Cole. *The Matter of Tim McVeigh.* Time. p. 2. (August 19, 1995)
- Collins, James; Patrick E. Cole and Elaine Shannon. *Oklahoma City: The Weight of Evidence.* Time Magazine (1997).
- Condon, Patrick. *Bomb Ingredient Restricted in 2 States.* The Boston Globe. (June, 2004)
- Crogan, Jim. *Secrets of Timothy McVeigh.* LA Weekly. (March 24, 2004)
- Davis, G. *Victims by the Hundreds: EMS Response and Command.* Fire Engineering 148 (10): 98–107. (1995)
- Davey, Monica. *Nichols Found Guilty of Murder.*

San Francisco Chronicle. (May, 2004)
- Dixon, David. *Is Density Dangerous? The Architects' Obligations After the Towers Fell.* Perspectives on Preparedness (PDF) (October 2002)
- Driver, Don. Marty Sabot. *Rescuers Search through Chill for a Miracle. San Antonio Express-News* (April 23, 1995)
- FEMA Urban Search and Rescue (USAR) Summaries (PDF) Federal Emergency Management Agency.
- Fox News. *FBI: Explosives Found in Nichols' Old Home. Associated Press.* (April, 2005) Archived from the original on (April, 2011)
- Fox News. *Trentadue interviewed-trial set to go forward in missing OKC Bombing tapes.* (September, 2013)
- Hamilton, Arnold. *New Life, Identity Await Fortier as He Leaves Prison. The Dallas Morning News.* (February, 2006)
- Hewitt, Christopher U.S. Department of Justice. *Understanding Terrorism in America.* p. 106. ISBN 0-415-27766-3. (October 2000)
- House of Representatives, *Federal Building Security: Hearing Before the Subcommittee on Public Buildings and Economic Development of the Committee on Transportation and Infrastructure.* 104th Congress, Interview with Dave Barram, Administrator of GSA, p. 6 (April, 1996)
- Indianapolis Star. Library Factfiles: *The Oklahoma City Bombing* (August, 2004)
- Johnson, Kevin. *Okla. City Date Nears, Militias Seen as Gaining Strength. USA Today.* April, 2010.
- Lewis, Carol W. *The Terror that Failed: Public*

Opinion in the Aftermath of the Bombing in Oklahoma City. Public Administration Review 201–210 doi:10.1111/0033-3352.00080 (May/June 2000).
- Linder, Douglas O *The Oklahoma City Bombing & The Trial of Timothy McVeigh. Famous Trials: Oklahoma City Bombing Trial*. University of Missouri–Kansas City. (2006) Archived from the original 2010.
- Loe, Victoria. *Berlin-Based Team's Design Chosen for Bomb Memorial; Winning Entry Evokes Images of Reflection, Hope. The Dallas Morning News.* (July, 1997)
- Mallonee, Sue; Sheryll Shariat, Gail Stennies, Rick Waxweiler, David Hogan, and Fred Jordan. *Physical injuries and fatalities resulting from the Oklahoma bombing. Journal of the American Medical Association* (1996)
- Martin, Gary. *President Demands Execution for Bombers. San Antonio Express.* (April, 1995)
- McLeod, Michael. *Hundreds still live with scars of Oklahoma City bombing every day. The Orlando Sentinel* July, 2007
- Means, Marianne. *Search for Meaning Produces Scapegoats. The Tampa Tribune. (May, 1996)*
- Morava, Kim. *Trooper who arrested Timothy McVeigh shares story. Shawnee News-Star.* March, 2009)
- Nadel, Barbara A. *Oklahoma City: Security Civics Lessons.* Buildings.com. (April 2007)
- Nadel, Barbara A. *High-risk Buildings Placed In a Class All Their Own. Engineering News-Record* (April, 2002)
- New York Times. *White Supremacist Executed For Murdering 2 in Arkansas.* Archived from the

original. (May, 1995)
- New York Times. *12-Year Sentence Given Again to Witness in Oklahoma Bombing.* October, 1999. Archived from the original in (March, 2011)
- Oklahoma City Police Department. *Alfred P. Murrah Federal Building Bombing After Action Report.* (PDF). Terrorism information.
- Oklahoma Department of Civil Emergency Management After Action Report. Department of Central Services Central Printing Division. (1996)
- Ostrow, Ronald. *Chief of Oklahoma Bomb Probe Named Deputy Director at FBI. Los Angeles Times.* (August 9, 1995) Retrieved (February, 2011)
- Ottley, Ted. *License Tag Snag.* Tru TV (April, 2005)
- Pellegrini, Frank. *McVeigh Given Death Penalty Time.*
- Pfefferbaum, Betty. *The Impact of the Oklahoma City bombing on Children in the Community.* Military Medicine. (April 2010)
- Public Broadcasting Service. *Bombing Trial.* Online Focus. (May, 1997)
- Rocky Mountain News. Nichols' Lawyers Say Government Leaked Information to the Media. (September, 1997)
- Rogers, J. David; Keith D. Koper. *Some Practical Applications of Forensic Seismology* (PDF). Missouri University of Science and Technology. pp. 25–35. Retrieved (July, 2010)
- Rohrabacher, Dana; Phaedra Dugan. *The Oklahoma City Bombing: Was There A Foreign Connection?* (PDF). Oversight and

Investigations Subcommittee of the House International Relations Committee. Retrieved (March, 2009)
- Romano, Lois. *Prosecutors Seek Death For Nichols.* The Washington Post. p. A3. (December, 1997)
- Russakoff, Dale; Serge F. Kovaleski. *An Ordinary Boy's Extraordinary Rage.* The Washington Post. (July, 1995).
- Scarpa, Greg Jr. *Report of Possible Subcommittee Inquiry into Oklahoma City Bombing, Recent Intelligence Concerning (a) Involvement of FBI Informant; and (b) Imminent Threat.* (PDF). Forensic Intelligence International. Retrieved (August, 2009)
- Smith, Martin. *McVeigh Chronology.* Frontline (Public Broadcasting Service). Archived from the original on (February, 2011)
- Solomon, John. *Gov't had missile in Murrah Building.* Associated Press. (September 26, 2002)
- Swickard, Joe. *The Life of Terry Nichols.* The Seattle Times. (May, 1995).
- Tim, Talley. *Man testifies axle of truck fell from sky after Oklahoma City bombing.* The San Diego Union-Tribune. (May, 2004).
- Thomas, Jo. *McVeigh Defense Team Suggests Real Bomber Was Killed in Blast.* The New York Times. (May 23, 1997)
- Thomas, Jo; Ronald Smothers. *Oklahoma City Building Was Target Of Plot as Early as '83, Official Says.* The New York Times.
- Thomma, Steven. *With his Swift Response, Clinton Grabs Center Stage.* Philadelphia Inquirer. (April 23, 1995).
- Tramel, Berry. *Emotion makes Memorial*

different. *The Oklahoman.*(April 29, 2006)
- United States Court of Appeals for the Tenth Circuit. *Petition for Writ of Mandamus of Petitioner-Defendant, Timothy James McVeigh and Brief in Support. Case No. 96-CR-68-M.* (March 25, 1997)
- United States Department of Defense. *Design of Buildings to Resist Progressive Collapse* (PDF). General Services Administration. p. 14. (January, 2005)
- United States Department of Justice. *Justice Department Issues Recommendations For Upgrading Federal Building Security.* WBDG Safe Committee (July, 1996).
- Vulliamy, Ed. *Oklahoma: the day homegrown terror hit America. The Guardian.* (May, 2010)
- Washington Post. *Judge Won't Delay McVeigh Execution. Associated Press.* Archived from the original (2012)
- Whitehouse.gov. *President's Statement on Tenth Anniversary of Oklahoma City Bombing* (Press release). (April 19, 2005)
- Winthrop, Jim. *The Oklahoma City Bombing: Immediate Response Authority and Other Military Assistance to Civil Authority (MACA). The Army Lawyer.* (July 1997).
- Witkin, Gordon; Karen Roebuck. *Terrorist or Family Man? Terry Nichols goes on trial for the Oklahoma City bombing. U.S. News & World Report.* (September 28, 1997).
- Witt, Howard. Torment lingers in OK City. *Chicago Tribune.* (April 17, 2005)
- Zucchino, David. Tracing a *Trail to Destruction; The Clues from the Oklahoma City Bombing Have Led to; A Small Circle of Malcontents – Not a Wide Network. The Philadelphia Inquirer.* (May, 1995)

Media Resources:

- Ambrose Video. *Witness to History Episode 10 (1990-1999)* VHS (2000)
- Aquarius Video *September 12: Life after Tragedy* VHS (2003)
- Court TV News. *The Oklahoma City Bombing Case: The Second Trial.*
- Davis, Jayne. *The Third Terrorist* 2004 Compact Disc. Books in Motion Spokane, WA ISBN 1-59607-151-6
- Discovery Channel. *FBI's 10 Most Wanted.* DVD (2009)
- Free Mind Films LLC. *A Noble Lie: Oklahoma City.* (1995)
- Garner, Joe 1998 *We Interrupt this Broadcast.* Published by Source Books, Naperville, Illinois. ISBN 1-57071-328-6. Compact Disc and book.
- Homeland Security Television. *A Study of the Oklahoma City Bombing.* (2006).
- National Geographic *Aryan Brotherhood* DVD. National Geographic Inc. (2007)
- National Geographic Channel. *The Bomb in Oklahoma City (Oklahoma City). Seconds From Disaster. Season 1.* (July 20, 2004)
- NBC News Report. *Timothy McVeigh is apprehended* (Video, 3 minutes). (1995)
- Oklahoma Today Magazine. *9:02 The Official Record of the Oklahoma City Bombing* ISBN 0-8061-9957-1 (2005)
- Rich-Heape Films Inc. *Black Indians: An American Story.* DVD Dallas, Texas (2000)
- Rosa Parks Story (2007) DVD Xennon Pictures
- Rush. *Clockwork Angels.* CD Anthem (Canada) Roadrunner. (2012)

- Sanders, Kathy. *After Oklahoma City: A Grieving Grandmother Uncovers Shocking Truths about the bombing and Herself.* Master Strategies. Arlington, TX. ISBN 0-976648504 (2005)
- Warner Brothers. *A Time of Healing, Oklahoma City Memorial Service.* Compact Disc (1995)

Reference Books:
- Burns, Vincent and Peterson Dempsey, Kate. *Terrorism: A Documentary and Reference Guide* Greenwood Press Westport CT. ISBN 0-313-33213-4
- Gulbrandson, Don. *Landscapes-Visions of the American West.* Compendium Publishing Ltd. United Kingdom (2007)
- Miller, James *National Geographic: Almanac of American History* 2006 Washington D.C. ISBN 0-7922-8368268-6
- National Geographic Society. *Historical Atlas of the United States-Centennial Edition.* Washington D.C. Copyright (1988)

Historic Timeline of Events

April 19, 1775 The battles of Lexington and Concord. The first armed conflicts of the American Revolution against Great Britain.

November 29, 1864 United States Army Colonel John M. Chivington and his troops massacre an estimated 163 Cheyenne and Arapaho Native Americans, mostly unarmed women and children along Sand Creek, Colorado.

November 26, 1868 United States Army Colonel George Armstrong Custer and his troops surprise attack a band of Native Americans who believed they were on a protected reservation along the Washita River near Cheyenne, Oklahoma. Chief Black Kettle and his wife were both shot in the back and killed.

April 19, 1943 German Nazi forces burn the Warsaw ghetto in Poland, killing or deporting over 56,000 Jewish families imprisoned there. A day celebrated in racist organizations.

March 2, 1977 The Oklahoma Federal Building named after judge Alfred P. Murrah opens at construction cost of 14.5 million dollars.

December 25, 1979 Soviet Union enters Afghanistan to provide security. United States funnels billions of dollars in weapons and money through the C.I.A. to the Afghan rebels, including Osama Bin Laden.

April 18, 1983 An Ammonium Nitrate Fuel Oil (ANFO) truck bomb explodes at the United States embassy in Beirut, Lebanon, killing 63 people including 17 Americans.

October 23, 1983 A deadly truck bomb explodes at the USMC barracks inside the Beirut International Airport, Lebanon, killing 241 American service members and wounding 128 others.

April 19, 1985 Bureau of Alcohol, Tobacco and Firearms surround the Covenant, the Sword, and Arm of the Lord's compound in Elijah, Missouri. Founder James Ellison is arrested and convicted of weapons charges in addition to Federal racketeering charges. He is sentenced to twenty years in prison.

August 1988 Abdullah Yusuf Azzam and Osama Bin Laden create the terrorist group called Al-Qaeda, meaning "the base" in Peshawar, Pakistan.

September 1988 Osama Bin Laden sends his brother-in-law, Mohammed Jamal Khalifa to Manilla, Philippines, to organize and join forces with allies of Al-Qaeda for planned attacks on the United States.

August 2, 1990   United States and Coalition forces began Operation Desert Storm against Iraq to liberate Kuwait. It is a resounding and bitter defeat for Saddam Hussein.

August 21, 1992   FBI surrounded the cabin of white separatist Randy Weaver in Ruby Ridge, Idaho. Using excessive force, they kill Weaver's young son and wife. Weaver is eventually awarded a 3.1 million dollar settlement. Chief of FBI E. Michael Kahoe pleads guilty to obstruction of justice for destroying evidence in the case and receives 18 months in jail.

September 1, 1992 Ramzi Yousef comes to the United States using a falsified Iraqi passport. He is arrested along with Ahmed Ajaj who carried fertilizer bomb making manuscripts and evidence of terrorist connections. Yousef is detained briefly then released.

December 1992   Osama Bin Laden funded fighters shoot down United States helicopters in Somalia during famine relief efforts.

December 5, 1992 Terry Nichols and Timothy McVeigh both move to key locations where Al-Qaeda is recruiting terrorists to join their network.
December 29, 1992 Al-Qaeda launched their first attack in Aden, Yemen, at a hotel. Bin Laden and Mohamed Khan claimed responsibility.

February 26, 1993   Ramzi Yousef, the nephew of 9/11 planner Khalid Sheikh Mohammed and Abdul Rahman Yasin, detonate a massive (ANFO) truck bomb that rips through three floors of the World Trade Center parking garage in New York City, killing six and injuring over one thousand.

February 28, 1993   Iraqi national Abdul Yasin, who mixed the chemicals for the powerful ANFO bomb detonated in the World Trade Center, escapes back to Bagdad.

April 1993   Iraqi dictator Saddam Hussein plots to assassinate President George Bush during his visit to Kuwait.

April 19, 1993   BATF and FBI launch an unconstitutional final assault on the Branch Davidian compound in Waco, Texas, killing 76 people, mostly women and children.

October 12, 1993   Tim McVeigh ticketed on Arkansas Highway 59 for prohibitive passing twelve miles outside of Elohim City.

July 1994   FBI informant Carol Howe places Pete Ward, Andreas Strassmeir and Timothy McVeigh together at Elohim City.

September 1994   Ramzi Yousef and Khalid Shaikh set up operations in Manila with funding by Osama Bin Laden. They intend to launch attacks called *Project Bojinka*, which includes bombing Federal buildings and hijacking airliners to be used to attack other important targets in the United States.

September 13, 1994 Tim McVeigh stays in hotel a few miles from Elohim City the same day as the Grand Jury concluded he formulated the bomb plot. He participates in military training directed by Andreas Strassmeir.

September 30, 1994 Terry Nichols along with Tim McVeigh, who was using the alias Mike Havens, purchased 40 bags weighing 50 pounds each of ammonium nitrate fertilizer. The purchase was made at the Mid-Kansas Co-Op in McPherson, Kansas, for $228.74 according to Robert Nattier the President of the business.

October 18, 1994 Terry Nichols and Tim McVeigh purchase another 40 bags of ammonium nitrate fertilizer from Mid-Kansas Co-Op for $228.74.

November 5, 1994 Roger E. Moore, a gun dealer in Royal, Arkansas, is allegedly robbed by Terry Nichols and Tim McVeigh to raise funds for the bombing in Oklahoma City.

November 22, 1994 Terry Nichols is detained by airport security before his flight from Las Vegas to the Philippines for carrying two stun guns. Terry Nichols travels to Cebu City in the Philippines where he meets with Edwin Angeles, co-founder and commander of the Abu Sayyaf, a branch of Al-Qaeda along with Mohammed Jamal Khalifa the brother-in-law of Osama Bin Laden. Nichols joins the groups involved with the *Project Bojinka*, which entails bombing Federal Buildings and hijacking airliners to attack important targets in the United States.

December 22, 1994 Tim McVeigh and Michael Fortier pose as job applicants and inspect the Murrah Federal Building floor by floor.

January 6, 1995 Ramzi Yousef and Abdul Hakim Murad cause an apartment fire while mixing chemicals for bombs to be used during *Project Bojinka*. Authorities uncover the plot and arrest Murad at the scene.

January 7, 1995 Ramzi Yousef escapes from the Philippines.

January 11, 1995 Wali Khan Amin Shah is arrested in connection with *Project Bojinka*, but breaks out of prison and flees the country.

January 17, 1995 The FBI arrives in Manila to examine documents concerning *Project Bojinka*. Terry Nichols flees the Philippines for the last time.

January 31-Febuary 15, 1995 Tim McVeigh stays in Kingman, Arizona, while meeting with members of the Arizona Patriot movement.

February 3-8, 1995 Members of the Midwest Bank Robbers including Stedeford, McCarthy, Langan and Guthrie, camp near Kingman, Arizona, and plan their next robbery.

February 7, 1995 FBI catches Ramzi Yousef in Pakistan living in one of Bin Laden's guesthouses named Su Casa.

February 16, 1995 Tim McVeigh buys 100 pounds of ammonium nitrate fertilizer and 600 pounds of ammonium phosphate from the True Value hardware store in Kingman, Arizona.

February 27, 1995 Congressional task force on terrorism and unconventional warfare issues a warning stating an Iran-sponsored attack on U.S. soil was imminent.

March 3, 1995 Director of a congressional task force, Yossef Bodansky issues an alert, "Terrorist plan to strike heart of United States."

March 10, 1995 Danielle Wise Hunt, the director of the daycare at the Murrah Federal Building in Oklahoma talks with Tim McVeigh during his visit there. He states he is looking for a new daycare since being stationed close by with the U.S. Army. She becomes suspicious of his story when his companion labeled as John Doe #2 seems to be casing the place.

March 16, 1995 Arkansas Governor orders Richard Snell's execution scheduled for April 19, 1995 in the conviction of killing a State Trooper.

April 8, 1995 Several witnesses including employees see Tim McVeigh, Andreas Strassmeir, Michael Brescia and Hussain Hashem Al-Hussaini together at Lady Godiva's strip bar in downtown Oklahoma City.

April 14, 1995 Tim McVeigh along with other men of Mid-Eastern descent, checked into room 25 at the Dreamland Motel in Junction City, Kansas.

April 15, 1995 Tim McVeigh reserves a 20-foot Ryder truck from Elliott's Body Shop in Junction City Kansas. He pays $280.32 in cash to the owner Eldon Elliott. According to his phone records, McVeigh immediately places a call to Elohim City.

April 17, 1995 Tim McVeigh, along with another man identified as John Doe #2, rent a 20-foot Ryder truck from Eldon Body shop in Junction City, Kansas.

April 17, 1995 A Federal Grand Jury hands down a sealed indictment charging Hillary Clinton with bank fraud pertaining to embezzling 47 million dollars from a Federally Insured

Savings and Loan in Arkansas. It includes benefitting from secret offshore accounts payable to Vincent Foster Jr. All evidence and indictments are stored at the Alfred P. Murrah building in Oklahoma City, while awaiting trial.

*April 19, 1995   Alfred P. Murrah Federal building in Oklahoma City is bombed, killing 168 people, injuring 680 and causing an estimated 652 million dollars in property damage.

April 20, 1995   An imprisoned Abdul Hakim Murad, a key soldier with Ramzi Yousef's terror cell, claims responsibility for the Oklahoma bombing in the name of the Liberation Army, an arm of Al-Qaeda. He repeats the claim to the FBI the next day.

April 21, 1995   Terry Nichols surrenders to police in Herrington, Kansas.

May 2, 1995   The Director of the F.B.I. Larry Potts and Danny Coulson, Special Agent in Charge, are dismissed from their positions without notice and forced into retirement. The Federal investigation of the Oklahoma bombing takes a dramatic turn, focusing solely on Tim McVeigh and Terry Nichols. All other evidence implicating additional conspirators is destroyed or remains missing.

May 20, 1995   Hillary Clinton's Federal indictment concerning the Whitewater fraud investigation and connections to the Mena Drug Smuggling Ring through Arkansas are dismissed because of lack of evidence that is reportedly lost in the bombing of the Murrah building. The overwhelming evidence was secretly transferred from the Federal courthouse in Little Rock, to the Murrah building just a week prior to the tragedy.

May 21, 1995 Congressional hearings are scheduled regarding the BATF's misconduct at Ruby Ridge and the Waco massacres, but canceled due to the files being destroyed in the bombing.

May 23, 1995 The Murrah Federal Building is quickly demolished without a thorough investigation from bomb experts. All crucial evidence is hauled away to guarded landfills.

July 1995 All video surveillance evidence obtained from twelve separate cameras on the morning of the bombing disappear while in FBI custody. These are key videos that corroborate over 35 witnesses placing two men in the Ryder truck during the bombing.

August 21, 1995 Kenneth Michael Trentadue is severely beaten and hanged in his cell at the Federal Transfer Center in Oklahoma City. Trentadue's family receives a million dollars in a wrongful death suit against the US Government.

August 31, 1995 Despite overwhelming evidence against him, World Trade Center bombing suspect Mohammed Jamal Khalifia is mysteriously acquitted of all terrorist charges and released from Federal custody. His personal effects, which included bomb making manuals and terrorist contacts, are returned to him.

November 13, 1995 Five Americans are killed in Riyadh, Saudi Arabia, from a truck bombing at a US-operated Saudi National Guard training center.

January 15, 1996 Richard Guthrie is arrested after a car chase in Cincinnati, Ohio.

January 18, 1996 Peter Langan is arrested in Columbus, Ohio, after a one-sided shoot out with authorities. Langan was unarmed and barely escapes death.

May 8, 1996 Oklahoma Police Sergeant, Terry Yeakey, is severely beaten, tortured and shot execution style, three days before he was to accept a Medal of Honor of Valor for his heroism during the bombing. Yeakey witnessed several unexploded bombs inside the Murrah building and was currently running his own private investigation on the cover up. All of his personal records including photos, notes and videos were stolen out of his car after he was left for dead in a field in El Reno, Oklahoma. His tragic murder is inexplicably ruled a suicide.

May 22, 1996 Scott Stedford is arrested and convicted in a Philadelphia court with robbing seven banks while working with the Midwest Bank Robbers.

May 24, 1996 Kevin McCarthy is arrested for several bank robberies. He testifies against Langan and Stedeford and receives a light sentence of five years before going into the witness protection program.

June 2, 1996 Without precedent or lawful jurisdiction, Judge Richard Matsche inexplicably places all video tapes of the bombing illegally confiscated from businesses by the FBI under an Official Seal, never to be released to the public. The McVeigh defense team to no avail adamantly protests against this illegal and unethical conduct.

July 3, 1996 Richard Guthrie pleads guilty to 19 bank robberies across the Midwest.

July 12, 1996 Days after disclosing to the media he wants to write a tell-all book about the Midwest Bank Robbers extensive connections to the Oklahoma City bombing, Richard Guthrie is found hanging in his jail cell.

September 5, 1996 Ramzi Yousef receives life in prison for planning *Project Bojinka*.

November 12, 1997 Ramzi Yousef is sentenced to 240 years in ADX Supermax Federal Prison in

Florence, Colorado, for planning 1993 World Trade Center bombing.

May 1998 John Miller of ABC News, interviews Osama Bin Laden at a training camp in Afghanistan, where Al-Qaeda officially declares war on the United States.

May 27, 1998 Michael Fortier is sentenced to twelve years in prison for his role in planning the Oklahoma City bombing and failing to notify authorities of the pending attack.

August 7, 1998 Al-Qaeda suicide bombers detonate truck bombs at U.S Embassies in Nairobi, Kenya, and Dar es Sallam, Tanzania, causing 224 deaths and over 4,000 injuries.

August 21, 1998 President Clinton orders missile strikes on three Al-Qaeda training camps in Afghanistan. Bin Laden, Al Zawahir and Mohammed Atef all escape unharmed.

December 19, 1998 The House of Representatives impeach President Bill Clinton for perjury and obstruction of justice. By a narrow vote, the Senate eventually acquits him.

January 5, 2000 Al-Qaeda summit in Kuala, Lumpur. September 11th attacks and *USS Cole* bombings are planned during this meeting.

June 11, 2001 Timothy McVeigh is reportedly executed by lethal injection at a Federal correctional complex in Terre Haute, Indiana. Witnesses state that he is still breathing long after the procedure. No medical examination is done proving death, no autopsy is completed and his body mysteriously disappears without a trace.

September 11, 2001 Al-Qaeda hijacks four commercial airliners. Flight 11 and 175 were flown into the Twin Towers in New York City. Flight 77 hit the west side of the Pentagon and Flight 93 crashed in a field close to Shanksville, Pennsylvania. Over 6,000 people are injured and 2,977 innocent people are killed in the attacks.

October 7, 2001 United States and United Kingdom launch Operation Enduring Freedom into Afghanistan when Taliban forces controlling the country refuse to extradite Osama Bin Laden.

November 14, 2001 Mohammed Atef, the military commander of Al Qaeda is killed in Kabul, Afghanistan.

March 1, 2003 Khalid Sheikh Mohammed, confessed mastermind to the September 11 attacks, is captured in Rawalpindi, Pakistan.

March 20, 2003 The United States and multi-national coalition forces launch a surprise attack on Iraq without a formal declaration of war and eventually capture Saddam Hussein.

November 8, 2003 An Al-Qaeda sponsored truck bomb detonates outside the Al-Mohaya housing compound in Laban Valley, West of Riyadh, Saudi Arabia, killing 18 people and wounding 122.

November 15, 2003 Al-Qaeda linked terrorists groups set off four separate truck bombs in Istanbul, Turkey, killing 57 and wounding over 700 innocent civilians.

March 11, 2004 Islamist terrorist with ties to Al-Qaeda bomb Madrid train station in Spain that killed 191 people and wounded more than 2,000.

May 26, 2004 After a questionable trial in which the prosecution is accused of suppressing, destroying and failing to turn over key evidence, Terry Nichols is found guilty of the Oklahoma City bombing. He is sentenced to 161 consecutive life terms and sent to ADX Supermax in Florence, Colorado.

March 2005 The FBI locates a substantial cache of explosives hidden within a crawl space at Terry Nichols home in Herrington, Kansas.

May 9, 2005 Salt Lake City federal Judge Dale Kimball orders the FBI to produce all documents previously unlawfully held concerning connections with the Oklahoma City bombing, Elohim City and the Midwest bank robbers. FBI admits that they have over 340 documents connecting the groups, but refuses to release them.

January 2006 Michael Fortier is released from prison after serving only 10 ½- years of his 12-year sentence for his role in the Oklahoma City bombing.

December 30, 2006 Saddam Hussein is executed by hanging at Camp Justice in Bagdad, Iraq, for crimes against humanity.

February 3, 2007 Al-Qaeda detonates a large truck bomb in Bagdad, Iraq, that killed at least 135 people and injured 339.

March 27, 2007 Al-Qaeda detonates two massive truck bombs in Tal Afar, Iraq, killing 152 people and wounding at least 347 townspeople, mostly woman and children.

September 20, 2008 Al-Qaeda detonates a truck bomb at the Marriott hotel in Pakistan killing 54 people and injuring 266.

June 16, 2009 Dennis and Daniel Mahon, using the organizational name of White Aryan Resistance (WAR) are both charged in mail-bombing the City of Scottsdale, Arizona, Office of Diversity and Dialogue. Dennis claims responsibility for the Oklahoma bombing.

May 10, 2010 A coordinated series of bomb and shooting attacks by Al-Qaeda caused the highest death toll in 2010, which killed over 100 and injured 350 people.

May 2, 2011 U.S. Special Forces in Abbottabad, Pakistan kill Osama Bin Laden. Photographic proof of his death are never released before his body is supposedly dump at sea.

December 18, 2011 The last United States troops leave Iraq.

April 12, 2015 Despite an exhaustive list of alleged criminal behavior and unethical activities including money laundering and fraud accusations which span decades, Hillary Clinton announces a second campaign for the Presidency of the United States. Her announcement is made in Oklahoma City at the site of the bombing.

April 19, 2020 This date marked the 25-year anniversary of the Oklahoma City bombing.

Author Bio

Photo Credit: Brett Wilson

Jeff Wilson has three amazing children and is a lifelong resident of Independence, Missouri. Jeff is the Founder of Novella's Bistro. *Oklahoma Ghost Dance* is his second novel.

Past Projects -

Queen Anne's Revenge. Novel-Fiction-Historic Mystery. 2013

Made in the USA
Monee, IL
16 August 2023

41104080R00218